A Fare to Hell

LEON FRANKLIN

FRANKLIN

A Fare to Hell

DEDICATION

To my grandchildren, Lior, Bella, Noa and Aytan

Published in 2021 by Leon Franklin

Printed and bound by Kindle Direct Publishing

ACKNOWLEDGEMENTS

Having originally decided to write this book in January 2018 and then finishing it in October 2019, there are a number of people that have gone the distance with me and deserve my thanks for their patience.

First and foremost is my wife for forty-five years plus, Jennifer. A constant support, sounding board, fielder of frustrations and giver of compassion, understanding and much more. Also, of course, there are my daughters, Lois and March, always ready with encouragement, pithy observations, and also love. Then, son-in-law, Dan, quiet, thoughtful, reliable and again very supportive. All have read and enjoyed the book.

Then we come to those other friends and family, who we road tested the book on, who gave many useful comments, that enabled me to keep the book pointed in the right direction and have constantly wanted an update on how it was all going. Larry, Malcolm and Beryl, my brothers and sister; Marilyn Gold; Felice Levine from the USA; Carol Wylie, who encouraged me to just do it; Ian Leader; Daniel Levy; Mary Hardie and Theresa Gibbs; Gary Appel, yet another cab driver; and not forgetting 'Uncle' Cyril Sheffrin, also no longer with us, but the father of my wife's oldest friend, Marilyn, and the person responsible for me going 'On The Knowledge.'

In addition, a special mention to Elaine Levy, who expectantly waited for more chapters weekly and so kept me going. Thanks, Elaine, many more chapters for more books coming your way!

Writing at length is not something that came easily, unlike talking, but, as always, it is best to choose a subject that is familiar, and being a cab driver is, and has been for forty years, full of interesting stories, situations and experiences. Hence the lead character, Lenny, and a chance situation in the cab that got me started. A lot of the names of characters are fictitious, but there are people I have met over those forty years and from my youth, that have great names, plus those that I have come across throughout my political involvement over thirty years. So with great thanks for the use of their names: Chris Hayward, Michael Atwell, Stewart Scott, David (Barney) Barnes, sadly deceased, and Martin Long, also deceased, as well as all the other names I have used that have been mixed and matched and made for interesting characters.

Finally, thanks to Ian Hughes and his team at Mousemat Design for their help, advice and guidance through the editing, copy editing and cover design, and also to Marc Goldberg, for his recommendation. Thank you for all your support, expertise and for doing an excellent professional job in bringing my book to life.

Hope it's been a good read and you liked it enough to get the sequel *The Return Fare*, that's coming very soon!

CHAPTER

1

It was the first Sunday of the New Year, and London was cold, dark and unwelcoming. By late afternoon, the earlier drizzle had almost stopped. The roads, though, were still wet and a mist was starting to form.

Despite that, Lenny Resnick had dragged himself from the comfort of his four-bedroomed semi-detached house in North London. He'd left behind his wife, Jody, who was working on an interior design for a new client, and their two teenage daughters, Ella and Jess, who were watching some early Sunday evening game show, having completed their school assignments.

Lenny was now pondering his life, as he sat in his cab on the taxi rank at South Kensington, waiting for a job. The work had been slow, but it was early in the New Year, and so he had time to let his mind wander.

He was immediately startled out of his meanderings by his mobile phone ringing. He looked at the display to see who it was, and realised it was work of a different sort.

He answered with a short "Yes."

"19.30 pick up at The Good Earth in Brompton Road. The guy will hail you. He knows your registration," said the voice at the other end.

"Okay," Lenny replied, and the line went dead.

The expensive Chinese eatery was actually about half a mile away, so he had plenty of time to squeeze another job in before 19.30. He wondered what was so urgent for Matt Flynn to call him at this hour, on a Sunday, with this job.

He had known Matt for some time, as they had met in Israel, when

Lenny was with the Israel Defence Forces (IDF) on secondment to the interior security services (Shin Bet). Lenny had spent a couple of days briefing British intelligence agents, including Matt, on a number of problems in and around the Middle East, that had the potential to get exported to the wider world.

Although Lenny was born in Israel, his parents came to the UK when he was ten years old. However, when he reached the age of eighteen, he decided as he still held duel British/Israeli citizenship, to go back to the land of his birth and fulfil the duty of all Israelis by committing to National Service. When his two and a half years were about to finish, he still wanted more, so he signed on for a further term in the IDF. It wasn't long before his talent for leadership and ability to maintain a calm head under pressure were noticed by the interior intelligence service, Shin Bet, and so he was then seconded to them.

He had kept in touch with Matt during his time in Israel and, when he had grown restless after another six years of active duty in both the IDF and Shin Bet, he returned to the UK to seek a fresh but quieter challenge. Much to Lenny's surprise, Matt made contact to see how things were with him and what his plans were.

Now at forty-two, and still a very fit 6ft specimen of a man, weighing 200lbs, Lenny thought about his life over the last twenty-four years: from a young eighteen year old conscript in the IDF, through his original two years six months of active service and then his secondment to internal security. After his marriage to Jody, he had had to make a decision about what to do after they returned to England, particularly with two small girls.

Once settled here, he realised he could have done a number of things related to his security experience. Jody's dad was a partner in a financial management company and he could have worked there, but he was not the office and desk job type of person. However, he did want some freedom and had always thought of trying his hand at cab driving. He had a number of relatives and friends who were in the cab trade and so he canvassed their thoughts on the idea. He also asked Jody's Uncle Cyril, who, at the age of fifty, had decided to become a cab driver. He looked into what was needed to get through the knowledge to earn that precious 'green badge'. After weighing up his options, he decided that he would commit to it; after all, how hard could it be, he had thought to himself. It would certainly be a lot quieter! Jody was aghast when he told her, but he was determined, and he began the process. It took him two and a half years, so much harder than he imagined, and after a number of odd jobs along the way, he earned his right to be a London cabbie. So, twelve years later, here he was, still enjoying the work and the freedom, and he had built a very comfortable life for himself, Jody and the girls!

As soon as Lenny had got his licence as a London cab driver, Matt had seemed even more interested in how he could put some 'work' Lenny's way, and did so from time to time, like this evening. Although Lenny had guessed that this was more than just another cab ride, based on all he knew about what Matt Flynn did for a living, he realised that this, like some of the other work he had done for Matt, would need special care.

With all that still running round his head and the fact that time had now passed so that any job other than the one at 19.30 was now irrelevant, Lenny pulled off the rank. He made his way along the Brompton Road towards Harrods. He made a u-turn and parked up outside the Bunch of Grapes pub, just along from the restaurant, and waited.

At 19.29 Lenny started the cab and drove very slowly the hundred or so metres towards the restaurant. When he was twenty metres away, a waiter stepped out. He looked very carefully and then, when Lenny was almost there, the arm came out. Lenny stepped on the brake, pushed the button and the window went down. The waiter looked at him.

"I've got two guys who need a cab to Sussex Gardens; you wait a minute or two?" Lenny nodded, put the meter on along with the handbrake, shifted the gear stick into neutral and waited for his passengers to come out.

A couple of minutes later the restaurant door opened and four men of Middle Eastern appearance stepped out. They were in good spirits and seemed content. After an exhaustive round of cheek kissing, smiles and handshakes, two of the men got into Lenny's cab and instructed him that the destination was Sussex Gardens via Hyde Park Square. Lenny set off eastbound towards Hyde Park Corner.

After a few minutes, it became clear that one of the men was having fun looking at and talking to a young woman, who was sitting in the back seat of a bus travelling next to the cab. But she couldn't hear him. She was taking pictures of the cab and the passengers with her smart phone, much to the mirth of Lenny's passengers. Curiosity got the better of Lenny and he grabbed a look at the woman. "Very nice," he thought to himself, "Certainly wouldn't kick her out of bed!" He quickly pulled his thoughts in and concentrated again on the road.

On the way from Brompton Road into Knightsbridge, the bus stopped at the traffic lights by what was the Burberry shop. Lenny noticed that, although the bus was still on his inside, the young woman was still snapping away on her phone. She then stopped, took a brief phone call, after which she resumed pointing her phone at his passengers. The thing that intrigued Lenny throughout this was why she was taking so many pictures of the cab and particularly his passengers. One of the men had resumed a conversation with his friend, but noticed the woman was still watching them. Again he began to wave and smile at her. She saw this, smiled, and waved back, but kept capturing them on her phone.

The lights changed and he moved off. The bus kept pace with Lenny's cab, until he got caught in traffic and the bus moved on.

Lenny approached the junction at Hyde Park Corner. He pulled up about fifty metres short of the lights. There was a line of buses waiting at the bus stand on his left hand, nearside.

As he sat there waiting, Lenny caught a glimpse of a tallish woman walking towards the cab. His passengers, who were now in deep conversation, were unaware of this. She then disappeared on the other side of the parked buses and reappeared moments later, almost at the nearside passenger door. Lenny turned around to see what was going on. It looked like she had a black face, but he thought something was seriously wrong. He looked again and saw there was something in her right hand. As she opened the door with her left hand, he realised what he had seen was a gun. Without thinking, and in a moment of self-preservation, he wrenched his mobile phone from its holder, opened the door and dived onto the ground, as close to the cab as he could get. He peered under the cab, watching the woman's feet. Before hitting the ground, he'd heard four muffled shots.

"Shit!" he mumbled, "What the fuck is going down here?" He quickly looked under the cab, and then behind, but she had gone. He slowly stood up and opened the passenger door his side, and there they lay. Both dead, two bullet holes in each, with blood, human brain matter and flesh tissue all over the back of the cab. One in the head and heart of each. Lenny looked in horror at what had, obviously, been a professional hit.

He pressed the speed dial on his mobile, it rang twice and then Matt Flynn answered.

"Hi, Lenny. What's up? You okay?"

"No, Matt, I'm not okay. I've got two dead passengers! Both shot head and heart!"

"What the fuck, Lenny…? What happened, for Christ's sake?"

"Too long to explain."

"Okay, where are you?"

"Hyde Park Corner, eastbound by the side of the underpass."

"Judas H Pri . . .! Okay, I'll be there in ten. Play nice with the cops till I arrive. Just be a cabbie, and keep them talking, and tell them as little as possible. I'll sort it when I get there."

He clicked off.

As he stood up, Lenny could see the police arriving … in numbers. Up above was the whirring noise of helicopter blades, holding the machine at a hover, with its spotlight now on the scene. It was going to be a long night.

CHAPTER
2

Relaxing in the luxurious opulence of his suite at the Jumeirah Etihad Towers Hotel in Abu Dhabi, the capital of the Emirates, Sheikh AbdulWahab Al Zakani was content. His plan had been as professional and as fruitful as could have been expected so far. All he was now waiting for was confirmation that the final part of stage one could be completed in a matter of months.

The Sheikh, who had just turned fifty, was an extremely wealthy oil producer and businessman. He had been born into wealth, as his father and his father had before him. The difference, though, was AbdulWahab's obsession in funding Hezbollah terrorism, both inside and outside Israel. His hatred of the Country State, recognised after the partition of what he considered Arab lands in 1948, knew no bounds. This was a long way from his father's and grandfather's positions. They had been given guarantees by the negotiators and friendly supporting nations as part of the partition agreement, that along with other Arab leaders, they would be granted special rights and privileges over lands and oil wealth, a sweetener he found distasteful, despite inheriting all of the family lands and wealth.

He had many other obsessions, or maybe they were idiosyncrasies. His gluttonous habits, with food always on his mind, meant he just loved to eat. He also felt the need to procreate at will with his four wives, and he had become almost legendary since he had managed fourteen children with them, and didn't feel the need to finish there.

However, his latest dalliance was now with the West: he was determined not only to see the 'great' and 'little Satan' and their allies expelled from the Middle East, in whatever way achieved that result, but also to end the dominance of western ideas in Islamic lands once and for all. Expelling the 'Infidel' had also now become obsessive. To that end, and because of how he hoped the day's events would play out, his latest terrorist plan would now be properly constructed. If in the end the overall result was successful, it would be talked about in a similar way to the now legendary events of September 11 2001.

He had expected the call at any time, from his contractor. It was now 01.00 local time and 21.00 in London. If he didn't hear in the next hour, he would have to make enquiries. Something he was loathe to do, as it meant other people would have to be involved and there would be repercussions, more than would otherwise be wanted or necessary.

AbdulWahab was on the brink of ignoring his own thoughts, but in the end decided to give it that extra hour. Then, if there was nothing coming through, he would have to assume that this particular and necessary part of the plan had failed. That would be very upsetting as, if he wanted to continue, he might then have to find another professional to accomplish this mission.

He was a substantial man in many ways and his wealth helped him accomplish all his needs and wishes. But the wait was now making his need for food insatiable, so he called room service. He decided eating, which was his favourite pastime, would bring a satisfying and calming air to a wait that had now become intolerable.

Within ten minutes there was a knock on the door with the recognisable "Room service." About time, he thought.

Thirty minutes into his feast, his mobile phone started to buzz. Sheikh AbdulWahab immediately stopped and grabbed the phone in excited anticipation.

"Yes?"

"It's done."

"Both of them?"

"I said it's done, you don't need the rest. If you want more, turn on the TV."

"Okay, just making sure!"

"You'll deposit the remainder?"

"Inshallah, I am a man of my word. Besides, I will have some more work for you in the near future, as I had originally promised. That will be even more rewarding for you."

"Thank you. I look forward to it."

She clicked off.

AbdulWahab did want more, so he took the advice and switched on the TV. Sure enough, it was the lead story on Al Jazeera as well as BBC News 24, ABC, CNN, Sky et al. He watched for a while and, to his displeasure, saw a man, described simply as 'the driver of the cab' talking to uniformed police officers and another man in plain clothes, presumably a detective. AbdulWahab's level of concern was now raised.

That concern got the better of him and he picked up his mobile phone, texted "*WHAT ABOUT THE CAB DRIVER?*" and sent it.

He didn't have to wait long as the message came back, "*HE'S NOT A PROBLEM. I WORE A WIG AND DISGUISE, AND HE WOULD NEVER KNOW ME, AND CONSIDERING THE AMOUNT OF NOTICE I HAD, THERE WASN'T ENOUGH TIME!*"

AbdulWahab was a little easier at this, and replied, "*OK FOR NOW.*" Nothing came back.

* * * * *

In North West London, Ella and Jess Resnick were in their TV room at home, watching a music channel and playing some DVDs, when Ella's phone pinged with a message from one of her friends. "*TURN ON NEWS 24 NOW.*" She quickly grabbed the control and turned on the news. The story of the shooting was being covered and details of it were repeatedly scrolling across the screen, as well as commentary that flashed up on the side. It went live to the scene and they both let out a loud yelp.

"Mum!…Come quick!…It's Dad. He's been involved with this shooting!"

A loud crash, as something dropped to the floor in the kitchen, was followed by a worried Jody Resnick rushing in to see what was happening.

She sat with her girls on the sofa and watched. Then calmly she got up and said, "I'll ring your Dad." As she did so, her thoughts went back to his former life in the military and security service in Israel, and the worry and anxious times while he was serving.

She brought up her speed dial and pressed Lenny's number, which went straight to voice mail. After the obligatory beep, she left a message. Her tone would tell her husband everything he needed to know about her worries and what she was thinking.

When Jody got off the phone, both girls looked at her expectantly. Sounding concerned at seeing how her mum looked, Ella said, "What's going on, Mum? What's happening with Dad?"

"I don't know, sweetie, but I'm sure Dad's okay. We'll know soon enough, I expect," Jody replied, as naturally as possible.

But she wasn't sure at all. She was fairly certain she had seen Matt Flynn on the TV, standing with a police officer, as he was questioning Lenny. If she was right, then it definitely wasn't all right; nothing really ever was when Matt Flynn was involved…and Jody wasn't a believer in coincidences.

After an anxious three or four minutes' wait, Jody's eyes narrowed when her phone buzzed: it was Lenny. Taking a deep breath, she pressed answer. "Hello," she said, her nostrils flaring as she heard the greeting.

"Hi, honey. What's up?" There was a longer than normal pause before she answered.

Lenny was standing with the two uniformed police officers who had been first at the scene of the shooting.

It wasn't long before a more senior officer appeared and spoke with the two uniformed officers, and then introduced himself to Lenny as Commander Stewart Scott, from the Counter Terrorism unit. They spoke for a minute or two, but before Lenny could get into details, the next person to join them was someone he knew. Matt Flynn had arrived in a hurry, making his way through the security cordon and joining Lenny and the Commander. He asked the Commander if he could have a quiet word. The Commander nodded, noted the credentials that Matt produced, and he and Matt walked away to discuss the situation.

Matt spoke first.

"Sorry to have interrupted you, Commander, but we have an interest in this situation."

"And what might that be?" queried Scott.

"Well, I can't disclose too much at this time as it is a security services operation, but suffice to say that the cab driver was taking the two men in the back to a meeting. They had some information we were interested in."

"So presumably there had been a leak and it had become known – hence the assassination and two dead bodies?"

"Yes, that about sums it up. Look, I don't want to interfere with police work and we have to be seen as following the correct procedures, so let the forensics do what they need to do and tow the taxi in for examination. This is clearly your domain, and once you have put out the usual appeal for witnesses, we'll liaise with you, of course, but we will begin our own investigation to find out who did this. We had hoped to have some of the answers, but this now puts us back and we are aware that something more serious may be occurring."

"I see," said Scott. "We will, of course, work with you as our national security is paramount, but we are Counter Terrorism, so I will expect full disclosure any time soon. I need to prepare my officers for anything that might be about to occur. Particularly the armed section."

"Fully understand that, Commander. My boss at Millbank, who I'm sure you know, is Mike Wyndham, and I'll brief him when I get back, after we've had a chance to talk to the cab driver. He's an old acquaintance and was doing the ferrying for us."

"Okay," said the Commander, "But I would appreciate a sight of the debrief, as it may help us in other areas in the investigation."

"Don't think there'll be any objection to that. I'll let Mike Wyndham know your thoughts. Maybe you can call him tomorrow. He'll be up to speed by then, and I expect the Home Secretary will want some eyes on the situation too."

"Yes, I expect so."

They parted company and Matt walked back over to Lenny.

The other officers had waited with Lenny, in the meantime, and made a few notes when Matt Flynn rejoined them. Credentials still in hand, Matt showed them to the officers. They listened for a few moments to what Matt had to say and then he asked the officers a few brief questions about any notes that they had taken. They replied with short, but explanatory, answers and Matt alluded to the fact that this was a national security issue and that Commander Scott would probably require their notebooks. They looked a little worried at this but Matt explained that they had nothing to be concerned about and they should move on and see if there was something more productive they could do. The two officers took their cue and slipped away.

Matt then turned to Lenny, but before he could say anything he was on the receiving end of, "What the fuck is going on, Matt? Who were they?"

"All in good time, Lenny, but I do need you to come back to Millbank to debrief."

"Yeah, well, I've got to call Jody; she left me a very terse message and is not happy, as she saw us on the news!"

"Okay, but make it quick, this is really urgent now."

"Matt, it'll be as long as Jody needs."

"Yeah, I got that."

Lenny walked away to find a quiet spot and hit the speed dial for his wife. It rang twice and then he said, "Hi, honey, what's up?"

There was a pause that felt like an age.

"What's up? WHAT'S UP?" Jody shouted. "Are you kidding me, Lenny? I've just seen you on the TV being interviewed by the police, and Matt bloody Flynn was lurking nearby, and you ask me what's up? What's going on, Lenny? And no bullshit please."

"Honey, if I knew what was going on, I probably couldn't say, but really I have no idea."

"Lenny, I don't do coincidence. What's happening?"

"Honey, I picked up the two guys and was on the way with the job … and you obviously know the rest! But I will find out. And, by the way, I'm fine."

"Yes, I can hear that and saw you, remember? But something's going on and I don't want you anywhere near it."

"Honey, I hear you, but seriously I knew nothing about this and I'm as angry as you are. But Matt does have to de-brief me, so I'll be a little while yet."

"Okay, but please call me straight back. I've been really worried and so have the girls."

"Yep, will do, and give them a hug for me."

They both clicked off.

Lenny went back over to where Matt was standing and said, "Okay, good to go."

"Really?" said Matt.

"Yeah, spitting bullets, and she's really not happy about you, but she knows we have to talk."

"Well, I'm not surprised about how she feels about me, but good to know she at least understands."

"You got that right, and she understands because she married me, warts and all, but she isn't happy with me having any connection to my former life."

"Yeah, got that too."

With all that in mind, and Lenny realising his cab was part of the crime scene, so wasn't going anywhere, he followed Matt to his car and the prospect of several hours of de-briefing. But it crossed his mind that the longer it took the more he was dreading facing Jody!

* * * * *

Jody had put the phone down and heaved a sigh, more out of relief knowing that Lenny was okay than of worry.

Both Ella and Jess were waiting for her to say something, but their attempt at being cool evaporated out of sheer frustration.

"MUM!" they both yelled, "Is Dad okay? When's he coming home?"

"Okay, you two, listen up. First, stop shouting at me and second, yes, Dad's okay and he'll be a while yet as he has to talk the police through what exactly happened."

"But is he really okay?" asked Ella, as Jess looked even more concerned.

"Yes, he sounded fine, if just a little hacked off this whole thing has happened, but he's got to make a statement and a few other things as well, and then see if he can identify the person who shot the two men. We'll see him later. Anyone for food?"

Things began to get back to normal when Ella and Jess, sensing a chance, both said at the same time, "Takeaway would be great." Jody didn't argue with them: she was too tired. She picked up her phone, dialled their favourite restaurant and ordered, not knowing how long Lenny would be, but glad he was okay.

4

Lenny sat at the table in the conference room of Section D, in the Thames side Millbank building of MI5. Also around the table were Matt Flynn, the section chief Mike Wyndham, and one other senior officer from the section, as well as Wyndham's deputy, Jennifer Hardie.

The formalities began with Matt introducing Lenny to Wyndham and Hardie, but before anyone could say very much else, Lenny jumped in.

"Before we go any further, can somebody please tell me what the hell I'm doing here?"

Expectantly, Matt looked at Wyndham, who nodded.

"Lenny," Matt began, "The two guys who you picked up were people of interest, in the sense that they had some information we needed and were on their way to talk with us, when they were assassinated."

"Okay," said Lenny, a bit calmer, "I'm listening."

"We've picked up chatter over the last months about something big being planned. The two guys were going to give us a name and that would've been a really helpful focal point of our enquiries, but that has now been put to an end."

"That's putting it mildly," said Lenny.

"Yes, and obviously the conclusion is that their intentions were discovered and subsequently their execution was ordered."

"Okay, that much I sort of figured. Y'know, I do have some experience here."

"Lenny, I'm telling you what we know, so cut the sarcasm."

At this point Wyndham held up his hand and they both stopped.

He looked at Lenny for a drawn-out moment, and then spoke, with a certain calmness.

"Lenny, or would you prefer Mr Resnick?"

"No, my friends call me Lenny."

"I'm much obliged," Wyndham said. "We appreciate your experience and the help you have given us over the years, both in Israel and the work you have done for us here. However, right now we need you to help us in any way you can. We believe that someone from an unidentified organisation is planning an attack on us here in the UK in one or maybe more of our cities, as some sort of spectacular terrorist attack. Will you help us?"

The request visibly stunned Lenny and, for what seemed an eternity, he was silent from the shock of what he had just heard. Wyndham then motioned to Jennifer Hardie, who opened a file and began.

"We first got wind of something around September of last year, about the time of the anniversary of 9/11. There is not much else except that the two men killed in your taxi had previously given us information that was good solid intel and that led us to prevent attacks and make arrests. They were, we believe, going to give us the main name. The assassination, we are fairly sure, was carried out by a top professional hit man to prevent that happening."

Lenny interrupted, "Wait a minute, why have you assumed it was a man, or am I missing something?"

Hardie responded, "Why do you say we assumed? We're saying we don't know of any female assassin capable of pulling off a hit like that."

"Well, excuse me for saying, but I think you're wrong!"

Wyndham was now looking even more concerned at the possibility that their intelligence was, or could be, so far off-beam.

"What makes you think it was a woman?" he asked.

"Well, for starters," Lenny continued, "Her hair was blonde and long. Now that could have been a wig, but when I was on the ground, I looked under the cab to see where she was before the shooting and then again after, but she had gone." Lenny thought for a few moments, then it dawned on him: he looked at Hardie and Wyndham. "Yes, for Pete's sake, I knew there was something strange, the shoes SHE wore had about a 2 inch heel, not stiletto, black, and I'd say around a female size 6. My wife is about the same size, and what I didn't get, until now, was that she was wearing a sculptured black mask, you know, like one of those theatrical types."

Wyndham was now even more disturbed, as he realised his team had wasted too much time on assumptions. Not having the chance to speak to the informants had put them back to square one.

"Okay, this is not good. We have the distinct probability of a large-scale terrorist attack somewhere in the country and we don't know where, when or what form it will take. So, someone please tell me, what the hell do I tell the Home Secretary? He'll probably have me sectioned for being insane or more likely, fire me!

He turned to Lenny and asked him again for his help.

"Lenny, I am aware, obviously, of your connection to Matt and your previous work with Israeli internal intelligence. We . . . err, I would really appreciate your input for the foreseeable future. I'll get you clearance as a matter of urgency and we need to start talking to assets in the Middle East, as well as contacts in Mossad and Shin Bet too. I'm assuming I won't have a problem getting you clearance?"

Lenny shrugged and, with a mischievous smile, replied, "Shouldn't think so, I am a fit and proper person, after all." Matt felt himself grimace while Wyndham left without understanding and Hardie smiled, but out of pretence. It was another cab reference.

As Matt and Lenny left to develop a strategy, Matt turned to Lenny, "Did you really need to go the fit and proper route?"

"Well, did he really need to ask the question?"

They walked on and found a quiet room, where Matt told Lenny to wait while he found some coffee and food. It was now nearly 02.00 and Lenny realised that Jody must be pacing like mad and in a really bad mood. He decided that at this time of night it would be best just to text. He pulled out his phone and completed the message in less than a minute.

The reply came back almost immediately *"WHATEVER YOU ARE DOING OR ABOUT TO DO, REMEMBER YOU HAVE A FAMILY. Jody X."* Lenny felt a lump form in his throat. The need to reply was urgent.

"HONEY I AM JUST TRYING TO HELP. THEY WANT ANY INPUT FROM ME AS WELL AS AN OPINION AND SOME PERSPECTIVE. LOVE YOU AND THE KIDS LOTS. Lenny X." He pressed send; nothing came back.

A few minutes later Matt returned with a large coffee pot, two mugs and a plate of freshly made sandwiches and snacks.

They ate the sandwiches and snacks, and drank a lot of coffee over the next few hours, during which time they went over every detail of what had happened, especially the girl on the bus and how the incident played out right up to the shooting.

Matt asked Lenny about the assassin again. What was she wearing? How tall, what colour hair, did he see her face? At that point Lenny said, "Damn" again. Matt replied with, "What have you remembered?"

Lenny closed his eyes and replayed the incident in his mind over and over for a few minutes. When he opened his eyes he spoke in a very measured tone.`

"I thought she was black, but she was, as I said, wearing one of those sculptured masks." He paused for a moment and then continued, "She had on a beige trench coat, and strangely not what I said before about the shoes, they were definitely about a 3 inch stiletto heel, not your regular assassin! But one thing she had I suspect it's standard equipment was a Glock 9mm automatic and a suppressor."

Matt thought all this through for a few minutes and then pulled out a file that contained pictures and profiles of known assassins. Most were male, but two were female. They both had little detail and no pictures; however both were of similar height and the choices were either West Bank Palestinian with certain links to Hamas, or Iranian original with an obvious Hezbollah link.

"So there it is. We are looking at a female who has had obvious training, and probably one of these two."

"OK, we've made some progress, so let's reconvene tomorrow. I'm sorry, I mean later today," (as it was now 05.00) "Let's say around midday?"

"Well, I will have to sweet talk Jody a little, but midday should be fine."

"Let me know when you're here and, hopefully, Wyndham will have your temporary clearance ready."

They got up and simultaneously stretched to shake out the stiffness from sitting so long. Matt walked Lenny out of the building. They shook hands and Lenny stepped outside into the still dark and damp early January morning. He zipped up his leather bomber jacket and turned up his collar to keep the wind off. Then he walked a few paces, turned and hailed a passing cab. He asked the driver for Green Park Station, where he would take the Jubilee Line back to Stanmore. From there, it was a short walk to his home.

Forty-five minutes later, Lenny was walking through his front door. Jody was waiting. They looked at each other for few seconds before she ran and flung her arms around him and held him as tightly as she could. They pulled gently apart and shared a loving kiss. Then he said, "Honey, I need to sleep as I have to go back to debrief at midday, so I need some food and then bed. I'll explain everything I can when I get home tomorrow. I'll need a few days off anyway, as the cab was part of the crime scene."

"Well at least they can rent you another cab?" She started to laugh.

Lenny also started to laugh.

"Look, they're not going to get my help for free. It's fine Matt will sort it!"

"Matt?" she questioned, "I knew the minute I saw him on the TV at the scene, you were bound to be roped in somewhere! He always knew where to call you when we were in Israel, and it nearly always ended with trouble!"

"Honey, it's not like that. They need my perspective since I have some expertise on Middle East stuff, and that's all I can say right now. So, can I please have some food now? I'm starving! I'll grab a shower and be down in ten."

Lenny ate the large plate of food Jody had prepared and drank the lemon tea, his tea of choice, and then went to bed. He lay awake for just a few minutes, thinking of what had occurred over the last fourteen hours or so, and then he fell into a deep sleep.

Eight hours after the shooting, Banu Behzadi arrived back at her apartment in the Arab quarter of Marseille, not far from the port.

The journey had been a little more hectic than expected, but luckily she was travelling light and had only one piece of hand luggage. She had quickly broken down the weapon into individual bits and disposed of them in litter bins that she had scoped out previously, on the way to St Pancras International. She caught the Eurostar to Gare du Nord in Paris and then from Gare de Lyon she travelled by the fast train down to Marseille, her adopted home city. Amazingly, the journey was pretty quick as it only took a minute or two shy of six and a half hours.

Although she had eaten on the train, it wasn't much mainly because she always had knots in her stomach for several hours after completing an assignment. She found it difficult to eat anything more than a small snack. After entering her apartment, she quickly checked that everything was okay and none of the security procedures she'd put in place had been triggered. They hadn't. Banu put her bag and hand luggage in her bedroom, quickly changed into more comfortable clothes and went to her well-equipped and very modern kitchen; she was now feeling hungry, as her appetite had returned.

She made herself a salad with leaves, humus, falafel, goat's cheese and some quartered fresh figs. She toasted pitta bread and poured herself a glass of white wine, a Sauvignon Blanc from Languedoc. She was a Muslim but she did like her wine, especially from the Southern French regions.

Banu finished her meal, poured herself some more wine and settled at her laptop to check one of her untraceable bank accounts, to make sure the Sheikh had been as good as his word. He had! She knew he would, but in her line of work the feeling was to trust nobody, that way the chances of survival were greater. Sure enough, her account had grown substantially. "Inshallah," she thought, it had been done.

She settled back onto her favourite sofa, realised her wealth was growing and began to reflect back on her humble beginnings with her family.

Her parents were anti-Shah teenage activists prior to the 'bloodless' Islamic Revolution in 1979 and were overjoyed when the Ayatollah took power and became the Supreme Leader. Very quickly, he moved the Iranian state from its position as a Royal dictatorship to an Islamic State.

Banu had been born six years after the revolution and grew up hearing stories from her mother, Leila, and father, Golam, about the struggles against the Shah's pro-western policies and the actions of his secret police SAVAK, as well as their notorious methods of interrogation and torture.

Both had suffered at the hands of SAVAK, an organisation similar to the Gestapo, in the years prior to the takeover. They were identified as troublemakers and spent several months at a time on a number of occasions being the recipients of torture and other vile practices.

As she grew up, her antagonism towards the West became even stronger because of her parents' teachings and the prolonged anti-West propaganda that had poured out from the state-run news service. By the time she had reached 19, a year after the second Iraq war, the evil dictator Saddam had been removed by the Western allies, along with some help from Muslim countries. As an Iranian, though, she had not lost her hatred of Saddam Hussein, the man who had fought a ten year war against her country; but this hatred now sharpened to an objective to expel the western intruders from Islamic lands and, as a further aim, to destroy the 'evil State of Israel'.

Also, by the time she had reached nineteen, Banu had learned much about the cause she was now totally wedded to, and sought the next step. She travelled to Syria, where she was taken in by Hezbollah. She spent a couple of years earning their trust, training hard, impressing her teachers and learning everything she could about terrorism. From bomb-making to planning suicide missions, using all sorts of hand guns and other weaponry. She carried out terrorist attacks over the border in Northern Israel, along with other like-minded activists. The thing she grew impatient with was the constant use and misuse of interpretations in the Quran. Her parents had taught her the reality and the true meanings of the Holy Book, but the interpretations of many of the zealots she trained with she found an abomination. It was contrary to what her parents and many of the moderate clerics had taught her.

She had carried out a number of terrorist activities by the time she reached her twenty-third birthday, and, though she had remained true to her Islamic beliefs, she had begun to realise that there was always more than one side to an argument. The trick was to be on the right side of that argument, or get well paid for not being.

Then she found Marseille, white wine from Languedoc and great southern French-Arabic cuisine. She didn't take long to make the choice to live in this fascinating and diverse place. It was almost home from home. She had accrued money from all of the private missions she carried out and was quick-witted enough to realise that she needed to set up accounts where some of the spoils of her illegal terrorist actions could be secreted away. Using some of the trusted contacts she had made over her time in 'action,' she had set up a secure network to make sure incoming and outgoing funds were untraceable.

News of her 'availability' got around and she was meticulous in her acceptance of any 'work' that came her way, having a number of checks that she could carry out to make sure she wasn't being set up. As time went on, she developed a very sophisticated system that she constantly kept updated, keeping ahead of technology, so she felt secure enough to maintain her life in France and her anonymity.

During her time in the Hezbollah training camps, Banu and others were sent out on incursion missions into northern Israel. They were generally small in size but were meant to keep the Israelis on edge and in constant fear. They would enter a small kibbutz settlement to terrorise and kill, and then they would exit as quickly as possible.

On her last mission into Israel, and the most difficult at that time, the incursion was expected and the Israeli defence and intelligence services were waiting for them, having received some very attributable information that had been confirmed through reliable sources.

Banu and her group had made the incursion in the same way as they had done many times before. The group had stealthily moved into the kibbutz area and began the build-up to the action and the terror they were about to cause, when all hell broke loose.

As her group came out into the open, something seemed wrong. There was no one around, no music, no laughter, no sounds of TVs and no noises of mechanical engines of any sort. Banu somehow sensed this and slowed her pace; the rest of the group missed this and carried on moving towards designated targets. Banu crouched and waited.

Then, without any warning, arc lights came on and lit up the area exactly where her comrades were. Heavy automatic weapon fire started. Her group of eleven were cut down in seconds and then the firing stopped. Shortly after, out stepped a man in combat fatigues with no army markings, followed by what was obviously a specially trained IDF unit, probably Sayeret Matkal (Special Forces), but he seemed to be in control. He was young, but older than she, and barked out orders. Banu was surprisingly calm, despite having just seen her group completely wiped out. After about twenty-five minutes, the Israelis had finished loading the dead terrorists onto trucks and had moved off. The total lack of noises remained. After several minutes more, Banu slowly made her way back to the border. This took much longer than she would have liked, but she had to be totally aware of what was around her since it was pitch black. She couldn't use any sort of light, but managed to find her way back to the border using a compass. After crossing back into Syria, she had made her mind up that her life needed to take another turn.

Going back to the camp was now not an option, especially as she was the only survivor and there would be questions. She decided to make her way into Lebanon, where she had several friends in and around Beirut; they had all trained with her in the camps, knew her and she knew she could trust them.

She suddenly remembered the face of the Israeli in the unmarked fatigues: she hadn't thought about him until about nine hours earlier, when he fell out of the driver's door of a London cab, after she had assassinated the two treacherous informants. She wondered if it was meant to be.

CHAPTER

6

It was 11.00 hours. Standing by the river side entrance of Millbank SW1, his back to the Thames, Lenny was looking at the building he was about to re-enter, nearly seven hours after he had left. It followed what had been a very harrowing day, one he never thought he'd experience again, since coming back to the UK for a quieter life.

He took out his phone, went to speed dial and pressed Matt Flynn's number. It rang twice. Flynn answered.

"As prompt as ever. You outside?"

"Yep on the river side, looking at the building."

"Okay, meet you by the front door in two."

"Okay."

Lenny clicked off, crossed the road and walked up the steps. As he reached the door, it opened and Matt ushered him in, and handed Lenny his temporary credentials.

"Wow, that was quick. I am impressed. No problems then?"

Matt smiled.

"No, it's not what you know," he said. They moved through the security smoothly, as Matt nodded at the two heavily built security guards.

They walked up to the second floor, went through the electronic security doors and into Matt's grid section. Matt was senior field officer, a step down from section chief, so had pretty high-level security clearance. He led Lenny into the conference room they'd used earlier. Waiting for them were Station Head, Mike Wyndham, and Jennifer Hardie.

Wyndham smiled.

"Good morning, Lenny. Hope you're rested and ready for a pretty full on session to try and find some answers?"

Lenny returned the smile and nodded, with obvious reservation on his face. Something that Wyndham noticed, but decided to say nothing about.

"So, let's get straight to it," Wyndham continued. "We need to establish, ASAP, on whose behalf our assets were taken out, who financed the killings, are they different people or one of the same? Also, what is the end game and who the hell carried out the hit? We also need all this in hours, not days, because whatever is planned is obviously serious enough to have warranted a hit like this to make sure that there were no leaks. So unless we stop it now, it will cause utter mayhem!"

"Obviously, the Met are involved via Anti Terrorism and we will be co-ordinating information with them as well as keeping serious crime updated too," Jennifer Hardie added, "They'll do the spadework, looking for answers around the crime scene. Also, Matt, we have asked for the notebooks from the two police officers at the scene that Lenny spoke with."

"So, any ideas?" asked Wyndham.

No one spoke for what seemed an age. Then, as if to jog everyone's memories, Lenny said, "Anyone any ideas or info on a possible female shooter?"

Again, silence broke out, as they all seemed to look to him for something more.

"Look, that's all I have. Remember, I saw female shoes, 3 inch stiletto heels and approximately a size 6. Oh, and long blonde hair, possibly a wig. So, apart from the wig and a sculptured black mask and the stilettos, I'm convinced it's not a guy, it was definitely a woman!"

Wyndham looked at Jennifer Hardie and nodded. She opened a file in front of her.

"Lenny," she said tentatively.

"It's okay," said Lenny, "As I said, my friends call me that!"

She half smiled with a relieved look and continued, "After your earlier suggestion, we looked again at some of our sourced material and reviewed chatter, and although the two possible suspects in the file were a fit of sorts, there is now a third and more likely candidate."

"Okay," Lenny jumped in. "Who is she and where is she?"

"That's a little more difficult," said Hardie. "Anything more is sketchy, and we are trying to confirm further details. The only possibility of a link is that she could be Iranian."

Wyndham now re-entered the discussion.

"Lenny, we think it might be time for you to speak to some of your former colleagues in Shin Bet or Mossad."

"Me? Why, you don't have channels?"

"Unfortunately, our current political masters are having problems with the Israeli government and their security services are being a little less forthcoming."

"You mean they're giving you the run-around?"

"Yes."

"Langley involved?"

"Quite probably."

"Okay, I'll get on it as soon as Matt can show me where to sit and use a secure phone."

"Well, this is MI5 so the phone will be secure, but," Wyndham paused and all eyes now fixed on him expectantly, "What may be needed is a face to face with them, you know, a bit more personal."

"Okay, where do I meet them? Are they over here?"

Wyndham cleared his throat, "Lenny, this is a face to face with them, over there."

"Oh no, no, no! I'm already running a fine line with Jody. Any deeper and my marriage is toast!"

"Why don't you make a holiday out of it, take the family? After all, you've all had a nasty shock and your cab won't be ready for at least ten days, so make the most of it."

"Fine, and, by the way, who's paying? I don't have a fairy godmother!"

"Lenny, you're helping us. We'll take care of it."

"Okay, not to put too much pressure on…but when do you want me to go?"

Wyndham glanced at Matt, before answering.

"Well, as soon as possible, in a day or two, if that's good for you!"

"Um, you're kidding?"

"No, and we need Matt there too."

"Well, that'll really please Jody!"

"Lenny, we need to get as much information as soon as we can.

You can tell Jody what you need to, but I'll keep out of the way," said Matt.

"Look, Matt, you know why she's sceptical about me being around you. We had some real nasty moments in the past and "never again" she said, and really I can't argue with that."

"Lenny, I get all that, but this really is a matter of top priority. I mean, it's national security. We've had some worrying chatter and someone, we don't know who, is possibly planning something that rates as horrific, and we need to know who and where, and of course, when. We need to talk to the Israelis face to face, ASAP!"

Lenny resigned himself to the fact that there was not another option available. "Okay, I'll call Jody and tell her the good news."

"Good news?" ventured Wyndham.

"Yeah, she's going on holiday! It could be a sweetener."

Lenny and Matt stood up, glancing at their watches. It was now 14.40. They agreed to do what was needed and meet in twenty minutes to develop a list of contacts to visit in Israel.

They split up and Lenny found a small, empty room. He took out his mobile phone, looked at it for a few unnerving moments, and then dialled Jody.

It rang twice. Jody answered, "Lenny…what's happening?"

"Hi, honey…nothing much…how'd you fancy a holiday?"

"Okay, Lenny, what's going on? I don't think I became an idiot overnight!"

"Nothing really, but we've got a chance of some sun and relaxation in a warm climate."

"So let me guess…ooh, let me think where it could be at such short notice…"

"Okay, Jody, cut it out – we're going to Israel for 10 days."

"So is that R&R or will you be working?"

"Well, I may have some stuff to do."

"Thought so! Matt going too?"

"Not with us, he's not, but he will be there for some of the time… yeah."

"Just keeps getting better," she sighed in a resigned way.

"Honey, we're getting a trip paid for, so I need to go and talk with some of my contacts over there. Information is needed."

"So why is Matt going? There's always trouble when he's around."

"Look, honey, it'll be fine, and that's a little unkind."

"Hmmm."

"Okay, I'll be home in a few hours. Get things packed, not sure what flight we'll be on."

He clicked off.

Lenny found Matt and they went to the canteen for food and coffee, and began to put together a list of people to see in both Tel Aviv and Jerusalem.

They spent just over two hours constructing a plan of action together, when Jennifer Hardie found them and said that there'd been a small breakthrough and they were re-convening in the meeting room straight away. They both instantly got up and followed her to the room, with a sense of increased expectation.

Wyndham motioned for them to sit.

"We have bits of what may be the weapon used by the assassin."

"How come and how many bits?" interrupted Matt.

"Three bits, suppressor, barrel and empty magazine, in three separate rubbish bins around Marble Arch."

Lenny entered the discussion.

"There's a couple of questions – why and how has she gone to Marble Arch? What has she done with the rest of the contents of the magazine? And any CCTV?"

"We're getting that looked at now and forensics are checking the weapon parts for anything relevant."

"Don't hold your breath on that. This woman was a pro."

"You were right on the gun though: it was a Glock. Good spot, Lenny," Wyndham added.

Matt looked at Hardie and asked her if there was a directional sequence in the disposal of the gun parts.

"Yes, Great Cumberland Place, just up from the Cumberland Hotel, George Street, east of Baker Street and Marylebone High Street outside the Waitrose shop," replied Hardie.

"Hang on," said Lenny. "That sounds like part of a cab route going north east." "That's great, Lenny, and I'll expand the CCTV search," Wyndham interjected.

He left the room speedily.

"Something I said?" quipped Lenny.

"Don't know, but obviously something has triggered an idea. I've never seen him do that before," Hardie said. "He usually takes his time to think things over first."

"Well, I'm sure we'll find out in due course," said Matt. They finished the meeting and left.

Matt and Lenny walked back to the grid, and chatted about the proposal to sit down with the Israeli Intelligence Services. Lenny wasn't sure that much would be gained, but it was probably worth a try. Matt looked at his watch and they both decided that as it had been a long twenty-four hours, it was time to call it a day. They agreed to meet back at the grid at 09.00. Matt told Lenny that if the time changed or if Wyndham needed them back earlier, he would call him, so not to be without his phone. Lenny agreed, and left for home. He needed a good night's rest.

Since the assassinations in London, Sheikh AbdulWahab Al Zakani had spent every waking hour scanning news services for any information related to the incident, particularly about the cab driver.

Usually he wasn't so concerned about such trivia, but Banu Behzadi had messaged him with a request. Although he found this puzzling, he reassured himself she was just covering her bases. The thought did cross his mind that somehow the cab driver may have actually seen her, and could possibly give a description to the police or intelligence services; however, he decided to accede to her request. Given the nature of her work, he wouldn't ask too many questions as it might upset her and he was still in need of her talented services.

He was ensconced in his luxury suite at the Jumeirah Etihad Towers Hotel in Abu Dhabi. Enjoying the small triumph he had initiated against the two traitors, he was now even more emboldened to push his plan forward to a successful conclusion. He got up from his large and luxurious sitting room and moved to a smaller room just off of the main area, which he used as an office. He opened a file sitting on his desk and started flicking through it. The file wasn't very thick but was full of names and contact details.

He found what he was looking for relatively quickly, wrote down the number of the contact he had searched for, put the file back in a drawer, and then picked up his phone and dialled the number.

Omar Hussain was the son of a relatively wealthy Saudi businessman, who also happened to be a friend of Sheikh AbdulWahab. Omar's abilities and skills base were somewhat limited in business areas, but the job he carried out was well within those limitations. Sheikh

AbdulWahab had pulled some strings to get Omar a job in the diplomatic service some years earlier, something that he took to, and having spent ten years in Saudi Embassies in other parts of the world, he had achieved a level that warranted a promotion. He had now been posted to the prestigious London Embassy.

The property that housed the Saudi Embassy was the formerly named Crewe House. It was a beautiful 18th century mansion located in Curzon Street, in London's Mayfair district. The house was built in 1730 and was owned by a couple of generations of Lords Wharncliffe from the early 1840s before being bought by the Marquis of Crewe in 1899. It was then renamed Crewe House. It was turned into offices around 1937 and sold to the Saudis around 1988.

It was a busy day, as people were still on alert after the incident at Hyde Park Corner a few days earlier. Omar was at his desk in the Embassy, when his mobile phone buzzed. He picked it up, saw it was an international call and answered with caution.

A voice that sounded familiar said, "Is that Omar?"

"Yes," was the hesitant response, "Who is this please?"

"Omar, it has been a long while but I didn't think you'd forget my voice that easily."

"Oh my…Sheikh AbdulWahab, a thousand apologies, how stupid of me, how can I be of assistance?"

"It's all right, Omar, I was just joking, no harm done, but I do need a favour."

"Yes, of course, Sheikh Abdul. How can I be of help?"

"Omar, I need you to get some information about someone, but I need you to be the model of discretion and nobody must know why or who asked you. In fact, it would be best if you did this without anyone else's involvement, I'm sure you understand?"

"Of course, Sheikh, I understand. What or who is it you want me to find?"

Sheikh Abdul gave the details to Omar and told him it was important that secrecy be maintained. Omar, as subservient as he could be under the circumstances, said all the right things and told the Sheikh he should be able to obtain the information he wanted. Although it would need discretion so as not to arouse any unwanted questions, he would do his best but it would take a little while. The Sheikh, somewhat agitated, told him speed was of the essence, but that he understood because he realised it was complicated. He would await his call. With that and many humble apologies from Omar, he and the Sheikh ended the call.

Sheikh Abdul went back to his luxurious lounge where a fresh supply of food had arrived via room service. He settled back and began to feast, satisfied that he would have the information requested by Banu Behzadi reasonably soon. He allowed himself a brief smile and then ate.

About the same time at the Saudi Embassy in London, Omar Hussain dialled a number, and after two rings a man answered. They spoke for about five minutes and then he hung up. Omar was satisfied he'd get the information he needed, just not sure when, although there would, no doubt, be a quid pro quo.

Matt Flynn put his phone down and sat for a moment in thought. He got up, hesitated momentarily, then left his desk and strode purposefully to Mike Wyndham's office. He knocked, waited and walked in.

Wyndham looked up.

"Matt, what's up?"

"Think I just got a break with the 'who'."

"How so?"

"A Confidential Informant that I hadn't heard from in a while, just called me and asked for some details on someone, and said a Middle Eastern gent wanted to know."

"I presume that someone is our cab driver friend?"

"Yep."

"So who's the Middle Eastern gent?"

"He wouldn't say too much. But some oil Sheikh who spends most of his time in Abu Dhabi."

"Okay. When does he want the info?"

"ASAP."

"What did you tell him?"

"Said I'd see what I could do."

"Okay, no mention of this. Let's try and drag this out 'til we've made our own enquiries. I've got people checking Lenny's suggestion on the CCTV, but it's time-consuming and could take a few days."

"What about my CI?"

"Stall him. If he's serious, he'll wait. Give him false but believable titbits for now."

"Okay, but I really think he has something to trade. I've known him a while."

"As I said, Matt, let's get our plan up and in the game, and then we can see what he's got. Give him something to whet his appetite for now."

"Will do."

Matt closed the door behind him and stood for a few moments, before returning to his desk to make some enquiries of his own.

He had a few people he knew from the Foreign Office, who he could rely on to check Omar's 'circle' of family and friends and, although there was a certain problem between the two main intelligence services, there were one or two people at Six he could rely on and talk to in confidence.

His first call, though, was a contact at the Foreign Office, Petra Green. She was a senior officer in diplomatic protection attached to the FO. Matt knew her from their time in the Met and they saw each other now and again. Platonic, and just friends, though Matt had once thought that there was a spark of something, until she intimated "men weren't her thing," so he concentrated on just talking shop.

He called Petra and told her about the possibility of an as yet unknown 'activist' from either Saudi or the Emirates organising something big in the near future. She said that she hadn't heard anything specific, but asked if it was related to the latest incident at Hyde Park Corner. Matt said that he didn't really have anything concrete on that, but it was probably connected.

They agreed to update as and when, and that lunch was a good idea some time soon. Matt put down his phone and sat for a minute or two, deep in thought.

He was wondering how it was possible someone new had got to a level of planning so far under the radar that there was little or no intel from anywhere, especially chatter from GCHQ. That, he thought, would be his next port of call. But it would have to be in person, as any delay could exacerbate the situation. He decided, however, Lenny should go too, and he would have to delay their impending trip to the Middle East, at least for a day or so.

He would have to call GCHQ to arrange the visit and run it by

Mike Wyndham, and then he would let Lenny know and would call to break the news about the short delay after getting the okay. He realised that this was just another black mark against him, as far as Jody was concerned. But it was what it was, and any enmity she had for him, because of events years previously, would have to be worked out or at least parked, whilst the current situation was unresolved.

Matt picked up his internal phone and dialled Wyndham's number. He usually went to his office and talked situations like this over, but was clear in his own mind what was needed in this particular instance and he also knew he had Wyndham's confidence to make well-judged decisions. Wyndham answered. "Matt, something wrong?"

"No, Mike, just wanted to get your okay on a visit to GCHQ, something I think we need to do, and I need Lenny to come with me, before we go to Israel." He explained his thinking and it didn't take long before Wyndham saw the need. He told Matt he would make the arrangements, as he knew the person to speak to at the listening facility. He would call him with the details, and in the meantime Lenny needed to be told of the slight change of plan. Matt agreed and said that he would call him. He put the phone down, picked up his mobile, scrolled through his favourites list, found the number and pressed the button.

CHAPTER
8

After speaking with the Sheikh, Banu Behzadi became impatient to find out about the London cabbie she had recognised at Hyde Park Corner a few days before. However, she realised that her now private vendetta against the man she was sure was the same Israeli commander who had been in charge of the unit that had ambushed her group those years ago in Northern Israel, would be on the back burner. Her immediate commitment was to her current contract with the Sheikh and that had to be fulfilled, not only because she wouldn't break a lucrative contract, but also because to do so would damage the excellent record of reliability and reputation she had enjoyed up until now, in getting a job finished in accordance with the clients' wishes.

Sheikh AbdulWahab had contracted her to see through his plan as its leader on the ground. After all he was paying her very well, a king's ransom in comparison, and she didn't want to mess it up. So she would wait for the details of the cab driver and deal with the problem in her own time, when it was more convenient to carry out what would be an act of vengeance for her dead comrades.

She had already begun to research how, where and when she could relocate, once the contract was completed. There would be a massive security crackdown everywhere, especially in Arab quarters like hers, as they generally harboured many people of interest to the authorities. Banu didn't want that inconvenience as she wanted to remain as uninteresting as possible in the immediate aftermath because she would still want to complete that personal business. It would still be a number of months to the proposed action. There was much to do in the meantime and many willing 'helpers' to recruit and instruct, to carry out the proposed attack on the Infidels of the UK.

But for now, her need to relax and restore her energies was uppermost in her mind and so she moved into her kitchen area and checked on her evening meal that was slowly roasting in the oven. She had prepared a shoulder of lamb, pomegranate molasses, cumin, onion, garlic, lemon juice and olive oil, and put it in to cook slowly for three hours. The aroma was just how she remembered it from her mother, Layla. Banu had planned to eat it with a pomegranate seed salad, and washed down with another of her favourite French white wines, this time from the Loire Valley.

Banu still had some time, so she decided the recruitment needed to begin urgently. She called a close friend and also a former resident of the Hezbollah camps to help. His home was now in Beirut, which was two hours ahead of her, but he was a man of habit so she didn't hesitate and called. When the man's voice answered, she said excitedly, "Hossein, it's good to hear your voice!"

"Banu, my dearest friend, how are you? Where are you?"

"Hossein, as always, a gentleman! Yes, my friend, I am fine, thank you, and keeping busy. Where am I? Well, at this moment I'm in my apartment."

"Oh, Banu, as always the mysterious one, and a blocked number too! After all this time, you don't trust me?"

"No, my friend, of course I do, but in my line of work you can't be too careful. I block my number as a habit, but I will text it to you when we've finished."

"Of course, and rightly so, and thank you, that would be most helpful. Anyway, what is it that I can do for you?"

"Well, it's very delicate and too difficult to explain in a phone call. Are you travelling at all, any time soon?"

"Travelling? Anywhere particular you had in mind?"

"Western Europe!"

"Banu, I think the world of you, I'm sure you know that, so tell me what is it you think that's so important for me to travel to wherever you are?"

"Hossein, it is of such importance that you must come, it can't be done in a phone call, Skype or FaceTime. It must be face to face!"

"Banu, you are beginning to worry me."

"Really, I'm okay but it's work and I need your assistance."

"Okay, but you will owe me big time! So where do I need to get to for this important meeting?"

"Hossein, please, it's not a joke. I have a lot riding on this. Can you get into Marseille without too much trouble?"

"Yes, of course. How long have I got?"

"Okay, can you do it in two days?"

"Well, it's a bit tight, but it should be all right."

"Good, call me when you have your place and time of entry, and I'll meet you."

"Expect to hear from me in forty-eight hours."

"Safe journey and thank you."

They hung up.

Banu sat thoughtfully for a moment or two and sent Hossein her mobile number. The aroma of her cooking wafted past her nostrils. She longed for the beautiful flavours to tease her taste buds. She went into the kitchen and checked her slow roasting shoulder of lamb, realised it still needed more cooking for the meat to soften completely, so she set the timer for another forty minutes.

Meanwhile, her thoughts wandered once again to the London cabbie that seemed to have reappeared in her life after so many years. It brought back the pain and the vision of all her dead comrades. He would pay with his life. She poured another glass of wine and began to feel relaxed. On her favourite sofa, she set her glass down and drifted off to sleep.

She woke with a start, as the buzzer on her timer sounded in the kitchen, telling her the food was ready. She got up from the sofa and stretched her arms over her head. With a long yawn, she rubbed the sleep from her eyes and set about satisfying her appetite.

As she sat and ate the delicious food, interspersed with sips of wine, she thought about her times with Hossein, how their friendship had begun in the training camps and how it was him she went to for comfort when her group had been wiped out that fateful night in Northern Israel. Hossein was the one that helped her through that dark time, and gave her the encouragement she needed to rebuild her life and move on. Even now, though, she was still not totally clear about his history, except that he was Lebanese, and his family had all been killed, by both Israelis and other Arab terrorist groups, because he was a Hezbollah operative. He was a couple of years older than her, and had always been there for her after her many missions over the border. He was a master at planning attacks and was always ready with a solution to any problem. Now, however, she needed him again; after many years fending for herself, his many useful contacts were needed. She knew he wouldn't say no.

Banu cleared the dishes away, tidied her kitchen and began the next part of the preparation. She particularly needed specialists in armaments. Turning several pages without success, she finally found a couple of profiles that she felt were a perfect fit! Yes, she thought, exactly what's needed, both before and after . . .

Satisfied she had identified a major element that had been necessary, she set about the task of co-ordinating the plan, so as to produce and maximise the best effect. How the infidels would pay for their invasions of Muslim lands! That would fulfil the brief that she had received from Sheikh AbdulWahab, and as he was paying her an enormous fee for her services, she felt obliged to embrace some of his more zealot-like intentions. She also knew that when Hossein arrived, she would need to spend a few days with him, making sure he thought her plan was workable. Also to help her with the necessary changes that would make it so, for although she was very professional in the work she carried out, this was the first time she had taken on something of this magnitude. That was why she had called Hossein: he was the critical eye she needed. But for now she would wait for him to send his arrival time and date.

Also being the suspicious type she needed to be, she checked a few security scenarios so she could prepare to meet Hossein. She would also need to send him instructions from whichever entry point he arrived at. There were about three possible, so she compiled details on them all.

Even though she had slept earlier, she was now beginning to tire. She finished up, walked to her bedroom, undressed and got into her comfortable bed, and drifted off into a deep well-deserved sleep.

Lenny had arrived back at Millbank about forty minutes after getting the call from Matt. He was a little bemused to be called back so soon as he had only just got home, specifically to help everyone get ready for the trip to Israel.

On arriving, he made his way up to the grid and was met by a worried-looking Matt. Seeing this he said, "Okay, what's up? What was so urgent I had to come in?"

"There's been some new intel and we need to take a trip somewhere else before getting on the plane to Israel."

"What?" said Lenny angrily, "You're kidding me?"

"No, Lenny, I'm not," Matt replied semi-apologetically. "As I said, we've had some new intel, and we need to go to GCHQ at Cheltenham to talk to some people out there. Look, it's a delay of thirty-six hours tops. You want me to explain to Jody?"

"You wanna live a long and productive life?"

"Yeah…of course!"

"Then I'd better tell her!"

"Well, I hadn't planned to be telling her face to face!"

"And here was I thinking you were a real tough guy."

"Judas H…Lenny, what did I do that made her hate me?"

"You want me to tell you?"

"Yeah, I do…it really can't be that bad…can it?"

"Seriously, Matt, we haven't got time!" A mischievous smile started to appear on Lenny's face. Matt saw him and he gave Lenny a sharp look as if to admit defeat.

"Okay, enough of this now." As Matt's business tone took over, Lenny sensed the need to stop the clowning.

"Okay, Matt, what's the plan?"

Matt explained what the trip would entail: it was a maximum of a one night stay and the purpose was to try and establish any connection with known terrorist groups and if not see if there were any embryonic cells that were leaving any semblance of an electronic footprint. In addition, there was an urgent need to see if there was any intel on the assassin, as CCTV results had been sketchy.

When Lenny heard that last piece he looked totally bemused. Matt noticed immediately that his 'friend' wasn't happy.

"Okay, Lenny, spit it out. What's the problem?"

"Matt, I practically gave you the route a cab would have taken. What happened? The cameras didn't work?"

"The cameras work fine, Lenny, but there's nothing to suggest a cab picked the assassin up or that any more bins were used for disposal."

"What about ballistics and forensics?"

Matt explained that the barrel of the gun was damaged substantially but that although reconstruction was possible, it would be painstakingly slow. As far as forensics, it was so professional that there were no prints or fibres.

"So she is certainly a very careful and clever lady then," Lenny added.

"You're still going with the female theory then? The high heels gave it away?"

"Matt, the more I think about it, the more I'm sure. In fact my gut tells me we may get more when we talk to the Israelis. That's why we need to get there ASAP."

"First things first, Lenny, GCHQ, then we go."

Lenny nodded his agreement, albeit reluctantly. Matt reminded him of the phone call he needed to make, which made Lenny grimace, and as he left he turned to Matt and mouthed "COWARD," and moved on quickly.

Lenny found a quiet area and sat. He wanted to tell Jody as much as he could, but knew that was almost impossible as she was more likely to pull the plug on the trip or at least make it uncomfortable for all concerned. He knew she was worried for him and the girls of course, but he was involved in something, although by accident, and had been asked to help. Something he didn't want to do, but couldn't refuse.

He brought up his favourites on his speed dial and hit the top one, which just said Jody. She answered on the third ring.

"Hi honey," she said, "You on your way back?"

"No, not yet, still a few things to sort out…" His pause alerted Jody.

"Lenny, what's up? And no bullshit!"

"Nothing's up, honey, just a small change of plan."

"Okay, Lenny, how small? What, the trip's cancelled?"

"No, no, of course not, just postponed for thirty-six hours maximum. Matt and I have to go to Cheltenham to talk to some people out there, and it may be an overnight stay."

"Cheltenham? What, the SAS?"

"No, they're in Hereford; this is the listening place. Matt said he'd call you in case there was a problem." He felt his face grimace and wished he hadn't said that.

"Really? Then tell Matt Flynn he's lucky he didn't!"

"Yeah, I already told him."

"So when you going?"

"Tomorrow early and I will probably be back sometime the following afternoon."

"And then what?"

"Well, depending on what we find out, it should be back to the original plan."

"Do I need to unpack then?"

"Nope."

"Okay, lucky for you then! Wouldn't have wanted to be in your shoes, coming home to tell me and the girls that their holiday had been cancelled because you had to go somewhere else!"… There was a brief silence that was broken when Jody started to giggle.

"Okay, honey, you got me! I'll see you later," replied Lenny.

He clicked off, released a long hard breath of relief and broke into a smile. He thought he'd have some fun at Matt's expense. But first things first. Time to see if his assassin theory was holding up!

Matt was waiting for Lenny, and they went over some more details where Lenny kept up the pressure about his female assassin theory. The necessity to keep repeating this was borne out of the frustration of having to deal with a security service, set in its way, particularly when their ideas were put under scrutiny. The time passed quickly, so they decided to leave it for now and wait to see what the trip to GCHQ produced.

Lenny left Millbank and got home around 23.00. Although Jody was still up, there wasn't much to talk about as he was very tired and had to be up around 05.00 for another early start.

Matt got to the Millbank building in Westminster around 06.00 the next morning. To his astonishment, he heard someone running up the stairs behind him as he reached the front entrance. It was Lenny.

"What's up, Lenny, couldn't sleep?"

"Nope, slept like a log, totally rested!"

They walked in and went through security, then moved straight up to the second floor, where Jennifer Hardie was waiting for them. She ushered them into the small conference room, where Mike Wyndham was going through some papers. He looked up and motioned for them to sit.

He went through some preliminary information, and then more detail as to what they needed to ascertain, if possible, from GCHQ. Matt then asked if the ground had been prepared for their visit and who they would be met by. Wyndham, a little disdainfully, replied that the Director of the Intelligence Analysis Unit, Chris Hayward, would be there to meet them.

As soon as Wyndham had finished, the phone in the small conference room rang. Hardie picked it up and listened for a few seconds, then acknowledged and replaced the phone. She looked at Wyndham, who nodded, and she turned to Matt and Lenny to tell them their transport was waiting for them at the rear of the building. Matt and Lenny got up and left.

On their way out, Lenny asked, "What's the transport? Thought we were going by train?"

"Change of plan obviously. Wyndham thought it would be quicker and more productive to get there and back by car, because we may not find as much as we'd like, making the Israel trip even more urgent."

"Okay, so how long have we got at Cheltenham then?"

"Maximum twenty-four hours, just an overnight and back early tomorrow, and then Israel tomorrow night or early morning the day after. You can tell Jody when we're finished at GCHQ."

"Okay, can't wait!" he said, through gritted teeth. Matt looked at him and just smiled.

They left by the rear of the building, where the car was waiting. Matt knew the driver from previous trips and just enquired if he knew the details, at which the driver nodded and started the engine. Matt and Lenny both sat in the back, belted up and relaxed as it was about an hour and forty minutes' drive.

They chatted for a while, but Matt sensed Lenny was tired, so he stopped talking, and sure enough Lenny's exhaustion from the events of the last few days caught up and he slept. Meanwhile, Matt made some calls and did some prep work, ahead of the visit to Cheltenham.

Ninety minutes later they turned off the main A40 and started the drive up Hubble Road toward the entrance to GCHQ. As if sensing this, Lenny woke up with a start.

"Welcome back. Enjoy the nap?" asked Matt.

"Yeah, great, we here?"

"Couple of minutes."

"Looks like a flying saucer."

"Yes, a bit, they call it the Doughnut, as there's nothing in the middle."

"What, not the Bagel?"

Matt didn't respond.

They pulled up outside, got out and walked in through what was obviously the right entrance, where they were met by a tallish, balding man, Chris Hayward.

He walked towards them and greeted Matt, who in turn introduced Lenny. They spoke briefly before walking through security and then to Hayward's office.

Hayward was a tallish man, balding and of quite a genial disposition. However, this exterior hid a deeply serious inner strength that was reinforced by his belief that his job was a major part of the nation's security. Anyone who mistook this as a sign of flippancy was soon made aware of their error.

After a few minutes of chat and explanation by Hayward, as to where they were going and what their analysts had managed to discover, Hayward's phone rang. He picked it up and spoke, then listened for about a minute. He put the phone down and said, "Gentlemen, please follow me." He took them along the corridor from his office and in through a door marked 'Analysts'.

Lenny looked impressed by the level of industry and low hubbub of noise emitted by the operatives, Hayward noticed.

"Anything comparable in Israel, Mr Resnick?"

"My friends call me Lenny, and no, not that I'd remember, as I haven't been involved for some time, but you probably knew that?"

"Err…yes…indeed," Hayward replied rather sheepishly, and quickly moved to where two of the operatives were working and looking expectantly at them.

"Matt, Lenny, this is Tom and Sarah, two of our top analysts. They've pulled out as much as has been available. I hope it helps. Come and see me when you finish."

"Thanks," said Matt, "Much appreciated."

Hayward left and went back to his office.

Tom and Sarah began showing and explaining the amount of detail they had on all the different threads they could find, since they had been given the information sent from MI5.

"The difficulty we've had is that there's not been much chatter about the incident that we can confirm," Tom said, "However, we are confident that this was a precursor to something that may be in planning or has been planned for some time in the future. We are confident, though, that whoever is bankrolling or planning this 'new event' has been involved with other things previously but has become impatient and wants to move on now with his/her plans. The two victims who were shot/assassinated had obviously been discovered as informants, so were taken out."

"What about the assassin?" asked Lenny.

"Yes, we were just coming to that," Sarah chimed in, "We have looked at female profiles and although no real information, i.e. pictures or informed biographical detail, has been confirmed, we have had some chatter about a woman, early to mid 30s, possibly originally Iranian, and a product of a Hezbollah camp, not sure where she is, but we know she is now active."

Lenny looked at Matt with a certain amount of satisfaction that his theory was probably right. Matt noticed this but chose to ignore it.

"What about the money and Mr Big behind all this?"

"Yes," ventured Sarah, "We've looked at the possible connection in Abu Dhabi and have a couple of people of interest. One is an oil wealthy Sheikh and the other is a very wealthy businessman, mainly tech-based but also in armaments. Both live there more or less permanently. Not much else to go on right now but we can keep digging."

Matt thanked Tom and Sarah for their efforts and asked for the information on hard copy only, as they didn't want any electronic mishaps. They both looked at him in an incredulous way, but Matt just looked back and smiled.

Tom changed his expression and told Matt that a copy of the information would be with Mr Hayward in ninety minutes or so.

Matt and Lenny both left the room and found their way back to Hayward's office. They knocked and were beckoned in and motioned to sit, as Hayward was on the phone.

When he finished, they had a brief conversation about the day's events so far and agreed that they would take a break as it was now around lunchtime. As they had at least an hour and a half to kill, they asked where the canteen was.

Hayward gave them directions and told them to be back by 15.30. They went to hunt down their lunch.

The text appeared without warning, from an unknown number, but she knew it was the one expected. It was almost forty-eight hours since she had spoken to him. She read the text: *"ARRIVING AT GARE MARITIME FROM CORSICA 17.30."* Banu's heart began to beat faster and she just replied, *"WILL BE THERE."*

The Gare Maritime is the port where ferries dock, coming in from Corsica, Sardinia, Algeria and Tunisia. Banu thought, typical of Hossein to avoid the obvious, and realised her worry probably wasn't necessary.

It was now 12.30 so she had time to prepare. He would be tired and hungry, she thought, and would want to bathe. None of which was a problem as her apartment, on Rue Jemmapes, had two good-sized bedrooms with en-suites, and she always had the spare room ready for last-minute visitors.

She knew what he liked to eat and drink, so made her way to the local market. She wasn't sure how long he would stay, but she would be prepared for any eventuality.

Banu spent an hour or so in the market. She settled on hake, which she would serve with a particularly Mediterranean Provençal sauce and spiced couscous, with some seasonal herbs. They also had similar taste in wine, mainly because he had taught her how to appreciate it, so she bought two bottles of one of her favourite whites.

Her apartment was only a few minutes' walk from the market, which in turn was also a five minute walk from the Gare Maritime.

She arrived at her apartment and took her shopping through to the kitchen. She spent some time preparing the food and stopped when the only thing left to do was to cook it, and that wouldn't be for a while.

She returned to her files and sorted through possible candidates for the different tasks needed to complete the 'mission'. She was meticulous in her selection process and only those with experience in the field were kept for further approval. She needed experienced and battle-hardened activists, ready to shoot but also willing to die for the cause, as well as those willing martyrs who would receive their rewards in 'paradise'. For that, particularly, she needed Hossein's help.

She rested for a while and then thought about the best route to meet up with Hossein. Banu decided to be cautious, as she still had no idea if there had been any further complications or leaks. So the plan, she thought, was go to the ferry arrivals and wait for Hossein to exit the terminal. She would text him instructions to her apartment and then wait, just in case he was being watched or followed.

Just after 16.30 Banu unlocked a cupboard door in her lounge sideboard and took out a locked, strong metal box. She picked up her keys, found the one that fitted, and opened it. Inside was her preferred weapon of choice, a Glock 19 semi-automatic pistol, similar to the one she had used in London. She used this one over others, Beretta, Sig Sauer etc, as it was easier to carry and conceal, and, even with a suppressor, for her, it was the ideal weapon.

She took out the pistol to carry with her to meet Hossein. Over many years now, she had become wary of people she met. Basically, because her business was a lonely one, strangers and acquaintances had to earn her trust, although they never knew it. As for Hossein, even though she hadn't seen him for years, her instincts took over: caution was always the byword.

She found the warm jacket that she had added a pocket to, where she could conceal the weapon and its shape. Nobody would look at her wearing an outer garment, as it was winter and even though Marseille was a Mediterranean city and port, it was cold in January. She put on her jacket and concealed her weapon, then donned her hijab, an accompaniment she used when necessary, and left her apartment.

Banu found a spot down by the port with a good view of the exit. Although it was early evening, by the time Hossein's ferry arrived and he came through, it would be dark, but the port was well lit and she had settled in for what she hoped would be around a forty-five minute wait. She had also brought with her a set of small theatre-style binoculars, but with a more powerful range. It was near the time now and the ferry should have arrived. With any luck, Hossein would be coming out fairly soon. She had prepared a text message with instructions for him to follow. That would get him to her apartment. Meanwhile, she could observe Hossein and make sure he wasn't being followed. If he was, she would take care of it, hence the Glock and the hijab, as well as dark glasses she had brought with her, even though night would have fallen.

At about 17.45, Hossein appeared at the exit gate, looking around and just a little concerned. His phone buzzed. Looking at the screen, he began to smile. Banu could see this and saw him start to walk off, according to her instructions. Banu trained her binoculars behind him and watched for a few seconds. There was no movement and, after a few more seconds, she moved off.

She found her pre-planned spot and watched again. To her dismay, Hossein had picked up a tail. This was now problematic, but she would deal with it, far enough away from her apartment so as not to cause a problem. Fortunately, and by design, she had sent Hossein a longer way round, in case of something like this happening.

Banu thought quickly and ran to the alleyway she knew Hossein would come through. She found the sunken doorway she had pinpointed previously, and pressed herself against the wall. The wait wasn't long, as Hossein passed by her, still looking at the instructions on his phone. She took out the Glock, attached the suppressor, cocked the gun, as there was already a round in the chamber so no need to rack it back, less noise, and took off the safety catch. Sure enough, the tail, a man, passed her by. Banu stepped out and coughed. This startled the man and he turned around. Horror etched on his face when he saw the weapon pointing at him. That was his last thought, as he was hit in the chest by two bullets that entered directly in the heart area. As he went down, Banu stepped up close and fired another to the forehead for certainty.

She looked at him momentarily, took a picture with her smart phone and thought probably CIA. She then stepped out of the alley from the other direction to where she had entered, gun and suppressor concealed again, and then quickly made her way home. She knew she had time as Hossein would still be following her long route. She sent a text saying, *"ALL CLEAR SEE YOU SHORTLY."* Hossein looked at this, a little puzzled, but smiled. He continued to make his way to her apartment.

Six minutes later, he was at her door, and as he raised his hand to press the buzzer, the door opened and he saw a beaming smile that he hadn't seen for several years. Their feelings for each other, often hidden, were suddenly unleashed, as they embraced and kissed with great passion. She led him towards the bedroom and they didn't reappear till mid-morning the next day.

CHAPTER 11

It was now 19.00. Although Lenny and Matt had received the GCHQ intelligence dossier with the information they'd expected three hours earlier, it was late and they were still not much further forward.

They had already pieced together much of what was in the dossier, and, despite the fact it didn't yet give them the new leads they had hoped for, the two new pieces of intel were positive on the information Matt had received. This confirmed his thinking that an as yet unknown financier had bankrolled the hit and was possibly looking at something bigger. He was probably living in one of the Emirates, likely to be Abu Dhabi. Also, the theory of the assassin being a woman with a background of terrorism was now confirmed by GCHQ, since they had a snippet of intel on a contractor that had carried out a number of successful hits over the last eight to ten years and there had been a suggestion that it was a female, which was almost unheard of. That, however, was all a number of intelligence agencies had. Not much to go on in number, but nevertheless significant. Some of that intel had, encouragingly, come via Mossad! Matt and Lenny, on reading this, now believed a trip to Israel was a matter of urgency.

Lenny was going through some of the file, just to review the intel once more, in case there was anything else relevant, when Matt came back with some hot coffee.

"Just spoken with Mike Wyndham and he's now saying the Israel trip is top priority. We need to be on the plane by at least 10.00 tomorrow."

"Well, that's all fine, Matt, but getting Jody and the girls ready by then is a stretch. Plus we're not even in London and that's a two hour drive, if we leave now."

"It's all arranged, Lenny. Phone Jody and explain that she needs to be ready with the girls by 08.00. We'll send a car to pick them up and get them to Northolt for wheels up at 10.00. We'll sort out the formalities for the plane and they'll go straight through."

"Okay, so this is real serious stuff now, Matt. I'm wondering what I'm getting into here."

"Lenny," Matt ventured, "This part is intelligence-gathering, so nothing untoward is expected. It gets tougher when we find out what is being planned and when."

"Yeah, okay, why am I having serious doubts about it?"

"Lenny, just go phone Jody and tell her to pack you some clothes and, when the car gets there tomorrow, to call you with the registration number, so that I can check and also get the guy's name. And before you say anything, I'm being cautious. Now go and make the call!"

Lenny found an empty room just down from where they were and spent the next twenty minutes explaining to Jody and reassuring her that the trip was just a formality. She took some persuading, but finally relented and mundanely asked him what he wanted in the suitcase.

Feeling a little more secure with the knowledge she was on board, they rang off and Lenny went back to the room where Matt was, now on the phone to Omar at the Saudi Embassy.

"Omar, all I've got right now is he's one of 24,000 cab drivers. The police have his details and I spoke with him briefly at the scene. Any other details are not available as the police Anti-Terrorist unit are running this one for now, but I expect something more in a week or so."

Omar thought for a moment and then spoke, "Mr Matt, I have a fairly big fish on the line asking. I think he could be very interesting to you, surely there must be something more?"

"Omar, you have got what I know, but rest assured, when there's more you'll have it. So does this big fish have a name?"

"All in good time, Mr Matt, all in good time!" The phone went dead.

Matt filled Lenny in about Omar with as much as he thought he needed to know. Lenny looked at him as if to say, "What aren't you telling me?" Matt saw this but ignored it.

"So it's getting late, what's happening?" Lenny enquired.

"We're booked into a hotel not far from here, but we can get dinner first, and then sleep. We'll get a wakeup call for 06.30 and be on our way straight to Northolt for about 09.45."

"Good job I brought a change of clothes then!"

"Yep, me too. The car and driver are still here, so we'll drive to the hotel, check in and then get food."

"Sounds good to me. What about the driver?"

"He's on duty till he drops us off at Northolt in the morning."

They found their driver and car, and arrived at their hotel about fifteen minutes later. They checked in, left their bags in the rooms, met back downstairs and headed for the restaurant and bar.

* * * * *

Omar Hussain had sat at his desk, wondering for a while about the conversation he had previously had with 'Mr Matt'. It wasn't so much that the news wasn't what he had expected, but there was definitely something that Mr Matt wasn't telling him! However, it was what it was and the conversation he was about to have with Sheikh AbdulWahab would be a difficult one.

Omar hesitantly pressed the speed dial, it rang once … twice … a third time, just as Omar's confidence sapped and he was about to end the call, the phone was answered. Sheikh Abdul spoke, "Omar, my dear boy, how are you? I was beginning to think you'd forgotten about our recent chat!"

"Oh no, Sheikh AbdulWahab, of course not. I have been waiting for the information you requested."

"You have it?" the Sheikh asked expectantly.

"Err, um … not exactly …"

"Well, come on, Omar, don't keep me waiting. What do you have?" The Sheikh's patience started to wane and he was beginning to wonder if something was wrong.

"The person I spoke with, Sheikh AbdulWahab, was unusually vague. All I have right now is that the name of the driver and his details are not known and won't be released until after enquiries are complete."

Sheikh Abdul thought for a moment.

"Omar, you realise that is utter nonsense and you are getting the run-around? Who is this person you spoke with?"

"Sheikh Abdul, I can't say, as he is a useful source of information and I don't want to spoil that."

"Well, I understand that but is he someone with access to what I need?"

Then came Omar's mistake.

"Oh yes, Sheikh Abdul, he's security services…" As Omar said it, a shiver went through him and he wished he could take that back, but it was too late.

"Omar, I did say to you be careful who you ask. How could you be so stupid?" The phone went dead. Omar held it and stayed looking at it for what seemed an eternity, before throwing it on his desk, and letting loose a tirade of Arabic swear words. It was as if he had committed a mortal sin. His only thought was that his loose tongue could change his life completely.

* * * * *

Sheikh AbdulWahab stared at the food laid out before him, but couldn't even think of eating. He was still consumed with the idiocy of his friend's son, and the problems his actions had now, more than likely, caused. He thought for a while and then realised only one course of action was possible, and, as sad as that would be, nothing would be allowed to interfere with the plan.

Sheikh AbdulWahab picked up his phone, found the number and texted *"WE MUST SPEAK URGENTLY."* He put the phone down and waited.

Banu lay in her bed, recalling the wonderful night she had just experienced. She turned her head a little, just to look at Hossein. He was fast asleep, but she just wanted to watch him, and the way his body moved with every breath he took. She had never known such passion and pleasure.

Her phone buzzed. She turned away from Hossein and picked it up. It was a text message. Just four words, but with meaning and possible danger in every one of them.

She got out of bed, put her robe on and walked into her lounge, closing the door quietly behind her, so that Hossein could sleep.

She dialled the number and was answered almost at once.

"What is so urgent?" she asked.

"I need you to go to London and see someone, who has become problematic."

"When?"

"ASAP."

"With what in mind?"

"Peace of mind for me."

"Information or something else?"

"Both."

"Okay, the usual rates and conditions apply."

"Yes of course. I will do that now and send you the details. When will you go?"

"I will go within the week."

"No quicker?"

"No, I am in the middle of some planning for other events, but will go in a few days. Send me the details."

"Okay, I suppose it will wait a few days, but it is urgent and a problem!"

"I don't break agreements."

"No, I understand, but it is urgent as it could affect the planning."

"Okay, I understand."

"Oh, and the information you requested, you need to try and elicit that before the contract is completed."

Banu was puzzled, momentarily.

"Ah, it didn't work out as you had hoped?" she enquired.

"You could say that. I'll send the details and wait for your confirmation."

Banu went to speak but the phone was dead.

She went back to her room. Hossein was just awake, so she took her robe off and went back to bed for more pleasure.

CHAPTER
12

Matt and Lenny's car pulled off the main A40 dual carriageway at the junction known as the Polish War Memorial. They drove along the slip road and took the first exit off the roundabout. After another quarter of a mile, they turned left toward the gates at Northolt Airport. They flashed their credentials at the Military Police and, as they had been expected, were waved through.

Although it did have some regular passenger flights in and out, Northolt was ostensibly a military (RAF) establishment, hence the need for MPs on the gate.

There was a distinct chill in the air around Northolt airport, on the outer edge of Greater London, particularly now as it was mid-January and, despite what calendars say, it was now midwinter. Jody and the girls had arrived. She had done as Matt had instructed when the car came to collect them and had spoken with the driver, and his instructions all checked out. They all gathered in the small, but comfortable departure lounge. Now Lenny was with his family, having an animated conversation with his daughters.

Jody left them to it and made her way over to Matt. His surprise at this encounter was apparent, as Jody stepped closer.

"Jody, how are you? You're looking well!"

"Hi, Matt, I'm afraid I'm not sure if that's just pleasantry, surprise that I came over or just because you think you need to… but no matter."

"Well, I suppose…"

"Look, Matt, it's great we're getting a holiday out of this and the girls are excited and inquisitive as to what's going on, but I sincerely hope you're not putting Lenny in harm's way. I mean, we've been down a similar road before now and so you need to be clear with whatever is happening right now."

"Jody, I promise you, this is just an information-gathering trip to see some of Lenny's old friends … and the situation is serious enough for us to use whatever we have, but no, I'm not putting him in harm's way."

"Matt, you know what he's like. He can go all gung-ho if he thinks it'll help."

"Yes, I do, but that's not in the plan right now."

"It's the right now that worries me."

"Figure of speech."

"Hmm…we'll see."

Jody started to walk away.

"Why do you hate me so much?" Matt asked.

"Matt," she answered, "I'm sure we will be boarding soon and in any case it would take too long to explain. However, I don't hate you, but it goes back to the things you and Lenny got up to in Israel." Her face broke into a wry smile and there was a little wink as she walked away.

Matt's mouth stopped gaping long enough for him to reply, "Funny, that's almost what Lenny said!"

Jody carried on walking back to Lenny and the girls.

"Okay, you three, what's all the excitement?"

There wasn't time for an answer as they were called to board the plane.

The flight to Ben Gurion Airport, just outside Tel Aviv, took just over five hours, so apart from eating and the occasional drink, Lenny and the family took the opportunity to catch up on some sleep. Matt, as dutiful as ever, caught up with paper work and the latest intel.

The plane landed around 15.15 local time. They put their watches forward two hours and then disembarked. Although very damp and cold back home, Tel Aviv was sunny and very mild.

They all gathered outside the still relatively new and luxurious terminal building, and waiting for them were Mercedes Taxi type saloon cars. Matt came over to Lenny and ushered him and Jody and the girls to the first car.

"Okay, so here's the plan: you, Jody and the girls take this one. Your luggage is already loaded and he knows where to go."

"Um, sorry, did I miss something? I mean, I know we were asleep, but what happened?"

"Nothing. You're going to a company apartment at the Tzamerot complex. It's all fully equipped and there are pools and restaurants. Just charge everything to the apartment." Lenny's jaw almost dropped to his chest, Matt noticed.

"You in pain, Lenny?"

"Err, no, just astonished!"

"Well, Mike Wyndham promised this was on us, given that you agreed to help, and he always keeps his promise. So enjoy!"

"Okay, I'll thank him."

"Plenty of time for that. Right now we have work to do."

"Right, when do we start?"

"You've got a couple of days to relax, and then we're off to Jerusalem for a meeting with your old friends at Shin Bet. Then, and we're trying to pin them to a time, probably a meeting with Mossad! Hopefully, the day after as they're in Tel Aviv, as you know."

"Okay, that sounds like a plan. Shin Bet still in Kaplan Street?"

"Yep."

"Thought so, but now under the 'Office of the Prime Minister,' which is not great."

"Why?"

"Let's just say he's not my choice."

"Okay, least said…"

"Suits me, so who's the lady?"

"Oh…you mean Petra? She's from the Foreign Office."

"So is she babysitting, or a special friend?"

"Not that you really need to know, but she's FO 'special section' and definitely not our type, but excellent at her job!" Matt looked straight at Lenny and smiled.

Lenny smiled back, then turned, walked over to Jody and the girls and explained what was happening. He looked back at Matt, who just mouthed, "Will call you later." Lenny nodded and joined the family in the black Mercedes. It sped off to their 'holiday' home where they would spend the next ten days or so.

It took about thirty minutes to reach the apartment from Ben Gurion. Driving through the gates, Jess and Ella yelped with delight as they saw the facilities available to them during their stay there.

"Wow, Dad, how did you swing this one? It's amazing!"

"Your father didn't swing anything, Jess. He's helping the authorities out, and they've brought us here and are just making sure we're comfortable, whilst Dad completes the work he has to do for them."

"Is that right, Dad?" asked Ella.

"Pretty much. You can enjoy yourselves, whilst I'm working, so I shouldn't think you've much to worry about on that score. There's plenty for you here, shopping, eating and so on, and you can charge it to the apartment. That's before you even think of swimming or sunbathing, even in January." Jody started to smile at the idea.

Lenny's thoughts at that time were moving elsewhere and wondering what, if anything, he, Matt and Petra would find that could be useful in discovering who was responsible for the murders at Hyde Park Corner and what else was in the pipeline. He was certain that he should pre-empt any possible shock discoveries with a few phone calls to some old friends in the right places. Today was too late, but first thing tomorrow was the plan, nice and early.

January in many parts of Israel was winter to the locals, but to most Northern Europeans it was akin to a balmy, spring day. Lenny got up early and walked around the complex. Having found the trainers, gym shorts and shirts Jody had packed, he then set off on a jog. About forty-five minutes later, he got back to the apartment, soaked with sweat and ready for a shower after a strong five mile run.

The apartment was a hive of activity, with Jody and the girls busy getting everything ready.

"Hi, honey, good run?"

"Yeah, haven't done that for a while, but it felt good."

"Hope you warmed up properly?" She looked at him and smiled.

"What do you think? I'll just grab a shower and be right back for food, smells great."

Fifteen minutes later, Lenny was back, showered and dressed, ready to sit down and have a family breakfast. They all tucked in to fresh fruit, yoghurt, fruit juice, pancakes and syrup. There was talk all through breakfast, and Lenny had to think back to the last time they were together as a family. It seemed a long while, probably the last family holiday, but whenever it was, this felt really good. Particularly as he looked at their faces and felt the relaxed atmosphere.

With breakfast now cleared away, he sat in the living room. Jody was first to ask what was the plan for the day. Lenny looked at her and the girls.

"Okay, so here's the thing. I know Matt said we have a few days for a bit of R&R, but I need to speak to some people, before I see them with Matt. It will take a few hours to locate them and get what I need. So how about we have lunch at this really great shawarma place in Ramat Hasharon around 1 o'clock? Mum knows the one."

Both Ella and Jess looked at their mum.

"Yes, I'd almost forgotten about that place. Hmm, yes, as I remember their food is really good. Hope it hasn't changed."

"I don't think so, honey. It's a family run place and they've been there for about forty years now, and they do have plenty of family."

"Okay, that's 1pm then. We'll do a little shopping around the complex and meet you in the restaurant. Presumably, you need to make the calls now?"

Lenny nodded and smiled, and said, "Thanks."

Jody and the girls got themselves ready and, within about five minutes, Lenny was alone.

He had gone to the bedroom to get his mobile but, as he came out, a nagging feeling that his phone could be tracked and even listened to made him wary. The choice was to go to the nearest phone shop, and get a burner with an Israeli sim, but not at the complex. He remembered seeing a small shopping mall across from the apartments, and, although it was a bit of a punt, he would see if there was a shop selling the type of phone he needed. Lenny waited about ten minutes to make sure he was on his own and no prying eyes. He didn't really think there would be, but always better safe than sorry.

Forty minutes later, he was back in the apartment and assembling his Israeli phone. He made four calls in all to people he knew or had worked with, when he was seconded to Shin Bet. All, to his mild surprise, knew he was coming over and with whom, and generally all would be pleased to see him, although concerned that he was mixed up in something that could develop to a dangerous conclusion.

He was grateful for their concern and, with one exception, none of them could add to what Lenny already knew.

That one exception was Lazar Spiegal, a guy he'd worked with several times, while with Shin Bet. He was now with Mossad, but had started the same way as Lenny, national service, signed on for longer, graduated to Sayeret Matkal, Israel's SAS, and then to Mossad. It was while Spiegal was in the Sayeret Matkal that Lenny met him, the night they wiped out a terrorist insurgency in the northern border area with Syria. Although it was Lenny's command, it was Spiegel's unit. After the clear up, they spoke often and had become friends. Lenny hadn't seen him for several years, but was now glad he had called him, since the news he received from him wasn't what he wanted to hear.

Banu Behzadi had experienced more pleasure and passion in those three days and nights than she had in her whole life. She and Hossein had only left the bedroom for essentials, but now it was time to plan, then to travel: they had a job to do.

She had received from Sheikh AbdulWahab the part-payment and details of the person he wanted her to deal with, and she would need to travel back to London for that.

Banu and Hossein had spent another few days planning how to maximise the unexpected time in London. First, she would deal with the Sheikh's problem. Then they would travel outside London to a few places they had identified, specifically to enlist the help they required for upcoming and future events.

It was agreed that travelling together, whilst preferable, was not a great idea as it might arouse suspicion, and that would be unwelcome. Banu seriously didn't like flying, so she used alternative means whenever possible. She only flew when the journeys were too long, and flying was the only option. Hossein, however, would fly to Gatwick Airport from Marseille and then take the fast train to London Victoria. Banu would use Eurostar, although she would have to take care not to over-use that form of travel for her own safety: however, she would, of course, change her appearance and passport. She had several passports to choose from, all in different names, nationalities and appearances. She had paid top prices for them, from people who were good at what they did and therefore she trusted them, as they did her. That was probably because they feared what might happen otherwise.

Banu would book the hotel after they had decided when they

would travel. There was a hotel she knew of, which was recommended, although she had not stayed there previously. The Park Grand in Devonshire Terrace was a five minute walk from another mainline station, Paddington. She would take a cab there from St Pancras, and Hossein could either do the same from Victoria, or catch the tube, but that would involve changing lines, so a cab was thought to be better.

Banu was anxious to deal with the Sheikh's request first, as it was in her best interest to find out from the Saudi Embassy guy what information he had on the cab driver she had recognised from Hyde Park Corner.

After that, they had to go to Birmingham and Manchester to meet with possible helpers for the task, even though it was still months away. Good planning took time and it would be necessary to iron out any possible drawbacks or problems. They agreed, for speed, they would hire a car in London, and drive. There were several in the Paddington area, owned by 'sympathetic' brothers and sisters to the cause.

They stopped for food, and then resumed after a good meal and some enthusiastic conversation about their feelings. They realised, though, that they had to put those thoughts away for the time being, as they had to finalise the aims of the trip and their disguises whilst in London. It was a city that had one of the world's largest networks of CCTV cameras and other information gathering technology, so a different identity was necessary, whilst there. Travelling to the other places, where they would be with 'friends' meant that a more relaxed disguise would do. Banu would add a different hair colour and a hijab, as she was used to wearing one and it was respectful to those who they would be meeting, although adherence to the custom for her had long passed. For Hossein, it would be a beard and then no beard, but he would stick with casual clothes. The people that he would take Banu to meet knew him and expected a more relaxed western approach, even though they themselves would be dressed more traditionally, especially the Imams. They respected that some of the faith's more observant didn't follow in the way they did, but fought for the cause in their own way for the 'greater good': their motive was the same, to move closer to the world caliphate they desired.

They completed their planning and decided, once they had checked availability, the preparation would need just a little more adjustment, which meant travelling would be in two days.

With that in mind, Banu had to arrange weaponry. She had her disguises already, but travelling with any weapon was totally out of the question. However, she had a contact in London, to the east of the city, someone who she knew would be able to help. She made the phone call. After a number of coded questions and answers between them, her contact was satisfied it was her, so she explained what she wanted and when. For the sake of haggling, the contact complained that "it was a bit short notice", but Banu was used to this and said the usual rates would apply and of course cash in whatever currency they wished. The contact sighed, indicating an acceptance he wouldn't win, and they agreed the terms and rang off.

Whilst Banu was on to her armourer, Hossein had phoned and booked his flight and arranged the hire car from a friend in Paddington. Once Banu had finished, she booked her Eurostar seat, just one way as had Hossein with his flight. They had no way of knowing how long the trip would be, although they hoped not too long. Banu then called the hotel in Paddington she had previously identified, and booked a double room. Might as well enjoy more pleasure whilst working! Being late in January, the hotel was happy to take the booking, since there were a number of rooms available.

With the travel and accommodation completed, as far as was possible, they set about finalising the details of the attack that Sheikh AbdulWahab had contracted her to fulfil. Although she didn't know where exactly, she did know that he wanted it to happen sometime in the summer, either late June or early July. Just a little intrigued by the small amount of detail, Hossein asked her, "What could it be that will take this long to prepare?" Banu was a little wary of the question, but then thought that maybe she would be inquisitive too, if the roles were reversed. She answered him, though, by saying that the Sheikh had outlined a plan to do something spectacular for the cause, that money was no object and he wanted as few people as possible to know where it was to happen. That way leaks by informants of the security services would be severely limited.

Hossein understood this and they moved on to the next part of their travel plan: where they were going and who they would be meeting with. They decided that after the London part had been completed, and it would need to be as inconspicuous as possible, so as to facilitate a worry-free journey, Banu would go from Euston station and take the train to Birmingham New Street station. Hossein would drive up and meet her. They expected to be there three to four days and would then drive to Manchester to finish the recruitment. Travelling back to France would carry a small risk, but the best option would be to drive to Hull on the East Yorkshire coast and take the car ferry to Zeebrugge. Once there, they would drive to Lille, in France, about ninety miles away over the border. They would park up at the international station, and the car would be collected at a later date. Then they would catch the first fast train back to Marseille.

With that all agreed, they decided to get some air, although it was now late afternoon. A walk down to the harbour and back seemed the best thing, and then supper and sleep. There would be more details to cover the next day and then pack and be ready for their travel the day after.

Some forty hours later, they both left Banu's apartment and went their separate ways to the different points of departure. Hossein took a local taxi to Marseille airport, which was situated around seventeen miles from the centre of the city, and Banu made her way to the Gare de Marseille-Saint-Charles, where she would catch the Eurostar direct to St Pancras International station in London.

Banu travelled dressed as a modern western French woman with an immaculate hair style, expensive two-piece suit, small heeled fashionable shoes, shoulder bag and a short stay travel case on wheels that she pulled along behind. Once at London St Pancras, she navigated her way through immigration and customs without any hitch and made her way out to the taxi rank on the Midland Road side of the station.

She had decided to change her plan slightly. She thought it best to go and see her armourer first and then make her way to the hotel. She had text the new plan to Hossein, who hadn't replied, probably because he was still in the air, as his plane departure was around three hours after her train had left. She had also messaged the armourer that she would be arriving today to pick up the equipment ordered and had received a response, telling her that it was ready for her.

She got into the first available cab and told the driver that she wanted to go to a road just off of Bethnal Green Road. She wanted him to wait, then to go onto a hotel near Paddington Station. She noticed the driver's excited nodding; she got in the cab sat back and relaxed. About twenty minutes later, the driver turned into Hemming Street and drove slowly, looking for the number. It was, unsurprisingly for the area, a converted railway arch. She got out of the cab, gave the driver £50 and told him to wait and keep the meter running. He nodded and smiled again but this time there was a "Yes, love, will do." Banu walked up to the door of the converted railway arch, and pressed the intercom. Within thirty seconds, the door opened slightly and she entered.

Banu spent twenty-five minutes with her armourer and paid the agreed amount for the merchandise she had ordered: a Glock 9mm with trident suppressor and 3 spare magazines of 17, 9x19mm rounds. She returned to the waiting cab and gave him the details of the hotel in Devonshire Terrace. He moved off and, after another twenty-five minutes, pulled up outside the Park Grand hotel. Banu noticed the fare was now £68.80. She took out a further £40 and gave it to the driver, then thanked him for waiting and got out of the cab. She wasn't worried that he could give a description of her, as she wouldn't appear in this way again.

Walking towards the hotel, she noticed that someone was moving towards her. It was Hossein. They looked at each other and momentarily smiled, as they continued to walk towards the hotel. Once inside, they set their luggage on the floor beside them and embraced, spoke a few words about their journeys and then booked in. Banu gave her credit card to the reception and it was swiped and approved. Their room was on the third floor and they were shown up by a porter, who had taken their small amount of luggage for them. Hossein tipped him and he left. They talked for a while and ordered room service, and carried on the conversation during their intake of food. Both had had unremarkable journeys and were satisfied that this first part of the plan had gone smoothly. They were now pretty tired from the travel and went to bed earlier than normal because they had a lot to do over the next few days. Tomorrow, the first thing was to rent the car and then begin to check the area around the home of the Saudi Embassy worker.

They woke early the next morning, showered and dressed, and went out to a cafe Hossein knew, in the Edgware Road a few hundred yards up from Marble Arch. It was a Lebanese restaurant and they tucked into a hearty Middle East breakfast. When they had finished, they decided that the car, from Hossein's contact, was not far from where they were eating, so that would be the first task. Then they would find Bathurst Mews.

The car rental went very smoothly. Hossein paid his friend in cash and arranged for the car to be collected when they had finished. The friend was not concerned where it would be left, as he had family all over France.

The car was a modern saloon with a satellite navigation system. Hossein drove and Banu programmed in the post code of the address in Bathurst Mews. They realised that they were about three minutes away and soon arrived at the destination. Bathurst Mews was a narrow street that ran between Sussex Place and Bathurst Street in the W2 Bayswater area of London. It was a street with very expensive but small cottage-type, mews properties. Some of the houses were single owners and others had been turned into flats.

They found the property they were looking for and, as inconspicuously as possible, took several pictures, concluding that there was only one entrance and exit to the property. This posed the problem as to what needed to be done. It would have to be after dark, but the upside of that was nothing would break news wise until many hours later. Banu had the details of Omar's regular work pattern and they decided that tonight was as good a time as any. They had seen as much as they needed and decided to make use of the time by going over how they would accomplish the task.

They arrived back at the mews just before 17.30, a little before the regular time their target got home from work. They knew that was around 17.40 to 18.00. Just after 17.45, a man of average height, of Middle Eastern appearance and smartly dressed, got out of a cab, by the entrance to the mews in Sussex Place. He paid the driver and walked into the mews. Banu studied the man's face as best she could. Although it was now quite dark, the street lighting was good enough. She looked at the picture she had been sent, just to confirm it was the right person, while he went up to the house. He took out keys, found the one he needed and let himself in.

Hossein moved closer to Banu and whispered, "I'll go and knock on the door. When he answers, I'll pacify him. Give me about a minute to move him further inside and you come up after that and interrogate him."

Banu nodded and pulled her weapon out to check its readiness, something she always did even though it really wasn't necessary.

Hossein walked quickly but calmly up to the mews house, rang the bell and waited. Almost immediately, the door opened. Omar stood there, startled for a moment, just looking at Hossein in surprise.

"Yes, can I help you?"

"Are you Omar Hussein?"

"Yes, why do you ask?"

"Well, if you are, I have something for you."

He motioned for Omar to come closer. In his naivety, Omar leant forward. That was stupid, thought Hossein, and, within a second, his fist smashed into Omar's face. Omar went crashing to the floor with a groan of pain and passed out. Within seconds, Banu was inside the house and the door was locked.

Hossein carried Omar into the living room and sat him on a chair. Using the plastic ties they had acquired earlier, he bound Omar's legs, pulled his arms back behind the chair and bound those as well. There was a groan from Omar, so Hossein taped his mouth. As he finished doing that, Banu came in and told Hossein that it was all clear and that Omar was alone, as per the Sheikh's information. His wife and two children were back in Saudi Arabia, taking a holiday with the family. After a few minutes, Omar awoke, his eyes full of fear. His body began to shake.

Completely motionless, Banu was looking at him; this made Omar even more fearful. After another minute of silence, Banu spoke, "Omar, it is Omar, isn't it?"

He nodded.

"I'm afraid you've upset someone very important, by your rather rash action of speaking to certain people you shouldn't be."

His eyes now grew wider at the realisation of what might happen.

Banu nodded to Hossein to remove the tape, but before he did, she looked at Omar.

"We're going to take the tape off, but if you yell or scream, I will kill you, understand?"

Omar slowly nodded. The tape was pulled off with a sharp tug. There was a yelp.

"Now then, I'm going to ask and you're going to answer truthfully and tell us what we need to know, yes?"

Omar just nodded. Banu took him through a series of questions, and, to begin with, he seemed genuine because he really had no knowledge of what the Sheikh was planning or involved in. Or he was a brilliant liar. She thought not. Then she got onto his indiscretion of speaking with the security services.

"Why did you speak with the security services? Which one was it, and who did you speak with?"

"I think he is Special Branch or one of the others."

She knew that was a lie because the Sheikh had told her otherwise.

"What is his name?"

"Err, umm, I think…"

Banu cut in, "Omar, you're lying to me. I know you know whoever it was, now last chance."

She took out the Glock and fixed the suppressor on. He let out another yelp and, in as defiant a voice as he could muster, said, "Does it matter? You'll kill me anyway."

Banu grew a little weary.

"Omar, I'll not do that if you just tell me the truth. Now again, who was it you spoke with? Which service are they? And what did you say to him?"

Omar relaxed a little.

"His name is Matt, that's all I know on that and he said he was MI5."

"Okay, that's good. Now, just a few more questions. What did you say about the Sheikh?"

"Nothing, he is a friend of my family, nothing honestly."

"So how do you know this Matt?"

"I was at a meeting with the Crown Prince and representatives of the British Government a while back, about some arms sales, and he was there and we started talking."

"Had you spoken with him much?"

"On occasions."

"About what?"

"Nothing much really. It always seemed small talk."

"And this last time?"

"I thought he might be able to get the information the Sheikh wanted about the cab driver…" It suddenly dawned on Omar why this was happening.

"And what did he tell you?"

"He said he couldn't get it straight away, as the case was still being investigated and no information was available."

"What, even to the security services? Ridiculous. You believed him?"

"I had no option."

"When did he say it would be available?"

"He said maybe in a week or so."

"How long has it been?"

"About ten days."

"AND?" Her voice grew louder with impatience.

"Nothing, really nothing…I swear!"

"You fool, Omar…he's playing you and obviously he asked you something and you've said something that has linked in to the event at Hyde Park Corner."

"No…No…I said nothing." His voice was now starting to plead.

Banu had heard enough to know that he wasn't being totally honest, but no matter, she had her instructions. She picked up her weapon and, despite the terrified look on Omar's face, she fired. The first bullet hit the middle of his forehead and she knew he would be dead, but she still fired another into his chest at the heart. Omar's body was now limp and bound. As they left, Banu turned to Omar and uttered, "I make no apology, but the Sheikh does and your family will be looked after, but you had become expendable."

They closed the door behind them, walked back to where the car was parked and drove off, a fruitless mission and a dead body, very unsatisfactory, especially for Banu.

CHAPTER
14

Sheikh AbdulWahab al Zakani had just finished a telephone conversation with one of his senior employees. He had put his mobile down and was about to indulge himself with a late snack, when his phone buzzed. He looked at it, saw who it was from and brought up the message. As he read the first sentence, his heart missed a beat. He sat down and finished reading the rest of the text. Feeling very heavy with sudden grief, he began to reply.

"ARE YOU SURE IT WAS HIM?" And sent it. The response was almost immediate.

"YES OF COURSE. I DON'T MAKE MISTAKES!"

He responded:

"WAS IT QUICK? DID HE SUFFER?"

The response again was instant.

"YES.IN THE END! BUT THE INFORMATION WAS NOTHING WE DIDN'T ALREADY KNOW. BUT HE WAS DEFINITELY KEEPING SOMETHING BACK AND WAS LYING ABOUT IT!"

He sat and pondered this before responding.

"YES I THOUGHT AS MUCH, BUT VERY SAD FOR ME, AS A FRIEND OF HIS FATHER. BUT NOTHING WILL BE ALLOWED TO STOP MY PLAN."

He pressed send.

"YOU WILL MAKE IT RIGHT FOR HIS FAMILY?"

"OF COURSE, AS I HAVE SAID BEFORE I AM A MAN OF MY WORD. INSHALLAH, IT WILL BE DONE."

"OKAY. IT WILL PROBABLY BE NEWS TOMORROW OR THE DAY AFTER."

That was the last text she sent on the subject.

Sheikh AbdulWahab sat on one of the sofas in his luxury suite; tears welled in his eyes for the death of his friend's son. He wiped them away and thought, "What a fool Omar has been. If only he had just made an excuse. Yes, I would have said what an incompetent he was, but he would have been alive. Still, if he has been playing both sides, that's an avenue now closed. However, what's done is done. I will wait for the news to break and contact the family."

* * * * *

Lenny and the family had enjoyed a relaxing time over the previous few days and were just getting used to the leisurely lifestyle, particularly by the pool and the many other attractions on the complex, when his phone buzzed. He left it for a few moments, as he had seen who it was from. He picked it up and answered, "Hi, Matt, thought you'd forgotten about me."

"No chance, matey. Time for work, I'm afraid."

"Okay, when?"

"I'll pick you up in an hour; we have an appointment in Tel Aviv."

"Giving me plenty of time then?"

"Sorry, the meeting time just got arranged, and it's ASAP. So see you in an hour."

They both clicked off.

Lenny looked at Jody, but she knew Lenny's playtime was over for now.

"It's okay, honey. We know why we're here. Go get ready."

He hurried off to shower and change. He was ready in thirty minutes, so spent some time looking through his phone's text messages. To his surprise, there was one from Lazar. It seemed he was expanding on the original conversation with Lenny, who read on and was even less happy when he got the full extent of the text. His problem now was to judge whether or not to let Matt know what he'd found out. He thought for a moment and decided to wait and see what Shin Bet had for them. His phone pinged. He checked: it was a very short message from Matt, *"OUTSIDE"*. Lenny moved swiftly out of the room and downstairs.

Matt was waiting in a standard issue new four door saloon car. In the passenger seat was Petra Green. Matt introduced them. Lenny nodded, smiled and got in the back.

Just over half an hour later, they were entering the city, and another ten minutes saw them inside a small Government Campus, and parking the car. The three of them got out and walked to the entrance of the building. To Lenny's surprise, Lazar Spiegal was waiting just inside the lobby. Lenny got a look from his friend: it was a look he'd seen before. Lazar walked toward them and held his hand out.

"You must be Matt? I'm Lazar, Lazar Spiegal, senior intelligence officer here."

"Hi, yes, I'm Matt Flynn. Pleased to meet you. This is Petra Green from our Foreign Office, and I expect you know Lenny?"

"No, not really. We met briefly many years ago but, of course, I've read our file on him." Lazar shook hands with Petra and Lenny. He then asked them all to follow and he took them up one flight of stairs and found the meeting room, where Lazar's boss was waiting for them.

Sat at the head of a medium-sized oval table was Lior Schiff, the Assistant Director in charge of external terrorism. He was dressed smartly but in a casual Israeli way. He was in his early forties, obviously very fit and a veteran of IDF and Sayeret Matkal (Special Forces).

He motioned for them to sit.

"Good morning, gentlemen and Ms Green. I hope you have enjoyed your stay here so far. Now what can we do for you?"

Matt was first to speak.

"Thank you for seeing us so promptly. We have a matter that we think you may be able to help with."

"Ah yes," said Schiff, "The assassination of the two men at Hyde Park Corner?"

"That's right," Matt went on, "We seem to have a gap in our information as to who the shooter was and why. What we also need to find out is who ordered the hit and who funded it. We also believe the two men were killed because of what they knew. So we, on Lenny's,…err…Mr Resnick's advice, sought your assistance."

"I think we can dispense with the formal bit, Matt, if that's okay?"

Matt nodded and smiled.

"Thanks, that's helpful."

"Yes, we were wondering if you would ask for assistance! As soon as Lenny's name came up on our radar, we thought you might be in touch."

Lenny felt his stomach churn, and knew his face was turning red with just a little embarrassment.

"So can you help at all? All we know so far is we have a female assassin, maybe originally Iranian, Hezbollah trained, and also from our informant, probable funding from someone in one of the Emirates, possibly Abu Dhabi."

"Matt," Schiff intervened, "Your informant, was he a Saudi Embassy official?"

"Yes, but how…?"

Schiff lifted his hand.

"Matt, we had this in just as you arrived."

Schiff handed Matt a piece of paper. Matt read it, put his hand to his mouth and took a sharp intake of breath, and then he exhaled with a cry of "Oh shit!"

"Omar?" Lenny asked, looking at Matt.

Matt, now with hand on forehead, just nodded. At that point, Petra Green looked at both of them and asked, "Would someone please tell me what's happened?"

Matt just handed her the paper.

"Oh my god!" She looked at Lenny, and was about to ask Matt, but he answered her before she did.

"Omar Hossein was my CI; he had come up with some good intelligence, in the past. He was a middle ranking Saudi Embassy official and the son of a very wealthy Saudi businessman."

Lenny chimed in, "He was also interested in me, and someone had asked him to get my details."

"But after talking with Mike Wyndham," Matt added, "We decided the trip here was more important and so we stalled him. We also think he had a name for us as to who ordered the assassination."

"So 5 had all this going on, but nobody thought to tell the Foreign Office?" Petra responded, impatiently.

"Well, we were okay with keeping him happy till we had more information from this trip and then we would have done whatever was necessary to get more info from him."

"Oh, great," Lenny raised his voice, "So, what, you were going to hang me out to dry?"

"No, Lenny, we wouldn't do that. We had a plan, but that's irrelevant now. Someone obviously suspected something and decided to eliminate him and prevent the possibility of a leak. Can't think of any other explanation."

Lior Schiff held his hands up in exasperation at the tone of the conversation that was taking place in his office.

"Please, everyone, this office is not for internal British security service family spats. You were invited here to see if we could help you with the possibility of an imminent terror attack in the UK. We have some information you might find helpful!" Matt, Lenny and Petra stopped instantly. They looked at each other, Matt apologised and then they sat quietly.

Schiff explained what information they (Mossad) had managed to gather. He shared the information they had, that a resident of one of the Emirate states, Abu Dhabi, was the money behind recent events, Hyde Park Corner being the most recent. He went on that the assumption, a very astute one by Lenny, was that the assassin was a female, around mid to late thirties, probably Iranian and the product of Hezbollah training camps in Syria. Unfortunately, no name had come up yet but it was evident and highly probable that she had come from one of many groups that made several incursions into northern Israel causing a great deal of death and mayhem. Matt glanced at Lazar, who had briefly caught Lenny's gaze.

Lenny was now even more certain that what his friend had told him when they had spoken and messaged by phone earlier, put him right in the line of fire. His attitude now changed from ambivalence and being in the background, to worry and concern, not just for himself, but also for his family.

Matt then proceeded to ask a few more questions that remained unanswered, primarily because some of the information that had been coming through was still sketchy or just unreliable. Feeling that there was little more to be achieved, Matt thanked Schiff for being able to share information with them. Schiff was polite enough to say that he was only sorry it wasn't more helpful. Matt smiled, nodded and commented that every little bit helped.

Lenny spoke briefly in Hebrew to Lazar as he walked them out. It was a general thanks for the heads up, with a couple of other more pertinent comments added. Lazar replied with "B'seder" (okay). Matt turned and shook hands with Lazar, as did Petra, and they walked back to where their car was parked, and drove off back in the direction of Herzliya.

Matt was quick to ask Lenny about the conversation he had with Spiegal, and why the necessity for Hebrew. Lenny explained that he was asking him how long it had been since he was in Sayeret Matkal (Special Forces), and had thanked him for his input, particularly, and he'd said okay. Petra was listening, but said nothing. Although she knew what Lenny had spoken to Spiegal about, being fluent in Hebrew, as a requirement of her job, she decided to leave it for now.

* * * * *

In Abu Dhabi, the news had now broken about the killing of Omar Hussein, in his London home. The Arab Middle East media was quick to point to the Israelis and Mossad. That, in a strange way, pleased Sheikh AbdulWahab as he now felt it time to speak with his friend, who would be grieving over the death of his son.

He made the phone call. It was a difficult situation, as he had to be as compassionate with his friend as he could, whilst making sure not to give anything away that might make his friend think anything was suspicious.

They spoke at length, with his friend sobbing from time to time, and with loud wails of grief and crying coming from his wife, Omar's mother, and the family. Sheik AbdulWahab was greatly distressed by this and his grief, as far as his friend was aware, was genuine. However, his guilt faded whenever he thought of the treacherous deeds that Omar might have been part of, and again promised himself that nothing would be allowed to interfere with the plan. That was what gave the Sheikh all the justification he needed for this latest action. They finished the phone call with Sheikh AbdulWahab promising his friend that he would always be there for him and his family, and that all he needed do was ask, Inshallah (it would be done).

CHAPTER
15

Banu and Hossein had completed their business in both Birmingham and Manchester. As far as recruiting was concerned, both places had been very productive and encouraging. Several prospective candidates had been identified and it was now up to the 'friendly Imams' to 'educate the soldiers of the cause'. Over the next couple of months, all would be put through their paces and set various tests of competence and loyalty. Many would be cast aside for the greater good, and their lives would be short thereafter. No chances would be taken on people being upset and willing to talk out of turn. For those who were accepted, there would be further training to prepare for the task and mission ahead.

Sheikh AbdulWahab al Zakani had been specific in his requirements and it would soon be the time when the 'target' for the mission would be made clear to Banu and, in turn, Hossein, mainly because they would need enough time to plan the attack and the getaway, as well as making sure all the logistics were in place.

Hossein was now starting the long drive across a wet, windy and cold northern part of England. The route was pretty straightforward, the M62 motorway went all the way from Manchester to Hull. It was approximately one hundred miles and would take about two hours, conditions permitting. Banu was now asleep in the passenger seat beside him, and his concentration was firmly on the road in front. They had plenty of time, as they had made sure the ferries were sailing and that there were spaces available. All of that was in order and it was clear, all things being equal, they should be in Zeebrugge by around 09.00 the next day, as they were catching the 18.30 ferry from Hull. With a journey time of around fourteen and a half hours from there, the drive to Lille was ninety kilometres and the train to Marseille approximately another five hours. It was a long way round, but security was everything now. At least they had a bed for the night on the ferry, thought Hossein.

Hossein switched on the car radio and listened to the news. Although the story about Omar's death had broken some days earlier, it still featured as a news item, but of lower priority. He smiled to himself in the knowledge that the security services and police were still at a loss to know why he was murdered. "How stupid these people can be", he thought, "No wonder they are such an easy target. This democratic open society really has its pitfalls."

He carried on driving for another hour or so, and Banu began to wake.

"Where are we?" she yawned.

"About another half an hour from the ferry terminal."

"Oh good, I'm getting a bit hungry. Are we okay for time?"

"Yes, thirty minutes before sailing is check-in and we'll be there with an hour to spare. We should be able to board and get to the cabin, then find a restaurant for food."

"Okay, food and then bed, that sounds great!" She looked at him and smiled. He briefly looked at her and smiled back, with great affection.

About thirty-five minutes later, they were driving towards the check-in. When the paperwork was confirmed, they drove on to customs. The French border police were on this side, so they used French passports in the names they had booked in, and all went without any problem. They were shown to their parking berth and finally got out of the car, stretched their stiff bodies and made their way to the reserved cabin. They put their bags in a built-in cupboard/wardrobe and went down to the dining area, and picked a restaurant. A waitress came over and took their drinks order, and told them about the specials of the day. They ordered a bottle of white wine and a pot of black coffee. Then they got up and went to the carvery to chose their food; two trays were made up for them and they returned to the table to eat. Waiting for them was the waitress with their drinks and a bill for everything. Hossein paid and they ate their meal.

By the time they had finished, both began to feel quite tired. It had been a long few days and they needed to sleep, amongst other things, as there was still a lot to do before they got back to Marseille the next day.

They awoke at 06.30 the following morning, both happy that they had accomplished more than just a night's sleep. Having showered and dressed, they went down to breakfast. After their meal, they made their way back to the cabin, collected their things and returned to the lounge area, where they waited for the ferry to be near docking before going back to the car.

At around 08.20 the docking processes began and by 08.30 Banu and Hossein were ready to get into the car and wait for the all-clear to disembark. The ferry crew saw them off in an orderly manner and they followed the line of cars through the port to the customs check and then out onto the road. They picked up the signs for Lille and drove the fast route. They made it to Lille at around 09.00. Once they had found the long stay car park at the international station, they locked the car, took a picture on Hossein's smart phone, and sent it to his friend in London to let him know where the car was parked. They put the key in a small bubble package and posted it to the pre-arranged address of the friend's family member, on the way to the departure platform for Marseille.

There was a slight delay for the train and so it ended up entering the Marseille St Charles station in the centre of the city almost six hours later around 16.00. Although it wasn't far, they took a cab to Banu's apartment where they dragged themselves in with their bags, which they left in the living room, and went to bed, this time just to sleep, as the following day the serious planning would begin.

CHAPTER
16

It was now early May. Lenny had been back in his cab for about six weeks. The vehicle had been forensically stripped down and rebuilt by the MI5 engineers and a technical team. Nothing of much consequence had been found, but they had checked and double-checked to be sure.

He was now firmly back in his work pattern, but, even though he enjoyed doing the job, it had begun to feel just a little mundane after the excitement of the last few months. He replayed the events of that early January evening over and over again in his mind, but had this curious feeling that there was something he'd missed.

The trip to Israel had lasted eleven days in all. Jody and the girls had enjoyed the break and had made good use of the free time and the hospitality, as well as the 'charge it all to the apartment' offer. However, after the final meeting with Shin Bet in Jerusalem, and with Mossad in Tel Aviv, Lenny had been busy going over intelligence with Matt and Petra, whom he still couldn't make out, although Matt had said that there was certainly more to her than met the eye! He had found out, though, after Matt had left them for a few minutes, that she was fluent in Hebrew. It rattled him momentarily, but he composed himself enough to respond in Hebrew and with a smile! He realised that she knew what he and Lazar had spoken about, but she hadn't told Matt and nothing more was said. But Lenny then wondered if she was just 'Foreign Office' or something a little more? He concluded it was probably the latter.

The work on the cab, through April and May, had been slower than normal, mainly because of Ramadan, being observed by the Muslim Community, so there was not much of that particular business for the cab trade. But the thought of the slowness of work was tempered slightly, as he knew that in another couple of weeks it would be the Chelsea Flower Show, and that was when the work usually picked up, and in general lasted through till late September. His mood began to lighten, just little.

Driving around most days, as he did in the cab, it gave him time to think. It was, he thought, therapeutic in some ways as he could have a 'conversation' with himself, in his mind, and develop answers to problems and situations. However, his recent excursion back into the world of security and intelligence reminded him of some of the better things, as well as the dangers, he had experienced in his former life. Before he had taken on the responsibility of being a husband and a father.

However, any thoughts of moving back into that world would be met with strong resistance from Jody, and she was probably right, whatever he thought about it.

Not for the first time his train of thought was interrupted by his phone. He saw who it was from and pulled over, even though he had his Bluetooth on. He answered and heard Matt say, "Lenny, how you doing?"

"Fine, until the phone rang!"

"Okay, not what I expected, but never mind, we've caught a break. You need to come in."

"Hang on, Matt. I thought my part was finished?"

"Well, it was, but this new intel includes you, so you need to see it. Same deal applies."

"Matt, d'you really need me?"

"Wouldn't ask if we didn't think it important. How long will you be?"

"Oh for Pete's sake…I'll be twenty-five minutes"

"Okay, I'll meet you in the lobby. We still have your creds, so will see you there."

"Well, how about that? What a surprise!"

"See you soon." The phone went dead.

On the rank in Smith Square, Lenny found space where he could leave the cab, without having to worry about getting a ticket or being towed, and walked round to Millbank. As he walked in, Matt was waiting.

"Okay, Matt, you have my attention. What's up?"

"You'll see in a minute. Come with me."

They walked through the usual security checks and up to Mike Wyndham's office, where he was waiting with Jennifer Hardie.

"Ah, Lenny, good to see you again. Hope you and the family are well? I presume they enjoyed their break in Israel?"

Lenny decided to be a little irreverent.

"Hi, boss, good to see you too! Yeah, they had a great time, thanks, and we're wondering if they could make it a regular thing?" Lenny smirked.

Wyndham's facial expression turned serious.

"Okay, Lenny, to business, I think! Matt will go through it in detail, but the bare bones are that one of our 'embedded' operatives has come to the surface briefly, and we now have a bit more intel that has added some significant pieces to our puzzle. Matt, it's your guy, so carry on."

"Okay, well we've had embedded operatives in a number of organisations in the Middle East, Afghanistan etc, for many years. Sometimes we get a regular stream and sometimes nothing for many months or even years. Well, this one has just re-surfaced."

"And you know this is reliable because…?" asked Lenny.

"Because they had all the right answers."

"Isn't this 6's domain?"

"Yes, it can be but we have to do this too, particularly if it affects our internal security."

"Okay, with you, but where do I come in?"

"Well, your theory on the assassin is now formally confirmed."

"See…I told you…"

Matt held up his hand.

"Okay, Lenny…there's more. It appears she was the only survivor of a raid into Israel some years ago from the Syrian border. You, apparently, were in charge of the operation that night at the kibbutz near the Golan. She was the one asking for your details." A cold shiver went right through Lenny as he realised what that raid was and when.

"Shit…she must have recognised me, as I was the Shin Bet agent overseeing the Sayeret Matkal unit that was commanded by Lazar Spiegal."

"Thought you didn't know him that well?"

"We all have little secrets, Matt. Thought it best to keep it that way as he had given me a tip off about the female before we met with Mossad, but it wasn't as informative as what I've just heard."

"You didn't think to say something?"

"Well, I thought your friend Petra would've. You know she speaks fluent Hebrew?"

"What? Lenny, if this is some kind of joke?"

"No, Matt, I'm serious. You are right about Petra. There's more about her than you think!"

"That wasn't what I meant, but good to know. I mean I had no idea!"

Wyndham held up his right hand as if to motion stop.

"Okay, it's probably an appropriate time to put a few things right. Petra is MI6 with special responsibility on the Middle East. Yes, Lenny, she is fluent in Hebrew, as well as a number of Arabic dialects. So, Matt, her talents and position up till now have been on a need to know basis and up till now there hasn't been…a need to know. Also, we need all the input we can get."

"Well, I'm glad we cleared that up!"

"Okay, Matt, I think we can move on now. We've more important things to do, haven't we?" Wyndham's body language was noticed by Matt, who realised now was a good time to calm his petulant thoughts.

"Okay, let's talk about what we know from the latest intel gathered via the resurfacing of our embedded agent. Shouldn't Petra be here though?"

Wyndham became impatient and his terse response to Matt was a signal for him to move on, which he did.

Interspersed with input from Jennifer Hardie, Matt went over the new intel and explained, mainly for Lenny's benefit, that the woman they were looking for was Iranian born, trained in Hezbollah camps, mainly in Syria. She had been part of a group that regularly infiltrated northern Israel to terrorise, kill and destroy infrastructure in and around kibbutzim. That had stopped after the ambush by Lazar Spiegal's Sayeret Matkal unit, under Lenny's charge as the Shin Bet Officer in the field.

"So you're saying that this is now all connected to the killing of the two guys in my cab, the request to Omar to get info on me and then his murder? Do we know yet what is planned and when?"

"Only that the target is London and maybe mid June, and that the money man backing this is a Saudi Sheikh living mainly in the Emirates. Which is a darn sight more than we had back in early February."

Matt stared straight at Lenny expectantly. He didn't have to wait long.

"So did it occur to anyone that the lives of my family, and obviously me, are now in danger?" Lenny's voice was now getting louder.

"Lenny, there's no need to raise your voice. We've got this under control and we can act accordingly."

"That's easy for you to say, boss. I'm the one she wants to know about and probably because she recognised me from the cab! If it's right about the northern Israel raid intel then, although I was sure we got them all that night, it seems that somehow she survived."

"Lenny, the intel we have is pretty accurate," said Matt, "It seems she was at the back of the group, as she was aware, instinct probably, that something wasn't right. She watched what happened, laid low and then made her way back over the border."

"Okay, well if she saw me, then she saw Lazar too. Has anyone told him?"

"The Israelis know," Wyndham added, "But you had a conversation with Spiegal about this, so it's no real surprise is it?"

"Yes, I had a conversation, but this wasn't known, and presumably that's from Petra Green?"

"Correct."

"Well, she's either missed bits out, or her Hebrew isn't as good as you think, but I fucking doubt that!" Lenny grew agitated.

Wyndham looked at him, stony faced, "Firstly, there's no need for the colloquial language, and second, as I'm sure you know, Ms Green's Hebrew is excellent! She obviously précised the information, but we got the message."

Lenny sat there for a moment and tried to calm himself before speaking again.

"Okay, I've got all that, so what now? I carry on as normal, or do you want me to stick around? And what about my family?"

"We have no reason to suppose they are in any danger, or you for that matter, but we will need you to work with us until we can stop whatever is being planned, or take out the terrorists before they get here."

"Yeah, that's what I was afraid you'd say."

Lenny was silent, thinking about that night in Israel and wondering why he'd decided to go to work that dark and dreary night in January.

In silence, Matt and Lenny walked back to Matt's desk on the grid, and both sat there deep in thought for what seemed like an eternity.

"Look, Lenny, I know you are reluctant, but this is about the country's security as well as the safety of your family."

"Well, glad you included them."

"Okay, I know you're angry and want to remove the personal danger, but the two things are compatible. We stop the attack, more than likely we get the assassin and the finance man behind all of this too, and save lives at the same time."

"You see, Matt, it's the 'more than likely' that worries me. My family is the most important thing to me!"

"I get it... no, really I do. I don't have the same family ties but I have siblings who I worry about, particularly at times like this, so not quite the same but still..."

"Matt... I get it too, okay! Let's get this done, the sooner the better. Hell knows what I'm going to tell Jody... she really isn't going to like this!"

"Right, well, that I'll leave to you. Tell Jody whatever you need to. Don't sugar coat it, she'll be really hacked off with the don't worry, it'll be okay but, should it go tits up!"

"Just what I needed to hear. Thanks for that."

"Just trying to be honest."

"Matt, you're a spy, don't make me laugh!"

"Okay, Lenny we have work to do, so let's get started. The major part of the intel you already know, but we also know that she, the assassin..."

"Still no name?"

"No…but we're working on it. Anyway, we know she was in London with a man and they are probably responsible for Omar's murder."

"How come?"

"Fortunately, there is CCTV all over the central area, especially around strategic buildings and points where people congregate. As you now know, Omar lived very near Paddington Station and we concentrated around Bathurst Mews. We had the Super Spotters from the Met's Anti Terrorist unit look at the CCTV and managed to get pictures of two possible individuals as well as a licence plate of the vehicle they used. They hired it from a rental office just off the Edgware Road, which is run by a Saudi. He's given us details from the documentation they filled out. The names are, of course, false, and the pictures from the CCTV couldn't show us any facial features that we could use with our recognition technology."

"So what happened with the car rental guy?"

"He gave us what he had."

"Really? You believe him?"

"Why?"

"Well, for starters why did they use that particular car rental place in the Edgware Road that was owned by a Saudi? Why didn't they use a regular rental place or something further afield?"

"Probably because they were staying somewhere local."

"Or they knew the guy, and they reckoned on him giving you a plausible story."

"Okay, we'll get him back in, see what else he knows."

"Yeah, like where's the car now? Has he got it back?"

"No, he said it had been rented for a week, but it hasn't as yet been returned."

"How convenient! And you don't find that suspicious?"

"Yes, of course we did. We had eyes on it through the CCTV and we know it went north to Birmingham. Then it got a bit sketchy so we did an all ports and got lucky when we found it had been booked onto a ferry from Hull to Zeebrugge."

"So what then?"

"Trail stopped there."

"Great, where's that near?"

"It's a southern Belgium port not far from the French border and about ninety miles or so from Lille."

"Then I suggest that's the next port of call."

"Oh, that's funny."

"Best I can do right now."

Lenny picked up the phone and made a few calls to the Belgian Ports Police, then the French Customs and Transport police. All this took a while, but he had some sort of picture that they would try to confirm, once they had looked at their surveillance cameras. They would call him back as soon as they had anything concrete.

Lenny left Matt to find a quiet space and phoned Jody. It went better than he expected as she, realistically, realised the importance of his input to the security services as well as his probable need to 'scratch an itch'.

Knowing that the information would take time, Lenny decided that a walk and fresh air was a good idea. He left word for Matt and exited the building. Walking round to Smith Square to check his cab was okay, he left the square by Dean Bradley Street. He turned right onto Horseferry Road and walked towards Marsham Street. As he crossed at the junction, he saw several cabs parked up around the sandwich and coffee place, Pret A Manger. There were a few cabs there that he recognised and he decided that coffee and a little light relief were in order.

About an hour went by, with lots of laughs, jokes and cab driver chat. One of the cabbies, a guy called Barney, was the chair of the proceedings and in pretty good form, so Lenny's mind temporarily forgot that he and his family could be in danger.

The jollity was broken when Lenny's phone buzzed.

"Lenny, where are you?"

"Horseferry Road."

"Okay, need you back now. We've more to go on."

"No problem. On my way."

He looked at his friends, "Sorry, guys, duty calls!"

As he stood and moved towards the door, Barney shouted, "What, another one out to the flyers, Lenny?" He turned round and saw them all laughing and replied with a smirk, "You never know, Barney, you never know!"

He jogged back to the building and went straight up to Matt in the meeting room. Jennifer Hardie was also there.

"Lenny, we traced the car! It was at Lille for a few days, and then someone collected it and brought it back to London, back to the rental place."

"You got the rental guy?"

"Yes. SO15 picked him up earlier. He's in Paddington Green and has been sweating for a while," added Jennifer Hardie.

"Okay, any more on who left the car and where they went after Lille?"

Matt took out a folder and opened it.

"Yes, all the details are here." He gave a copy to Lenny and Hardie. They studied it for a few minutes.

"But no positive description. All it says is it's a man and a woman?" Hardie said.

"Well, yes it does, but the more interesting thing is this." Matt took out another sheet of paper and continued, "We have a man and a woman leaving Lille for Marseille the same day as the car was left. We then got intel from our 'friends at Langley,' who have only now, nearly four months later, told us that one of their guys was found dead in an alley in Marseille…shot twice."

"Head and heart, yes?" Lenny added.

"Got it in one!"

Hardie then looked at Matt inquiringly, "Does our local station have any more info on this?"

"About as much as we've had from Langley, but the local French security say they believe the dead guy was tailing a person of interest and then went off the grid until he was found in the alley."

Hardie thought for a moment, before picking up the phone and calling Wyndham. They spoke for a few minutes before ending the call.

"Mike just had Petra on with the same details, except that the CIA guy was tailing a suspected terrorist recruiter who was based in Beirut. He thinks a trip to Marseille would be in order to see if there is anything else, maybe get some local info? Three of you."

"Matt, and who are the other two?" asked Lenny.

"You and Petra, as it's her domain as the foreign service agent,"Hardie smiled.

"Hang on, hang on…I understand Matt and Petra…but why me? What input can I help with?" Lenny stared straight at Hardie.

"Lenny, you are helping us with this situation. You are a different set of eyes, and something may jump out at you! We need you to go… please! It's no more than information gathering."

"Great, just what I wanted, a trip to Marseille… not!"

"Well, if all else fails, you can converse freely with Petra in Hebrew!" Hardie picked up her papers and left, and as she did, she turned to Matt and Lenny. "Enjoy the trip." She smiled and closed the door behind her. Lenny and Matt just sat there with their mouths wide open.

Canary Wharf formed a section of the complex in the part of London known as Docklands on the Isle of Dogs, which is an area north of the River Thames, past Tower Bridge.

It was the brainchild of a former CEO of Credit Suisse, to build a modern financial district of London similar to Manhattan, with all the pizzazz and zing of the real thing on the island. It encountered several financial problems early on and was taken over by a consortium of Canadian entrepreneurs, who bought the failing project in 1988.

Construction began that year and, in 1991, the first towers were opened and named Canada Square. The 'Island,' as it is now known, has a skyline that resembles a mini Manhattan, and is home to many global organisations, in banking, finance, insurance and accountancy. Like other areas similar to this development around the world, it has other attractions that could just be identified as 'sex, drugs and rock and roll'. For the more mundane, it has an extensive shopping mall and many varied restaurants, as well as a number of very well known hotels. Expansion of the site continues in all directions, including upwards, and at a gathering pace.

Lucretia and Haider Mikhail, twenty-five year old twins of parents, Raheem and Farrah, had both escaped from southern Iraq when Saddam restored his reign of terror, soon after the unfinished first Gulf War in 1991.

Raheem and Farrah were from the Basra area in the south of Iraq, and were much affected, mentally not physically, by the bombing and gassing of the Marsh Arabs by Saddam. They managed to escape with help from British forces, and came to England, where they were given refugee status and were allowed to settle. Raheem was an engineer and Farrah was training as a lawyer. On arrival in England, they were found accommodation in East London and were helped to find work. They were only just married when the invasion of Kuwait happened and then the bombing, by the coalition forces, made them certain of the fact that it wouldn't be safe for them if or when Saddam survived.

They had become settled into their new country and, although it was hard for them, they had found a sort of peace. However, they had hoped that one day they would return to their native land. Even though they kept in touch with Iraqi communities in London, they tried to integrate into the British way of life. A few years later, their twins were born and, all through their formative years, the twins were made aware of their heritage and history.

As the twins grew, the teachings of their parents about western interference in their homeland stuck with them and, by the time the second Gulf War had finished, they were almost nine. By this time, they had developed an acute awareness of the tragedy that had been visited upon the country of their heritage. They also became aggrieved when the reason for the war, the search and destruction of Weapons of Mass Destruction (WMD), was found to have been an excuse for regime change. It wasn't so much the coalition had removed the homicidal tyrant, Saddam Hussein; it was the reason for invading Iraq for the second time in twelve years. That became embedded in the psyche of Raheem and Farrah and, over the succeeding years, the twins took on board their parents' teachings and opinions. Even at such a young age, they understood and felt the pain of their parents.

Now at the age of twenty-five, both Lucretia and Haider had graduated with honours degrees from Cambridge and, having completed four years of legal training, had taken up lucrative offers with a large finance corporation at Canary Wharf.

They were both surprised and delighted to have landed such great jobs with such a prestigious organisation, particularly as there were many applicants. They were excited, but thought no more about it.

One cold, early evening in April, after finishing around 17.30, they were met by a man, standing alongside a black limousine. He said he was a friend of their parents, and he asked them to step into the car, as there was an important VIP who wanted to meet them. Slightly bemused and more than a little hesitant, they were quickly put at ease by the reassuring manner of the very large and well dressed Middle Eastern man sitting in the back of the car.

They drove several miles west, and the journey ended when they pulled into a long driveway that finally led to a very large country mansion in West Oxfordshire. On the way, the Middle Eastern man explained to the twins that he had a large stake in the company they worked for and that it was mainly because of his associates and connections inside the British army, before they were born, that he was able to facilitate their parents' escape from Iraq and entry into the UK. He also made them aware that he had maintained a link with their parents who, despite their sadness in leaving their homeland, were very grateful to him for getting them out. He had told them at the time that one day they would repay him if and when he needed their help.

As they approached the mansion, the twins were agog that a place like this existed, such great wealth and opulence they had not seen before. They were shown to their rooms and their host told them to relax and be at ease, and to meet for dinner in an hour.

Smart, casual clothes had been provided for them, nothing was formal as was the tendency in some other old English estates. He also told them to call their parents, if they wished: they could use their mobiles. What he didn't say was that any other suspicious calls would be monitored, just as a precaution.

Lucretia and Haider's rooms were very large and adjoining. They agreed to change and meet in Lucretia's room and then phone their parents. They also agreed that no other phone call would be made, until they had clarified exactly who this mysterious Arab man was, and if he was genuine.

About an hour later, the twins went down, as requested, for dinner. Dressed in the expensive clothes provided for them, they found their host waiting for them at the entrance to the dining room. He greeted them warmly and asked how their parents were. A little taken aback by this, Lucretia answered.

"They are very well, Sheikh AbdulWahab; they asked after you and send their regards."

"That's very kind of them, my dear. I will call them tomorrow, but first we will have dinner and then I will chat with you about some plans that I would like you to help me with." As he ushered them into the dining room, the twins looked at him inquisitively. Noticing this, the Sheikh just smiled and thought to himself, "All in good time, all in good time!"

The dinner was sumptuous and had a number of courses, some of which the twins just moved around their plates, as they were not used to such a feast. It was now 22.45 and the Sheikh took them into another room, a study, where they could speak privately. They spoke for an hour or so, and the Sheikh explained to them the outline of his plan and their role, should they undertake it. He had taken a risk in doing this, but time was now of the essence, as there were only just over two more months to execute the plan. He was skilful in making them aware that their intelligence and expertise in certain areas were key to the success of that plan and they would be very well rewarded. Both of them sat back and listened intently, and, unless he had read the signs incorrectly, he was confident that the twins would agree to help him.

After he had finished and taken their questions, he said, "I think it best, due to the lateness of the hour, that we meet at breakfast around 08.30 and talk some more." They nodded in agreement and the twins went up to their respective rooms without any conversation, except to say "Goodnight."

They both lay awake, thinking about the proposition before them, and after tossing and turning, they set alarms for 07.30 and fell asleep.

When their alarms went off, it felt like only a few minutes had passed but it was now five hours later. Despite their reluctance to get out of their comfortable beds, they managed to drag themselves to the bathroom to shower and then dress.

They made their way down to breakfast, chatting intensely and quickly, almost garbled, but it was an excited tone and one that, because of their closeness, they understood.

When they entered the room, the Sheikh was already seated. His metabolism was such that he couldn't wait and had already started eating. He loved kippers, and was tucking into two of them with grilled tomatoes and buttered toast. He looked up, smiled and waved them in to sit. They did so, and took their places either side of him at the large, oval antique oak table. As they sat, the butler asked for their choices of drink. Both ordered hot black tea with slices of lemon on the side. The butler nodded and hurried off to fetch the tea.

All through breakfast, the Sheikh studied the two of them whilst enjoying his food. He was becoming even more certain that his 'offer' would be accepted.

When he finished, he looked at them both, from side to side, as he sat back in his chair.

"So what did you decide?" he asked.

Haider spoke this time and started a little hesitantly, which worried the Sheikh. "Sheikh AbdulWahab, we have thought about it and although we are not exactly sure of what it is you require of us, although we have a reasonably good idea, I think it's fair to say that we are a little…"

At that point Lucretia grew impatient, held up her right hand as if to motion stop.

"Oh, for goodness sake, Haider, stop dithering!" she exclaimed.

Haider did, looking at his sister in silent protest, but Lucretia had already gained the Sheikh's attention and carried on, "Sheikh AbdulWahab, we are very interested in your plan, so far, and are of a mind to agree the proposition. However, we will need more information, of course, and a guarantee that our parents are completely taken care of as well as us, as you have already promised."

Trying to control his delight, the Sheikh looked at her.

"Lucretia, my dear, everything you have asked, *Inshallah,* it will be done," he said, with a feeling of satisfaction. They all smiled with contentment and finished the rest of the meal in silence.

As they walked out, the Sheikh explained that he had taken the liberty of booking them three weeks' leave of absence from work, which he had cleared with their bosses, on the basis he needed the twins to represent him in the Middle East on a personal matter.

He then told them to get ready to be driven back to their apartment near Canary Wharf, as they needed their passports and other items for a trip to France, where they would stay for about fifteen days.

They were to fly to Marseille and would be met by one of his associates, who would take them to the hotel that had been arranged, and get them checked in. The chauffeur had all the relevant tickets and hotel information and would give these to them at the airport. They looked rather bemused at the speed of developments, but nodded in agreement. Very soon after that, they were in the Sheikh's car, leaving West Oxfordshire and heading back to London for the things they needed for their trip to Marseille.

Late spring in Marseille was a special time for Banu. Ramadan was almost finished, Eid was a day or two away and it was now the time when her part of Sheikh AbdulWahab's plan would be nearing its climax. Although there was, it seemed, still much to do.

Hossein had returned home in late March. They had planned much, although the main target was still only mooted. However, by intelligent deduction, she had a good idea what the Sheikh wanted and Hossein had recruited enough 'willing martyrs' to accomplish the spectacular event. They had been placed in friendly accommodation around London, with minders to make sure they didn't stray or speak out of turn to anyone outside their groups. However, the constant repetition of their roles continued every day. The promises of eternal martyrdom and the gifts from god were all laid out to give them incentive and courage. What they didn't know, then, was if they faltered on the day, the detonation would be out of their control anyway.

The two young people, sent by Sheikh AbdulWahab for training, were going to prove to be extremely useful in accomplishing the task that they had been set. Their skills were wide and varied, particularly with fire arms, and the three weeks she had with them had taken her back to the days in southern Syria and Lebanon when she and her group infiltrated Northern Israel and carried out targeted terrorist attacks there.

The weather in Marseille at this time of year was wonderful: warm spring days around 23°C and a very comfortable 12-14°C at night. Her time was spent going over the plan, where to attack, where to use the suicide packs and, of course, how she and Hossein would escape.

The element of surprise would quickly dissipate, so they had to hit hard and then get out and away as efficiently and as stealthily as possible, using the mayhem to its best effect.

She had spent many hours reviewing her plans, and she was now becoming impatient, as the time grew ever nearer. She was used to planning for short-term incursions into Israel with her comrades from the camps, as well as scoping and executing a singular liquidation for a client. This, however, was on an altogether higher level. She was glad she had enlisted Hossein's help. Without his expertise, recruitment would have been much more difficult and time- consuming, and, of course, there had been the fringe benefits. Her mind wandered for a minute, back a few months to when they spent a number of wonderful weeks together.

She could feel her body aching at the thought of his love and tenderness, and it made her more determined than ever to want to be with him. She began to wonder about what to do after this was over. She harboured the thought that she would leave this life. After all, this contract would enable her to be free to do whatever she wanted without the need to work anymore. Living and having a family with Hossein in a place far from all this was idealistic, but in her mind and with her acquired wealth, it was all possible.

The daydream ended when her phone rang. She picked it up and answered. It was the Sheikh.

"Sheikh, to what do I owe this unexpected pleasure?"

"Banu, my dear, you came highly recommended to me, particularly as you had flown low under the radars of most intelligence agencies. But we had an incident flagged up regarding the death of a person in Marseille a few months back who, we understand, was an American CIA agent. What can you tell me?"

"Sheikh, he was an unnecessary risk to the situation, and had to be eliminated."

"So you took it upon yourself to make this decision?"

"There was no time, if I had left it any longer, the person he was tailing would have led him to my apartment, and then who knows what the outcome would have been. I would have been discovered, Omar would still be alive and who knows what you would be doing right now!"

"What do you mean by that, how could you have known?"

"Instinct, Sheikh AbdulWahab, that's what has helped me survive for so long. Omar was lying to you, of that I am convinced, and with the right pressure the British security services would have interrogated him and he would have given you up. He was a weak individual."

"But he didn't tell you anything, did he?"

"No, but I didn't have the time with him that the British would have had, and, again, then where would you be?"

Banu became frustrated with this irrelevant conversation, and while the Sheikh took moments to think, she again spoke before he had time.

"Do you want me to carry on or not? I have invested much time, energy and effort putting in place the necessary arrangements. To cancel now will be a great shame and costly."

"Money is not a problem."

"I wasn't specifically speaking just about money!"

Sheikh AbdulWahab felt a shiver go through him at the thought of what she had said. His weakness took over and he tried to regain composure with what was obviously a nervous laugh. Banu sensed this and kept quiet, waiting for his response.

"Banu, my dear, of course this continues, I was just being careful. I rely on your expertise completely."

"Thank you, Sheikh, that is good to know. When can I expect the final detail of the target? I need to finalise the exit strategy, and, of course, payment to others as well as the rest of my fee. It will be compensatory, as my work will suffer for quite some time after."

"Yes, of course. You will have all you need in a few days' time. The plan is for this to happen in mid June. You will have everything well in advance and the rest of the fee two days before. I trust you to complete." With that, he hung up.

Banu put her phone down, satisfied that she had made the Sheikh succumb to her demands. Something, she was sure, was a consequence of her implied threat regarding his future.

Thinking back over the conversation, though, the comment the Sheikh made about the incident in the alley near her home made her wonder how the news got to him. There were no reports in the French media and she had scoured the American and European media too, so who was watching her, or Hossein for that matter? Was the Sheikh watching her or did he have contacts locally? She would need to find out, and soon.

Her mind stopped wandering and her thoughts returned to the present. She decided that, as it was such a lovely afternoon, she would walk to the shops near the harbour and get some air. Although she didn't normally wear one, she picked a hijab and put it on with a pair of very dark shaded sunglasses. That would give her some anonymity and wouldn't look out of place. There was a back way out of her apartment, which she used only occasionally, and she felt the need to use that today. On leaving, she quickly made her way back round to the main street and then she would go down to the harbour. The fresh sea air felt good, the sun was very warm and pleasant, and the walk, although not too long, was enough for her to feel a little more relaxed.

Her route to the hypermarket and port took her past the Commissariat de Police. As she walked by on the other side of the road, she noticed that a large saloon car had just parked and three people, two men and a woman, had got out and were met by two local police officers, one uniformed and the other in a day suit. They were shaking hands, chatting and smiling. As they walked towards the building, one of the visitors looked round. Banu stared briefly and wondered why he seemed familiar to her. The five of them disappeared into the police station and Banu walked on. After about fifty metres, it suddenly hit her. It was him…the one that looked around…the cab driver from London…the Israeli from that night in Northern Israel! She felt her legs give way momentarily, and she put out her arm against a wall to steady herself. As soon as she recovered, she found a small café and sat at an outside table to gather her thoughts.

This was a distracting turn of events and it had happened very soon after the strange conversation she had had with the Sheikh. Was it just a coincidence? Maybe, she thought, but why now? A waiter came over and she ordered coffee, with an apricot Danish pastry: she needed something sweet.

By the time her coffee and pastry arrived, she had composed herself and begun to think about what to do. Although it would be an ideal opportunity for her, she thought, calm and logic had returned to her thinking. To take her revenge on him now would put the whole contract with the Sheikh in jeopardy. To kill him at this time could put her in a dangerous situation, for many reasons.

She usually planned well in advance and always had a plan B. Now wasn't the time to depart from her usual modus operandi. However, she now needed a much keener sense of awareness in place, so as not to disrupt her plans before she returned to London to complete her contract.

She put money for the coffee and pastry down on the table; she stood up firmly, her head now clear, and walked off toward the hypermarket.

* * * * *

"Good afternoon, Mademoiselle Green and Messieurs Flynn and Resnick. I am Commandant Guy Beringer and I understand that you would like some information about an incident that happened a few months ago?"

Petra Green was first to speak.

"Thank you for agreeing to see us, Monsieur Beringer. Yes, we have obtained some information regarding the mysterious death of a man in Marseille, as you say, a few months ago. We believe that it may be related to our ongoing investigation into the deaths of two men at Hyde Park Corner, London, in January this year. We also have reason to believe that the man killed here, a few months ago, was a CIA agent, although Langley won't officially confirm this to us. However, their unofficial response to us was that they had been following a strong lead and a person of great interest regarding a possible terrorist threat. This was finally confirmed and we now believe that these three deaths and that of a Saudi embassy official in London are related to a probable terrorist attack on the capital, in the not too distant future."

Beringer had listened intently, thought for a moment and then excused himself, and left his office. They sat there for a few minutes, wondering what next, when he suddenly returned with a medium-sized folder. He sat back at his desk.

"Well, Mademoiselle Green, Messieurs, luckily we too have contacts at Langley as well as our Interior Ministry. As soon as we received your request for this visit and the reasons, we were in contact with both organisations. You may take time to look through the information in this folder; it will not leave this room, but make any notes from it that you wish."

He got up and left. On the way out, he told his secretary to supply coffee and refreshments, as his visitors would be in his office for a while. The office door closed and the three of them worked their way through the documentation. Much of it was known. However, there were a few nuggets of information that filled in some of the gaps, and, using his smart phone, Matt took pictures of all the relevant documents. The whole process took a few minutes short of two and a half hours.

Commandant Beringer came back for a brief discussion with them, before escorting them back out, where he bade them farewell at the main door to the building. He was sincere in his comment, when he told them not to hesitate if there was anything else they needed. He also told them that on their way back, to stop off in Lyon, where the Headquarters of Interpol France was situated. He said he had been in contact with Interpol France earlier and they had suggested a brief visit there, as they might be able to add more information to what had already been obtained. Petra Green thanked the commandant and agreed that the small diversion to the Quai Charles de Gaulle in Lyon would be a good idea.

The car took them back to the main station in Marseille where, after about an hour, they caught the fast train to Lyon. From there they would return to London St Pancras, ready to debrief Wyndham, Hardie, and probably the Home Secretary, as a matter of urgency.

CHAPTER 20

Lenny, Matt and Petra had now returned from their trip to Marseille and had travelled home from there, via Interpol in Lyon. They had briefed Mike Wyndham and Jennifer Hardie on their information-gathering trip, and that information had been disseminated.

Matt and Petra were now in Wyndham's office, along with Hardie. They were listening to the result of that dissemination of the intelligence they had gathered and the next course of action.

Because of what they now knew, they had narrowed any possible terrorist attack down to between the 10th and 24th June. The main focus was currently on where the possible targets would be, and how it would be carried out, a task somewhere between finding a needle in a haystack and sticking a pin in the newspaper to find the winner of the Grand National. However, unlike the films, although intelligence work like this was sometimes laborious, it was an integral part of building the picture that would tell the right story.

Wyndham spoke, "Matt, you're with me this afternoon; we are briefing the Home and Foreign Secretaries, so, Petra, you will need to arrive with your FO hat on, but your main boss from our friends across the river will be there too, as well as the Met's counter terrorism chief."

They all nodded. Jennifer Hardie, looking a little left out, handed over the new draft intelligence reports that had been finalised from the information Matt, Petra and Lenny had gathered from their excursion to Marseille, along with the other more revealing information, now confirmed, from the visit to France Interpol HQ in Lyon.

It appeared that Interpol had received the details of the death of the CIA agent in Marseille and had discovered he had been killed whilst following a suspected terrorist who had come into Marseille via the ferry terminal at Gare Maritime. The local gendarmerie had been able to track the suspect and CIA agent for part of the way until they went into an alley, but the agent didn't appear at the other end. Only the suspect came out, but then disappeared into another area not covered by CCTV. The only other thing that was memorable was what looked like a woman who appeared about five minutes later from the same entrance the CIA agent hand entered. They lost her when, again, she disappeared into the same area of the city without CCTV.

"A woman? Well that at least is a probable connection to our Hyde Park Corner shooter," Matt said.

"Yes," Wyndham replied, "Although it is no more than a possibility in reality, it is certainly more than a coincidence, and I don't believe in those."

"So have the Marseille authorities any ideas yet who she is or where she lives, if indeed she is based there?" asked Matt.

"No, she was well disguised and, cleverly, wore dark glasses and a hijab, so no chance of facial recognition, even if there was better CCTV coverage."

Matt thought for a few moments, realising that they had about as much information on the killing in Marseille as they could have at this time.

"So, okay, we've hit a wall on that for now, but I suspect in time more will materialise," Matt said, "So what time do we meet with the ministers?"

Wyndham collected his thoughts and said, "Let's all get some lunch, those that are leaving with me need to be back here for 14.00. We're due at the Home office at 14.30. Petra, we'll see you there."

Petra Green nodded, picked her papers up and left.

"Matt," Wyndham said, "Can you inform Lenny of where we are and that he can stand down for the time being. But I'm sure we will need him again, and tell him thanks for his efforts."

"Will do, chief. He'll appreciate that!"

Matt made his way out of the building and called Lenny, on the way to the Horseferry Road branch of Pret A Manger. The conversation lasted around three minutes, and Matt's general impression was that Jody and his kids would be delighted to get their husband and dad back, hopefully for good. However, he realised Lenny was wise enough to know that it was only over, when it was over!

Matt decided to eat in the restaurant, and collect his thoughts. He was still concerned that although their intel had enabled them to narrow down the time frame for a possible attack, unless they obtained more information on where, they were still practically working blind, and he wasn't comfortable with that thought. Covering all possible targets would stretch resources to the limit. He finished his meal and made his way back to his desk.

Just before 14.00, he made the short walk to Mike Wyndham's office, knocked and went in. Wyndham was sitting at his desk going through paperwork he needed for the afternoon briefing at the Home Office, but looked puzzled.

Matt saw this.

"What's up, chief?" he asked.

"Not sure. We've had something in that is strange and even possibly troubling."

"How so?"

"Well, as I said, I'm not sure, but it could be a problem or just something rogue."

"Okay, you've got me. What are you trying to say?"

"Remember we had, after a long time silent, intel from an embedded informant that led to you going to Marseille etc?"

"Yes, I do. What about it?"

"The strange thing is it's to do with Lenny and the assassin. Someone has been trying to find out his details even after Omar was killed, probably because they didn't get the information they wanted, and now there are more 'enquiries' being made by someone and there is a lot of money being splashed around to get his details."

"Oh, shit and, just less than an hour ago, I told him to go back to his day job as we didn't need him. Now he needs us more, not less! What is it they know about him?"

"Again, I can't be sure, but possibly that his name is Lenny and he drives a black cab. We think that may have been leaked by someone in the Marseille police department."

"I need to let him know. We'll have to protect him and the family!"

"No, Matt, not just yet. There are nearly 25,000 cabbies in London and there must be plenty of them named Lenny. I've spoken with the Mayor's office to apprise them and Transport for London (TfL) and told them to make sure that any request for details on drivers, however innocent it may seem, is to be referred here for checking, so we will wait and see how this plays out. Now, we have to go to the Home Office."

As they walked out to the waiting car, Matt became increasingly unsure about not letting Lenny know just yet; he was thinking up some way of informing his 'friend', without causing panic. For the moment though, they had an important briefing to give at the MoD and the country's security was his first priority.

The meeting at the MoD lasted for just over two hours and Matt, Wyndham, as well as Petra Green, arrived back at Millbank just before 17.00. They all went straight up to Wyndham's office, where they were met by Jennifer Hardie. They had been given the go ahead by the Home Secretary to find out by any means possible, short of anything that could be construed as illegal sometime down the track, what the possible target was, who was behind it and where the money was coming from, although they had got closer to answering that question. They began a discussion on known informants, as well as others susceptible to what would be termed 'gentle persuasion'. They drew up a list, that, whilst not extensive, contained a number of names, including the car rental guy just off of the Edgware Road; he had rented the car used by the people who had killed the Saudi diplomat, Omar Hussein.

They broke at 19.30 for food, and resumed at 20.30, when they worked through more names and a plan of action to bring in any of those on the list they deemed 'people of interest'. Around 00.30 they decided that they had had enough, and agreed to resume at 09.00.

Matt left the building on Millbank and hailed a cab. He gave the driver the address and sat in the back. Closing his eyes briefly, he began to think about the possible danger to Lenny. Over and over in his mind, he kept posing the same question of what to do.

"Do I tell him or not?" he thought. Telling him about the latest turn of events that threatened his life was surely something he needed to know, but he was conflicted by his duty to the security of the country, and didn't want to fall foul of that responsibility. He had decided what to do by the time he got home. Suddenly aware how tired he was, he climbed into his bed and went out like a light as soon as his head hit the pillow.

CHAPTER
21

Matt was woken from his sleep by the sound of an alarm. He sat bolt upright as if to prepare for a swift exit. He relaxed, however, when his phone fell on the floor beside his bed and he realised that it was the phone's alarm that he had heard.

He sat for a moment, wondering if his response was caused by fear, exhaustion or just pressure of the current caseload.

He put his feet firmly on the floor and walked into his bathroom. Twenty minutes later, he was showered and dressed and in his kitchen making scrambled eggs, toast and coffee. He looked at his watch: it was 07.45 and his pre-booked cab was due at 08.20. He ate his cooked breakfast and managed two cups of coffee, with most of that time spent thinking of what and how to warn Lenny. He was shaken from his thoughts when his phone buzzed. He looked to see who it was and realised his pre-booked cab had arrived. He grabbed his keys, jacket and small rucksack bag. He locked up and went down one floor via the stairs, found the cab and got in.

It wasn't a long journey as Matt's flat was in one of the mansion blocks opposite the south side of Battersea Park. The driver stayed south of the river along Nine Elms Lane, passed the new US Embassy and New Covent Garden Market south of Vauxhall Bridge, then the MI6 building, along Albert Embankment and over Lambeth Bridge. He dropped Matt outside the building in Horseferry Road just past the junction with Millbank. Fifteen minutes after starting the journey, Matt was walking into MI5, ready for another long day. He wondered what it would bring and how close they were to finding intel that would move them into a position of control.

* * * * *

David Barnes had been driving a London cab for over thirty years and was once again working the late shift, which for him meant that 03.00 would be when he got home to his flat in South London.

It had been a pretty good day and he was now waiting for a job outside a popular venue for A&B list celebs, as well as a preponderance of Middle Eastern and Russian residents. He was second on the rank and it had just gone a little quiet, so he picked up his book and began to read.

After a few pages, something distracted him and his mind wandered back to the conversation and chats he had had with his friends over dinner earlier.

David and three others regularly met up most nights for food and chat at what was generally described as an 'up market greasy spoon' in the Kings Road Chelsea, around the part known as 'The World's End'. It was an Italian pasta pizza place with a varied menu and reasonably priced, hence it was frequented by several discerning cabbies.

After returning to his book, the cab in front got a job and David was now next cab off. After another five minutes, a young, very attractive, blonde girl came out of the restaurant and bar, and walked to the cab. She asked him to take her to a place in Kensington, wait for her for a few minutes, and then go on to a place just over the other side of Battersea Bridge. David smiled and nodded for her to get in. He started the engine and moved off. She gave him the address, just off Kensington High Street and very near to the Kensington and Chelsea Town Hall.

David was an old school cabbie: he liked to chat with his customers but didn't push it if he could see they wanted some privacy. He always found being pushy a bit out of character for him, although he was a gregarious type and always ready with a joke or a story when needed. Very often, he kept his friends well entertained during their dinners together.

He sensed reluctance from the passenger, so he toned it down and just made small talk. He detected, from her short replies, an accent of some sort, but couldn't get it exactly. He would normally ask, but on this occasion he let it go. Five minutes later, they arrived at the address in Kensington. She told him to wait and that she would be back in a few minutes, as she was collecting a parcel. She got out and went in to an apartment block. David watched her and saw her let herself in. Usually, he would ask for a deposit, but on this occasion it felt like he didn't need to.

A few minutes passed and the young woman appeared from the front door of the apartment block, carrying a smallish parcel. She got back into the cab and she told David the address in Battersea.

On the way there she managed to reply very generally to his comments, while she fiddled with what David presumed were the contents of the package. David thought himself pretty good at accents but he was stumped with this customer, but settled on mid to Eastern European.

He finally arrived at the destination in Battersea, a short road and not very wide, just the other side of Albert Bridge. She told him to pull over into the space that was on his left, which he did. He couldn't see too much from behind, but heard some rustling, which he assumed was the woman searching her purse so as to pay the fare. In fact, she was taking the contents of the package out and making sure she had everything ready to deliver it. The Glock 19 was in her right hand and, as she raised it, she said, "Sorry, but nothing personal." Before David had a chance to say anything, she fired the weapon. The bullet hit the Perspex partition from close range and went through it to hit the back of David's head. It passed through his brain, collecting fragments of it and tissue before exiting his forehead and making a hole in the windscreen. The round was suppressed, so there was little noise, but blood and bits of flesh and bone fragments now covered the window. As quickly as she could, she got out of the cab, put on a baseball cap and dark glasses, took out a piece of paper and laid it on the now dead and slumped body of David Barnes, who had taken his last job.

Satisfied that all was as she had planned, she took out from the package an untraceable mobile phone and dialled 999. She gave just enough detail, and then hung up. Then, whilst walking to a car she had parked earlier, she took the phone apart and distributed the bits of it into various waste bins away from the crime scene, but kept the sim for disposal later. Her parked car was about two hundred metres from the taxi and she used an indirect route to get to it, even though she could hear sirens in the distance. In a matter of minutes, the place would be swarming with police. She reached her car, started the engine and drove off, as naturally as possible, away from the scene she had just created.

* * * * *

Matt was suddenly woken by violent banging on his door and the ringing of his phone. He quickly answered the phone, then heard Wyndham screaming, "Matt, answer the fucking door, I'm outside!"

He'd never heard Wyndham swear before and was now really concerned. He unlocked his front door. An agitated and red-faced Mike Wyndham was standing there.

"Mike, what the fuck is going on? It's 05.30, for Christ's sake. What happened? Did the attack…?"

"No, Matt. We have the body of a dead cab driver, very near here, and this was on it." He showed Matt a plastic document holder with paper inside and printed on it were the words *'Lenny is next!'*

Matt froze for a moment and exhaled, as his first thought was about Lenny.

"What the fuck happened?"

Wyndham looked at him.

"A cab driver was shot and killed, and left in his cab in Anhalt Road about four hours ago," he replied, in a calmer tone. "An anonymous call came into the police and they were first on the scene. Local CID found the note and one of their senior officers called Counter Terrorism, who retrieved the note from the local CID. They then called me."

"Shit… I thought… when you said a cab…"

"Yes. I realised you might, but this is going live pretty soon, so we need to get in front of it with Lenny. He needs to come in now, and the family need protecting."

"Okay, I'll call him."

"No, Matt."

Matt jumped in too quickly.

"Why the hell not, Mike?"

"Because, if you'd waited for me to finish, you'll realise that you need to go there and speak to him and the family, and try to keep them calm, while we arrange things."

"Okay, sorry…what things?"

"Well, first we'll need to take care that they don't find out which 'Lenny the cab driver' he is, and then we need to consider how to protect the family. That's why you need to go there right away."

"You've got to be kidding. Me, boss? I must be their public enemy number one."

"No, Matt, I'm not. There's a car waiting for you downstairs. He'll take you, wait as long as you need him to and then bring Lenny and his family back here, and we'll get a team together for round-the-clock protection. As low key as possible, obviously. We don't want any speculation by the neighbours!"

"Are you really sure about this, boss?"

"Yes, now go."

"Okay, on my way!"

As Matt left his flat, he gave Wyndham a spare key to lock up, and then went down to where the car was waiting. It was now 06.20 and Matt reckoned that with a bit of luck they'd be at Lenny's by around 07.15. At that moment, he had no idea what he was going to say. But he had forty-five minutes to think, all the time hoping he would get there before they saw or heard the news.

* * * * *

Banu Behzadi was in her apartment in Marseille. It was late, but she had lots to do before she relocated temporarily to the UK, where she would complete her contract with the Sheikh. Her phone buzzed, she picked it up and saw the message.

"BAIT SET, NOTE LEFT "LENNY IS NEXT" WATCH NEWS SOON."

Banu stopped what she was doing, went into her living area, picked up the remote and turned on the TV. She flicked through the news channels until she found BBC World News, nothing yet, then Sky, then CNN, but still nothing. She looked at the time, 03.00 which meant 02.00 in London. "Obviously too soon for anything yet," she thought, "They must only just have cordoned off the area and no news crew will be allowed there yet!" She decided to finish what she was doing and watch later after she had slept. She texted back, *"NOTHING YET BUT NOT SURPRISING. WILL LOOK LATER."*

Bilquis Anzorova was originally from Chechnya. She had fled with her parents from their home, a small village just outside the capital Grozny, when she was a small girl. They left because of the crackdown on Chechnya by the Russian Government after the breakup of the old Soviet Union.

Like many of the other former Soviet states, the Chechen people, predominantly Sunni Muslim, wanted independence from Russia. However, the powers in Moscow were adamant that would not be allowed and had sent several army units down to the 'Russian Provence' to prevent that from happening. Naturally, civil war ensued and many, including Bilquis and her family, became displaced. They fled across many countries and finally ended up in Beirut, Lebanon. Her parents found work and a safe place to stay, within the Sunni community. Bilquis went to school, but the structure and excitement of the training camps enticed her. It was there she met Hossein and his friend Banu.

She and Banu became good friends, and, over the years that followed, carried out a number of terrorist activities, directed by Hossein. However, when she was in her mid twenties, her parents were killed in a car crash just outside Beirut. This devastated Bilquis for some time, but throughout this Banu took care of her friend. When Banu relocated to Marseille, Bilquis went with her, and subsequently helped her with a number of her private contracts, giving her a good deal of financial security. When Bilquis decided to leave, Banu, although disappointed, was not surprised as she realised that her friend was ready. Bilquis had been to London several times with Banu, and there was a growing Russian community there. It meant that a number of them were possible targets, for retribution, because of the atrocities that had been carried out in her homeland, in the name of Russia.

Whenever Bilquis carried out a 'task' in retribution, it involved a large sum of money, before she ended their lives. That allowed her to continue to build a considerable amount of wealth that had enabled her to live very well in her large apartment in Kensington, west London.

This latest contact with Banu was all part of a greater plan that she had been made aware of. However, finding the cab driver, who had picked up the two traitors she had followed that Sunday evening in January whilst on the bus, had now become personal to her friend.

Bilquis was always ready to help, and had devised the plan to 'flush him out' with Banu. Now she had to wait, as did her friend, for the next part of the plan to develop.

Matt's driver pulled up outside Lenny's house at 07.20, just a few minutes later than anticipated. The house appeared to be quiet and no visible movement was obvious. He gave the driver instructions to park up somewhere inconspicuous and said he would call him when he was needed.

He got out and the driver pulled off. Matt walked slowly up to the door, glancing all around in case there were unwanted eyes on him. Lenny's cab was in the drive, so obviously he wasn't yet out to work. He rang the bell and waited. About thirty seconds went by and he was just about to ring again, when the door opened. A sleepy Jody wearing a dressing gown suddenly opened her eyes wide and shouted up, "Lenny…you'd better get down here…your bad penny just turned up!"

She left the door open and walked back in. Matt followed her, but stopped at the lounge.

Lenny came down the stairs, rubbing his head and yawning.

"Matt, what the hell are you doing here so early?"

"Well, good morning to you too. Were you working last night?"

"Yeah, got home about 01.30, why?"

"I wanted to let you know that around about 01.30 a cabbie by the name of David Barnes was murdered in his cab just south of Albert Bridge. I need to know if you knew him."

"Shit, yes, but not generally by that name. Most of his friends called him Barney. Do you think this is something to do with the case and, in particular, me?"

"Yes, I thought you might know him. Unfortunately, that makes what I am going to tell you even more problematic and extremely worrying."

"Matt, for fuck's sake, spit it out. You're beginning to worry me now. Are my family and me in danger?" Matt hesitated just long enough for Jody to have come back, when she heard the shouting from Lenny.

"What's going on?"

"Lenny, Jody, sit down.We have a problem."

"Okay, Lenny, let's have it. Is the murder of 'David, Barney, Barnes' something to do with me?"

"What?" screamed Jody, "What the hell is going on, Matt Flynn? Are we in danger? All Lenny has done is help you, and this is what we get, just more crap!"

"Jody, Lenny, believe me, this is something nobody could have foreseen. We did know that the woman that carried out the Hyde Park Corner attack had somehow recognised Lenny, but from where we're not sure. We think it was years ago in Northern Israel, when he was with Shin Bet. But we have no idea exactly who she is. She obviously has a grudge and her seeing Lenny has raised the possibility of revenge. Hence this…" He showed them a copy of the note left on the body of David Barnes. Jody saw it and gasped. She stared at it for a moment before speaking.

"Okay, Matt, this is obviously now a very scary situation for us, so what are you and MI5 going to do about it? If anything happens to Lenny or my kids, believe me, I will hold you personally responsible."

With that, she walked over and put the TV on. The screen came up on BBC News 24 and, sure enough, the main story was of the murder of the cab driver in Battersea during the night. They stood and watched the TV in total silence for several minutes, as they heard the TV correspondent's take on the confusion and what may have happened to the cab driver. No mention was made of the note, as that hadn't been released to the news media, plainly as the security services didn't want to start an unnecessary panic, amongst the cab driving fraternity. They needed the news of the murder of the cab driver to seem random.

The silence in the Resnick lounge was broken, when Jody looked at Matt sternly and said, "So, 'okay Mr got it under control Matt Flynn', what now?"

"That's why I'm here, Jody, to work with you and to find the best way to keep you and the girls safe."

"Me and the girls? What about their father?"

"Obviously, that is our main priority, and they want Lenny to come back with me, where we can use all our resources to protect him more effectively."

"Oh well, that's just great," the cut of the sarcasm wasn't missed, "So what do we do in the meantime?"

After watching and listening to Matt and Jody meta-phorically tearing lumps out of each other, Lenny decided it was time to speak. There was a pause in the hostilities, so he seized the opportunity.

"Okay, you two. I think we've got a grasp of the feelings involved here, but it's wasting time." He turned to Matt, "Look, I did know the poor guy, but this is personal now. They've viciously killed a non-combatant to try to get to me, I don't know why, but, given the intel we have had, I have a pretty good idea. So let's stop the crap, that's taking us nowhere. We need to make sure my family are safe and I'm covered. At the moment, they don't have any useful information of my whereabouts, so when my family are safe, we can move on with finding these assholes and put them where they need to be, dead or in prison."

"Six feet under, preferably," Jody said.

"Well, whatever we need, I expect," answered Lenny.

Matt then began to set out what the options were, although there was only one real choice open to them, and that was to keep Lenny close to MI5 protectors and either install Jody and the girls in a 'safe house' or get them out of harm's way, maybe back to Israel, till whatever it was that was coming, played out or blew over.

Jody wasn't too happy, but, by this time, Jess and Ella were listening to the conversation at the bottom of the stairs and squealed with delight at the thought of going back to Israel. Lenny, Jody and Matt all looked round at the girls when they heard the noise. Jody decided to damp down on the joy.

"Don't get too excited, this will not be a holiday, if indeed we go anywhere. You will have to take schoolwork with you, as you're not going to fall behind. This is a very important year for both of you," she said. Their facial expressions changed to serious.

"How serious is this, Dad?" Jess said. Lenny looked at Matt, then Jody, before attempting to answer. Fortunately, Matt helped out before Lenny could answer. "Look, guys, we have a very probable threat to the country. Your dad has helped us out and now, through no fault of his own, he has had a credible threat made against him. A man died last night as part of the threat. It was cowardly and despicable, and we need to find who did it, and your dad is going to help us with that too! But the safest thing for you and your mum now is for us to protect you any way we can until we have resolved the problem. That means one of two things, a safe house here with 24/7 protection or a much safer place away from this country until it's over."

Jody stopped wondering what he might say, as she was astonished at Matt's frank explanation.

"Well thanks, Matt, for not sugar coating it. I'm sure we all appreciate it."

Then Lenny took his opportunity.

"Matt, you know I'm ready to help in any way I can, and I also appreciate your candid comments, but what we are looking at? How long do we have before it all kicks off?"

"Lenny, you know I've gone beyond where I maybe should have, but that's my choice. As for when and how long, you know we've narrowed the time frame to mid June, so that's around three weeks, and we're squeezing out info as we speak. As for the threat to you, we're probably looking at it being personal to whoever has a beef with you, so that is likely to be after and not part of the attack, if as we believe the two things are connected." The girls groaned, shrieked and grasped each other, and Jody went and held them both. She looked at Matt and said, "I think we've heard enough and got the gist and you and Lenny have probably lots to talk about, so we'll go and start arranging for our time away." With that Jody, Ella and Jess went upstairs and started to sob, softly.

Matt and Lenny went and sat in the lounge, and Matt produced some paperwork and files for them to go over.

Over the course of the next few hours, they arranged for Jody and the girls to leave later that day, with the same accommodation for them as their previous trip, but this time it was open-ended. Lenny would move into Matt's spare room for the duration, hopefully no more than four weeks, by which time they hoped that whatever was coming had been successfully dealt with.

It was now mid afternoon and Matt had arranged an EL AL flight from Heathrow, departing at 23.30 and arriving at Ben Gurion, Tel Aviv around 06.40 local time.

Matt organised the car to Heathrow, the travel documents and necessary funding arrangements that would arrive with the transport. Lenny had spoken with Lazar Spiegal to explain the situation, and Lazar agreed to take care of Jody and the girls on arrival and also to maintain a discreet surveillance, throughout the course of their stay. Lenny thanked him for that, and Lazar assured him that thanks were not necessary, as Israel owed him a lot more for his previous service.

Jody came back down and prepared food for everyone. When Lenny told her about the arrangements, she turned away and began to cry. Lenny knew what she was thinking, and moved to her and embraced her, but she attempted to shake him off. He held her even tighter and he felt her stop resisting. She turned to him, her face reddened with her tears. She put her arms around his waist, buried her head in his chest and held tight. He held on tight too, and gently kissed the top of her head, in a loving way. They stayed like that for a moment, then Jody pulled away, looked at Lenny and said, "I'm scared, Lenny, really scared."

He looked at her and responded, "I know, honey, so am I, but we're going to make sure we get through this, and then get back to normal as soon as…"

"Of course you will," she interrupted, "But I know you, Lenny Resnick, don't go being a hero! Your family already know you are… and we need you back in one piece."

Lenny looked at her and began to well up. Seeing this, Jody said, "Come here, you big lump."

She pulled his head towards her and they kissed, hugged and held that for what seemed an age. They pulled apart when the girls came in and saw what was happening, and then joined in for a family hug.

CHAPTER 23

The car pulled into a drop-off bay at terminal 4 of London's Heathrow Airport. Matt had borrowed a Peugeot 5008 from the car pool and drove Lenny, Jody, Ella and Jess. It was part guilt and, in another way, something he felt he needed to do.

They all got out. Lenny opened the hatch back and started unloading the bags, whilst Matt found some trolleys to put them on. Matt said his goodbyes to Jody and the girls, and handed Jody a medium-sized envelope with travel documents and other essentials, including a company credit card. Jody looked at it quickly and zeroed in on the card. She looked at Matt and said, "Okay, thanks, is the card for real?" She knew it was, but still wanted an answer. Matt had been around long enough to understand.

"It's the least we can do in the circumstances!" he said.

"Damn right it is, so why do I feel it's like a bribe?"

Matt noticed there was hint of mischief in the comment, but answered it anyway.

"Let's just say, for services rendered. We can decide what the services were when this is all over!"

Lenny joined them and so did the girls.

"Okay, let's go check you in and get the formalities done, and then you can settle, get some coffee and wait to board," said Lenny.

"I hope you're not thinking of leaving just yet?" said Jody, a little put out.

"No, honey, I'm waiting till you get called to board, and Matt is waiting to take me back to his place. He's minding me for the duration!"

Jody looked at Matt and reminded him about the warning she

gave, should any harm come to Lenny. Matt was clearly tuned into this.

"Jody, I am fully aware of your comments and so is my boss, because he's on my case too. So I will stop at nothing to make sure my friend comes through this unscathed," he responded very quickly, to remove doubt.

Before she could say anything, Lenny intervened again and started ushering Jody, Ella and Jess into the terminal to check in. Matt said his goodbyes, then went back to the car and waited for Lenny.

In the EL AL Terminal check-in, the flight had opened, just. Thankfully not too many were in the queue yet, and there were only between six and eight groups to check in. Three check-in desks opened and very soon were weighing their baggage. An Israeli girl, in her mid-twenties wearing the EL AL uniform, was very efficient, and processed everything very quickly.

With the formalities completed, Jody and the girls went to sit down, and Lenny went to find coffee and Danish pastries. Mission accomplished, he brought them back to his waiting family.

They drank the coffee and eagerly consumed the very good pastries, an activity that muted the feeling of impending separation and possible danger for Lenny, Jody's husband and the father of their two daughters.

However, when Lenny finished, he looked at Jody and his two growing, beautiful daughters, with immense pride. Fighting back the emotion, he pulled them all up, gathered the three of them in his arms and squeezed them tight, kissing each one in turn. When they pulled away, none of them had a dry eye. He wiped away the moisture from his eyes and then spoke.

"I know this is hard to understand, but I need to know you will always be safe, that's why we have to do this. You will be safe in Israel and I can then do what I need to do to end any more threats to our family. Matt is a top professional and he will keep me as safe as he can. Call me, FaceTime me every day, I want to know you are all okay. You all agree?"

They said nothing, but all nodded and the tears reappeared. Lenny then held both the girls tight and whispered something to each of them and they repeated the tearful nodding, but this time they managed a weak smile through the tears. Lenny hugged and kissed both of them and told them how much he loved them, and that they should remember to call every day.

"We know you have to do whatever this thing is, dad, but please, please be careful. We need you back soon!" Ella said.

Lenny felt a lump form in his throat and fought back the urge to cry. He coughed and cleared his throat, breathed a little and put his arms around both of them again. He held them for a moment and then said, "Sweetheart, I'm not intending going anywhere, but you're right – I have to do this, and I'll think of you and Jess so I can finish it as quickly as I can."

With that, the call to board the plane came over the public address system. He looked at Jody and she came towards him. They embraced, kissed and held onto each other tightly for about thirty seconds. They pulled apart slowly, looked at each other and smiled briefly.

"Honey, I'm really sorry we're having to do this," Lenny said, "It's not what I planned right now, or even for the foreseeable future, but there is danger out there and I've got to sort it, otherwise it's going to keep coming back."

"I know that, Lenny, but it's hard, especially for the girls."

"Yes… They're smart and know why I need to do this. Now, come on, let's get you on that plane."

They walked hand-in-hand, with Ella and Jess either aside of them. They arrived at the beginning of the boarding phase, had one last group hug and then Lenny kissed all of them again and reminded Jody that Lazar Spiegal would meet them at the airport. He watched as they walked on through.

Jody looked back twice and waved. Lenny waved back, as they disappeared, hoping that it wouldn't be the last time he held them close. He walked out of the terminal and headed to where Matt was parked. Matt flashed his headlights when he saw Lenny looking for him. Lenny picked up his pace to the car and got in.

"Tough?" Matt asked.

"You could say. Beginning to regret going to work that Sunday early in January now!"

Matt drove off and not a word was said for the majority of the way back to Battersea. The silence was broken when Lenny said, "Where do you live, by the way?"

"Prince of Wales Drive."

"What, one of the mansion blocks?"

"Yes, Overstrand."

"Okay, very nice. And there's room for me?"

"Of course. Keeps everything nice and neat, just like my boss wants it to be."

A few minutes later, they pulled up and parked outside the block where Matt's flat was, Lenny took his bag out from the boot and they walked up to the first floor.

Matt unlocked the door and turned on the lights. He pointed out all the amenities, showed Lenny his room, and went into the kitchen and put the kettle on to make a hot drink.

Lenny tested the bed, opened his case and took out all of his toiletries. Then he sat on the bed, held his head in his hands and just let his thoughts wander. They started with his service in Israel, that night in the north when he and a company of Sayeret Matkal (Special Forces) ambushed an insurgent group from Syria. The intel they had had was spot on and he had always wondered how it was so accurate. He remembered it in every detail, right down to the body count. There were eleven all taken out, literally in minutes, but it now appeared there was a survivor and she was out for revenge. Then his thoughts moved to the murdered cab driver, Barney. "Poor guy," he thought, "Just doing his job and murdered because they think it will flush me out." Then it occurred it might just be a distraction from the main event, whatever that might turn out to be. All the time, though, his thoughts were on the fact that his wife and family were in danger and they had had to flee. Non-combatants that had nothing to do with his past had had to flee for their lives. "Well, lady," he thought, "Whoever you are and whenever you come for me, I'm ready, so you'd better be very good, because it's you or me and I'm not going anywhere any time soon!"

Just then Matt called out, and Lenny emerged from his thoughts and joined him in the lounge.

They spent the next few hours discussing the case and what Lenny's role would be. The desire was to keep Lenny away from the action, as far as possible, but the more they spoke, the more they came to realise it would be almost impossible. So the next option was how to incorporate his participation with the activities of the Security Services. By now, it was the early hours of the morning and their brains were starting to shut down, so they agreed to continue at 08.00 the following morning.

They met in Matt's lounge around 07.30. After a quick coffee and chat, they decided to resume on the grid at MI5. The journey was made in the car Matt had used from the car pool and they took the route south of the river, as that was always quicker. It looked like being another lovely early summer's day: the sun had been up for a couple of hours and there was already a virtually clear blue sky, with just a few white vapour trails from high-flying passing aircraft. Matt and Lenny arrived at the Millbank building around 08.15. The previous day had been a pretty long day of activity, culminating in an intense session of information-gathering at Matt's flat, and as well as sifting through all of the intel, to see what was useful and what was just speculation. Eventually, they had become weary from the effort, although they'd found a few nuggets, whilst they trawled through the information. On arriving back at Millbank, they discovered that the whole team were now following all of the intel, to see where it led. Once they got to Matt's desk on the grid, they found Jennifer Hardie there, ready to take them to the meeting room, where Wyndham was waiting. Also with him was the anti terrorism officer both Lenny and Matt had seen on that fateful Sunday evening at Hyde Park Corner, Commander Stewart Scott.

"Matt, Lenny, come in. You know Commander Scott?"

They smiled, nodded and took their seats.

Wyndham continued, "Commander Scott is here as he has some ideas and thoughts as to what the targets for an attack might be in the coming few weeks, now that we have a time frame for any, now probable, terrorist action. So over to you, Commander…"

Commander Scott, cleared his throat and began, "Thanks, Mike. Over the last few months, we've been going through the major events, as I'm sure you have too. We now believe that the targets can be pinned downed to a maximum of three: Royal Ascot, the cricket Test Match and a late one – unknown a couple of months ago – the State opening of Parliament on the 22nd."

"Surely, Commander Scott, the State opening should be discounted?" Matt interrupted, "We knew months ago that some sort of 'spectacular' attack would be attempted before that was even on the horizon."

"Yes, Matt, you're quite right, but from the information we all have, it wouldn't be too difficult to change the focus of any attack. We are very confident that they will want to take out as many civilians as possible, and it would be totally random. So that's probably suicide bombers, and we can't discount the use of automatic weapons either. Whichever way, this will be an attempt at some sort of spectacular suicide mission." There was a deep intake and exhale of breath around the room.

Lenny then decided to say something. "Commander, I understand the intel has obviously been checked, but if we have this much detail, why don't we have anything more specific? I mean, two of those events are spread over four or five days. Do we have the resources, including people, to cover them for that amount of time?"

"It's a very good point, Mr Resnick…"

"Lenny is fine."

"Okay Lenny, thanks. No, we don't, in short, but we are hoping for more intel, at least MI5 are, from the recently re-surfaced mole."

Wyndham broke in, "Yes, that's still a work in progress. We still don't know exact details, but as soon as we have anything else, we will be able to be more specific. However, in the meantime, we have an immediate problem, particularly after the murder of the cab driver the other night.

"It was a different MO from the January shooter and the murder of the Saudi diplomat, Omar Hussein, so we are looking for a second or third possible assassin. There is obviously a cell or the makings of a cell possibly here or on their way. They will also have recruited more terrorists too, probably from here. We know from other intelligence reports that some unknowns visited mosques of interest in both Birmingham and Manchester, probably to recruit some of the necessary willing 'martyrs' they need. That's why, we think, Omar was killed. It was information we are now confident that he had. But that's still a bit speculative," he went on, "So we still have a lot of work to do. Matt, you and Lenny carry on your search through the other possible people of interest, use up to four more officers from the section, until we have a more complete picture. We can't take our eyes off other areas at the moment. Back here tomorrow at 08.30. Jennifer will contact and get latest info from GCHQ and anything too from Petra at 6. Commander Scott, hopefully you'll have more for us, so we will expect you tomorrow, if that's okay?"

"Yes, that's fine. I'll see you at 08.30, then." He picked up his papers and left.

Wyndham looked at Lenny.

"How you holding up, Lenny? Sorry you are involved with this, must be tough?"

Lenny was taken aback at this show of empathy.

"That's okay, boss. Thanks for the concern, but I'm glad my family are safe and out of harm's way."

"Good to hear, Lenny, so let's get out there and find these bastards, before they carry out this atrocity."

CHAPTER 24

London in early June, when there was a warm sun under a deep blue sky, was a place that enchanted many visitors each year, and provided a wonderful opportunity to take in the many marvellous historic sites, as well as the modern structures, theatres, castles, palaces and the beautifully maintained parks and gardens. There was also the joy of being able to sample menus of some of the finest restaurants anywhere in the world.

The month of June also brought with it the regular round of society and sporting events that meant summer had arrived. This year, though, June had seen an extra event, a snap General Election had been inserted by the Government to seek approval for its new round of policies, after what was becoming a very messy divorce of the UK from the European Union. Unfortunately for the government, they lost twenty-six of their, already depleted, numbers, leaving them way short of being able to command a majority in Parliament and now five seats behind the other main party.

As a consequence, the Socialists, Scottish Nationalists and a couple of Northern Irish Social Democratic and Labour Party members (SDLP) constructed a coalition, which gave these three parties a notional majority. The Welsh Nationalists and the one Green MP were also expected to support the coalition. This gave power to a very left-wing Prime Minister, who four years earlier had been dismissed and characterised as a no-hoper. Because of this, there would now be a State Opening of Parliament, unusually on a Thursday, on the same day as the Royal Ascot meeting. The Queen would be accompanied by the Prince of Wales at the State Opening, in order to deliver the new government's programme to Parliament. As soon as this was completed, she would be driven back to Buckingham Palace to board a waiting helicopter that would take her to Windsor Castle, in time for lunch and then the procession of the carriages to open the day's proceedings at Royal Ascot.

* * * * *

Banu Behzadi had made the journey from Marseille to London and was now settled in an apartment not too far from travel links, sourced for her by her friend, Bilquis. It was just a short walk to Kensington High Street in West London. Banu had paid for a six-month rental, so as not to raise any suspicion, but in reality she would only need it for four weeks at most.

The journey from Marseille had had to be a little circuitous, in case she was being watched. She had made an effort, despite her dislike of flying, by taking a plane to Berlin, where she spent two days in a hotel making necessary arrangements, before flying from Berlin to Paris. Even though it was taking a chance, she returned by Eurostar from Gare du Nord to London St Pancras International. All this was made possible by using three different passports and credit cards to match, on accounts she had set up some months earlier.

The arrangements made from her Berlin hotel were to make sure that all of the 'tools' needed for the 'event' would be in place at the right time. She had also ascertained that the first half of her substantial fee, agreed with Sheik AbdulWahab, had been paid into the designated bank account that would be difficult to trace. Satisfied that all was now in place, she began to finalise the list of things she would need to do from her temporary Kensington home. Once there, she would be able to confirm that all of the recruits were in place, trained and ready to be deployed when the time came.

During the conversation she had with the Sheikh, she was told the target, as well as any secondaries for further disruption, if there was time. She pondered that for a while, before coming to the conclusion that the resources they had available might only allow for one secondary, and it would have to be only a short distance from the main target. She informed the Sheikh of this and, with some reluctance, he agreed.

After the conversation had finished, Banu thought long and hard.

She realised that any secondary action would have to be part of the main one, so she set about planning the deployment of the group to best effect.

Now settled in her apartment in Kensington, she had contacted Hossein using an untraceable phone and discussed with him the best way to use their resources. She didn't know where he was but that was best, and, in any event, she would see him very soon.

During their conversation, Hossein had agreed to meet her by the Serpentine in Hyde Park, to try to finalise details, as preparation, particularly thorough preparation, was key. It was after Ramadan, and that area around the lake would be a good place to meet, as they would be among thousands of Middle Eastern visitors who came to London at that time of year to celebrate the ending of the holy month as well as enjoying a holiday from the extreme heat of the Gulf States and Saudi Arabia. They would practically be unnoticeable. In her mind, she could see them together in her apartment in Marseille, and longed for the day when they could spend more time, in fact all of their time, together. After all, her fortune was now very impressive and she would be able to do anything she wanted when this mission was all over, and settle once and for all her private business with the cab driver.

She broke off from her thoughts and took out her untraceable mobile to text Bilquis. The message was brief: *"COME OVER SOON, MUCH TO DO!"*

The reply came within a few minutes, *"OKAY WILL BE 45 MINS."*

She was okay with that: it gave her time to prepare some food, as they would have to spend a good few hours going over what needed to be put in place over the next week or so.

Almost exactly forty-five minutes later, the buzzer on Banu's intercom sounded. She moved out of her kitchen and answered, "Yes?"

"Hi, it's me."

She pressed the button and let her friend, Bilquis, in the main door. She stood by her door and waited. Within a few seconds, Bilquis appeared from the lift and, seeing Banu, she ran straight to her and they hugged for what seemed an age. Although they had kept in touch by messaging and phone calls, they hadn't seen one another for several years.

Banu took her into the apartment and showed her around,

forgetting that it was Bilquis that had sourced the apartment for her. When she realised this, she just started to giggle, along with Bilquis.

After a few minutes, they both calmed down and Banu poured them a glass of white wine. They raised their glasses and toasted 'friendship and success'.

They spent the next hour eating, drinking and reminiscing about their exploits and friendship and Hossein. Bilquis was delighted to hear that her two closest friends had finally got it together.

"I knew you would, it was only a matter of time."

"How on earth did you know? I didn't know myself until we met in Marseille earlier this year."

"I could tell. I've had a lot of experience with men and intuitively felt you were good together. However, I still have not found the right one, but I know I will!"

They finished their food and reminiscing, and adjourned to the lounge, where they got down to the planning. Banu had already laid out some maps and lists of things to do before the main event.

They sat for hours talking, planning, and going over and over again what the options were that could become the secondary attack, so that it would be near the main target and easier to achieve the full effect. They had devised a couple of dummy targets too, as a misdirection, to try and weaken the resources of the police and intelligence services.

Time passed quickly and it was now after midnight, so they agreed to finish for the night and return to the plan around midday. Banu walked her friend to the door and said goodnight. Bilquis went out into the warm Kensington air and decided that it was too nice to do anything else but walk. It would take about ten minutes but she didn't mind: the fresh air would do her good. As she turned off of Kensington Church Street, into her turning, two men in their early twenties were following her. She had been aware of them and kept her pace steady and without any sign of concern. The two were English and a little worse for wear because of the drink they had consumed, which only made them stupid in their intent.

Bilquis kept listening and realised the men had picked up their pace and were very close to her. They started to call her, asking if she 'wanted a good time'. She ignored them until they were almost behind her, at which point, she spun around and looked at them. They were a sorry sight, but she asked them calmly, "What do you want, boys?"

"We thought you might be up for some fun…so how about it?" replied the bigger of the two.

"You are mistaken then. I don't do young boys!"

"What? Don't tell me you're a lesbo!" he responded with a sneer which quickly turned into a snigger.

"No, you are not listening. I said I don't do boys, I prefer proper men, which you really are not."

As she finished speaking, the bigger one moved towards her, shouting out, "I'll show you how much of a man I am…bitch!"

As the last word came out, he was only three feet away. Bilquis had just swayed slightly back and then pushed off from her back foot. Her momentum and timing were perfect because, when he was one foot closer, her bent arm came up at pace and, as she came level with the side of his face, her elbow smashed into the side of his head. Stunned and with a glazed look, he collapsed instantly. His friend now panicked, turned on his heels and ran. Bilquis checked to see if the boy was breathing. He was. She then took out her phone, dialled 999 and requested an ambulance, stating that there was an unconscious drunk man who had collapsed on the street and hit his head. She waited until she heard the sirens and then disappeared into her apartment, fifty yards further along the road.

The lounge window of her first floor apartment faced the street. She watched as the ambulance crew tended the stricken, very foolish alpha male. She had dealt with many like him over the years and seen them all off, mainly because of her training in the camps in Lebanon and her time spent with Banu and Hossein, which had toughened her up.

She saw the paramedics load the now semi-conscious male into the ambulance. Just before they closed the doors, the other boy reappeared. He spoke briefly with the crew, shook his head a few times, then nodded and got into the ambulance. It pulled off into the night with its siren on full.

Bilquis smiled briefly. She was pretty sure nothing more would be said, as no self-respecting alpha male would admit to being floored by a girl! She closed her blinds, went to her kitchen, found a glass and took out an open bottle of white wine from the fridge. She poured herself a large glass, returned to the lounge, sat, drank and pondered what the next few weeks and months would bring.

First, though, she had to carry out another task before she could relax. It would be time for another reminder to the security services about that cab driver, Lenny. Banu had asked her to send another 'message' to help keep them distracted and thereby enable her, and the rest of the 'activists', to make the final preparations for the attack. She wasn't a psychopathic killer, but when it was deemed necessary for the cause, she would never shy away from the task.

But now it was time for rest: her most recent exertions had left her a little weary. As she had to be back at Banu's tomorrow at midday to continue their plans, and as it was now into the early hours of the morning, she needed to sleep. Tomorrow would be a long day, difficult and probably dangerous, but also, she felt, exciting.

Hossein had arrived back in the UK at Stansted Airport in Essex to the east of London, via Tel Aviv, on an Israeli passport: he could pass for a Sabra – a Jew born in Israel. He made his way to central London, where he checked in at a hotel in Lancaster Gate, just off the Bayswater Road, north of Hyde Park.

He got there a few days before the meeting he had arranged with Banu, so had time to explore his surroundings and settle on a spot near the Serpentine Lake, where he would arrange to meet her. He hadn't told her when he would be there, mainly for safety. He didn't know if the intelligence services had him on their radar, particularly after the CIA had lost an agent in Marseille, or if they knew he was party to the liquidation of the Saudi Embassy official. How strange it was, he thought, that he had chosen to stay in a hotel just a stone's throw away from that action.

He had returned to the hotel late the previous evening, after many hours just walking around Hyde Park. Having ordered room service for breakfast, he went up to his room, which was luxurious, and larger than the standard double, with a sofa, lounge chair, good size desk and two more chairs, plus a large TV with access to phone charging points, wifi and a printer.

He slept well and was woken when room service arrived at 08.30. He let the waiter in, to set down the breakfast, tipped him and then saw him out. The only thing that was hot was the large pot of coffee; the rest was fresh croissants, butter, jam, fresh fruit, cottage cheese and yoghurt. He decided to shower first, and then eat, before contacting Banu.

After his shower, he shaved the parts of his face where there was no beard, dried himself and put on the comfortably soft, white bath robe provided. He touched the coffee pot – it was still hot – and then poured himself a cup. After a few short gulps of the coffee, he ate the croissants with jam and worked his way through the rest of the food. He hadn't realised how hungry he was. After the third cup, he sat back in the chair, picked up his mobile, which was untraceable, and called Banu.

Her phone rang three times before she answered with a hesitance in her voice. "H-e-l-l-o?" she said.

"Hello, my dear. How are you? It's been a while."

"Oh my god…it's you! I thought it was someone else."

"Who else were you expecting?"

"Oh nothing to worry about, but Bilquis had a spot of bother as she walked home last night, but it's all probably okay, nothing more than two young testosterone-filled English guys who thought that she might be interested, but they got it wrong and she showed them the error of their ways."

"What happened?"

"She used her elbow on the big one and the other ran. Needless to say, she did call the emergency service and watched as the ambulance took him to hospital."

"But what if he gives a description?"

"Well, I don't think that will happen. They were both a bit drunk, and, in any case, I don't think his pride will let him admit he was floored by a girl!"

"Yes, I forgot the English with their stupid pride thing."

"So, when can we meet? I can't wait to see you!"

"Well, how about the cafe by the lake on the lido side, around midday? Have you far to come?"

"No, that's fine. I can walk. It's a lovely day again and it will take me around fifteen minutes What about you?"

"Yes, I'm not far away either. Also about the same."

"Okay, I'll see you there at midday. Can't wait."

"Me neither, see you then."

Hossein clicked off the phone, took a small wire tool out, removed the sim and inserted a new one. She would call no doubt, he thought, but he would give her the new number when he saw her later. Attention to fine detail was what had kept him alive for all these years.

By now his coffee was cold, so he ordered more from room service, then asked them to come and clear his breakfast tray. He needed to make a number of other calls too, mainly to check that all the people who needed to be in place were.

The same waiter came with the fresh coffee and removed his breakfast tray. Hossein tipped him again; the man was very appreciative and smiled as he left the room. Hossein poured another cup and spent the next hour calling people in Birmingham and Manchester, and then the twins, to see how their training had gone.

Satisfied his enquiries had been successful, Hossein finished dressing. It was a warm day, and likely to stay that way, so he dressed in a light cotton polo shirt, a pair of lightweight chino trousers, cotton socks and a pair of boat shoes. He strapped on his watch and collected his wallet and money from the dresser, as well as some paper tissues, which he distributed evenly in the pockets of the trousers. He then picked up his lightweight windbreaker, slipped his phone in one pocket and zipped it up. He slipped his hotel entry key card into his wallet. After looking around to take in where everything was, he made sure his security measures were in place, and left the room.

Stepping out of the hotel, Hossein remembered his sunglasses were in the inside pocket of his jacket. He took them out and put them on. It was a warm, sunny day and, apart from shielding his eyes from the sun, the sunglasses gave him a certain amount of anonymity, which was always good.

He made his way across the Bayswater Road and into Hyde Park, via Victoria gate and then to West Carriage Drive. He walked past the car park, across the Serpentine bridge, and then towards the part of the lake where the lido was, and the café, where he had arranged to meet Banu. As he had thought, it was a favourite meeting place for many Middle Eastern people, who came to enjoy the summer in London every year, and so he felt very much at ease in this place because he blended in. It occurred to him that Banu might need to contact him if there had been a problem, or if she was running late. He was early for the meet, so he took his phone out to text his new number, with a short explanation. He didn't have to wait long, as her reply came back, that everything was fine and that she would be there at midday.

Hossein found a spot near the lake by the café, with a view in all directions. He sat with his back to the lake and so was pretty confident that he would be able to observe anything he felt was suspicious. As it neared midday, he could see a figure he recognised approaching him from the West Carriage Drive and the south west. He realised that if she had come straight here it was from the Kensington direction, as she had said. As she came closer, he could see the smile on her face and what seemed to be eagerness to get to him as quickly as possible. When she was about five metres away, he got up from his seat and smiled. She hurried across to him, he held out his arms and they embraced. He felt her body press close to his and he really wanted to press back, but knew his need for her would have to wait, since there were much more important reasons for them both being here, which had to take prominence. He held his position and she sensed this. As she pulled away, she looked at him inquiringly. He kissed her on both cheeks and then pulled back, saying, "How lovely to see you, my dear." She looked at him again.

"Is something wrong?" she asked.

"No, nothing, but we are now preparing to fulfil a contract that will enable us, when completed, to go away anywhere we wish and enjoy a wonderful life. Our passions will have to be put on hold until then. We are leading people to an event that is dangerous, so we have to remain totally professional."

She looked at him, and he could see her disappointment, but she nodded in agreement. Her mood lightened, though, at the thought of a life together with him.

He led her over to a table just outside the café. Again, he sat looking out over the park with his back to the window, and she sat facing him. A waiter came over and gave them menus, and asked if they wanted anything to drink.

Hossein asked for some iced water and said they would then order lunch. The waiter smiled and walked away to get the water.

They chatted while looking at the menu. The waiter came back with his drink and to take their food order. Both had agreed a fresh fruit starter with a lamb tagine, spiced couscous and Moroccan roasted vegetables. The waiter moved off and they sat for a few seconds, looking at each other. They spoke in general terms about the impending action they were to undertake and, although Hossein was now very curious as to the target, he knew to ask directly would only produce misdirection. As much as anyone wanted to know something, he had taught her, the more you must keep them waiting. She had learned well, he thought.

The one thing she did let him know was that there was to be a main target, as well as a secondary that was nearby. He was surprised at this, but she explained that it was what was required.

They ate their lunch and ordered coffee, afterwards discussing plans. Hossein had asked her about the incident involving Bilquis, but Banu removed his fears of repercussions, explaining they had checked hospitals and police stations for any reports of the incident, but had found nothing.

After Hossein paid the bill, they decided to walk through the park for a while, whilst they continued to chat about the event and how they would get away as quickly and efficiently as possible. They knew Bilquis was going to stay and keep low for a while, but they planned to get out of the city as soon as they could, so as to miss any lock down, probably go north and then travel to Wales, find a ferry to Cork in the Irish Republic, stay there for a week or so, and then fly to wherever they decided was safe.

Having settled on that as a necessary, but moveable, plan, they embraced once more and arranged to meet again in a few days. Then they went their separate ways. Once out of sight of each other, they both made significant phone calls to confirm plans.

After several days of sifting through information from all known sources, GCHQ, Anti Terrorism and the Met as well as MI6, plus intelligence from the CIA and Interpol, the team at MI5 were able to narrow the field of possible targets down to three.

Given the time of year when there were many sporting and society events taking place, they had meticulously gone through all the possibilities over and over and finally arrived at their conclusions.

Having gone through all the security protocols, and the possible areas where any attack might be targeted, they then spoke with the necessary agencies involved. The one thing, though, that eluded them was a definite target. They were all thought viable, as no risks could be taken.

Out of the three, they were not sure about one, primarily because the date was not known when this whole thing had erupted back in January. Although it could be a possible target, the security around the State Opening of Parliament was of the highest level, because of the Queen's involvement as well as that of the heir to the throne. However, it was on the list because history told them that nothing was impossible, particularly if the terrorists were determined enough, and the craving for a spectacular loss of life by those fanatics was a great inducement for martyrdom. Therefore it was included in that main list of probable targets. The other two events were of concern because they were held over a few days, where tens of thousands of people would attend. This really was a logistical nightmare, mainly because covering either would stretch resources to the limit on three of the days, as they would overlap, as would the State Opening because all of them were in that same week.

They were now just days away from what was possibly about to become the largest and most horrific terrorist attack in the capital, since the deaths of fifty-six innocent civilians and injuries to seven hundred during the attack on 7/7/2005. The despair and misery experienced then had turned into a steely determination on the part of government, security services and a large section of the population that this should not happen again.

With all of those possibilities still unresolved, they continued to check through their inquiries for any new intelligence reports. Matt and Lenny were at Millbank, going over all the latest information that had come in overnight, and it was now mid-morning. They were meticulously going through that latest intel.

Matt suddenly let out a loud cry of "S H I T!" Momentarily startled, Lenny looked up to see Matt staring at paperwork, with one sheet in his hand, which began to shake.

"Matt, what is it?"

Matt stared at him for what seemed like an age, then answered, "What is it? I'll tell you what it is. Some fucking idiot, I presume a lazy analyst, has passed this intel to us, obviously without reading it properly, hence no flags. It's telling us that we had reliable information, from our deep cover operative, where the attack is going to be and, therefore, what fucking day! And we've just spent the best part of three hours sifting through all this other stuff. So, yes, S H I T!"

"That should never have happened, but we'd better get it to Wyndham now," said Lenny.

They both stood up and walked straight to Mike Wyndham's office, knocked and walked in. Looking up, Wyndham saw Matt and Lenny staring at him with faces like thunder.

"Morning to you too, what the hell is the matter?"

"The matter is this, boss," said Lenny. He took the paper from Matt's still shaking hand, and placed it on Wyndham's desk. Wyndham picked it up and read it, then read it again to make sure he had every detail correct.

'It's the Lords on the 22nd and a secondary nearby,' was all it said. Matt had calmed himself by then and, as Wyndham looked up, Matt said, "Some fucking idiot got this through a day or so ago, put it on a pile and delivered it to us as and when he or she was passing, I expect. This is supposed to be the intelligence service, for Christ's sake, but I

— 140 —

think that must have passed them by when intelligence was given out! The only good thing is we still have a few days to organise a plan of action."

"Well, it's a good thing you noticed it then, isn't it?" Wyndham spoke calmly, if with a note of sarcasm.

Matt noted the tone.

"Sorry, boss, but our nerves and resources are stretched every which way, without having to worry about missed intel."

"Yes, I realise that and I'm liaising with all the other agencies to maximise those resources. But what is now worrying to the extreme is a secondary. What target and where would be good to know. Is this from our 'deep throat?'"

"Yes, it is. Presumably, they're near to the plotters on this?"

"As far as I'm aware, yes, and trusted." Wyndham thought for a moment before continuing, "We need to look at the area and see what other possible secondary targets might be. I mean it could be any number around Westminster… including here!"

Wyndham picked up his phone. He instructed his PA to contact Petra Green at the Foreign Office to come in for a meeting ASAP and to ask Jennifer Hardie to meet them in the small meeting room in twenty minutes. He put the phone down, looked at Matt and Lenny, and said, "Get whatever intel you have and we will meet in twenty. In the meantime we need to brief the Ministers and other agencies on this latest information in a few hours. I'll have my PA arrange it. In fact, this will now, more than likely, have to go to COBRA (Cabinet Office Briefing Room A) and the PM, so prepare for that!"

Half an hour later, they convened in the small meeting room. Both Petra Green and Jennifer Hardie were already there. Wyndham quickly ran through the current information and a discussion started about where the intel had come from, and how best to present it to the COBRA briefing that had been arranged for later that afternoon. Lenny, who up till now had been quiet, said, "Hope that doesn't include me, boss?"

Wyndham looked at him.

"Well, I'm not sure. It's your fault we're in this situation, so it might be an idea!" he replied. Lenny was just about to respond, but he saw the others in the room trying not to laugh, when Wyndham held up his hand, palm out, and said, "No, it's okay, Lenny, probably not a good joke, but hope it lightened the mood? Seriously you can stand down for this one: your help really has been invaluable, but I don't think the PM is ready for you just yet!"

Lenny managed a believable smile, sat back and just listened.

Wyndham then looked at the others and explained that the COBRA meeting would be at 17.00 and that they were all expected. The PM would be taking the chair and the relevant cabinet and security people who should be there, would be. Petra interjected briefly to say that she, of course, would be there with her bosses from the FO and 6. Wyndham also added that apart from Matt, Jennifer Hardie and himself, the DG of MI5 would also be travelling with them. With that, the meeting wound up and Matt and Lenny went back to their desks, and carried on sifting through the latest information to see if anything else had been missed or left in a pile that it shouldn't have been in. After about thirty minutes, Matt strolled over to Lenny.

"You know, you may as well go back to the flat. We might be some time at COBRA."

"Yes, I might, but I haven't spoken with Jody and the kids for a day or so, and I was hoping to call them or FaceTime them every day or at least as much as possible, so I'll do that before I leave, but there's still enough to do here anyway."

"How are they doing over there – enjoying themselves?"

"Probably, leastways the girls are, but I think at times Jody gets anxious, and it's a lot for them to take in right now, although Jody's sister Musha is with them quite a bit, and the girls think she's great, so they're having fun. I think she knows Lazar too."

"Is that an Israeli name, Musha?"

"Yes…well actually Hebrew, it's sort of a female name to correspond with the male version of Mark."

"Okay…got the idea! How old?"

"You fishing?"

"No… just interested and making conversation."

"Okay, well she's younger than Jody, by about six years, very fit, attractive, and is a dancer and teaches it as well. She's also done her army service and trained with another pretty tough unit, so don't go getting any ideas!"

"As if, but next time you go, mind if I tag along?" With that, Matt smiled, turned and walked back to his desk, before Lenny could answer.

Around 16.30, Wyndham and Hardie were at Matt's desk and motioned for him to leave with them. As Matt got up, Wyndham walked over to Lenny.

"Lenny, you may as well go when you can. I don't think we'll be back any time soon."

"Thanks, but I've still a bit to go through and, as much as I like Matt's place, sitting on my own for too long doesn't appeal," Lenny answered, looking up. "Besides I'm going to FaceTime Jody and the girls, as we haven't spoken for a couple of days."

"Okay," Wyndham said, on his way out, "But we could be in for an early start tomorrow. I feel there will be plenty of plans to go through." He smiled and walked briskly out to catch up with Matt and Jennifer, as the DG was waiting for them.

Lenny returned to his work; he knew it was laborious, but it had to be done and, as it was now quiet, he could get on with it without distraction. He would then speak to Jody and the girls, as it was almost suppertime there in Israel. He wanted to catch them all together, so he text Jody to say that he was going to make a FaceTime at 19.30 their time and was sorry he hadn't been in touch for a day or two, but it had been hectic. The reply was almost instant: Jody was so glad to hear he was okay and would have called him later anyway, but 19.30 was a good time as they would all be together, including Musha.

The DG, Wyndham and the others from MI5 arrived almost simultaneously with the group from MI6. They entered the Cabinet Offices and were ushered through into the briefing room. All the relevant people were there, the cabinet members, the Commissioner of the Met Police and Assistant Commissioner for Counter Terrorism, as well as the Chief of the Defence Staff of the Armed Forces and his two other heads of the armed services from the Royal Navy and RAF. They all took their appointed seats and, very shortly afterward, the Prime Minister entered the room with the head of the Civil Service. He motioned for them to sit and he spoke briefly. He then asked Mike Wyndham to update them on the information, which they spent around twenty-five minutes going through. They confirmed all the details, as well as the possible targets, and then moved to the person or persons believed to be behind the proposed attack.

After that, Wyndham took questions for another thirty minutes or so, and a discussion developed. The PM clarified a number of details and made known his anxieties at the thought of armed soldiers on the streets of London, particularly as they would be stationed at a number of different venues and would be very noticeable. It would certainly cause a great deal of alarm to the public. This was, however, countered by the defence chief, when he explained the necessity for the action because, unlike a number of other proposed attacks that had been foiled, with this one there had been few or no leaks or whispers emanating from the usual sources and therefore difficult to counter. This was supported by the head of SIS (MI6) and the MI5 DG. They both concurred that GCHQ had monitored assiduously, and that they had obtained as much information as had been available. Mike Wyndham confirmed this.

The meeting went on for several more hours and a number of scenarios were thrashed out, until an agreed approach was reached. The PM, now satisfied that all the intelligence services had a handle on the best plan, wound up the meeting and confirmed that, in case of there being a huge loss of life, due to anything unforeseen, there would be an immediate lockdown. This would, of course, be followed by a massive hunt for the perpetrators, whilst recognising that all known eventualities had been thoroughly covered. Nothing was left to chance.

Lenny had left the building on Millbank at around 18.15, having spoken to Jody and the girls, as well as Musha; he did mention Matt's interest, but got short shrift from Jody. They FaceTimed for about 30 minutes, ending around 18.00 London time, 20.00 in Israel. After leaving the building, Lenny walked around the corner to Horseferry Road, towards Pret a Manger. He noticed six or seven cabs there, and a couple he definitely recognised, so decided to go and have a bit of light relief with a few friends. He walked over to the drivers he knew to say hello, and was persuaded to sit a while and have a catch up. He went and ordered some food, paid for it and sat down with his pals. About an hour later, after some lively banter, and about three more infusions of caffeine, he decided to go. Lenny walked out of the restaurant onto Horseferry Road, whistled at a passing cab, which stopped. He got in, after telling the cabbie where he wanted to go, and was walking into Matt's apartment block about fifteen minutes later. As he walked in, he spotted someone of interest on the other side of the road standing by the railings of Battersea Park. He continued walking into the building but, as he did so, he took out his phone and dialled a special contact number for urgent assistance. He was answered in a matter of seconds and explained the situation; there was an immediate response. He continued to walk into the building. However, using his higher than usual peripheral vision, something perfected over the years driving a cab, he kept an eye on the person he had noticed, who was now doing stretching exercises against the railings of the park.

Nothing out of the ordinary, as many joggers did that, but why now? Was it by chance or had he been spotted or were they waiting for Matt? He let himself in and walked through to the lounge, as it fronted onto the Prince of Wales Drive side, overlooking the park. Being a beautiful summer's evening and almost at the longest day of the year, it was still light and warm.

He carefully approached the window to see if the person was still there. The thin blinds were pulled down, such that Lenny could see out but he was not visible from the outside. Picking up a pair of binoculars Matt kept on his sideboard, he used them to focus on the park, to see if the person was still there. They were, but at that moment a police patrol car was making its way along Prince of Wales Drive, heading towards the Chelsea Bridge end of the road. The person noticed this too, but carried on stretching; the car passed and kept going. A moment later, its blue lights were flashing and the siren started; then the police car sped off to answer an emergency call.

Lenny knew the police car wasn't the response vehicle: that would be an ordinary car parked up along the road, and with eyes on the person Lenny had seen. A minute or so later, the stretching stopped and the person jogged off in the direction of Albert Bridge Road. A car started up and pulled out about thirty seconds later, moving off in the same direction as the jogger. Lenny smiled and knew he was safe for the moment.

A few minutes later, the response car had spotted the jogger. They had gone through a gate in the park and had now increased the jog to a serious running pace. The operatives in the response car reported this and were told to abandon the call, as it appeared the person was just a jogger after all. The information was relayed back to Lenny, and although he accepted what he had heard, he wasn't totally satisfied.

He now started to wonder whether this was just a coincidence, a serious threat, or was his mind overworked and playing tricks?

Around 23.00 Lenny heard the key in the door and, a moment or so later, Matt walked into the lounge.

"Didn't think you'd still be up."

"Well, I had lots to think about, so my mind was still buzzing, plus there was an interesting development when I got back."

"What development? What the hell happened?"

Lenny then explained about the person, and that he was sure that he had seen them before; also, that he'd called the response unit, but it appeared to be a false alarm. Matt was intrigued by this and they talked for a while longer. Then Matt said something about the COBRA meeting, mentioning that there would have to be temporary road closures everywhere. Traffic would be hell and the bus timetables would have to be abandoned. Lenny looked at him for a moment and just stared.

"Lenny, what is it? What did I say?" asked Matt, a little concerned.

"You said buses that are …That's it…"

"That's what?"

"The buses… the jogger was the girl on the bus… you know the one taking the pictures…"

"Taking what pictures?"

"What pictures? The ones of the two guys shot in the back of my cab…those fucking pictures!"

"Oh, shit!" said Matt.

Bilquis ran around the park for about forty-five minutes, at a steady pace, making sure nobody was watching or following her. She reached her car, parked on the river side of the park in North Carriage Drive, not far from the famous Pagoda. She retrieved her keys from her bum bag and hit the unlock button on the fob. She took out her phone, found the number she wanted and text just four words *"I have found Lenny"* and sent it. The response was almost instantaneous. Her phone rang and she answered.

"How did you find him?"

"Sheer chance. I was jogging and stopped by Battersea Park. A cab pulled up outside one of the mansion blocks and a guy got out. I looked straight at him, whilst he was paying the cab off, and it was him."

"Did he see you?"

"Would it matter if he had? He doesn't know me."

"But he saw you on the bus."

"Only briefly, and I had the phone in front of me most of the time whilst taking pictures."

"So what else happened? Tell me everything you saw."

"Well, he walked into the mansion block. He didn't look round. I did some stretching and that was it! A few minutes later, a police patrol car came through but obviously had a call because the siren went on and the blue lights too. I was running the other way and went into the park. I did about forty minutes at a decent pace, and then made my way back to my car. The only other people I saw were other joggers and soccer players. Then I text you."

Banu thought for a moment.

"Okay, but be on your guard now: we are so close. But keep the memory of which block. We'll deal with him after the attack and before we leave!"

"Yes, will do."

She clicked off and drove home, but a small, yet significant, concern kept her wondering whether he recognised her from the bus, and it began to take hold.

After putting her phone down, Banu began to be distracted by the thought of Lenny being so close, and felt an impatience growing in her finally to avenge the deaths of her comrades all those years ago in Northern Israel. However, she quickly drove the thought from her mind, and reassured herself that, after the mission was complete, she would take the opportunity to make him pay for the killing of her comrades that night. She turned her attention to the upcoming attack, and went through her final preparations for the ever-nearing finale.

Tomorrow would necessitate a visit to her armourer, as well as confirming with Hossein that all of the trained people and the four 'martyrs' were in place and ready to go.

She had planned her next few days assiduously, as she wanted to make sure that there was very little, or even no, room for error. When satisfied she had checked everything, she called Hossein to complete the final details of where the 'martyrs' were to be deployed and at what time, as well as where the other activists would need to be. Because there were a number of events happening on the same day, the main priority was that the biggest impact would have to be on the original target, with any secondary attack being used as a distraction to enable them, and as many of the other activists, to escape. She knew at least four of them would die, but also expected some of the others to be eliminated too. That was the sad but inevitable truth.

Hossein's phone rang and she waited for him to answer. After the fourth ring, her anxiety grew, but unnecessarily, as he picked up just before the fifth ring.

"Banu, my dear, sorry to keep you. I was just in the middle of checking a few things. I'm glad you called."

"Well, it's good to hear you too. So what's the problem?" Her voice was calm and showed no sign of anxiety.

"No..., no problem, just that a few of the helpers are a little restive, but I have kept them calm. They are aware that the time for action is very soon. However, although they're settled and aware of the date, Lucretia and Haider are getting a little fidgety. Maybe a message from you, with your calming voice, will help settle them down?"

"Well, I really don't have time to babysit them. They know their part and how they get to the target, and when, so what more can I do?"

"Just a call will do. They need some reassurance, that's all. They need to hear your voice."

"Okay, text me the number. I will call them later. By the way, Bilquis has found Lenny."

"Really? Well, that's very helpful. But how?"

"Sheer chance. She was out running, and he pulled up in a cab near Battersea Park."

"Did he see her?"

"She doesn't think so, but he probably wouldn't know her anyway, unless he remembered her from the bus, but that was highly unlikely. Anyway, she says not, as he walked into the apartment block without looking round."

"Okay, but check anyone and anything now, no mishaps."

"Yes, you are right, of course. I will tell her to be vigilant."

"Good. We will speak tomorrow and arrange for the merchandise to reach those in need! And don't forget to call Lucretia and Haider."

"No, I won't forget. I will do it shortly. We'll speak tomorrow and arrange the meeting." They both hung up.

Banu put her phone down, realising that Hossein was right about the sighting of Lenny. "We will all need to be vigilant," she thought, and that prompted her to call Bilquis. The call was brief: they discussed Hossein's comments and agreed that, as the end game was fast approaching, extra precautions were needed, so as to be absolutely certain of the outcome they desired. Her phone buzzed with a text from Hossein with the number for Lucretia and Haider. She wrote it down and then deleted the message.

It was now late into the evening and she needed to eat. She had prepared some food. It was still a very warm summer's evening, so Banu had made a salad. She poured herself a glass of white wine to go with her food. She thought about what to say to the twins, to keep them from realising the enormity of their part in the plan. By all accounts, they had trained very well, becoming experts in the weapons they would use, and were fully committed to the cause. But, like many things in life that involve danger, the nearer you get to the action the more stressful it becomes. This was no exception.

Banu finished the food and wine, and picked up her phone. She looked at the piece of paper with the number, and then dialled. The phone rang twice and, before the third ring, a hesitant female voice answered.

"H e l l o?"

"Hello, Lucretia, Hossein asked me to call you, to see how you and Haider are."

"Okay, who is this please?"

"It's Banu, and well done for being cautious, just the sort of awareness that is expected."

"Oh, thank you. We trained and were very attentive with everything we were told."

"Good, very good, that is excellent! I am sure you know now the day for action is almost upon us. We need to keep clear minds and heads. That way we will see this through and it will keep us all safe. Now, have you anything you want to ask me? Sheik AbdulWahab recommended you and your brother very highly to me, and I note from one of your teachers that you excelled in the skills you were shown!"

"Again, thank you, that's very kind, and it is good to hear from you. I think we're just getting a little anxious, through boredom. But we are both okay now and are ready for our tasks ahead."

"Good, that's what I needed to hear. You have your destination and timings? It is imperative you reach your positions in plenty of time so that you can assemble the things you need."

"Yes we have all of the information we require, and we wait for the tools."

"They will be with you tomorrow. Someone I trust will bring them to you."

"Okay, we will wait for them."

Banu hung up, satisfied that the twins were all ready to go, and it sounded like all of their fears were dispelled. She got up from her couch, picked up the wine bottle from the table and poured out another large glass, knowing that after this drink, there would be no more alcohol until the job was completed.

She picked up her phone, and again dialled Bilquis, who answered after one ring.

"Hi, what's up?"

"Can you come to me around 10.00 tomorrow? We have to pick up some tools, and make sure they get to the people who need them. And I don't want to take a cab, as that could be too risky!"

"Okay, will be there at 10.00."

Banu then sent a text to Hossein to let him know that all was well with the twins and that although she had a lot to arrange the next day, she would meet him at 16.30. She asked him to let her know where.

The response came within minutes, saying that the time was fine and that he would let her know where, tomorrow. She put her phone away, went to her bedroom, found her briefcase, opened it and took out the plans that she had made and agreed with the Sheikh. She took them back to the living room and laid them out on the dining table. There were now a few small adjustments to be made, but, all in all, she was happy with the proposed concealment of the operatives and how the 'martyrs' would get to the target. She was certain that, because not many people had been party to the planning, the chance of executing the plan successfully was greatly increased. She was also happy that the escape route she had decided on was the best way out of the area. Once successfully away, she would turn her attention to the other item on her personal agenda. That, of course, was Lenny, and if anyone else got in the way, they would be eliminated too.

It was the second day of Royal Ascot, and the weather was simply spectacular. The sky was a clear, deep blue and not even the smallest cotton wool clouds could be detected.

Ascot was the Queen's horse race meeting that lasted for five days and generally began around the third Tuesday in June each year. It was held at the Ascot racecourse, merely a carriage ride from Windsor Castle. June was generally packed with sporting and society events, and this year, Ascot apart, there was the Ashes cricket series of Test Matches with Australia, which had begun in early June, Wimbledon tennis towards the end of the month, and a couple of garden parties that the Queen held at Buckingham Palace every year, each one usually attended by eight thousand guests.

On this day of the Ascot meeting, the crowds thronged the walkways and the various enclosures. The attendees in the Royal Enclosure were expected to wear morning dress and top hats for the men and smart cocktail day wear for the ladies, with extravagant hats to set off the many designer outfits. Generally though, most people, no matter which enclosure, were smartly dressed: the men mainly wore lounge suits, and the ladies excelled themselves with appropriate outfits and hats to match.

The racecourse was beautifully maintained. The members of the public with tickets for the other enclosures got as close to the rails as they could, to try and snatch a glimpse of the Royal party's procession of carriages, as they made their way from the castle to the Royal enclosure. Once the Queen's party had arrived, and the band had played 'God Save the Queen,' the racing could begin.

Although the security services had been able to rule out a possible attack at the Royal race meeting, the increase in armed police officers was very apparent, as was the increased presence of the military, and not necessarily for ceremonial reasons either. To that end, Mike Wyndham had felt it appropriate to be there, just in case, so he arranged for Jennifer Hardie, Matt and Lenny to go with him for the afternoon and monitor anything that might be deemed as suspicious. Apart from the obvious delight at actually going, it was, supposedly, a strictly business exercise.

On arrival, Wyndham showed his credentials at security, who'd already been told of their impending arrival, and they were waved through straight away, told where to park, and where they would find the senior police officer in charge. They didn't need any introduction, as that turned out to be Commander Stewart Scott from the Met's Counter Terrorism unit. He greeted them and ushered them into the control room.

"Good to see you, Mike. Sorry it's business, not pleasure."

"Yes, good to see you too. You know the rest of the team, of course?" They all nodded to each other. "So what can you tell us, Commander?"

"Well, nothing out of the ordinary, really, but obviously we have a higher presence of security, police and military. But it's all been run of the mill, so far, both yesterday and, so far, today."

"Well, that's good to hear," replied Wyndham, "And it probably bears out our thinking that any attempted terrorist act is now more likely tomorrow. As you know, we are looking at the Westminster area."

"Yes, we've been briefed, of course, in readiness for tomorrow, and made sure all leave for armed officers was cancelled so we'll be at full complement."

Wyndham stared for a moment at the TV screens, which showed the Queen arriving at the Royal enclosure.

"Well, that's good to know, of course," he said, "Because we aren't sure what form this probable attack will take. Our intel on this one has been very sparse, so that tells us the organisers are a small group and those, who may have known too much, were the ones assassinated."

"The good thing for us, though," Scott added, "Is that we are very mobile and can re-locate at a moment's notice, if needs be."

"That is good to know, and I assume you will have snipers on the roof tops?"

"Oh yes," confirmed Scott, "We've already scoped which ones, and the officers will be in place from early morning."

"That's great. Okay, we'll watch for a bit, take a walk around, and then head off back to London – heavy day tomorrow!"

"No problem, Mike. Whatever you need."

Wyndham and the others stood and watched the screens for about twenty-five minutes and then moved off from the control room to the outside. Matt walked with him, and Hardie and Lenny walked just behind. Matt waited to see if Wyndham would say anything, but he didn't, so Matt asked the question:

"Boss, as nice a day out as this is, did we actually learn anything by coming here?"

"Yes, Matt, we did. He's on his toes, and ready, and that's the most important thing. He answered my questions without hesitation, so that tells us he's planned with the info he's had. I've known some of these plods in the past think they know it all and, whatever happens, they can react. This guy is on the ball, thankfully!" Matt said nothing in response, as they carried on walking and taking note of the crowds and the way they were being marshalled, although the visitors were completely unaware of this.

* * * * *

Banu and Bilquis had made their early morning trip to the armourer in Bethnal Green, east of the City of London. Banu went in and Bilquis waited for about half an hour outside. When Banu returned, she directed her friend to drive to the rear of the railway arch and reverse as close to the doors as possible, and then open the boot. This was done, and they loaded the merchandise. Each package had labels, and Banu had written addresses for Bilquis to deliver the merchandise.

There wouldn't be any problems with delivery, as all of the recipients had been told that they were getting their tools that day and were required to be in to receive them. One or two of the drops were on the way back to west London, so Banu was with Bilquis for those, but didn't get out of the car. However, she made sure her face was partially covered at all times.

On the way back they talked at length about the aftermath of what they were about to do, how they would escape from the scene and how long they would have to lie low for. Although Banu was determined to settle her score with Lenny as soon as possible, she wanted to be away and start her new life with Hossein. After all, she would have all the money she needed, so living well wouldn't be a problem in the future.

Banu got out of the car a little way before her flat in Kensington. She had given Bilquis the details for the rest of the deliveries and told her to be back at her apartment by 08.00 tomorrow as it was likely be a day that the whole world would remember. She waved her off and, as it was near to the time when she was to meet Hossein, she didn't go home, but went straight to the arranged meeting place. She was a little early, but that was no bad thing. She walked into Kensington Gardens and found the place that Hossein had identified. He chose to meet by a small copse of trees, with a few tables and seating. No particular seat had been chosen by Hossein so she picked one to the left of the trees with Kensington Palace as the backdrop. She was not surprised to see he wasn't there yet, so she sat watching the direction that she had come in from, and at the angle she was sitting, her excellent peripheral vision enabled her to see anything coming from the palace.

Banu checked her watch, it was 16.25 and, as she looked again towards Kensington Road, she saw Hossein walking towards her. Once again, seeing him made her heart skip a beat and her adrenalin pumped through her body, which accelerated her excitement and yearning for him. As he drew nearer, she could see his wonderfully comforting and enticing smile. He straddled the bench opposite her and sat.

"Good afternoon, my dear," he said, "How are you?"

"That's very formal. Are we strangers now?"

"No, my darling, I'm being ironic!"

Unfortunately Banu didn't understand the irony, but she managed a believable smile.

"Okay, you got me!" she replied, "So are we all ready to go? All of the 'helpers' totally prepared and equipped?"

"Yes, of course they are, completely. They will all be in their positions for tomorrow. Glad to hear you spoke with the twins and were able to settle them."

"Yes, I think it was a little bit of stage fright. I'm certain they will play their full part."

"Good…good."

"Bilquis is finishing off the tool delivery, so we are good to go. We have our meeting point and we need to be there to observe and settle about an hour before. Bilquis will take me somewhere close, then I will walk to the place and she will move on to her position, leaving her car at least a ten minute walk away. That way she can move as soon as she has finished her task. There will be so much confusion by then, she will be lost in a panicking, screaming crowd."

"Excellent, excellent, a very well constructed plan, from a very well crafted mind. Impressive."

Banu could feel her face flushing red with embarrassment, but she looked at him approvingly and smiled.

"Your use of flattery, my darling, does you credit, but I, of course, learned from a master of terror!" It was now Hossein's turn to blush. He just looked at her.

"You're very welcome, my dear."

Banu smiled and sat there, looking at him and longing for this to all be over, for purely selfish reasons.

They stayed and enjoyed the sun and surroundings for a while longer, then stood, embraced and looked at each other.

"I will see you tomorrow," Hossein said.

"Inshallah, all will be done, Inshallah!" came Banu's reply.

They went their separate ways. Hossein walked through to the north of the Gardens and emerged out onto the Bayswater Road near Notting Hill, while Banu went out at the southern gate she had entered from and made her way to her rented apartment in Kensington Court. Her excitement rose and then dipped when she considered the possible outcomes tomorrow. After all, the British intelligence would probably have some information, but not enough, hopefully. But she knew that the targets would all have armed security; no matter how small in strength, it would be there.

She kept that thought with her as she reached her apartment. Inside, she made herself some coffee and pondered alternative escape routes, should it not go according to plan.

The twins, Lucretia and Haider Mikhail, had been back in the UK for almost three weeks, after their training stint in France, under the guidance of Banu and Hossein. They had been taken through their paces, physical and mental, during some long and intensive sessions with them both.

Their obvious intelligence and incisive minds had been a revelation to their two 'teachers'. They had shown an extremely impressive ability with firearms, both hand pistols and assault rifles. The weapons of choice were the Glock 19 hand gun (Banu had recommended that) and, ironically, the IWA Tavor X95, an Israeli manufactured assault rifle, but used all over the world because of its compactness and reliability, as well as its ability to dispatch between 750–950 rounds per minute. Hossein had recommended this weapon. Banu had initially protested because it was Israeli, but relented when she saw the devastating results of its capabilities. It wasn't the first time Israeli weapons had been used by Iranians as, unbeknown to many, Israel had supplied pieces of military equipment to Iran during the Iraq/Iran war, when no other country would.

All of the weapons the twins had needed were obtained for them, and were collected and delivered to a 'friendly' storage facility, a fifteen minute drive from their apartment near Canary Wharf.

After they had duly collected their 'tools,' they had taken them into their apartment late in the evening from their underground car park, stripped the weapons down and put the parts into separately coded and marked black nylon bags. They were the flimsy duffle type, the sort of things you might carry gym gear in. This made it easier to transport, as the bags could be carried on the shoulder. Haider had scoped out a disused and deserted light industrial area that was very easy to access, despite wire mesh fencing around it. There he had set up some small training areas and shooting ranges for the two of them to use.

They had gone at irregular intervals to their temporary 'training facility,' so as not to cause alarm, and that was interspersed with their work at the large finance corporation, in Canary Wharf, where they had returned to after their initial trip to Marseille in early April. However, after they had received a much fuller detail of what was expected of them and where they needed to be on the day of the 'big event,' they took every opportunity to practise and keep their skills honed in preparation.

It was now the day before the attack, so a good rest was needed, although probably unlikely. The twins had taken the day off and remained in their apartment, just going over and over the details of the task involved, as well as continually checking their weaponry.

It kept them busy while most other things couldn't. Their timings and travel details had been relayed to them and they would be dressed as tourists, with suitcases they would pull along as they walked to their starting positions, but, of course, they wouldn't be together.

The plan was to meet up after the main focus of the attack had been completed and then move onto the secondary target, if all went well. They had no illusions but they were prepared for whatever presented itself, in the knowledge that their parents would be looked after by the Sheikh. They had been assured that this had already been arranged.

On the day of the attack, the sun rose at 04.54 and the twins were already well on their way. They had woken up at 03.45, having set their alarms for that time, showered and then dressed in the tourist type clothes they had bought several days before. Their 'tools' were already packed in the black nylon bags and had been put into the luggage cases. They left their apartment at 04.30 and went to their car in the underground car park. They loaded the cases into the boot, then drove out in the direction of their makeshift training area.

On arrival, Haider drove the car into a covered area and parked. They both got out and lifted the cases from the boot. Haider locked the car and then took hold of the tarpaulin they had brought to cover the vehicle they would use again, once their task was completed. The tarpaulin had a draw-tie thin rope around the bottom edge that he pulled tight and tied a double knot at one end.

About ten feet away, acquired a month earlier, was an old 5 door Ford Focus, which they had made some alterations to. Haider had re-sprayed it white, and that made it pretty innocuous, as there were countless vehicles of that colour on the road. They had also changed the number plate and had erased the VIN (vehicle identification number) from the engine and the small alloy plate on the frame of the passenger door. They had paid cash for the car, which would be disposed of after it became surplus to requirements. They had made sure it would be untraceable.

The twins loaded the cases into the boot of the Ford. Haider took out the ignition key, sat in and started the engine to make sure it was working. It hadn't been started for a few days, but it started first time. He let the engine idle for a while, occasionally revving it. It sounded fine and he was satisfied that his interest in cars, when he was much younger, had proved useful.

They were both now hungry and decided to leave their temporary base and find a place to get some breakfast. They needed to travel towards the centre of London, but decided to stop short of the final destination, as they had enough time, as well as wanting to remain as inconspicuous as possible. The last thing they needed was to be near an area where there was an extended police and security services presence.

They drove from east London over to the Islington area, where they knew a few early morning working men's cafés, where they would get a decent breakfast. As things stood, there was a doubt as to when or if they would eat again. They found a parking spot just behind Chapel Street Market, paid the parking charge for two hours and walked across the road into a café. They found a table by the window and sat down, keeping a discreet eye on their parked vehicle.

* * * * *

About six miles away, Banu had just finished her round of calls, the last one being to the Sheikh, to seek confirmation that the contract was still on and was to be completed. He confirmed this and waxed lyrical about how it would be a great day for the cause and that dealing such a blow to the west would only hasten the departure of the

'Infidels' from Muslim and Arab lands. Banu listened to him for as long as he needed to talk, bearing in mind he was paying her a lot of money. Even the half he had already paid was substantial enough, and, to her surprise, the Sheikh advised her that the balance would be transferred within the hour. Then he clicked off. She thought about what he'd said, and considered it was very foolhardy but didn't complain at the time, as she would finish the job in any event. Breaking a contract was not an option, since in her business it was bad form and would severely diminish any future work that might come her way, should she need it. This was in the back of her mind because she was determined that, even though it was only a goal right now, she hoped this would be the last contract she would have to commit to. Except of course, the unfinished business with that damned Israeli London cab driver. After that had been attended to, she wouldn't need to consider the dangers in her current life any more, as a new life with Hossein was moving ever closer.

She busied herself with last minute distractions, and kept telling herself everyone was ready and that her plans must not fail, knowing that she had done everything she possibly could to ensure the result she hoped for. Her phone buzzed. She checked and saw it was Bilquis.

"Hi, all okay?" Banu answered.

"Yes, just checking in, in case there's anything last minute you need me to do."

"No, all good, and your fee has been deposited in the normal way."

"Well, thank you. I would never ask, as you are one of very few I trust my life with."

"That's okay, and that feeling is reciprocated."

"Okay, then, we shall speak later, all being well, and meet at the prearranged rendezvous."

"Yes, we will!"

They both clicked off.

Banu continued to finalise her affairs, as this was going to be her last day in the rented apartment. She had found another place, more secluded and away from prying eyes, in which to lay low in for as long as it took for the initial clamp-down to subside.

She had made arrangements with Sheikh AbdulWahab for him to oversee the usual round of claims as to which group was responsible for the atrocity; that way, the focus would be on known activists, which didn't, as far as she was aware, include her. She was quite sure nobody knew who she was or what she looked like. However, there was no need to take risks: caution was always the more sensible way. Were a few more days going to make a difference? She would soon be able to escape to anywhere she wanted to with Hossein, and fulfil their dreams, together.

Banu checked her watch. It was time. She picked up the phone, opened up the Taxi App and ordered a cab. Her luggage was already at the new temporary flat, so all she had to carry was a handbag with a shoulder strap and an attaché case that carried two Glock 19 handguns with three magazines each. A few minutes later, the taxi arrived and he confirmed this by text to Banu's phone, which pinged. She looked at the phone, noted the message and left her temporary accommodation for what she hoped was the last time! She walked up to the cab, was dressed in a trouser suit, had long blonde hair and wore large round Armani dark glasses. She told the driver where she wanted to go and got in. The cab came out onto Kensington Road, turned east and sped towards central London. It was to be a long, tough and, hopefully for her, successful day.

CHAPTER
30

The day after the summer solstice, there was once again a cloudless, deep blue sky with a very light gentle breeze and temperatures expected to reach 27°–28°C, or, as some still referred to it 'in old money,' 79–81°F.

Matt and Lenny had been in the office at Millbank since 06.45 checking all overnight intel. It was now just a few minutes short of 08.00 and they were about to go to the meeting room, where Mike Wyndham, Jennifer Hardie, Petra Green, Commander Stewart Scott and other operatives from Matt's section were waiting for the latest update or any new information that might help neutralise, or at least minimise, the expected, impending violent attack.

Wyndham was in the chair, as usual, and began by reading out a message from the PM and Home and Defence Secretaries. It was basically a pep talk and an in-advance thank you for putting their bodies and lives on the line in defence of the nation. It was heard in silent courtesy, but they swiftly moved on to the main business, namely using whatever resources they had to try and prevent a major catastrophe from any terrorist attack. Wyndham looked at Commander Scott and invited his update. Scott, the senior officer in charge of the Met Police Anti Terrorist unit, began by confirming that the numbers of armed police patrolling the expected target had been increased by fifty per cent. The extra officers had come from a reduction in some special protection duties and cancellation of all leave. The possibility of more than one target had also been taken into consideration and, although they would be stretched, he was confident of extremely good coverage depending, of course, on the nature of each additional attack. He also made the room aware that specialised army snipers had now been specially seconded for the duration of this emergency and that this had all been approved by both the Home and Defence Secretaries, after discussion with the PM at the last COBRA meeting.

"The snipers are from the elite Special Forces unit," Scott went on, "They are being seconded temporarily to the police armed protection unit and will be under my direction along with a senior Special Forces officer. They won't be in their regular unit cammies but in unmarked regular police issue and, while active, will be wearing ski masks for anonymity, should there be a skirmish."

The room stayed silent after taking in all of this latest information.

Commander Scott continued, "This is a special situation and the snipers used are highly trained in this sort of situation; in addition, each one of the snipers has a trained spotter, who they work with and trust. The snipers will be armed with the LA115A3 Long Range Rifle, the maximum distance of which is around 2400 metres, but obviously that shouldn't be required for this type of situation. They will be using .338 Lapua Magnum 8.59mm rounds, with an extremely effective range of 1100 metres, although the rifle has a maximum guaranteed effective range, if necessary, of around 2000 metres, again highly unlikely to be needed."

Again the room stayed silent.

Wyndham then looked at another person attending the meeting and nodded. This was the head of the Intelligence Analysis Unit at GCHQ, Chris Hayward. He had come at short notice to confirm the latest intelligence and to explain in detail, any possible ambiguities.

He began, "Chairman, thank you, I can confirm that all of the information you have so far is correct up to a point..." He was interrupted by Wyndham.

"Sorry, Chris, what do you mean – up to a point?"

"Well, Chairman, I was coming to that. The supposition that the attack may be aimed at the State Opening, and with a possible secondary target somewhere nearby, is of course still very plausible, but the two analysts that your colleagues met when they came to us a few months ago, have been following the intel as it has come in. They are concerned about some of the language, particularly the assumption of the target."

Wyndham now looked extremely concerned.

"Chris, how long have you known this?"

"Literally in the last twelve to fourteen hours, Chairman. Tom and Sarah, the analysts, have looked and re-looked, as they believe there is a doubt about the terminology used in identifying the target. Really, it was about the use of the word 'the.'"

Now looking extremely confused, along with the others in the room, Wyndham said, "Well, I'm wondering where this is going, Chris, over the word 'the'?"

"Well, Chairman," Hayward continued, a little agitated, "It's the way it was used in conjunction with the other two words."

Now looking very impatient, Wyndham said, as calmly as he could, "I can't wait for the punch line."

Hayward, astonished at the flippancy, carried on, "The information came in as 'It's the Lords' and we've all taken that to mean the State Opening at midday, as that part of Parliament is where it all happens. But going through the chronology of this whole threat, right back since January, we didn't know then that there would be a ceremony today. What we did know, and have obviously known for some time, and it's also been public knowledge, is that the Ashes Test match begins in London today. They will be expecting 30,000 plus people and, although it will be busy from about 09.30, the main focus, we believe, should be close of play at around 18.00 to 18.30. This is when the main bulk of the crowd will try to get out of the venue and go home or to pubs and restaurants, local train stations etc, so we think it is safe to assume that there were two words missing when the original intel came in and it should have read 'It's the Lords Test Match,' which makes a lot more sense."

Wyndham let Hayward finish, and then he informed the room that the information was correct, as his MI5 section had come across the same intel late yesterday and that Commander Scott had taken the snipers to view the area around Lords. He also apologised to Chris Hayward and the rest of the assembled representatives that the information hadn't been shared much earlier, but the lateness of the intel meant that things had to be changed very quickly. Hayward reassured Wyndham, saying, "Chairman, there's really nothing to apologise for, we are all working to the same end, but I would be interested, in due course, to know your source, if at all possible?"

"Thanks, Chris, I appreciate the comments. No real secret really, an embedded source, who we hadn't heard from in a while, got it through to us late yesterday." What Wyndham didn't say was that it was actually very early yesterday, but that was a minor detail at this stage.

The room had stayed silent for what seemed an eternity and then Wyndham looked around at a sea of faces, all looking quite bemused at what had just happened. Wyndham waited for someone to ask or say something, but their gaze was firmly fixed on him and Hayward, and they were focused on what had just been discussed. Realising that they were waiting for him, Wyndham also looked at Hayward, composed himself and spoke.

"So, just to confirm, what Chris has now told us is that all the planning we had put in was skewed because the two very important words, 'Test Match' were somehow lost in translation, making the original intel wrong, because the interpretation of that intel was wrong."

"That's correct, Chairman," said Hayward, "But it would seem that we all had assumed the main target would be Parliament and the Queen, and, as I said, the chronology of information we have had since January was a strange fit with an attack on the State Opening, and it now seems those doubts were correct. We also believe that murdering a huge number of civilians, out of the 30,000 that would be at Lords, is, for the terrorists, a spectacular way of very quickly turning public opinion against this country having a military presence in Muslim lands. That, we believe from our now updated intel, is the aim! Many people, particularly the rulers of those lands, would be totally opposed to the Queen being the target, as it would be seen as an open invitation for other dissidents to attack and overthrow their regimes."

"Okay," said Wyndham, "So we now know that this is the action planned, are we sure we know who is behind it, and who the person or organisation is funding it? And, Commander Scott, now we have diverted our resources from the State Opening, will we have all units in place in time?"

Hayward spoke first, "Chairman, we are confident it is one of the wealthy Saudi Sheikhs, who are mainly domiciled in Abu Dhabi, that has been identified and we are now monitoring 'traffic' from phones, computers and bank account movements to pinpoint which one. We are confident we will have that information within the next twenty-four hours."

"Okay," said Wyndham, "Keep a close eye and let us know as soon as you do."

Hayward nodded.

Wyndham then looked at Petra Green. "Petra, tell your boss at 6 that we need surveillance up and running on the two suspects in Abu Dhabi, and that we will need a specialist team to go out as soon as, to take the person out, once we know who it is." She also nodded.

Then he turned to Commander Scott.

"Commander, will all your units be ready?"

Scott had already prepared an answer:

"We have units staying to monitor the situation at Westminster, and even leaving them there, we have till about 13.00. By then, the ceremony will be over and the Queen back on her way to Ascot. The logistics won't be too difficult, as we can move the armed officers to the cricket ground fairly speedily. However, the scouting of positions for the snipers has taken a little longer than we thought, so we will need a bit more time but we're confident we will be ready. I will call the Special Forces Commander on the ground and get him to meet me at the venue in around thirty minutes. We'll get a more updated report then."

"Okay, everyone," said Wyndham, "We all know the urgency and seriousness of the situation. I'm not going to reconvene back here. We'll do the rest now by conference call. It's now 09.45, so we will speak at 13.30, when we have established where the operational base will be, and the Commander and the Special Forces have had a chance to set up the sites for the snipers. Okay, let's get to it." The meeting adjourned, with all non-MI5 personnel rushing out to get to where they needed to be.

Matt and Lenny looked at Wyndham and Jennifer Hardie. The other MI5 agents had also left. As soon as they did, Matt spoke, "Boss, how on earth did we all miss the real meaning of the intel?"

"It's not that difficult to work out, Matt. We all assumed it meant the House of Lords at Westminster because of the words used. I mean, the Royal family and Parliamentarians are and always will be targets for this and any other form of terrorism."

"So where do you need us to be, boss?" Lenny now asked.

"I think the best place now for you and Matt is the cricket ground," Wyndham said, "Matt, go down to the armoury and draw weapons.

Tell them if they have any queries about Lenny having one to call me! Lenny, you okay with that?"

"I was hoping you would ask. Yeah, no problem, boss. I've been keeping my eye in whilst at Matt's."

"Glad to hear it. Now go!"

They got up and left at speed, heading for the armoury.

* * * * *

Banu had kept track on the progress of all of her comrades; Hossein had organised the four 'willing martyrs;' Bilquis had been in contact with the twins, who had begun their journey very early; and Banu and Hossein between them had arranged for the other attackers to be collected and transported to allotted positions in plenty of time. None of the terrorists would be in the open, until it was necessary, thereby leaving very little time for them to be spotted by police or security services. Once the firing started, there would be enough of a diversion and panic deployed for the 'martyrs' to do what they had been trained for. They would become heroes and enter paradise in the company of seventy-two virgin maidens, according to the interpretation of the Quran by some Muslim scholars.

Just before midday, the Queen's procession arrived at the entrance to the Victoria Tower, the opposite end of the Palace of Westminster to Big Ben.

The security services had remained vigilant the whole time, and had made continuous sweeps of the area along the route the procession had taken and would take on the way back to Buckingham Palace.

Just after 12.50, the Queen's carriage and escort left the Palace of Westminster and began the journey back. The route, on the way, was watched extremely vigilantly by all the security services and they were all stood down, as soon as the procession had re-entered through the palace gates.

At 13.05 Wyndham began his conference call with the people he had met at his MI5 office earlier. Wyndham didn't include Matt and Lenny as he, or Jennifer Hardie, would bring them up to speed a little later, once the plan for the deployment of the armed officers and logistics were in place.

Matt and Lenny arrived at the venue. There were lots of people milling around, as it was now lunchtime at the cricket. They had scouted the area and had spotted a number of positions on the roofs of buildings that would probably be of use to the snipers, although they realised that the snipers themselves would make the final choices. Most positions they had found were pretty obvious to them, and they were sure that the 'professionals' would spot them fairly quickly. They would have to be on roofs, and set as far away from the scene as necessary but still effective. There were also unmarked vans, carrying armed police units, which would be strategically placed so as to be ready if and when needed, in order to minimise or indeed nullify the effect of the expected attack. Matt and Lenny completed their tour around the area and at 14.00 returned to their car. As they got in, Matt's phone rang. It was Wyndham, who had just completed the conference call with the other security branches. However, as the call progressed, Wyndham was interrupted by Jennifer Hardie, rushing into his office and looking extremely worried.

"Hold on a minute, Matt. Something's happened."

"What is it, boss?"

"Just a minute," said Wyndham. He quickly read from the paper Hardie had just handed him.

At that moment there was a loud bang and it didn't sound too far from where Matt and Lenny were.

"Shit, what the hell was that?" asked Lenny.

"It sounds like another car bomb has gone off, and could be related to the information I've just received," Wyndham said.

"What's that?" asked Matt.

"We've had a report in, that a car bomb has been detonated at the back of the Royal Courts of Justice at the entrance in Carey Street off Chancery Lane. We're checking for deaths and casualties and the emergency services are at the scene now. Okay, we've just had the details of the bang you heard. Another car bomb, this one is at Camden Town station, by the entrance at Kentish Town Road. It appears someone just pulled up outside the entrance, stayed in the car and detonated the bomb. There's been severe casualties – many dead and many more injured."

"Sounds like it's starting, boss. Do we stay or go see what's happening at Camden?"

"No, you stay where you are. I don't want any semblance of us running around like headless chickens. I'll get another couple of teams over there to both bomb blasts, and they can liaise with Counter Terrorism. This is going to cause a logistical nightmare now, and we still need to get the snipers and the spotters set up over there, at Lords."

"Sounds like the attack has definitely begun," said Matt.

"Yes, and, in all probability, the proposed attack at Lords is the finale. The terrorists must already be in the vicinity."

"We'll take some armed officers and do a walk about around this location to see if there's anything untoward. You never know."

"Okay," said Wyndham, "But be careful and keep me informed, and I'll get you some details on the other two bomb scenes." They rang off.

Lenny and Matt went to the main control room at Lords to speak with the senior armed officer and very soon realised he already knew what had just occurred, as he was in conversation and response mode. There were several TV screens in the room and all were tuned in to various news outlets that were showing the bomb scenes. It all looked like mayhem had just happened. There were several police and ambulance units at both sites and it became apparent that there were also multiple casualties.

"Jesus," said Matt, looking at the screens. "The bastards who've done this are out there and we need to find them." He spoke with the senior officer and told them what they needed to do. The senior officer agreed that a reconnoitre of the immediate area was needed and he also agreed that Matt and Lenny should accompany his officers, but insisted on them wearing protective jackets, as a precaution. They obviously didn't argue. As they were getting ready to go with the armed officers, Matt text Wyndham to let him know what had been arranged. The message that came back was short, *"GOOD, JUST BE CAREFUL."* Matt didn't reply, as he knew there was no need.

They spent around ninety minutes with the armed officers, checking for signs of possible car bombs, but there were none. They returned to the control room and Matt FaceTimed Wyndham to update him. They spoke for several minutes and Wyndham gave Matt the up to date details on the casualties. Over the two sites, there were at that time twenty-four fatalities at Camden Town and six at the Law Courts, but as yet no confirmed number of casualties, because it was a fluid situation. Matt let out a long exhale of breath, as he finished his conversation. Lenny saw this and asked, "How bad?"

"Bad," Matt replied, "And it will get worse by the end of the day, unless we can stop these bastards from killing any more innocent civilians.

After another hour had passed, Matt and Lenny were given instructions from Wyndham as to what was required and where they needed to be from about 17.00. Everything was now in place and the two earlier bombings were under control, but unfortunately the death toll and casualty numbers had risen. Wyndham also confirmed that new intel had come in and they were given the updates regarding the money man: they now knew that he was also the instigator. Orders were currently being carried out to discover his allies in the venture and all avenues were being explored to see if there were any up to date pictures of whoever they were. They had decided to wait to act on the updated information until after the expected attack had occurred. If the anticipated further attack did occur, they would need to act as quickly as possible afterwards, particularly in the case of the resident of Abu Dhabi, who would be dealt with in such a way that there would be no need for extradition. If no further attack happened, time would still be of the essence but not as imperative.

Matt and Lenny were a little surprised at this, but effectively they knew that it was probably the only way. They also knew there were operatives in the region, who were more than capable of carrying out what was necessary, without it being trailed back to the British government. They ended the call, and Matt and Lenny sat in silence for a few minutes, before Lenny turned to Matt and said, "I think I'm going to stretch my legs and call Jody and the girls. It's been a few days since we spoke. So much for calling every day!"

"Good idea," Matt replied, "And give my regards to her sister Musha."

Lenny replied, "Yeah…right!"

The afternoon of 22nd June grew hotter, as the blazing sun moved across the cloudless, deep blue sky towards its eventual setting, much later in the evening.

The first day of the cricket Test Match against the old adversaries, Australia, had reached the mid afternoon session in front of a packed 30,000 crowd at what was generally termed the 'Home of Cricket'. Lords Cricket ground was located in the district known as St John's Wood in North West London, named after its cricket-loving professional player and founder, Thomas Lord. The current site was the third one Lord moved to and it opened in 1814. It was also, as the crow flies, less than half a mile from the famous Abbey Road recording studios, where the Beatles recorded most of their hit singles and most famous albums.

There was an obvious armed police presence, particularly at the entrances to the stadium. Security checks were carried out on anyone entering with a ticket, intending to go and watch the match. There were more armed officers sitting in unmarked vans around a number of side streets near the ground, but available within thirty seconds of any incident occurring.

What was not so obvious to the public was the activity in other parts of London during the afternoon, regarding the two car bombs that had been detonated. The thinking of the security services was that as far as possible little or no information should be broadcast, except that there had been incidents that the security services were dealing with. However, the mere fact the two incidents were all over various news channels just made the original strategy extremely difficult to maintain. The security services had hoped that, by controlling the news flow, it would prevent the creation of panic and the possible escalation of a mass loss of life, especially if the 30,000 crowd decided to make a hurried dash for the exits. That would completely disrupt the ability of the police and security services to control the impending attack, particularly as other armed police anti-terrorism officers, as well as the Special Forces snipers, were setting up their positions on the roofs of several blocks of flats in the streets all around the cricket ground. The decision was taken, though, to stay with the original plan and hold up the crowd exiting the cricket ground for as long as possible, so that the terrorists would be out and easier to identify, when necessary.

The Special Forces snipers and their spotters had arrived at the scene of the possible attack as speedily as time allowed, and very carefully selected the four positions that they felt gave them the clearest sight, as well as having the least visibility from ground level from the tallest blocks. The sights covered the two main exits and entrances in St John's Wood Road, with two positions on each exit at crossfire positions. They built their temporary hides on sturdy but makeshift platforms, to give them the best angles and anonymity. The snipers were equipped with their standard issue L115A3 sniper rifles and were chambered with .338 Lapua Magnum (8.59mm), which had a totally effective range of 1100 metres, although the longest successful distance from this rifle had been 2400 metres in Afghanistan in 2009, when it took out two Taliban machine gunners. The rifles were also fitted with a Schmidt and Bender 5-25x56 PM11 day scope with 25x magnification and a suppressor, in order to reduce muzzle flash and noise signature.

Matt and Lenny were with Wyndham, Hardie and Commander Scott in the command centre inside the Lords perimeter. Joining them were the Met Police Commissioner and the Special Forces Senior Officer.

It was now 16.45 and the cricket was into its final session of the day's play. It had been a day of slow batting and fast bowling between the two old adversaries and the reckoning was that play would end around 18.30.

With that in mind, all of the security service operatives were told to be on high alert for anything out of the normal, but from 17.00 the alert would be at red and to expect the worst. Nothing else needed saying, bearing in mind what had happened earlier, and they were all professional enough to know what was required. Nobody questioned this command, as they all knew that if the terrorists wanted to have full effect, it would be at the close of the day's play, when around 30,000 people would be coming out of the stadium.

* * * * *

Banu, Hossein and Bilquis had rendezvoused at an agreed location just off of the Edgware Road, about a mile away from the cricket ground. They had monitored the execution of the first part of the plan, as Banu had been in contact with the 'martyrs' just before the bombs were detonated. Although it was possibly a danger to be in contact so close to the action, Banu had taken precautions by supplying Hossein, Bilquis and the twins, Lucretia and Haider, with new burner mobile phones. They had gone over the plan of attack several times, and relayed the final details to the twins. The four 'martyrs' were in position and being looked after by an old and trusted friend of Hossein.

They finished their discussions and agreed, all being well, to regroup at the pre-arranged place near Bilquis' apartment, as soon as it was possible to do so. Any delay more than three hours after the action and the worst would be assumed, and they would go about their escape plans individually.

Bilquis said to Banu, "What about Lenny?"

Banu looked at her and said, "I will have great pleasure in dealing with him, and settling an old score. As we know, getting out of the country after this afternoon will be difficult, so I will pick the right moment to deal with him!"

They both stared at her for a moment, and then returned to the business in hand.

Meanwhile the four 'martyrs' were being transported to the area and were being reminded of their rewards in paradise for doing this deed for the love of god and the cause. The bombs were now strapped to each of them and could not be removed. Should they not carry out their duty, the bomb would be exploded remotely using a signal sent from a mobile phone: both Banu and Hossein had the codes for this.

* * * * *

Lenny had excused himself and walked outside, ostensibly for some air. When he was out of sight of the control room, he took out his phone. Not his regular one as he knew it was being monitored, but an untraceable he had bought a few days before. He had entered just three numbers on the speed dial, selected the one he wanted and pressed the button.

It rang just twice, and was answered by a female, who hesitantly said, "Y-e-s?" Lenny knew she would be wary but quickly said, "Musha, it's Lenny. I don't have a lot of time. Say nothing out loud. If Jody is there, just hand her the phone." He heard her say, "Here…it's for you."

The next thing he heard was Jody's voice, hesitantly saying, "H e l l o"

"Hi, Jody it's me!" said Lenny. He heard Jody let out a sigh of relief and, before she could say any more, he went on, "Listen, I don't have much time as things are about to happen, and you'll probably catch it on the news later, but I'm okay and this should all soon be over."

"Well, I certainly hope so. We're all missing you."

"Well, thanks and the same here. Gotta go as I'll be missed! Will call you tomorrow. Love you and the kids lots!" He rang off.

Jody handed the phone back to her sister, and started to cry. Seeing this, Ella and Jess rushed to their mum and hugged her. Musha joined in and, before long, they were all crying and hugging each other tightly.

Lenny walked back into the control room. Matt looked at him and guessed something was wrong.

"Hey, what's up?"

"Nothing, just missing Jody and the girls."

"Oh…okay! Hopefully it ends today, and, if so, we'll get you on the first available flight."

"That'll be good, thanks."

"So," Matt began, "We have all our units in place; we've got most, if not all, of the options covered; we're fairly definite on suicide bombers and terrorists with assault rifles, making about ten, possibly twelve, terrorists altogether."

"Is that from confirmed intel?" Lenny asked. Wyndham stepped across and took over the conversation.

"Yes, that's right, Lenny, it is. Our deep throat managed to get us some very good intel and pictures of most of the terrorists, and the snipers and armed officers have all that detail."

"Does that include the female of interest?"

"No, nothing on that, but we're hopeful of something fairly soon."

"Well, it will have to be soon, as it's now getting a little close to the wire," Lenny added.

"Our main aim right now is to limit any casualties here, and take some alive, if possible. We'll get to the organisers after, if necessary!"

"Yeah, I get that, but does the intel give us detail on the shooter that started all this?"

"No, nothing more than our original suspicion, but it did confirm that she is Iranian, and we weren't wrong on Marseille either."

Lenny looked at Wyndham.

"Good to know my powers of observing detail are still good!" he said emphatically.

"You won't mind if I congratulate you later? I've got something else to deal with right now," was the rather curt response.

Wyndham then turned and moved to the control area, where he looked at the various CCTV screens that had the whole perimeter covered, and began getting more detail from the Special Forces Commander and Commander Scott.

Matt walked over to Lenny, who was feeling a little chastened.

"The one thing about Mike is that you need to know when to have a dig, and that wasn't one of them."

"Gotcha!" Lenny walked away from Matt and stood apart from Wyndham, but also watching the screens.

A few minutes went by and one of the communication officers received an incoming message from one of the snipers.

"WE HAVE EYEBALL ON POSSIBLE SUICIDE BOMBERS, FOUR OF THEM 2 AND 2."

"HOLD YOUR POSITION ALPHA 1 AND KEEP US POSTED ON ANY SIGN OF AGGRESSIVE ACTION," came the response.

"COPY THAT."

"OKAY STAND BY FOR MORE INSTRUCTION."

"COPY THAT."

The day's play at the cricket had ended at 18.10, and there was a steady trickle of people coming out of the Grace Gate and the Eastern gate in St John's Wood Road. Suddenly, there was a roar of van engines from either end of the road. They abruptly screeched to a halt, having swerved to cover the carriageway at both ends. The vans' side doors slid back and out jumped six armed terrorists from each van. They began shouting "Allahu Akbar" and then trained their guns on the exiting crowd from both gates. At the same time, the four suicide bombers, who at this stage were about to reach the now screaming crowd, took off their flimsy over garments and joined in the chanting of "Allahu Akbar."

The control room had seen everything and Commander Scott had given the go ahead to engage. Within seconds, the snipers had taken out the four bombers and were told to hold fire. Meanwhile, several people had fallen from the gunshots fired by the terrorists, but the armed police units were now on sight, and shot and killed all of the terrorist gunners. The promising future of the twins, Lucretia and Haider, had been extinguished when their lives ended violently.

Watching all of this from an apartment window opposite was Banu. Tears rolled down her cheeks as she watched the destruction of her willing helpers, particularly the twins. She cared not for the murdered infidels, and was determined that this was not finished yet. She watched, as armed police approached the dead bombers. She took out a phone, dialled a number and pressed send. Within seconds, the four bombs blew up, shrapnel and body parts flew in all directions and the eight police officers fell, either dead or maimed. Suddenly, there was a deathly hush as everyone watching stood opened-mouthed at what had just happened.

Tearfully, Banu called Bilquis, but there was no answer. She tried Hossein, but again there was no answer. She couldn't understand what had gone wrong. It was now plainly obvious that the police had known about the plan and were waiting, as they knew exactly where to be. But how could they? The time was moveable. Someone had leaked the details. But everything was kept secret till the last possible moment. She picked up her phone and dialled the Sheikh. The line was dead; she tried again, with same result. She screamed and swore loudly in Arabic, and cried some more. For the first time in many years, she had no idea of what to do next. Her emotions took over. She stopped and steadied herself, got up from the floor and peeked out of the window to look at the scene. It was mayhem, several people dead, many injured, and blood and body parts strewn all over the roadside and pavements. It brought some relief to her, seeing the plan had partly worked and now it made her think of how to escape and, hopefully, meet the others.

Back in the control room, it had started to resemble a war zone, with headless chickens running and shouting at the same time. It was, of course, a lot more controlled, as each different security branch had procedures to follow and were doing exactly that. Matt and Lenny were ordered to check their weapons and put on the necessary protection vests once again. Wyndham wanted them to do an initial reconnoitre of the carnage and report back ASAP. Scott ordered two of his armed officers to go with them.

Lenny and Matt went out, followed by the two armed officers. They moved slowly and carefully, their weapons cocked and ready alongside the armed police officers. Crouching low, they maintained a slow but sure pace sweeping their gaze evenly around the scene of the attack. As they reached each group of bodies, Lenny and Matt made reports through their comms packs, whilst the police officers kept watch. What they saw, the carnage and dismembered bodies, sickened them, mentally and almost physically, but they were both in professional battlefield mode and detailed everything. Once finished, they reversed their course back to the control room.

As they were returning to give their report to Wyndham, a second floor curtain pulled slightly back and the occupant of the apartment carefully peered from the window. Banu took a sharp intake of breath, when she saw who was out on the street. It shocked her, but once again she steadied herself and sat back in a chair.

"So it's you again. Once was bad enough, wiping out my unit that night in Israel, but to do this again is too much to bear. I will take my revenge on you, and your friend, as well as your family. That I promise. Inshallah, it will be done!"

She made herself ready, but wouldn't leave until it was dark. She would make her way to her hideaway, where she would stay for a few days and then get out of the country to be with Hossein, when finally this part of her life would be over.

But first she would exact her revenge and she knew exactly where that would be achieved.

CHAPTER
32

The summer heat in Abu Dhabi was very intense and there wasn't much respite in the night time either. Although air conditioning was an absolute essential, some opened their windows and sliding balcony doors just for the sake of whatever breeze there was along with fresh, natural air, even if it was warm. So it was with Sheikh AbdulWahab al Zakani. He had watched the news on Al Jazeera and had seen his plan only partially completed.

Dissatisfied, he had called Banu Behzadi, but to no avail: her phone was either unobtainable or trashed. Either way he couldn't contact her, which was worrying, or in any event, he thought, it was probably too dangerous. He decided that he would wait to see if she called him. Throughout the course of the day's events, he felt no responsibility, whatever had happened in London or to her, she had received all that she had asked for, and would by now have the balance, as most of the mission had been completed and the final payment had gone through hours earlier. The money didn't matter to him, as much as the outcome, which was all down to her: she had hired the help, made the arrangements and organised all the training; the failure, such as it was, was her responsibility. He didn't have any further need for her services and, as far as it went, her connection to him was over. She was probably dead anyway. His only thought in connection with the attack and the almost completed mission was that he now had to tell friends that their son and daughter, the twins, were dead, and that they somehow had, foolishly, been recruited to this lunatic cause, which had cost them their lives.

With that thought filed away in his mind, he ordered room service, ate heartily, raided his secret wine 'cellar' and, after consuming a large part of the bottle he had chosen, grew tired and went to bed.

The Sheikh had a restless night, partly due to the concern of having to talk to his friends about their children but, more than likely, it was the late consumption of the food and alcohol.

He woke around 03.00, local time; although sleepy, he heard very soft noises from his living room. Without thinking, he walked straight into the room, and was confronted by three men in dark clothing with ski masks and wearing NVGs (Night Vision Goggles). Before he could get any words or sound out, two of the men raised their suppressor-equipped Glock 17s and fired two rounds each at him. His life expired immediately. One of them checked to see if he was dead. Having ascertained that, the men carried out a thorough search of the luxury suite and took with them anything they thought useful, putting everything in soft cloth bags, which they slung over their shoulders. They then exited the building and made their way to the rendezvous point, where a helicopter came in low, collected the three of them and flew to the international airport at Dubai. It landed by a special British Airways diplomatic flight, which had wheels up within minutes of their boarding, with their cargo fully intact. All the details had been cleared through back channels at the Foreign Office by Petra Green.

The plane carrying the three Special Forces men landed at 07.00, local time, at Northolt Airport, West London, where a car was waiting. They were whisked away, alongside a special police escort. At 07.45 on Friday 23rd June, they were standing in a room at the MoD, less than fourteen hours after the carnage outside Lords Cricket Ground, in North West London, carried out by sixteen terrorist bombers and Islamic militants with assault rifles.

Apart from the sixteen terrorists, the toll of dead and injured were the eight armed officers, blown up when the bombs were detonated, and another thirty civilians, who had lost their lives. A further seventy-eight were injured, some severely, and along with the dead and injured toll from the other bombings, the numbers were still expected to rise significantly. However, the vast majority of the other minor casualties were expected to make a full recovery, physically. It could have become the worst terror attack in London after the bombings in the capital on 7th July 2005 and, had information not been gathered, it would have been much worse.

Given the nature of the attack and the consequences, the Prime

Minister had announced a three day period of national mourning, during a TV and radio broadcast, where he also announced that he had received condolences from all around the world. He went on to say that a major part of the capital would be closed off, to allow for the forensic work to be completed and a clear up and repair to be carried out. The new Prime Minister had been to see the Queen, at Windsor Castle, very late on Thursday, and they had both agreed to visit the site of the attack, as well as travelling to the hospitals, where the injured had been taken. This would all happen throughout the weekend.

What was also planned was a meeting of COBRA, so that the government could receive an up to date report from the security and intelligence services, which the new Prime Minister would chair, as soon as the up to date intel had been received. He would report to Parliament at the earliest opportunity, which would probably be Monday 26th June.

Matt and Lenny had worked through the night, along with their colleagues at Millbank. It had been a long session and they had taken it in turns to rest for an hour or so, before returning to the task in hand.

They all were aware that the mission to eliminate the money-man and presumably the brains behind the attack, had taken place successfully. They were checking all of their sources and records to see if he had been flagged anywhere. But that drew a dead end.

They were all now waiting for the arrival of the contents from the Abu Dhabi hotel suite, so they could sift through for prints and DNA to identify any or all of the terrorists involved. They were also hoping to put a name and a face to the mysterious Iranian woman, who had started the ball rolling back in early January, when she murdered the two Middle Eastern guys in the back of Lenny's taxi.

It was now 10.00 hours on Friday 23rd June and all the operatives and agents at Millbank had been working around the clock for at least thirty-six hours. They were now scrutinising the documents and hardware from Abu Dhabi that had just arrived. The paperwork documentation had been distributed between different groups at Millbank, with the hardware going immediately to the technical section for close investigation. They all knew that trawling through everything would take time. However, time was of the essence, as the Prime Minister needed something to take to the COBRA meeting later that day. So the likelihood of anyone seeing their own beds any time soon was a distant thought.

Lenny, Matt and Jennifer Hardie were in the small meeting room going through several documents, bank records and various other journals that had been taken from the suite in Abu Dhabi. Matt was just about to say something when the door opened and Chris Hayward poked his head in. They all looked up quizzically.

"Morning, all. I know you're snowed under, so I've brought some help," Hayward said. They looked a little bemused, but then realised what he meant when Tom and Sarah, the two analysts Matt and Lenny had met at GCHQ, walked in and smiled.

"Morning, how can we help?" they said.

Matt looked at them both, smiled and then looked at Hayward.

"Chris, that is really good of you. We needed some fresh eyes and these are just the sort we wanted."

"Mike Wyndham mentioned you might need something from an analytical perspective," responded Hayward.

"Might have guessed, but thanks," Hayward closed the door. "Okay, Tom, Sarah, good to see you, just in the nick of time."

Tom smiled briefly, "How can we help?"

"Well, we've just received a bag full of stuff, taken from the person who we believe was the originator of the plan, and the money man too, behind the attack today. What we need is your expert eyes to analyse this documentation, filter out what is of use and then give us as much information on who the activists were who carried out these attacks. We have some names, but we need to know more about them and if needs be we can get into a records database for pictures etc. We can organise a link up, if needed, with the CIA and Mossad, ASAP as our boss will be briefing the Prime Minister at a COBRA meeting later."

"We'd better get started then," said Sarah, "Is there any hardware we need to look at?"

"That's with the techies, but if you need access, Ms Hardie here can sort that out for you."

"Err… excuse me. What will *you* be doing?" Hardie enquired.

"Lenny and I need to go look at the scene around Lords again, and then take a trip to Kensington, as there may be a connection. I found some information in one of the documents I've looked at which has a reference to an apartment just near the High Street. It's worth a look." Hardie was not totally convinced, but she agreed.

"Okay two hours, no more. We really have to process this as quickly as possible, the new Prime Minister and Home Sec are all over us and he wants answers very soon."

"Okay, we'll be as quick as we can."

Matt motioned to Lenny and they left the room.

"Is this all for real? I mean going to the scene and then back to Kensington?" Lenny asked, looking puzzled.

"Yes, all legit. The explosions that killed the eight armed police weren't detonated by the bombers, and my guess is, whoever planned this was at the scene keeping a close eye on the suicide bombers, so that if there was any chance of any of them getting cold feet, the bombs could be detonated remotely. Also, there's something in the back of my mind that keeps nagging."

"Okay, what...did you find something?"

"No, it's more like what I think I saw yesterday, when Wyndham sent us out on that recon after the shooting had stopped."

"What...what did you see?"

"I saw a curtain move. There was an image, you know...like they were peeking around it, as it had been slightly pulled back."

"Where?"

"In one of the blocks of flats, on the second floor. It would have been the perfect place to observe the whole scene. And, of course, good for seeing what happened to the bombers and then, as I said, blowing them up remotely."

"Right," said Lenny, "Let's go to the scene first and then do the Kensington stop on the way back."

"Okay, you take us the quick route?"

"Well, what else...trust me, I'm a cab driver!" They both smiled and left the building, got into a pool car and headed for St John's Wood.

The traffic wasn't great, mainly due to road closures, but the car Matt was driving was fitted with blue lights and siren, and they were on for most of the way, with Lenny doing the navigation for extra speed.

Twenty minutes later, they were at the scene in St John's Wood Road, where they showed their credentials and were waved through the cordon. They parked up and saw that Commander Scott was there. They both went over and spoke with him. Matt told him the reason for the visit, and which block of flats he wanted to go and look at. Scott thought about this for a moment or two, and then agreed, but only on the proviso that armed officers went with them. He wasn't taking any chances. Matt and Lenny both agreed, without any hesitation.

A few minutes later, Matt and Lenny had been kitted out with suitable protection and were making their way across the road from the control room inside Lords cricket ground. They headed towards the block of flats Matt had identified as the one where he saw the curtain being pulled back. He realised, by looking at the block and remembering the incident of the curtain, the flat was definitely on the second floor. There was a porter's desk inside the main door, and, seeing them approaching, he moved quickly to let them in. Matt asked if there were any empty flats on the second floor that overlooked the road. The porter told him that there was one empty flat on the second floor. However, all the flats had front and rear views.

The porter looked at his list and pointed to a number. Matt asked him if it was the second floor and the porter nodded.

"Have you got a key? We need to get in and check the place out," Matt asked.

"Well, I don't know if I'm allowed to do that. I have to ask permission from the owner."

"Who's the owner?"

"It's an Arab gentleman," came the response, "But he's not here right now, and he's probably back in Saudi anyway."

"Look, I know you have a job to do, but this is national security, and we have reason to believe that the flat on the second floor is connected with yesterday's terror attack here," Matt said, in exasperation, "So you can either let us in or I'll have you removed to a maximum security police station and charged with obstructing a security services investigation, and believe me you don't want to go there!" Now almost a quivering wreck, the porter handed over the keys and sat with his head in his hands.

They made their way up to the second floor and found the door to the flat they were looking for. Caution was the watchword, so they donned the rest of the gear they had brought for protection, in case of any booby trap explosion when they opened the door. Matt had the key, and he got the others to stand well back whilst he undid the lock to open the door. Lenny and the two armed officers moved a good distance away. When Matt was satisfied, he inserted the key. He turned it anti-clockwise till it wouldn't turn further and the latch opened. Momentarily, there was a click. Matt dived for cover and waited for the explosion. He counted…nothing after five seconds; still he waited…nothing after ten seconds, still he waited. After thirty seconds, he was pretty sure that any delayed timing mechanism would have expired. He stood up and gingerly moved to the door of the flat and slowly opened it. Nothing, not a sound, the place was empty. Still wary, he motioned for the two armed officers to establish if indeed it was empty and that nobody was hiding anywhere.

The two armed police officers moved stealthily inside the flat, with their guns in front, making large sweeping movements with them. It took about five minutes, and then simultaneously Matt and Lenny heard "clear", so they too went inside. Shutting the door, they heard something drop behind them. They both fell to the floor but nothing happened. Matt looked up and saw it was a metal part of the latch that had come away from the doorframe and fallen onto the floor.

"Okay, it's all clear," said Matt, "Just a loose latch. Something tells me that someone has tried to break in recently, but did a lash up repair. In any event, we need a forensics team down here ASAP to see if there's anything significant we can use." He got on the phone to Jennifer Hardie, to tell her what they'd found and what they needed. She put that in motion immediately and gave him and Lenny extra time to get back, as significant progress had been made with the two GCHQ analysts. It had been an inspired idea of Chris Hayward's to bring them in, and they had saved countless hours in disseminating the documents and information from the hardware they had recovered.

Lenny and Matt looked around the flat, being as careful as they could not to disturb anything that might hold some piece of evidence indicating one or more of the terrorist attackers had been there. About twenty minutes after the call, forensic investigators arrived. Matt spoke with them and told them what he wanted. It would be a painstaking exercise, but Matt knew they would be thorough.

Both Lenny and Matt decided that they would go to Kensington and take a look at the other place on which they had intel. It was another flat, but in an even more expensive part of town just off Kensington High Street. Kensington Court was a strange configuration, as it was set out like a noose shape with one section running off in another direction. That caused a certain difficulty in locating how the numbers ran.

Lenny had a rough idea, as there was a general rule of thumb, which he applied, and managed to find the number they were looking for. The buildings themselves were Queen Anne Revival style but built in the 1870/80s. Originally large houses, most had had long since been converted into individual apartments. However, there were several that were either used as foreign embassies or diplomatic residences.

They found the one they were looking for and had arranged for an agent to meet them with the keys, as it was a rental property and it had been let recently to, supposedly, a tourist. They met the agent, who had obviously misunderstood the reason for the 'viewing'. However, he was soon made aware of the seriousness of the situation, when Matt produced his credentials and gave the young agent a brief explanation, took the keys and told him that they would be returned when any investigations were completed. He also gave him a card with a number to call if there were any questions. It was Wyndham's office line.

The young letting agent scuttled off, whilst Matt and Lenny made their way inside, up two flights of stairs and arrived at the front door of the apartment. There were two keys, one the regular type latch, although it was an expensive make and had a double lock action, and a mortise dead bolt lock. Lenny looked at Matt as he was unlocking the door.

"Don't you think that's a bit strange?" Lenny asked.

Matt paused.

"Not with you, explain," he said.

"Well…these apartments have got to be multiples of over seven figures each, the ground and first floor front doors are all modern with single security keys for lift and lock doors, but this one is the old fashioned style?"

"Good spot, Lenny, but I'm not sure what it is you're getting at."

"Well, this is an absentee landlord, who has a managing agent to do the letting, and we're here because we think a terrorist planned the Lords attack or the final part of it from the apartment. Or am I being paranoid?"

"No, I don't think you're paranoid, just getting more suspicious of things. So let's look around, and if we find anything of interest, we'll get forensics down here too."

Matt opened the door and they entered the flat. It was a large, well appointed and expensively furnished place, slightly dated but tasteful.

"Blimey," said Lenny, "Looks like my mother could have done the decor!"

"She's obviously someone with taste then?" Lenny looked at Matt, but he just smiled.

There was a large living room with a good dining area, two en suite double bedrooms and another smaller one, a very good size modern kitchen, study, utility room and an extra bathroom. They took their time looking round, finding very little of interest until they went into the study.

They both looked through the contents of the desk and found a number of documents that were certainly relevant to the attack. Matt decided that forensics would be needed, so he made a call. They both then looked at the laptop. It was switched off but open, and still warm.

"This has been used within the last few hours. Whoever used it is probably connected to the attack and has been back to wipe the disc, and is travelling as light as possible, so left it!" Matt said.

"Yeah, it may also be booby-trapped, so let's wait for the techies and forensic guys to give it a once over," Lenny said, stepping back.

"I'm going to call this in to Hardie. If she needs to, she can put this into the COBRA briefing papers later," Matt said. He made the call, while Lenny finished off checking cupboards and drawers for anything else of interest.

About twenty-five minutes went by and Matt's phone rang. He answered, "Hello…yes, it is…okay, where are you? I'll come out." He looked at Lenny, who seemed quizzical.

"It's the forensics etc, they're almost here," Matt explained.

"They should have taken a cab," Lenny mused and then laughed.

Matt went outside, just as the forensic team were approaching. They saw where he was and pulled over and parked up. The team leader got out and, as he approached Matt, there was a noise that sounded like a crack. The forensics guy looked round, while Matt fell to the floor. A split second later, the forensic guy went down too. But he was dead. Missing a major part of the top of his head. That was now splattered over the ground where he lay, as well as blood, bone, brain matter and flesh on Matt's clothing. Within seconds, armed police, on Embassy protection duty, had secured the scene and called it in. Lenny came rushing out of the building and saw Matt getting up.

"Matt, what…the…fu…?" he screamed. He stopped when he saw the body of the dead forensics guy on the floor and missing part of his head.

CHAPTER
33

She stopped running after two minutes. Fortunately, she was fleet of foot and had got away before the Embassy protection police had secured the area, where she had just killed the forensics officer.

It had been a mistake. Banu had meant the bullet for Matt, but the other man had walked across him as she fired.

Banu had been in the flat since the attack, having decided to stay and lay low instead of moving temporarily, as that may have caused unwanted interest. She had received a call from the letting agent to say that there were some people wanting to look at the apartment for a possible future long term let. She thought it strange, although not unlikely, as she had rented for three months and was only three weeks off the term being up. What had been more worrying was that she'd still not heard anything from the Sheikh, and had bad feelings, as he was weak and, if threatened, would easily give her away. He definitely would not have remained silent. She had gone out for some fresh air and groceries. However, she returned to find Matt waiting outside and the forensic truck pulling up. As a matter of habit, she had her weapon with her just in case and saw a chance to take some retribution. However, she had taken her gun out and had meant to kill Matt and then wait to see if 'the Israeli' cab driver had been there too. But it all went wrong. Now the security services would have her laptop and other stuff. Fortunately, though, the papers weren't that important but the laptop was full of detail. It was well protected, the passwords were sensitive to error and everything was encrypted, but good technical operatives would at some point be able to break the encryption. However, she had everything backed up on a memory stick and knew how to get into her laptop remotely from another machine. She just needed to get to one fast and wait till hers was turned on, before she could wipe it clean.

In the meantime, she needed to find another place to stay since she couldn't now go back to the flat. Bilquis was still in the same apartment off Kensington Church Street, as she too had decided that was the best place for her in the short term. Banu called her and explained what had happened. Without hesitation, Bilquis told her to come straight away.

It wasn't very far to her apartment and within five minutes, Banu was pressing the intercom. It had a CCTV camera and Bilquis pressed the entry. Banu heard the buzzer, pushed on the door, walked in and up the stairs to Bilquis' apartment. Bilquis hugged her and they walked into the living room, where Al Jazeera news was on the TV.

Banu watched in astonishment at the screen: the story that was running was coming from Abu Dhabi. To her horror, and then stark realisation, she realised why she hadn't heard from the Sheikh: he was now dead. Banu looked at Bilquis.

"Oh shit, when did this happen?" Banu asked.

"They think about ten to twelve hours ago. He was found earlier this morning by the regular room service people who took his breakfast in around the same time every day. Apparently the patio doors were open to his balcony, and the room was ransacked. All of his hardware, computers, phones and other records are gone. They're saying it was an Israeli hit squad, as there was information released that he was funding terrorists in Israel."

"As much as I despise the Israelis, there's no way they did that. They may have given some support but this smells of British Special Forces. Did they say yet how Sheikh AbdulWahab died?"

"No, just that he was killed and that a number of valuables were missing, so they're calling it a robbery that went wrong."

"Yes, well that's total nonsense, I'm sure. The truth would probably ruin the tourist trade and the big investors that go there!" After they had both stood watching for a few minutes, Banu said to turn it off, which Bilquis did.

Banu then looked at Bilquis, having calmed down a little, and said, "Okay, it really doesn't change much; just that we now have to work more quickly before we leave. The Sheikh was as good as his word and the money was deposited on the day so we are okay on that count. By the way, have you heard from Hossein? I can't seem to get him. His phone is dead."

Bilquis looked surprised.

"No, nothing, I would've thought he'd been in touch. You don't suppose he was captured or hurt?"

Banu thought momentarily.

"No, there would have been some sort of bulletin, saying they had someone in custody. Of course they won't have identified all of the bodies yet, so we will wait. If we hear nothing by the time we leave, then we must assume he didn't make it. We will also need to take extra care now; they may have a lot of detail about me, as well as the plans. The fact that MI5 were there at my apartment means they had information and are clever enough not to raise suspicion by telling the letting agents why they wanted access."

"Is that how you think they knew?"

"Sure, it can only be four people who had that information: you, Hossein, the Sheikh and me. I trust, er sorry… trusted, all of you, but of course the Sheikh is no more."

"Okay, so what now?"

"I have unfinished business, as I keep saying, with Lenny the cab driver. I know it's becoming an obsession, but he's the beginning of the problem and I intend that he will be the end of it too."

"How will you do that?"

"You said you knew where he was staying, somewhere near Battersea Park?"

"Yes, I saw him going into a mansion block; I think the apartment is owned by his MI5 friend. I made some enquiries, and the answers were very strange and confusing. So I asked around some of my old Chechen friends and they told me that the sort of run-around and lack of info probably meant security services, so adding it all together it must be his friend. His wife and family must be elsewhere, probably Israel, but more than certainly not in the country, as they couldn't guarantee the family's safety. Anyway, since I left the message on the body of the dead cab driver, I suspect they've been taken somewhere safe and will be there till it's all over."

"Bilquis, my dear friend, what would I do without you? That's brilliant. So tomorrow you need to go running again in that park, but keep watch on the apartment discreetly. If you see either or both, call me and I will come down."

"But won't it be too dangerous?"

"Yes but I have to do this. Besides I will be in disguise so nobody will recognise me."

"But you have no clothes."

"I know, and that's why early tomorrow, I will make a list of things I need and you will get them for me. When that's done, I can move around but right now I need to see my armourer. All of my belongings are in the apartment and I expect the security service have my other weapons and ammunition now, so I need to replace what I can."

"Okay, whatever you need. Inshallah, it will be done."

* * * * *

Matt and Lenny finally got back to the building on Millbank well into the evening. The briefing by Wyndham to the Prime Minister and COBRA had gone ahead, and it included the new information regarding the flats in St John's Wood and Kensington, and the death of the forensics officer. Lenny found a quiet room and phoned Jody. She wanted to know why he was still there, and he did his best to explain, without telling her the whole story. He told her there was still some more work to do clearing up the investigation, as to who was behind it and if there were still any terrorists around connected to the attack. She groaned and cried, and he did his best to reassure her, but she was, naturally, worried.

"Lenny, the promise was that as soon as it was all over, you'd be on a plane here, so what's going on?"

"Nothing's going on, honey; it's just the clear up. A few things to sort out, I promise. I'll be there in a day or so."

"Lenny, I know you too well. You better not be there unnecessarily, and you've gone way beyond the call. We're missing you and want you here ASAP."

"Honey, I promise you I'll be there in a day or so. As I said, there are just a few things to finish up and then I'm on that plane."

"Okay, you'd better be…take care, love you…"

"Love you lots too, honey."

They both hung up.

Lenny returned to the section, where Matt was talking to some other officers. He waited for Matt to finish. Matt saw him and walked over.

"Everything okay, Lenny?"

"Yes and no."

"Okay, I assume that means you've spoken with Jody?"

"Got it in one."

"Well this is MI5…and the clue is in the name…Intelligence!"

"Well, I'm glad one of us is feeling humorous, and, yes, I just got off the phone with her and she's wondering why I'm not there yet."

"Well, I hope you told her there's still some clearing up to do?"

"Yep."

"So?"

"So, she's still wondering why I'm not there yet!"

"For Pete's sake, you know this is one of the reasons why I didn't…" Matt tailed off and stopped mid-sentence, as his phone started to buzz in his pocket. He took it out and answered. Lenny went to speak but Matt held his hand up to stop him. Matt listened for a while and then just said, "Okay, got it, we'll be there in half an hour."

Lenny looked at him.

"What's up, what have they found?"

"See, I knew you'd be good at the job. We have to go back to Kensington. There's some stuff there they think will interest us."

"Okay, no gunshots this time please!"

"Can't promise, but let's go."

Matt and Lenny arrived back at the flat in Kensington around twenty-five minutes after leaving Millbank. It wasn't really that far, but traffic was still problematic with a number of diversions and road closures.

Having parked up, they entered the building, showing their credentials to the armed police at the entrance. They went straight up to the flat and were met by the forensics team leader and the senior investigating officer from the Metropolitan Police, Detective Chief Superintendant (DCS) Jack Atwell. He introduced himself to Matt and Lenny, and briefed them on what had been found.

He led them through into what was the master bedroom and laid out on a glass topped table were two Glock 19s with two boxes of compatible 9mm ammunition and three different passports, French, Iranian and Lebanese. The passports were all in different names, but with the same picture of a young-looking woman around mid to late thirties. There was also a large amount of currency in Euros, Sterling and US Dollars, as well as credit cards to match the names on the passports. The wardrobes contained clothes, obviously belonging to the woman pictured in the passports. There was also a small tablet computer, as well as paperwork that, at a cursory glance, could have been plans.

Matt looked at the computer.

"We need to get that to our tech guys ASAP. There's probably info on there we can use to try and close anything else down quickly," he said.

The DCS motioned to one of the uniformed officers to bag up the computer for Matt and Lenny to take with them.

"Well, this is a nice little haul," said Lenny.

"Yes, it certainly is, and wasn't difficult to find either," the DCS answered, "She obviously didn't think to hide it, probably not thinking she'd need to."

The officer came back with the bagged computer and handed it to Lenny. Matt and Lenny shook hands with Atwell and thanked him for the heads up. He responded by talking about 'joined up security' and told them that the rest of the evidence would be at the Anti Terrorism unit when they needed it. Matt asked Atwell to use the passport photograph for a handout to ports and airports only, but to be discreet, as they didn't want the publicity just yet. If there was a chance to capture her making an escape, there needed to be a shortage of detail right now. DCS Atwell told him not to worry, as Lenny had already mentioned it, so there no need to expand. Lenny and Matt smiled at each other and then at him, said goodbye and left the building.

On the way back to Millbank, Matt noticed that Lenny was particularly quiet. "Okay, Lenny, what's up? Don't like it when you go quiet on me."

Lenny thought briefly.

"Nothing, and everything. I thought, when I first came back here, after I'd finished with the cloak and dagger stuff in Israel, I wanted a quiet life, but it keeps pulling me back. Who'd have thought picking up a fare in the Brompton Road on a damp Sunday evening in January could end up being so dangerous? It's like I got the fare to Hell."

Nothing more was said between the two.

CHAPTER 34

Lenny and Matt spent several more hours at the Millbank building, sifting through documents and going through the tech information taken from the laptop and phone that belonged to Sheikh AbdulWahab, as well as the documents and rough plans retrieved from the apartment at Kensington Court. The guns and ammunition were sent for comparison testing, to see if any had figured in any of the recent and not so recent shootings.

They now knew names of some of the main activists, and Matt spent some time thinking about one name in particular, as he was sure he knew it from the fairly distant past, but couldn't place where or when. Lenny saw Matt staring at the paperwork with total oblivion as to what was going on around him.

"Matt," he called, but no answer.

"Matt!" he said louder. Finally, after one more go, Matt looked up and smiled. "Yeah, Lenny, what's up, mate?" he answered.

"Well, you, really, you seem distant?"

"Oh…er… no, I'm fine. Just one of the names on this list. I know I've seen it before, but can't figure out from where."

"It'll come. You're tired. Good night's sleep is in order."

"That'll have to wait till this is all sorted."

Around midnight they decided that they'd had enough and needed some sleep, no matter how little. They finished up and, after Matt had collected a few things, they left the building and hailed a cab to take them home, back to Battersea.

By the time they reached Matt's block of flats, it was 00.45. Matt paid the cab driver. Lenny looked at the driver.

"Be lucky," he said, to which the driver gave him a quizzical look.

Lenny smiled again, winked and headed towards the flats. As the cab drove off, the driver of a parked car across from the mansion block watched Lenny and Matt walk into the flats. The driver watched as a light went on in a room on the first floor. Matt looked out before closing curtains. The driver of the car turned and saw that the passenger was still sleeping. A tap on the shoulder and Banu woke up. She looked at Bilquis.

"Are they back?" she said.

"Yes, on the first floor, the window with the shaft of light between the curtains."

"Good, give it a few minutes and then we will leave." Bilquis waited and watched, and Banu had her eyes firmly fixed on the first floor window. Their patience was rewarded a few minutes later, when Lenny came to the window and peered out.

Sitting back, Bilquis looked at Banu, who was sat up straight and in deep thought for a moment, her eyes narrowed and nostrils flared.

"So the Israeli cab driver is cowered away here? Well, no matter. I will avenge my dead comrades right here and the new martyrs too, and they will finally be at peace," Banu said.

Oblivious to the fact that his nemesis was so near, Lenny closed the curtains and turned to see Matt holding out a glass with a good measure of single malt Glenlivet.

"Thought we deserved a nightcap!"

"You got that right," Lenny took the glass and lifted it, "Cheers."

Matt smiled, lifted his too and said "L'chayim. So, see anything outside?"

"No, just the usual cars, traffic and park!"

They finished their drinks and headed to their beds for a well-earned sleep.

Matt woke up and semi-consciously could hear his phone buzzing. He looked at his watch: it was 01.45.

"For Christ's sake, what the hell…?" he moaned. He reached out, picked it up and looked at the display. All it showed him was 'unknown number'. He just stared at it, wondering who on earth was calling him at this unholy hour. It kept buzzing and finally Matt answered, "H e l l o…?"

"Hi, it's 'deep throat.' I need to see you," came the reply.

"Okay," Matt said hesitantly, "When and where?"

"I'll come to you in about thirty minutes. I'll call you when I'm outside."

"You know what time it is? Can't it wait till the morning?"

"No, I really need to see you ASAP!"

"Okay, I'll come down and find you when you call."

"Good, just you and me, none of the bosses."

"Well, that's fine, but I've a friend here, who is helping us."

"Yes, okay, I know all about him, so no problem. Besides, what I've got to say he'll want to hear any way!"

Before Matt could answer, the phone went dead. He stood there for a minute, just looking at his phone in a state of semi-disbelief. Lenny, who had woken up by this time, looked at Matt, and waited for him to speak. But Matt didn't for several seconds, so Lenny did.

"Matt…,Matt…, what's up?"

Matt looked at Lenny and waited to compose himself.

"You remember earlier, when you asked if anything was up?" Matt said.

"Yeah, why something happen with the phone call?"

"Right…well I was trying to think of where I'd seen a name on the list I was checking, and they just called me!"

"Shit, how did they get your number?"

"Well that's another story, but it's now much clearer where the intel on the attack came from…him, and he'll be here in about twenty-five minutes."

"Shall I go?"

"No…No definitely not. He knows you've been helping, so, no, you stay."

"Okay, so what does he want?"

"Didn't say. But he wouldn't be breaking cover unless he had something to say that needed saying in person."

"Okay, so how you want to play this?"

"He's calling me when he's outside. I'll get him and bring him up. You wait in the bedroom, just for a minute or two, unless you hear anything you don't like. Come in after that. We can then find out what he has in the way of more intel."

"Okay, you have a weapon here in case?"

"Yes, it's in my room, top shelf in a shoe box!"

"Very original!"

"Well, it's better than under the bed!"

"Yeah, well, Uzis are a bit too big for shoe boxes, and we always needed them in a hurry and generally at night!"

"Okay, I'll get my Glock!"

Matt disappeared into his bedroom. Meanwhile, outside a car started, moved off into the balmy night and headed back to Kensington.

Matt came back in.

"Shoe box is in your room, it has a suppressor, so if there is any trouble, don't make too much noise. I have to live here!"

"Wow, my room, eh? Can't wait to leave really."

"There's me thinking we were really getting along!"

"Sorry to disappoint, but I am really longing for a good woman… my good woman. She's two thousand miles from here right now, but I live in hope."

"We'll get you over there, mate, just as soon as we can. Won't be too long now, hopefully."

"Yeah, I know, Matt, just hope it's very soon, I really am getting to the end of my patience of not being at home with my family."

Matt's phone buzzed. He picked up and answered. He listened and then said, "I'll be right down."

Lenny nodded and went into his bedroom, as Matt left the flat and went down the stairs. He opened the door to the street and looked around. About a minute went by before a man, dressed in a hooded top, tracksuit bottoms and trainers, turned into the entrance of Matt's block and walked towards him. Matt tensed: he had his hands in his pockets and was beginning to wish he'd brought the Glock with him, instead of leaving it with Lenny. However, the anxiety subsided when the man, although still covered by his hoodie, took both hands from his pockets and offered one to Matt in a handshake. Matt took it.

"Come inside. We'll walk up. It's only one flight," he said.

They walked up to the first floor and Matt led the man to the apartment. Once inside, the man took off his hoodie and the dark glasses he'd been wearing and finally Matt recognised him and smiled.

"Dan, my old friend, it's been a long time."

"Yes, Matt, far too long, so long in fact and so many names since anyone used my real name, I'd almost forgotten it."

"You've been in deep cover, so it's not surprising."

"I fear my cover is about to be blown and that will present many problems for me and, of course, your employers. The raid on the Sheikh and the papers, computer and phones recovered will no doubt have me all over them."

"Yes, afraid so, but not many of us know who you really are – we kept that very quiet."

"How about your friend. Is he here?"

"Yes he is, want to meet him? He's a former Shin Bet agent I met years ago."

"Don't have anything against Israelis, just their leadership!"

Matt called out to Lenny, "All clear, Lenny, come on in."

Lenny took a second or two and then entered the living room. Dan and Matt both stood up, and Lenny moved towards the guest and held out his hand. Dan reacted positively and shook Lenny's hand. They exchanged pleasantries and sat down. Lenny looked a little surprised to see this guy, but decided to go with the flow.

Matt looked at Dan.

"So why now, Dan? What has you worried?"

"It's not worry exactly. I've been in difficult situations many times, but the person that organised the attack is suspicious and you never know whether she has worked out the truth or not. She is also very skilled with weapons and has an accomplice just as skilful and dangerous."

"How did she get all the bombers and shooters together?"

"She had introductions, and the Sheikh arranged some of them too."

"What we can't understand is why we didn't get any chatter of substance that this attack was even a possibility. And what we had originally, the two informants got blown away."

"Yes, the Sheikh kept it very tight, apparently, but when he found out that he had a leak, he had it taken care of. In fact, even the suspicious nature of a phone call with a Saudi Embassy official made the Sheikh order his elimination too."

Lenny then spoke to Dan, "So do you know who the assassin is?"

"Yes, of course, but only by reputation and second hand information. But I managed to confirm all of that, over time."

"Why is she so concerned with causing me harm?"

"Look, from what I know, you've had intel on this and I don't think

I can add to anything you already have, except to say that she believes you are solely responsible for the destruction of her Hezbollah group in Northern Israel all those years ago."

"But we believed we got them all then. How did she survive?"

"You'll have to ask her. I don't know."

Lenny looked at Matt and again turned to Dan.

"So why didn't she shoot me at Hyde Park Corner? I mean I hit the ground pretty quick but she could easily have got to me."

"Again, that's a question for her, I think."

Lenny again looked at Matt, who said nothing. Lenny turned once more to Dan. "Why do I get the feeling there's something you are leaving out?"

"Ah, that wonderful Israeli suspicious mind shows itself," Dan replied. Lenny just stared at him, and could feel anger brewing. Realising friction was starting to emerge, Matt stood up.

"Coffee anyone?" he asked.

Dan instantly looked up at Matt and responded, "Oh yes, that would be great. Just black for me, please."

"Me too," said Lenny. Matt looked at them both.

"Is it safe for me to leave you two alone?" he said, "I mean, I don't want to be responsible for a new regional conflict starting."

"Matt, we're good. We are on the same side on this one, aren't we?" replied Lenny.

"That's supposedly the idea" said Matt.

"Then we're good?" Lenny asked.

"Yeah, I'm good", said Dan. Matt walked out and made coffee.

To his surprise, on his return he found the two of them babbling away in their almost common language.

"Well, just look at you two, peace in our time!"

"Okay, we've just proved that if the zealots left the sensible ones to it, we'd find a way," Lenny said. Dan looked at Matt and nodded.

"I'll be sure to tell the powers that be! Seriously anything helpful developed?" asked Matt.

"Only that Dan filled in the blanks as to why the female assassin wants to kill me! Which sort of helps and I suppose I understand in a strange sort of way. Although I suspect if it hadn't been me driving that day, it wouldn't have raked up the old memories or the probable guilt of being the only survivor of an ambush by Israeli Special Forces unit."

"Well, all that means is, it is now number one priority that we find her and whoever she's working with, and that it's urgent!" Matt looked at them for a direct affirmation, and got it.

They spent the next few minutes arranging future meet ups, places and times, over the next few days. Dan now had both Matt and Lenny's mobile numbers and they had his. Dan put his hoodie back on and his dark glasses too, although it was still dark outside. They said their goodbyes and he left. He walked out of the mansion block and turned right towards the Chelsea Bridge end of the road.

Keeping his head down, he stayed alert for a passing cab, as around there public transport wasn't too good. When he neared the junction with Queenstown Road, a parked car started up and pulled out in the same direction that Dan was walking. He got to the end of the road and spotted an empty cab which he quickly hailed. The cab stopped, Dan told the driver the destination, he got in and the cab moved off. The car followed at a discreet distance.

Matt looked at Lenny, who had just got off the phone to Jody and the girls. It was a conversation that went through a whole range of issues, including why she wasn't speaking to him face to face in Israel at that moment. It had been a difficult conversation with lots of tears and emotion from all of them, and was particularly poignant as they had been able to see each other on FaceTime. Although emotional, Lenny had seen that Jody and the girls looked tanned and fit, and wished he'd been there with them.

"All good, Lenny?"

Lenny looked at him despairingly and said, "What do you think?"

"Look, Lenny…" Lenny held up his hand to Matt, palm out. Matt stopped and let Lenny speak.

"Look, Matt, you, inadvertently, got me into this, so not anyone's fault. It was sheer chance the events have turned out the way they have, and I will finish the job, so don't worry. I'm not going anywhere till then. Sure Jody's upset, but she remembers the days in Israel when I was with Shin Bet and the ever changing dangers that were around then and it was certainly one of the reasons we came back, with the girls, to England. As soon as we're finished, I'm taking a long break."

"Thanks, Lenny, but I'm still sorry that you're involved. I do understand what you went through in Israel, believe me. When this is finished, your long break is on us. Wyndham has already got it sanctioned."

"Thanks," said Lenny, "I really appreciate that."

"No need, you've gone above and beyond the call. Now it's been a long day, so I think sleep is a good idea, so we're ready to go again tomorrow." Lenny nodded, and they went to their bedrooms and fell asleep easily from exhaustion.

They had both been awake since 07.30 in the morning, after meeting Dan about five hours earlier. They met in Matt's kitchen for coffee and toast. There wasn't much small talk, as they had exhausted their ability to chat over the last few days, particularly yesterday. Matt's phone buzzed. He looked at it and answered. It was Wyndham.

"Morning, boss." He listened for a minute or so, and then said, "Okay, be there in about twenty-five minutes." He looked at Lenny.

"Come on, let's go. Wyndham wants us there, ASAP. We have a plan for today."

"Okay," Lenny answered, "Raring to go."

They grabbed their jackets, Matt took his keys and they left the flat. They walked down to the ground floor and out onto the street. Luckily, there was a cab just about to pass. Lenny whistled and the cab pulled over. As they walked over, Lenny recognised the driver, Posh Michael, they called him because he'd been to public (fee-paying) school as a youngster and spoke with a posh accent. He was now, however, a staunch Socialist. Lenny never understood that.

They exchanged pleasantries, before Lenny told him where they needed to go. Michael looked at him and, before he could say anything, Lenny said, "Don't ask because if I tell you, you may end up like poor old David Barnes!"

Michael looked at him.

"My god, Lenny, what on earth are you up to? Barney was a real shock," he said.

"Well, yes he was, but then you knew him well, whereas I only knew him as an acquaintance. Nevertheless, it was a complete shock. So how did his family take it?"

"Well, he wasn't married, but he had a brother and sister-in-law, as well as a niece and nephew. Several of us went to the funeral in south London, near Eltham, and then onto a pub afterwards, where there was food and drinks. About fifty people turned out, probably around twenty cab drivers. We gave him a good send off!" Lenny had sat on the pull-down seat behind the driver, so that the conversation could continue while they were being driven to the building on Millbank. On arrival, Matt directed Michael to the rear entrance where he and Lenny got out. Matt went to pay and Michael looked at Lenny. He nodded at Michael.

"Take it, Mike. It's all down to HMG." Michael nodded and took the payment, including a tip, gave Matt a receipt and, as he went to drive off, Lenny said, "Careful how you go, Mike."

"Thanks, Lenny," he replied, "You too, mate, and be lucky." And off he went.

Lenny and Matt went straight up to the meeting room, where Wyndham was waiting for them along with Jennifer Hardie.

"Morning, boss," said Lenny, as he walked in alongside Matt.

"Morning, you two. We've got plenty to do today and we've had more intel in about Sheikh AbdulWahab. It appears he had a number of things planned, apart from the most recent one. We're fairly sure that there was a secondary target, after what was supposed to be a massacre at Lords. We think that it was probably meant to be one of the synagogues in the vicinity – there are three. However, the one opposite Lords is discounted, as it wouldn't be secondary. The one in Abbey Road would have been too far away for a quick secondary attack, so the obvious and most prominent is the main orthodox one in Grove End Road, literally a minute or two away, even on foot. It also happens to be one favoured by the Chief Rabbi. We have been in touch with local police as well as the Community Security Trust (CST), in case of anything impending we may not have intel on yet."

"So, where do you want us to start today? We had a visit last night from an old acquaintance that I hadn't heard from for several years, but is obviously still involved with us," Matt offered.

"Who was that?" asked Wyndham, with a look of concern.

"His name is Dan; he's our deep cover informant."

"How come you're just telling me now? Didn't it occur to you that he may have been doubling? You should have called it in!"

"Yes, it did occur to me, boss, but Lenny was with me and we took effective precaution in case it went south. In any event, he gave us some good information and also told me why the assassin is looking for Lenny."

"Okay, Matt, but you still should have called it in."

"Yes, sorry, boss, but it was late and he was pretty unrecognisable, as he had kept his identity well hidden under a hoodie and dark glasses. Plus the fact that we spent hours talking and going through different intel and, by the time, he left we just crashed out."

"All right, we'll need all of that in a report and then Jennifer can do a face to face de-brief with you and Lenny." There was a groan from Matt, as he realised that would take some time, and he wanted to carry on with his investigation and to try and get the person or persons responsible for the attack.

"Boss, can't this wait? We really need to be out there looking for the terrorists, especially as we know that Lenny may still be a target."

"Lenny is with you, Matt, and I have every confidence that between the two of you, Lenny's safety is in good hands! Now go do the report, and the de-brief, a couple of hours max, then you can get back to the search. In the meantime, Anti Terrorism is conducting their investigation and we are liaising with them and sharing intel of course…now go."

Matt and Lenny left the meeting room and returned to their grid stations to begin the report of the previous evening's events. On the way, Lenny looked at Matt and said, "So that went well then?"

"Don't…, don't. Wyndham's right. I should have called it in as soon as he got to us. A stupid, elementary error."

"Look, Matt, don't beat yourself up. We're okay. Let's just do what we have to now and get back out there. The sooner we finish, the sooner I get to see Jody and the girls."

"Okay, let's get to it. Couple of hours…max!"

* * * * *

Banu was back in the flat with Bilquis. They knew where they would execute the plan and it was now just about getting the timing right. They would continue to keep watch on the flat in Battersea and pick their moment to complete the final part of the mission, by taking out the MI5 officer, as well as the cab driver.

However, Banu was still worried that she hadn't heard from Hossein and had kept trying his mobile numbers, but they were all out of service. She had made calls to people she knew, that Hossein might have contacted, but nobody had heard anything. Her heart was breaking at the thought that he might have been killed and she tried to shake that thought out of her head. But it was a recurring fear, one that wouldn't go away easily.

They had developed a plan for how they would deal with their targets and had kept an eye on them. They knew that the only time they spent in the flat in Battersea was when they went there to sleep, and anything outside of that would probably be fraught with all sorts of dangers. Besides which, Banu was determined to kill the Israeli, face to face.

They had revisited Banu's armourer in Bethnal Green and obtained handguns (Glock 19s) with enough reserve magazines for what was needed. However, Bilquis still had her weapon, and would stay using it. Banu had also managed to arrange replacement passports and credit cards from a known and reliable source. In the meantime, Bilquis had sharpened up her make-up and disguise skills, after purchasing some equipment that included skin-like latex and adhesive, along with nose and cheekbone moulds to fashion subtle appearance-altering changes. All of this had been necessary because the new version of Banu had needed to be photographed for the new passports.

Bilquis had also become worried that her friend Banu was growing obsessive about revenge against the Israeli and that it could be her downfall. She decided to put in place a plan for herself, should things take an unexpected turn. As much as she was Banu's friend, there was still the need for self-preservation inside her, probably instilled at an early age through her parents and the troubles that the collapse of the Soviet Union had visited upon her homeland, Chechnya.

They needed some food supplies so they decided to go out into Kensington High Street, to the whole food store. They didn't know how long they would have to wait, so they would buy enough food to last a week. It would also be safer to eat in the apartment; that way they reduced any risk of being seen.

They both put on a hijab, along with dark glasses. This wouldn't be out of place as the area of Kensington had a high proportion of residents from Muslim and Middle Eastern origin, and the warm sunny weather made sunglasses regulation attire. As soon as they were both ready, they walked out of Bilquis' apartment, along Kensington Church Street and then turned left onto Kensington High Street. They crossed the road at the pedestrian lights and walked into the store.

Walking and talking on the way, they hadn't noticed a man had watched them come out of the apartment block and followed them down to the High Street. He had thought to use his phone to take pictures of them, so they could be used for facial recognition but with the dark glasses and hijab, it wasn't much use. Nevertheless, he had seen enough to know it was who he needed to be watching. He remained discreet and tried to be as anonymous as possible. Once the two women were out of sight, he scrolled through his phone contacts and sent a message via WhatsApp to the number he'd selected. A couple of minutes later, his phone rang.

"Hi, you found her then?"

"Yes."

"You sure it's the right person?"

"I can't be hundred per cent sure, because of the shades and scarves, but I'm as sure as I can be. Certainly for one of them anyway, but, as I said, the shades don't help."

"Okay, well at least we know where they are. We just need to think of the best way to deal with them without causing too much of a scene."

"No problem, you want me to continue watching or pull off?"

"Yeah, just see if they come back and show their faces, if not, then there isn't much point hanging around anymore. See where they go back to and then pull off and come back. We can meet up later, but we certainly want a positive outcome in the next few days."

"Okay, will do. I'll see you as soon as."

Not long after, Banu and Bilquis left the store, laden with several bags of food that would keep them going for a week, if necessary. The man watched them closely, took note of where they went to and pulled off the surveillance. He walked back to his car and drove back to meet the man who had sent him.

Banu's phone rang. She looked to see who it was. It was an unknown call with no identified number showing up. She answered hesitantly. Her relief was visible, and also audible, as she shrieked with joy when she heard Hossein's voice. Concerned, Bilquis ran in from the kitchen, but stopped when she saw that, although tears were falling down Banu's cheeks, she was actually smiling.

"My god, Hossein, where are you? Are you okay?"

"Yes, Banu, my dear, I'm fine. I smelt a rat so made myself inconspicuous and watched helplessly, as the carnage to our great martyrs took place. Such a tragedy. After it was over, I discarded my phones and anything traceable, then made my way to the best place to exit the country."

"So why did you not let me know? Bilquis and I have been worried sick. So where are you now?"

"As I said, I discarded all my electronic things. I've been travelling since Thursday and am heading for home!"

"Okay, well, we're still waiting here. I've not quite finished yet, but as soon as we are, I'll come to you and then we can decide what's next. I assume you heard about the Sheikh?"

"Yes, very sad, but unsurprising. They're saying it was the Israelis, but that's probably not so. They wouldn't want any part of that action."

"So who then?"

"Probably a Special Forces black opp. We must now assume they have details about us, so we need to be careful with our communication."

"Yes, we were thinking the same. When I've completed my last action and am out and away from here, I will call you. Text me a number."

"Will do. Now please be careful and I'll wait for your call."

"Fine." Her phone went dead.

"So he got out okay then?" asked Bilquis."

"It would seem so. He's on his way home. He said he's been travelling since Thursday and he had discarded all his electronic equipment."

She stared at Bilquis, who asked, "What is it? You look strange."

"I don't know, probably just relief that he's okay." As Banu said that, her phone pinged. It was a text. She opened it and saw a phone number and message that read, *"LOOK FORWARD TO SEEING YOU SOON x."* She smiled when she saw this, looked at Bilquis and said, "It's okay, seems I worried for nothing!"

"That's wonderful, now we can concentrate on the job in hand."

"But first we eat! I'm suddenly very hungry!"

They sat down and ate, drank some wine and chatted, but all the time Banu thought about Hossein and where they would go to be together. After they had finished and cleared away, they sat at the table and discussed where, when and how they would execute the final part of the plan to take down both Matt and Lenny.

After much discussion, they agreed to keep watch at the flat in Battersea for another few days. Also, they decided to see what would be the best way into the block without being spotted. They knew there were cameras, and needed to find out if there was a back way into the block, so as to avoid them. Bilquis thought a run around the park with a little diversion behind the flats would give them a better idea of what was possible. She would also take some pictures as discreetly as possible: that way a more concealed entrance might be evident.

The following day, around 18.00, Bilquis parked her car at the same place as she had previously. She already had on her running gear; she took her phone and placed it in the holder on her arm, secured by a Velcro strap. She put in her wireless ear buds, so that she could listen to music while she ran and wouldn't have wires to deal with, when she needed to take some pictures on the phone. She got out of the car, locked it and put the key in one of the zipper pockets in her Lycra sweatpants.

It was again a warm evening, as she started to jog, and she noticed there were several other runners in the park, as well as people on the tennis courts. Towards the centre of the park, there were a number of matches taking place on the artificial football pitches. Bilquis ignored them and just ran. Her objective was to get to the south side of the park, exit at the gate by Queenstown Road (the Chelsea Bridge end) and then run the block front sides and back, once without stopping, keeping a close eye on any access to the rear of the building that was of interest.

She got to the gate she needed and turned right along Prince of Wales Drive, keeping an eye on the blocks to her left. She needed to pay particular attention to the third block along. As she neared it, she slowed a little and crossed the road. She was now by the block of interest and jogged a little further. Finding the side road immediately past the block, she turned left into it. Whilst maintaining the jogging pace, she kept looking to her left for any possible entry to the rear of the building. Nothing was obvious, so she speeded up to a run. She turned again left on to Battersea Park Road and ran along the block, until she reached the next corner, where she turned left again.

As she slowed to where there seemed to be a side entrance to the mansion block, she took her phone from the holder on her arm, found the camera and took some pictures of what appeared to be a suitable entrance to gain access. Having done that, she replaced the phone, and secured it again, with the Velcro strap. She continued to jog and, as she turned again onto Prince of Wales Drive, she picked up the pace and ran towards the gate at the junction with Albert Bridge Road. She entered the park and ran north along the western side of the park.

Once she had returned to where she had parked her car on the Northern Carriage Drive, Bilquis got in, took her phone out again and called Banu. The call was answered on the second ring.

"Hi, did you find anything?"

"Yes, I think so. I found a side way in through an alleyway that goes along the back."

"Good, come back, and we'll go through it and see how possible it will be to gain entry from there. I've also made some searches and found the flat number we need."

Bilquis started the car and drove out of the park, north over Albert Bridge and back to Kensington.

She arrived back at her apartment, showered and changed, and then came into her lounge to find food and refreshment waiting for her, courtesy of Banu's cultivated culinary skills. Whilst they ate and drank, Banu asked a number of questions about the block of apartments and was impatient to see the pictures Bilquis had taken. Bilquis sent them directly from her phone to the printer. She then explained to Banu what she had found, before printing them out.

After they had cleared their supper away, they sat with the pictures, studied them and began to devise a plan of how they would gain access, without being detected. Finally, after a lengthy discussion, they settled on a course of action. They knew that it would need a couple of days of surveillance to verify that the targets would be there. Banu would then enter the building to carry out the plan. Bilquis would remain in the car, strategically placed out of sight of CCTV, and where Banu knew she would be, so that they could make a swift getaway. They would only take with them what they urgently needed and would drive as far away from London as possible, before they headed to an exit point.

They hadn't decided where that would be yet, but had a number of options. However, they would need to make bookings for several modes of transport and would need more than one vehicle or train route but, of course, only one would be used. They would take the next few days to get together everything required for the escape, as well as monitoring the movements at the target flat. They spent the rest of the evening deciding what they would take and what would be discarded.

Banu had a restless night and drifted in and out of sleep. By 06.30 the following morning, the adrenalin coursing through her body was enough to make her realise that more sleep would not be possible. She got out of bed, showered and dressed, then made her way to the kitchen, where she started to make some coffee. Within a few minutes, a very sleepy Bilquis walked in and asked Banu if she was okay.

"Yes, I'm fine. I just couldn't sleep any more, and I had too much buzzing around my head."

"Okay, give me a few minutes and I'll shower and dress, and then we'll have some breakfast and get things ready for our task today."

"It's all right: I'm not that hungry right now. Take your time. We can prepare when you're ready. We know that they won't be in the apartment most of the day, and we can check when we get there by pressing the buzzer."

"Okay, but no pressing buzzers, it will have CCTV and I don't think they will be expecting us!"

"No of course…sorry, not thinking straight."

"Come on, Banu, what's up?"

"No, it's nothing."

"I've known you long enough to know that there's something bothering you."

"No…well, it was hearing from Hossein again, and wanting to go and be with him…I just don't know what I want right now."

"Look," said Bilquis, "If you want to abandon the plan, we can always do it some other time. You never know, when the furore of what happened dies down, they will, as they always do, drop their guard and that may be a better time."

"No… no, I want to get this done as I don't intend to be coming back here any time soon. So we carry on!"

Bilquis smiled, turned, went to her room, showered and dressed.

After about fifteen minutes, Bilquis reappeared and made Banu some food. Banu drank more coffee. They prepared some provisions and other things, drinks and snacks, as it was likely to be a long day keeping watch in Battersea. They realised that, in all probability, most of the waiting would be fruitless, but it had to be done. Banu had always been meticulous with her preparation, and the conversation had snapped her out of her lethargy. Bilquis was glad their focus on the plans for the day had enabled Banu to forget her worries about Hossein, but wasn't that surprised, as she had thought her suggestion of a postponement might just do the trick, as it had, together with the planned surveillance.

Two hours later, they left the apartment. They walked over to Bilquis' car, put their belongings into the boot and drove off. They were so focused on their task, chatting as they pulled away towards Kensington High Street about what they wanted to achieve from this exercise, that they were totally oblivious to the car that pulled out and started to follow them.

There were two people in the car: one was the man who had been watching Bilquis' apartment; the other was the man he had been on the phone with when he had spotted them a few days before. The latter turned to the driver and said, "Good, keep a reasonable distance, and we'll sort them out at the best opportunity."

The driver turned his head briefly to him and smiled.

"Can't wait!" he said.

Bilquis had parked up. She had noticed the car stopping and parking about fifty metres behind them. She adjusted her mirror to a position where it was possible to keep an eye, without turning her head.

"I can't be sure yet, and don't react, but I think we've been followed," she said.

"Really, since when?"

"Not sure, but I noticed them when we got into Gloucester Road. I've kept my eye on them since. They're parked up now."

"Okay, we'll watch both situations and see what develops."

"In another hour or so, it will start to get busy along here and we can use the traffic to move on if we have to. It will be easy enough to lose them. Although it would be good to know who they are!"

"Well, they're either security services or police, although thinking about it, if they are, they probably would have stopped us by now!" said Banu.

"Right, so if it's neither of those, who?"

Banu shrugged, "I don't have an answer to that, but if they're still here later, we will find out, and deal with them!" She turned and looked at Bilquis, who also turned to look at her. There was a steely determination on both their faces.

Approximately fifty metres behind, the two men had settled and were keeping watch. The driver turned to the passenger and mused, "Wonder what they're doing, or how long they will be?"

"What's the matter? You gotta be somewhere?" the passenger asked.

"No, just wondering. I might want to take a leak at some stage, and there's nowhere here to get any food."

"Your habits are not my problem. We're here for a specific purpose and we're not going anywhere until we've finished."

"Okay."

"If you need a leak, you can find a tree in the park. There's an entrance just back there behind us." He pointed back to the set of traffic lights at the junction with Albert Bridge Road. They too settled in and waited.

After a few more hours of sitting in a cramped car, which included taking it in turns to doze for a bit, Banu and Bilquis decided a leg stretch was appropriate. Again, they took it in turns to get out and take in the surrounding area.

They both took the opportunity for cursory glances in the direction where the car that had followed them had been parked. It was still there, but both of them noticed that the two men had dozed off.

Back in the car, they agreed that the men were not with any of the security services, so who were they? Banu looked at Bilquis.

"Well, it doesn't matter who they are. We will have to deal with them, if we need to, at a later time," she said.

Bilquis replied, "Yes, if they follow us back, we can try and lead them somewhere quiet and then take whatever action is needed, just as long as it's not connected to here or in Kensington. I think I know just the place!"

Another few hours passed and they were getting a little fidgety. They'd eaten their food throughout the day and now they just had drinks left. It was nearing the end of June and the daylight still lasted till around 21.30. The day had been warm and sunny with a clear blue sky, something that was becoming the norm in the UK, after many years of indifferent summers.

Banu looked at her watch and shook her head.

"I think another thirty minutes and we can call it a day. We've spent enough time here and they're obviously working hard, trying to find us! So we'll not make it easy for them. The time is approaching when we will let them see us, on our terms!"

However, no more than five minutes passed before a cab pulled up outside the entrance to the mansion block. Lenny and Matt got out of the cab. Lenny exchanged a few words with the driver, and then they both walked in through the main door, Matt chatting as they did so.

Banu and Bilquis watched and waited. Sure enough, within a few minutes, Lenny appeared at the window and surveyed the scene outside. Then he stepped back, drew the curtains and walked away.

Bilquis muttered, "Certainly habitual."

Banu smiled and answered, "Let's hope so, for another day or two, at least!" They both giggled nervously, and sat for a few minutes.

Banu broke the silence and said, "Right, what will we do with those two idiots behind us? We don't need any more distractions, particularly as we are so close to finishing the task."

"Like I said, we need to lure them away from here to somewhere quiet. That way they're not traceable to us, and we can find out who they are. You know the rest!"

"Okay, but it will need somewhere undiscoverable for a couple of days."

"Yes, of course, I know exactly the place!" They both became silent, as if deep in thought, with a quiet satisfaction that all of this would soon be finished, with a new life beckoning elsewhere.

* * * * *

Matt poured good measures of single malt whiskey into a couple of glasses. He gave one to Lenny and they both raised their glasses and said, "Cheers." Matt asked if there was anything interesting outside, to which Lenny shook his head.

At that moment, two cars started their engines and moved off away from the apartment block. All of this was unseen and unheard by both Matt and Lenny, due to the soundproof nature of the secondary glazing in Matt's flat.

They had both worked hard on the intel that had come in from the different agencies since the attack and, apart from what they had learned from sources, including Dan, they were still at a loss to know a) if the suspects had got away and out of the country, b) how many terrorists had taken part, and c) was it just two females, or had they had, or were they still having, help?

Matt opened the file on the table and took out papers, printed from the confiscated laptop in Abu Dhabi. He sat on a sofa, with a coffee table in front of him. After putting down his glass, he picked up some of the papers and flicked through them. Then he looked at Lenny and paused a moment.

"The thing that I can't get to grips with is it's now been several days since the attack and, although we know who funded it, and he's been dealt with, we still don't have any intel on the whereabouts of the main perpetrators, or if they're gone or held up somewhere with a plan to escape."

"Look, Matt, we know that the person or persons who planned the attack are two females, with experience of activism in the camps in southern Syria and Lebanon. They were both trained by Hezbollah and raided Northern Israel on a number of occasions, and got away. They are obviously well trained and experienced in the art of knowing when to hide and when to lay low. To have planned this attack, they, or at least one of them, visited here on a number of occasions. So re-circulate the descriptions we have and let some of the super spotters go through CCTV for the last six months, to see if they can pick them up anywhere and trace their movements, as accurately as possible. You never know, we may get lucky, if they used public transport or taxis. Somebody must have seen them both, or just one of them, you never know."

"That's gonna be pretty painstaking, Lenny, and it will certainly take a while. And who knows if they have something else planned?"

"Highly unlikely to have planned something else. I suspect that they've gone to ground and are waiting for an opportunity to make their escape. As I said, they're experienced, but I'm pretty sure that someone has seen one or both of them and probably won't realise it. So we need to shake a few memories, as well as letting the terrorists know we are closing in on them. You never know, but if they have been seen, it may spook them into doing something irrational, if they think we're closing on them."

"Lenny, you know that's just about what we need right now, someone who has seen them or at least someone who thinks they may have but is not sure. We should have done this earlier, Lenny. What were we thinking?"

"Matt, don't beat yourself up. It was a major attack, where dozens of people have been murdered and it could have been a lot worse. It's bad, obviously, but had it not been for the diligence of the different agencies, it would have been a lot worse!"

"Yes, you're right, of course, but I'm gonna phone Wyndham to get the ball rolling on the super spotters." Matt walked out and called Mike Wyndham, hoping to get the spotters on to the task immediately.

* * * * *

Bilquis drove at a pace that was easy to follow, and the two men followed obligingly, thinking they were being careful but they'd obviously watched too many TV shows, as they were very easy to predict. She turned slightly to Banu and smiled, "They're still behind, how dumb are they?"

Banu replied, "Obviously very!"

"We'll be at the place shortly. I'll drive as close as possible to the bushes, so that you won't be seen. I'll pull further along the road and then stop. When I get out, it will be over to you to complete the manoeuvre."

"Okay, with these two, I don't think that will be too difficult." Banu laughed briefly. Then Bilquis went back to concentrating on driving and looking for the place she had identified to catch the two men out.

She turned into a street a few miles north west of where they had been. It was narrow and only allowed one vehicle at a time. As she turned the car in, Bilquis slowed and waited for the car behind to follow. She nodded to Banu, who opened her door and slipped out, and hid behind some bushes.

Bilquis drove on slowly for a further seventy-five metres, with the car still following, and then she suddenly stopped. The driver of the car shouted, "What the fuck…?"

Bilquis got out and stood looking at the two men in the car. The driver of the car stopped abruptly and looked at Bilquis. He turned to the other man.

"Yep, that's her, and she's now all alone. Let's have some fun."

But before he could get out, the rear offside passenger door of his car opened and they both turned around, about to shout, "What the fuck?" again. But they stopped when they saw a suppressed handgun pointing at them.

Her Glock 19 directed at the passenger's head, Banu said, "Turn around and follow that car in front, or your friend here dies."

"You wouldn't dare use that. We're in West London, for fuck's sake, not the Wild West!" the driver said.

"Just do as you're told and drive," Banu replied.

"And if I don't?"

"You'll both be dead right here, right now." She cocked the gun.

By this time Bilquis was back in her car, which she had started to drive slowly. The driver began to drive once more, following her and shaking all the way, till they had reached the destination Bilquis had pinpointed for privacy. It was a deserted old mews in the Ladbroke Grove area of West London. Bilquis parked across the entrance to the mews, once the other car had driven in. She walked in and stood at the near side front door of the car. When she looked in, she realised who the two men were. She got in the rear passenger seat, next to Banu.

"These are the two idiots who tried to attack me near the apartment," she said, pointing her gun at the passenger, "and this is the one I put in hospital."

Banu looked at the men.

"You really should have left it alone. Now you will pay a very heavy price for your drunken stupidity."

"What d'you mean, a heavy price? It was only a bit of fun."

"Sorry, you picked the wrong females. We don't do fun with infidels like you!"

"Infidels, what are you, fucking Muslims?"

"No, we're just Muslims, and that may just be the last time you blaspheme against Islam." She raised her gun and shot him through the right temple. Blood, brain matter and flesh splattered across the passenger door window and the windscreen, and he was dead. Before he had a chance to say anything, Bilquis had repeated Banu's action and shot the driver in the left temple with the same result: the man's life expired instantly.

The women sat briefly, disassembled their weapons and put them in a small duffle bag. Then they got out of the car and shut both rear doors as quietly as possible. They removed their latex gloves and put them in the bag with the guns. They returned to their car and drove the short distance back to Kensington in total silence.

Banu let the shower's hot water pour over her aching body for about thirty minutes. The ache, from the rush of adrenalin, started to ease. Meanwhile, Bilquis had finished showering; she felt herself cleansed from the hot running water and began to feel calmer. Banu came out of her room, wearing a bathrobe. She saw Bilquis was already there, and that she had prepared a light snack for them both, and had also poured out two large glasses of white wine.

Banu looked at her friend.

"It is now imperative that we finish the task we set ourselves, either tomorrow or the next day, as I fear we may be running out of luck. So we will sit over at the apartment in Battersea tomorrow, and wait for an opportunity to avenge the death of the many comrades who perished at the hands of the Israeli Special Forces, commanded by the Israeli cab driver, as well as our recently fallen martyrs!" Bilquis gave Banu her wine, they raised their glasses and together said "Fe sahatek" (Good Luck).

The end of June had arrived and its last day was yet another glorious one, with the vast majority of the country again bathed in very warm summer sunshine and cloudless blue skies.

Lenny and Matt were on the grid at the building on Millbank. Wyndham had given the okay to Matt's request for the super spotters and it had been initiated.

He had also included all CCTV footage from all ports and airports, including Eurostar and Eurotunnel.

Lenny was sitting at his station, but deep in thought. Matt spotted him and wondered what he was thinking about. He walked over to where Lenny was sitting.

"Anything happening, Lenny? You seem distracted."

"No, not distracted. Just running an idea around my head."

"Okay, go on."

"Look, we've got lots done and much more in place. But we seem to have hit a brick wall."

"Yeah, and…?"

"Well, it looks very much like the ones that organised the attack are probably still here, and yet nobody has seen them or even remembers what they may look like. Mind you, the details on them are sketchy. We need more intel to add to the profile of them."

"And we get that how? I mean, we do have a pretty decent high tech system!"

"Well aware of that, Matt, but we need intel that isn't being picked up. Street talk, you know the sort of stuff you'd maybe pick up in conversation, confidential informants, cab drivers or delivery people. Someone has seen them at some time. Look back and think where, like the one who killed David Barnes, the cab driver. I mean where he picked his killer up from. Was the cab inspected? The meter would have had details, if he was using an app for work that would have info too. Have these been checked?"

"Shit…I don't know. Why are you mentioning this now?"

"Well, it's just come to mind, and I've had time to think. Y'know, we've been a little distracted!"

"Yeah, yeah, okay, I get it. I'll get on it right away."

"Okay, I'll be out for a while!" Lenny got up, took a thin folder with him and then, as he turned to go, Matt called after him, "Hang on, Lenny! Where are you going?"

"Going to visit some old haunts of mine, a few watering holes!"

"You lost me."

"Sometimes I think, if only! Cab shelters, cafés, sandwich places. Where cab drivers stop for food and a chat. They do a lot of that!"

"Yeah really? Never knew!"

Lenny turned and left. He knew where he would start, and exited the building at the rear. He turned right onto Thorney Street, then left onto Horseferry Road and headed for the line of parked cabs, that were outside Pret A Manger, Leon, and the other places where cab drivers stopped to eat and chat. "As good a place as any," he thought. He strolled up and down a line of taxis, recognised one or two number plates, had a peek inside some of the eateries and finally found the cabbies he was looking for.

They weren't in either of the well-known restaurants; they were in a small, family run café just in Regency Street. He looked in and saw some guys he knew, strode in and stopped by a table where four cabbies were sitting: one of them was the one who he wanted to talk to. As he got to the table, that cabbie, Henry, looked up and saw Lenny, and he smiled.

"Blimey, look what the wind just blew in! Lenny, my son, how are you? Where've you been? Heard you were busy with something important."

"Yeah, you got that right. I am. Something very important, and I need to ask you some stuff. I'll need you to search your memories. It's really important!"

"Okay, Lenny old son, but I'm getting worried now."

"Nothing for you to be worried about, Henry, and if you guys want to hang around, you might be helpful too."

They all looked at each other, then at Lenny and nodded.

"Okay, so I'm helping out some people I know with enquiries regarding the death of David (Barney) Barnes."

Henry looked at Lenny.

"Okay, Lenny, what's going on? Barney was a friend of mine and we've told the police all we knew, which amounted to diddly squat anyway, so who are 'these people' you know? He needs to rest in peace!" Lenny wouldn't normally acquiesce, but Henry was a big guy and, even though he was in his mid- seventies, you wouldn't want to argue with him. He was an ex-Royal Navy Chief Petty Officer and at 6ft 4inches was still an imposing specimen. As a young man, he'd been in naval action in South East Asia. Lenny reached into his trouser pocket and took out what looked like a wallet. One of the other cabbies said, "Blimey, Lenny…you paying!"

A good deal of laughter broke out.

"Okay, okay, guys, yeah, I know, tight as baby's bum. Yeah, heard em all!"

He opened the wallet; it had his MI5 credentials inside plastic covering. He tugged at Henry's arm and motioned for him to move closer.

"What I'm about to show Henry is confidential and if it gets out, I'll know, so please, tight lips," he said to the drivers.

He showed Henry his creds. Henry looked at them and then back at Lenny. "Where did you get those from?"

"Where d'you think?"

"Well, I… um…"

"Okay, Henry, cut the crap. They are genuine and they're from the building on Millbank. I can get you an invite if you like!"

"You must be joking. It's full of public school twits. How come you're there?"

"Long story, but I'm working there and need information." Lenny opened the folder he'd brought with him and took out two sheets of paper.

"Now look, guys, these are well-sourced photofit pictures of two women we want to talk to. So just look at them and tell me if you've seen them, picked them up or know anyone who has. And this goes back to January." The four cabbies looked and studied the pictures, but came up with nothing. They all shook their heads and said they couldn't help. One of them asked if they were Arabs.

"Well, apart from the appearance," Lenny said, "Why you asking?"

The cabbie thought for a second or two.

"It's just something a mate of mine said a while back," he said.

"About one of the women?"

"Yeah," the cabbie said, "I remember him telling me about a fare he had from Eurostar…I think, he picked up this Arab woman and took her to a few places, before ending up dropping her at a hotel somewhere around Paddington…I think."

"Okay, what's your mate's name and where will I find him?"

"Well…I…err…"

"Look, I just want some info, so you need to tell me what you know. Or we can take a walk round to the security services and you can refuse to answer them! Sorry if that sounds heavy, but this is about National Security."

The man looked as though the blood had just drained out of his whole body. "Okay, okay…his name is Martin, and he usually stops to eat at the Mona Lisa, Worlds End, Kings Road around 21.00, or around the same time at a Turkish place in Warwick Way, think it's called the Mangal."

"Thank you, now that wasn't too difficult…was it?"

The cabbie, still looking ill, shook his head.

"Good, does he have a surname?" Lenny asked.

"Think it's Long, he lives out near Rayleigh, Essex."

"Brilliant, much appreciated."

Lenny thanked them all, stood up and went to the counter and paid their food bill.

"Who the hell was that, Henry?" said the man who had given Lenny the information, his face still pale.

"Lenny? He's an ex-Israeli soldier and formerly worked for one of their security services. He's a cab driver, but is now obviously helping out our lot, and, by the way, you did the right thing."

Lenny walked back to the building on Millbank and went straight to see Matt, to explain what he had found out and that he needed a search made for a cab driver by the name of Martin Long, in the Rayleigh area of Essex, and a mobile number, if possible. Matt told him that he could have asked for it himself, but Lenny reminded Matt that he was only temporary and hadn't realised he had clearance for that sort of thing.

In the circumstances, Matt made the request whilst Lenny was with him. About two minutes later, the information popped up on Matt's computer screen. He read it, and then printed it out and gave it to Lenny.

"What's the plan?" Matt asked.

Lenny thought for a moment, "Well, I don't want to waste time chasing him around. I'll phone him and ask him where he's eating later, so we can meet to have a chat."

"You trust him to be there?"

"Yeah, apparently he's the curious type."

"Okay, so you'll be back late then? I only ask as Dan called and wants to meet later. I told him to come to me about 21.00."

"Well, if this guy is fairly punctual, I reckon I'll need no more than half an hour with him, so should be back around 22.00, at the latest, so if you need food, text me and I'll get some on the way back."

"That sounds like a plan, will do. Let me know if you get anything."

"No problem."

Lenny went back to his station, picked up some keys and more papers, and left the building. He went down to the car pool, saw the security people there and showed his credentials. They checked and confirmed he was cleared to use a car, and gave him the keys to a Black BMW X1 67 plate. The security man told him that the tank was full, and that he should fill it before return, and would get the fuel costs back with a receipt. Lenny gave him a wry smile, thanked him and drove out, heading north.

On the way, he contacted the cab driver, Martin, who seemed to have been expecting a call. They chatted briefly and Lenny asked him if he would meet later, around the time he stopped for food. Lenny had told him that he was after more background information on the dead cabbie, David Barnes. Martin agreed and arranged to meet Lenny at the Mona Lisa restaurant in the Kings Road, Chelsea at 21.00.

That done, Lenny kept on driving and, around thirty-five minutes later, arrived outside his home in North London. He sat parked up for about five minutes, thinking about Jody and the girls, and how much he missed them. He was also thinking about how he had arrived at this point in his life.

He got out of the car, found his home door keys, opened the door and went inside, then deactivated the alarm. There was a mountain of post and junk mail that he picked up. He went through to the kitchen and placed it all on the table. He filled the kettle with water and turned it on, and then found the cafetière and the coffee. He put in three full spoonfuls, as he liked his coffee strong. Once the kettle had boiled, he poured the hot water into the cafetière, put the top on, gently pushed the plunger down to where it met the liquid and left it to brew.

He then went back to look at the post and separated out the junk mail from the bills. Satisfied there was nothing urgent, he returned to the cafetière, pushed the plunger down fully, reached into a cupboard for a mug and poured himself a large quantity of black coffee. He picked up his phone, went to speed dial and selected the number he wanted.

The number rang just twice and was answered by an excited Jess.

"Dad, oh my god, I so miss you. Are you okay? When can we see you?"

"Hi, sweetie, too many questions in one go. But yes, I'm fine and it won't be too much longer and I'll be there to see you, Mum and Ella, and I miss you too and love you lots." With that, she screamed, and handed the phone to Jody, who, without looking at the screen, said, "Hello, who is this?"

"Hi, honey, it's me. What, you forgotten me already?" said Lenny, a little taken aback.

"Oh, Lenny, thank god it's you. Jess was screaming, so I got worried. You coming over soon, I hope?"

"Well, nothing definite, but I don't think it will be too long now. We're nearing the end game, I think. How's everything there? Your sister still with you?"

"No, not at the moment. She pops back and forth, when they don't need her at work."

"Okay, but you're all right there? You have people around you?"

"Yes, don't worry. Lazar Spiegal comes around at least twice a week, and, although he hasn't said, I'm fairly sure he has people around making sure we're okay."

"You sure they're his?"

"Yes, don't worry. We're all fine, just missing you like crazy."

"Same here, I really do hope that I'll be over there very soon. We have got a few things happening that should prove useful and clear up the remaining issues."

"Well, that tells me something and nothing. Is that some sort of doublespeak?"

"Sorry, honey, it's about all I can say right now."

"Okay, I understand, but still miss you like crazy."

"Understood. I just popped home and all seems okay, plenty of post, mainly junk, and all else seems fine."

"Well, I can't wait to come home, really missing that place too. Don't get me wrong, we like it here, it's safe and comfortable, but home is home."

At that point Lenny had another call coming through, so he had to cut Jody short. They said their goodbyes quickly and Lenny promised to call her in a day or so. He pressed the phone screen that answered the other incoming call: it was Matt.

"Hi, what's up?"

"Where are you?"

"You need me to answer that?"

"What are you doing there?"

"I just felt the need to come back and check the house to see if everything was still okay. What's the problem?"

"We just got a call from the local police, saying there's a strange car outside your house and someone was in there."

"Good to know Neighbourhood Watch works then."

"Okay, you could have let me know. I'll tell the locals to stand down."

"Yeah, sorry, should have called. Just missing the place and wanted to check it out and be somewhere familiar."

"No problem, it's understandable. I'll call you later with the food order."

"Okay, thanks, should be on the way back to you by 21.45 the latest."

They both hung up. With that, Lenny looked at his watch and realised he needed to get back, as he wanted to be in position before 21.00 at the Kings Road meeting.

He reset the alarm, opened the front door, stepped outside and shut the door and locked up. He waited for the alarm to beep, meaning it was set, got back into his car and drove off towards his rendezvous in Chelsea.

As Lenny drove back towards central London, his thoughts remained firmly on the job in hand. He had the picture of Martin Long, who, by all accounts, was quite a loud person with a raucous laugh and a pretty straightforward view of life. According to his records, he had served in the army for five years as a young man, with a couple of overseas deployments in South East Asia, as well as some time in Germany, prior to the breakup of the Eastern Bloc. He'd been a cab driver now, though, for over twenty-five years, which made him late sixties.

Lenny found the place he was looking for in the Kings Road, and managed to locate a parking spot right opposite the restaurant. He was early, but he had a clear view of the place, so he would see who was arriving and leaving.

Just after 21.00, a black London cab drove past the restaurant and found a parking space. The driver reversed in first time, and stopped the engine. After taking a few seconds to pick up some things, he opened the door and got out. As he walked away, he pressed his fob to lock the cab and walked into the restaurant.

Lenny looked at the photo and details of the driver and confirmed to himself it was Martin Long. "Good, it's him," thought Lenny, "I'll give him a minute or two to settle." He watched him speak to the waiter there and put his things down on a table, and then walk down by the side of the counter and disappear. Three or four minutes went by and the driver reappeared and sat at the table, where he'd put his things. Lenny sat for another minute, whilst the man looked at his watch. Then Lenny got out of the car, locked it and walked into the restaurant.

As Lenny walked in, the waiter, who had spoken to Martin,

approached. "Buonasera, Signor. You would like a table?"

"No, it's okay. I'm here to meet with that guy there," he pointed at the cab driver.

"Okay, you mean Martin?"

"Yes, that's right."

The waited pointed the way and said, "Please, Signor."

Lenny walked over. When he reached the table, Martin stood up and held out his hand, which Lenny took, and they shook hands.

"Good to meet you, Martin."

"Well likewise, I hope," Martin replied. He was a good deal shorter than Lenny, and had a trim physique, as well as a firm handshake.

"For a man in his mid to late sixties, he's in pretty good shape," Lenny thought.

They both sat down.

"So how can I help? You said on the phone it was about dear old Barney?" Martin asked.

"Well, it is, but also other matters that are related."

"Okay, do I need to worry?"

"No, not at all. It's about someone who we think you picked up a while back, that wasn't the ordinary sort of punter."

"I see you've been learning the lingo."

"Surprised your friend didn't tell you that I'm a cab driver too."

"No, he didn't. How long and what are you now?"

"About fourteen years, and I still am, but I'm helping out with this for some people who need information that they think cab drivers can help with."

Martin was the inquisitive type, "So these people…MI5?"

"Well, I can neither confirm nor deny, but let's just say if I tell you…!"

"Kidding, right?"

"Am I?"

"Okay, now you're worrying me as to what I may be getting myself into."

"Seriously, Martin, there's nothing to worry about. I just need you to tell me if you picked this person up and where you took them."

"And that's all?"

"Yes, that's all."

"Okay, let's see what you've got." As he said that, the waiter came over and asked them if they wanted to eat. Lenny just asked for a black coffee, while Martin ordered gazpacho and the grilled fish. Opening the folder, Lenny took out the two pictures of Banu and Bilquis and showed them to him. Martin put on his glasses and looked at the one of Bilquis, shook his head and said, "No haven't seen her before." Then he looked at the one of Banu.

"Yes, picked her up from Eurostar, did a whole journey with a lot of waiting and then to a hotel in Paddington. She paid well over the top too!"

"So, where did you go after Eurostar?"

"Well, I thought it was strange, but she was well dressed in a very smart trouser suit. She wore a scarf thing, you know the Muslim women wear them."

"You mean a hijab?"

"Yeah, that's it, a hijab, and she had dark glasses on, and had a small suit case on wheels, and a shoulder bag."

"So what was strange?"

"Well, she said she wanted to go to this hotel in Paddington…"

"Which one?"

"The Park Grand on Devonshire Terrace."

"So where did you go before that?"

"Well, this was the thing – she went to Heming Street, Bethnal Green."

"What, where the taxi dealership is?"

"Yeah, that's right. Blimey, you really are a cab driver!"

"Yes, I said I was."

"Anyway, she went down Heming Street, near the end where there are railway arches, and went into one of them, and came out about twenty minutes later, carrying a parcel of some kind."

"So, what was strange about that?"

"Well, she sat in the back and, as we moved off, she opened the parcel. She did it in such a way that she covered what she was doing with her back. But there was a smell."

"A smell, what smell?"

"Look, I did five years in the army, and have been around enough guns to know certain smells. I couldn't be 100% sure, but I'd put money on it being some sort of gun grease."

"Really, you can tell the smell?"

"Yep, pretty much so."

"And you didn't think to mention this to…say, the police, maybe?"

"Well, err no, not really…I mean, I go into a police station and tell them I think one of my punters had some gun grease in the cab, they'd probably arrest me and take me down to the funny farm, wondering what I'd been smoking!"

"Well, not sure about that, but right now I need you to show me where you took her. We'll need to take a closer look at this place in Bethnal Green."

"What, right now? What about my dinner?" Just as Martin said that, Lenny's phone rang. It was Matt.

"Hi, just finishing up. Have got some new intel."

"Well, it will have to wait for now, as we have a situation. You need to get back to the grid ASAP."

"Okay, be there in twenty." He clicked off. "Well, it seems your night or your dinner won't be disturbed after all. I've got to go back to the office, but I'll need you tomorrow to show me this place in Bethnal Green."

"Okay, but don't make it too early. I work late."

"Don't worry, I'll call you, and thanks for your help."

"No problem."

As Lenny got up, the waiter brought the coffee and the soup, but Lenny apologised and gave him £20, saying that was for the meal and the coffee, and any over he could keep. The waiter smiled, took the money and said, "Grazie, Signor." Lenny rushed out, got into the car and sped off towards Millbank.

He arrived back at Millbank in just under the twenty minutes, parked the car and hurried up to the grid. When he walked in, Matt was waiting for him with Wyndham and Hardie.

"Okay, what's the rush? I had just got some really good intel on the assassin."

"That's great," said Wyndham, "And we'll get on that as soon as, but we have another problem now."

"Right, and that is?"

"Two men, late twenties, were found dead in a car in a very quiet mews not far from Ladbroke Grove. One shot in the right temple and the other, the left one."

"Two shooters?"

"Yes, that's what we think as the bullets were from two different weapons, both Glock 19s. However, and this is why it's come to us, the one shot in the left temple had a parabellum round from the same gun that killed the cab driver David Barnes."

"What the hell?" uttered Lenny.

"We don't know yet what the connection is, but taking it to its logical conclusion, the other weapon is obviously from the other female's gun," Matt said.

"So now we know this – they're either clearing up loose ends or it's totally unrelated. But one thing's for certain, they're still here and obviously active, and given the Iranian's feeling about you, Lenny, we want you at Matt's until this is resolved."

"Well, I may have got a little further on that score, boss."

"How so?"

Lenny explained the meeting he'd had with the cab driver, Martin, and said that he was meeting him the next day to go and take a look at the place in Bethnal Green. If, as he suspected and given Martin's comment about the smell of gun grease, Lenny went on, "We might find the link as to the supplier of the weapons, as the women certainly didn't enter the country with them. They used too many weapons to have travelled with them."

"Yes, I agree with that conclusion," said Wyndham, "So do that tomorrow, and take Matt with, and, if needs, be put armed officers on standby, as you never know!"

"Will do that," said Matt, "I'll get on to the armoury and make sure they are ready with weapons etc to sign out, plus I'll alert another six officers for possible action."

"Thanks, Matt. Now I suggest you get some rest, and, Lenny, make that meet with the cab driver as soon as possible, as we need to get this sorted."

"Okay, boss."

Wyndham and Hardie left, and Matt turned to Lenny and said, "Good work, mate. Looks like tomorrow could be busy."

"Yeah, certainly looks that way. So what happened with Dan?"

"Nothing really, as soon as I got the details in about the two dead guys, I realised that seeing him tonight was not going to work, so I text him and cancelled. If we're clear tomorrow, I'll call him and rearrange for tomorrow night. Although I suspect we may be turning over a hornets' nest tomorrow, so meeting with him may be a few days off right now."

"Any idea what he wanted, or was it just hangin' out with friends?"

"You know, you can be a real pain sometimes?"

"Yeah, but you wouldn't have it any other way. In any case, you got me into this, so suck it up, my friend!"

"Hmm…," was Matt's only response. They left and went down to where Lenny had parked the X1 and he drove them back to Matt's flat in Battersea. They arrived there around fifteen minutes later. Lenny parked as near to the entrance as he could, and they walked into the building, still in deep conversation.

As they opened the door, there was movement in a parked car about fifty metres away. Banu and Bilquis had been there for four hours or so, and were alerted when Lenny had pulled up in the black BMW.

They both sat up and watched the two men walk in to the mansion block. Banu felt the urge to touch her gun.

"That's not an option right now," Bilquis said, "We haven't planned for off the cuff action. We said we'll watch, wait and plan a perfect execution."

"Always the voice of sensible reason, thank you," said Banu.

"Look, it will be done soon enough, and we can leave here and go wherever we want, and you can meet up with Hossein, and forget about all of this, and you will have avenged our dead comrades in the process, as well."

"Yes," said Banu, "That is all that's left now between the old life and the new… vengeance! It will come soon."

Banu and Bilquis left the mansion block they had been watching, and drove back to Bilquis' apartment in Kensington. Not much had been spoken between them, as Banu was deep in thought.

When they arrived back, she finally spoke.

"My dear friend, and you really are, I have to thank you for your words and guidance earlier. Had I been on my own, I would probably have done something petulant and stupid."

"There is really no need. Knowing you, as I do, I know you would have paused at the right moment!"

"I'm not sure I have the same confidence that you do."

"Well, you should have. But we all have emotions, and you have had to deal with much recently, so a momentary lapse is excusable."

"Nevertheless, I still thank you!"

They got out of the car and walked into the apartment. They showered and changed, and met back in the kitchen where they had some food and drank some white wine.

Banu had made up her mind that the end of her stay in the UK would be in the next two days and no later. So her act of revenge, for her dead comrades, would be the next night. Then they would leave the following day. If that was not possible, the deed and escape would all be completed the day after.

During the course of the evening, she told Bilquis her plan and what arrangements would need to be made. Although for Bilquis the thought of leaving the place she had called home for the last few years caused her great sadness, it was very apparent from her face and in her demeanour that she realised it was now the only option. Banu saw this and felt a tinge of regret for her friend, but said nothing.

"So," Banu said, "Will you come with me? Do you want to come with me or travel elsewhere?"

"I think women of Middle Eastern appearance, travelling together with possibly a one-way ticket might look a little suspicious, so I think using separate departure places would be a better plan."

"Yes, of course it would. So where do you prefer to go from?"

"Well, hopefully we can get away before they find Lenny and his friend, and we will have to be quick at getting to our places of exit."

"I've been through Eurostar too many times over these last months, so you use that route to Brussels, and I'll fly, probably from Gatwick. Your talents will be needed to alter appearances, as I suspect they will have some sort of picture of us from the information they collected from the Sheikh's and my apartments recently."

Bilquis nodded and smiled.

"We will look very different, of that you can be sure," she said.

That agreed, they searched what was available and booked, using the new passports and credit card details from other accounts they had set up in the last few days, and had not yet used.

With all the planning completed, they drank some more wine and toasted a new life.

* * * * *

Matt and Lenny had walked up to the flat and made an impromptu meal, basically out of the freezer, into the microwave and onto a plate. They opened a bottle of red wine and talked at length as they drank and ate their TV dinner. Their main topic of conversation revolved around what they might find at the place in Bethnal Green. Lenny said he thought, in his experience of cab drivers, that Martin's story about him taking the woman down there may have had a little embellishment, so not to read too much into the gun bit as it could be subject to some exaggeration. Matt looked at him with a wry smile.

"Hang on a minute, am I hearing this correctly? You're saying that a cab driver has told the security services a porky?"

"No," Lenny said somewhat defensively, "I'm not saying that, he may well be right, just don't expect too much. And, anyway, I'm only technically security service."

"Yeah, well, we could have a conversation about that!"

"No, we really couldn't. Jody will definitely divorce me if anything gets made permanent."

"Don't panic, I'm just yanking your chain a little!"

"Well, I never would have guessed!"

After chatting for a while longer, Lenny said that he was going to phone Martin first, to arrange the meet for the next day, then Jody, and then go to bed, as they had an early start in the morning. Matt nodded and told Lenny he would confirm a meeting with Dan for the following day at the flat, obviously subject to what happened after Bethnal Green. Lenny nodded and walked off to his room, and Matt made his call.

It was quite late in Israel, but Jody was still up, talking to her sister, when Lenny called. The conversation wasn't a long one, as they were both tired. They rang off and Lenny sat for a while, thinking about what they planned to do the next day and where, if anywhere, it would lead. He let his mind wander for a while, thinking about the early start. Finally, he got into bed, turned off the light and very soon went to sleep.

Lenny was already awake, when Matt tapped on the door at 06.45.

"Lenny, you awake?"

"Yeah just about to shower," Lenny called back.

"Okay, I'll get the coffee and toast on."

"Great, be out in about ten."

Within ten minutes, Lenny walked into the kitchen, where Matt was dressed and had just put the toast and coffee on the table.

"So, what's with Martin? What time do we pick him up?" asked Matt.

"He's driving in this morning, and I said we'd meet him in Smith Square at 11.00. He can park his cab there."

"Okay, I'll let Wyndham know so that he can put armed units on standby, just in case."

"You really think we'll need them?"

"No idea, but if this place is where they sell weapons, there may just be more than one person there, and, if so, they may have multiple weapons available to them. So, yeah, better to be safe, don't you think?"

— 234 —

"Can't argue with that. Especially as Jody knows how to use a weapon, and, if anything happens to me, she'll come looking for you!" Matt gave him a cursory glance and caught Lenny smiling.

They arrived at the grid in the Millbank building around 08.15 and walked straight up to see Wyndham. They had a brief conversation, where he told them that the armed units had been arranged and that they would be in place on standby by 11.00. He also instructed Matt and Lenny to draw side arms from the armoury, as a precaution, and reminded them that, to use them, it had to be an exact and extreme reason to protect their lives and the lives of the general public. They both nodded and walked down to the armoury.

When they got back to the grid, Jennifer Hardie was waiting for them. She called them into her office. They walked in and sat down. Hardie opened a folder and took out a couple of papers.

"We've had more information in about the two men found dead in the car at the mews off of Ladbroke Grove," she said, "The one who was shot in the right temple, the passenger, had been taken to St. Thomas' Hospital about four weeks ago with a fractured cheekbone, some damage to his eye socket and concussion. His friend, the driver, shot in the left temple, was with him at the time and said it was due to him falling over, because they had been drinking heavily. They had been picked up in Kensington Church Street from an anonymous call by a female. However, the autopsy revealed that the passenger had suffered a blunt force trauma to that part of the head and that it's a good possibility that the injury was consistent with an elbow connecting with that part of the skull."

Matt looked at Lenny, then Hardie.

"So, the possibility is that somehow they must have come into contact with one or both of the women and obviously came off second best?" he said.

"Yes, I think we can assume that they were drunk, saw a young woman walking alone and thought they'd have some 'fun'."

"Only one ended up in hospital with a fractured cheekbone etc, and now they've both ended up dead! There are just some women you shouldn't mess with," added Lenny.

Matt nodded and said, "It adds up really, if you think about it, one of the women probably lives in the area, they've seen her and we have a good idea what came next. And being the types they are, they wouldn't tell anyone about coming second best with a girl, and concocted the story about falling over drunk. Then when the one with the cheekbone gets out of hospital, they plan retribution and watch out for her. When they finally find her, they follow and wait for the right time to execute their amateurish plan."

"Ending up dead and second again," Lenny added.

Matt and Lenny left Hardie to it, and walked back to the grid.

"Time to phone Martin, I think?" Matt said.

"Yeah, was just about to do that."

Lenny sat at his desk and called Martin Long. Matt saw that he was in conversation, so got on with some paperwork he had been meaning to deal with for days. Lenny finished the call and walked over.

"He's on his way, and will be here by 11.00. He knows where to park in Smith Square and I said we'd meet him there then. He asked if I was driving!"

"Why?"

"You have to ask?"

"What's wrong with my driving?"

"Did I say there was?"

"Well, err no, but why is he asking?"

"Okay, do you know where Heming Street is?"

"Bethnal Green."

"Yes, very good, I told you that, but where exactly?"

"Well…I…err…"

"Exactly, you've answered your own question. I won't need the sat nav or ask him where it is. With me now?"

"Okay, you drive. I'll sit in the back and listen to you do cab driver talk."

"It's called cabology, and I don't. It's boring."

"So you've got an ology…wow, did not know that!"

Lenny missed that bit of humour completely, turned on his heels and walked back to his desk. He took out his phone and text Jody. It was 10.30 in London and 12.30 in Israel, and he assumed that they would be getting ready for lunch. A text came back and, as he thought, they were just about to sit down and eat. Jody also said that Lazar Spiegal was continuing to keep an eye on them, and had been over and said that this might soon all be over.

He answered her saying that hopefully Lazar was probably near the mark, as there had been some developments, and so he was looking forward to seeing her and the girls as soon as possible.

When he finished, Matt came over and motioned to go. Lenny picked up his phone and keys, pulled open his desk drawer and took out the Glock 19 he had been issued with. He put it in the shoulder holster provided, then put his arms though, got comfortable and finally put on his lightweight zipper windbreaker. He looked at Matt and said, "Good to go."

They walked out in virtual silence. Leaving by the back door, they crossed over Horseferry Road and on into Smith Square. As they turned right, they saw Martin standing by his cab that he'd parked on the cab rank. Lenny and Matt went over to him, and Lenny did the introductions and then walked them over to where he had parked the X1. Martin looked at it.

"Nice car, mate. They're obviously paying well!" he said to Lenny.

"If only," Lenny said, "You get in the front with me, Martin. My friend here can watch."

Matt just stared at him and said, "Have I got to put up with this cab driver reunion the whole time?"

"Yeah, just for a while. Let's go," Lenny answered.

They all got in and Lenny drove off, Martin smiling and Matt with a distinct frown on his face that Lenny could see through the rear view mirror. He just smiled and kept driving.

CHAPTER
41

Lenny and Martin chatted most of the way to Bethnal Green, mainly about people they both knew, as well as swopping anecdotes on things they had experienced over their time as cab drivers.

Martin was quite a jovial character, who generally saw the funny side of most things and had a loud shrieking laugh that tended to go right through you. However, when he suddenly ventured into the details of why he was needed, saying "and what's it all about anyway?", Matt's voice came from the back of the car, "If we told you, we'd have to kill you." Martin suddenly stopped talking, turned and saw Matt's face: it was like stone. Martin turned back to look at Lenny and said, "He's joking... isn't he?"

Lenny answered, "That's the trouble you see, I can't tell."

"Hang on a minute, I didn't fucking sign up for this, that ain't funny!"

"No, Mr Long, it isn't funny. It's hysterically funny," and with that Matt burst into laughter. Lenny carried on driving, with a broad grin on his face. Martin, however, slumped back in the front seat, muttering to himself.

About twenty minutes later, they arrived at the road they were looking for, Heming Street.

"Okay, Martin, whereabouts did you drop her off and wait?" Lenny asked.

Martin seemed to have regained his enthusiasm to help and sat forward.

"About sixty to seventy metres past the cab dealership is a row of arches. If memory serves, about five. Four are working for servicing and repairs. The other has black double doors and a smaller normal one as an inset."

"Astonishing," said Matt, "You got all that from just dropping her off?"

"No, I was waiting for her about half an hour, and don't forget I'm a London cab driver, large hippocampus and all."

"Hippo what…?"

"Campus," said Lenny, "The part of the brain that controls the memory."

"Oh, don't you start as well," Matt groaned.

Lenny carried on driving slowly down Heming Street. As they neared the arches in question, he slowed and stopped ten metres short. He turned to Matt and said, "So how we going to do this?"

"Okay, you stay with Martin in the car. I'll go and knock the door. Put your ear comms in and we'll know soon enough, if we have to use the backup.'"

"Okay, what happens if they let you in?"

"Well, just listen to what goes on. I'm sure we will know soon enough if it's going south, in which case call for the backup. They are positioned, so it would be a matter of minutes. I'm Alpha one and you're Alpha two, and base, who will be listening, is Alpha zero. So comms in and turn the power pack on, and we'll be heard and traceable."

"Okay, copy that."

Listening to all this, Martin said, "Do I get an ear piece too?"

"You're lucky to be alive, remember?" Matt said. Martin again sat back and said nothing. Matt looked at Lenny.

"Oh…by the way, Lenny, get him to sign the form."

Lenny looked enquiringly.

"This one, the OSA." He handed it to Lenny.

"So what's that then?" asked Martin.

"The Official Secrets Act," said Matt.

"But…but…"

"There are no buts, Mr Long, it's necessary."

"What if I don't? It's my choice and I have helped."

"You don't have a choice, and we thank you for your help and service to your country!"

"I did my service nearly forty-five years ago. I think I'm good for it!"

"Yes, and we thank you for that too, now sign…please." Martin grudgingly took the paper from Lenny and signed it. Reaching over, Matt took it from him and put it in a folder. Matt then opened the door, looked at Lenny and said, "Remember, listen to everything that goes on and, if you hear it going bad, call in the cavalry."

"Copy that," said Lenny.

Matt got out and walked towards the arch with the black doors. On the way he radioed in, "Alpha Zero, this is Alpha One, am approaching identified target."

"Alpha One, this is Alpha Zero, Roger that, we will maintain silence and just listen."

"Roger that, Alpha One out." Matt continued towards the black inset door.

He reached the double doors and saw an entry phone system on the right hand side of the inset door. There was also a camera on the top of the box that included a speaker and just one button to press. Obviously, he realised his options were limited. He stood back and checked for any other CCTV cameras, but none were visible. Moving forward again, he pressed the button. No answer. He pressed again and waited. There was a crackling noise, like static, and a voice said, "Hello, what do you want?"

Without thinking, Matt said, "Banu sent me."

"Who?"

"Banu."

"Don't know anyone of that name."

"Well, don't think I got it wrong. You sure you don't know who I mean?"

"I already told you, never heard of them. Now go away."

"But she said you were the person to see about getting some hardware."

"What hardware? We don't sell hardware. You want hardware, there's plenty of those shops in Bethnal Green Road. We only do motor servicing."

The intercom went quiet. Matt stood there for a few seconds and, as he walked back to the car, he spoke, "Zero, did you get that?"

"Roger Alpha One. Obviously not the response we needed, but maybe maintain discreet surveillance and see what happens over the next few hours."

"Zero, yes, I was going to suggest that, and maybe we can get the okay to enter if we feel the need?"

"Copy that, Alpha One. We'll get on it."

"Roger that, Zero." Matt got back into the rear seat of the car.

"You get all that?" he said to Lenny, who nodded and switched off the comms pack.

"Yeah, got it all. The guy was obviously stalling for time, so we sit and wait now and see who, if anyone, emerges."

"Yeah, I brought some surveillance gear with me, in case we needed to stay for a bit. It's in the boot. We need to park up somewhere a little less exposed though, but with a good view. Is there a back way out of the arch?"

"No, some have a rear entrance but these back on to the railway banking, and, unless they've dug a tunnel, there's one way in and out," Martin said suddenly. Matt switched on the comms pack again and spoke, "Alpha Zero, you copy?"

"Roger Alpha One, we copy."

"Zero, can you get an up to date map of the area around the target. We need to make sure there isn't a rear exit."

"Copy that, Alpha One. We'll get on that now and send it over to your mobile."

"Copy that, Zero, thanks…out."

They found a less obvious place to park, where they had a view of the arches. Matt got the surveillance gear from the boot and set up the camera, a Nikon D7500 SLR, along with a Nikon AF-S FX Nikkor 24 – 120mm F/SGED vibration reduction zoom lens with auto focus, and a set of Bushnell Power View 20x50 Super High Powered surveillance binoculars: total kit price around £1900. Martin looked at the equipment.

"Okay, which one can I use?" he said.

"Thanks for the offer, Martin," Matt responded, "But I think Lenny and me have this covered!"

"Oh, spoil sport. So what do I do?"

"I think you've helped out tremendously, so thanks for that," said Matt, "We'll get you a ride back to your cab."

Martin, looking just a little crestfallen, sat back and muttered some more. Matt made a call on his mobile phone and requested a car to come and get Martin. Lenny looked at Martin.

"It's for your own protection, Martin," he said, "We're not sure what we may be dealing with here and we really don't want you to come to any possible harm."

"It's okay, mate, I understand. Just haven't had as much fun and excitement for years. Not since my army days, I think."

"Yeah, and I echo what Lenny said, Martin, and you really have been helpful, so thanks from me too."

"No problem, mate. Trouble is, I don't think driving a cab is going to be the same for a while, still I've got a few stories to wax lyrical about."

Matt said mischievously, "That's okay, of course, but don't forget the OSA!" Martin looked at him puzzled and said "OSA?"

"Official Secrets Act."

"Oh, for fuck's sake, I nearly forgot!"

"Good job I mentioned it then?"

"Yep, but I'll change the names and embellish a bit. That'll be okay, me old mate, won't it?" Before Matt could answer, his phone rang. It was the driver of a car that had parked up behind them. Matt just said, "Okay," and clicked off. "Your ride back is here, parked up behind us," he said to Martin. They said their goodbyes and thanked him again. He walked back to the car behind and got in. Then the car pulled out and sped off.

Matt got out of the back and joined Lenny in the front of the car. He handed Lenny the binoculars.

"Right, let's get to it," he said.

Matt's phone pinged. He looked at the screen, brought up the attachment to the email he had received and scrolled through it.

"Looks like Martin was right about the place – there's only one entrance and egress."

"Yep, he sure was, and the door has just opened," replied Lenny. Matt looked up quickly, raised the camera and started clicking away, as the man walked down the street on the other side to where they were. The man was dressed in a white kufi (skull cap), a dark tunic top and trousers similar to the cargo style. Over the tunic top, he had a lighter beige medium length waistcoat. He hurried along and was quickly out of sight.

"Wonder where he's off to in such a hurry," Lenny said.

"No idea," said Matt, "But I doubt if it will be too long. He wasn't carrying very much, so the wait could be a short one." Lenny nodded.

As it turned out, Matt was more or less right, because fifteen minutes later the man in the kufi came back, driving a medium-sized flat bed truck. He pulled up to the double doors of the arch, got out of the truck, opened the doors and got back in the truck. He then reversed it into the darkened interior of the arch, pulled the doors closed and locked them. Matt and Lenny waited a few more minutes and, to no real surprise, three other men arrived, all dressed similarly to the first man. One of the men used a mobile phone and, a minute or so later, the first man opened the inset door to the arch. The three men entered.

Matt looked at Lenny.

"Think it's time for the show to start," he said.

Lenny nodded, "Yep, think it's time."

Matt turned on the comms pack again.

"Zero, this is Alpha One, do you copy?"

"Alpha One, go ahead. What is the current status?"

"Zero, we have activity at the target. We think it's moving day."

"Copy that, Alpha One. Are you calling for the standby unit?"

"That's an affirmative, Zero."

"Copy that, Alpha One, we will initiate deployment."

"Copy that, Zero. Out."

They waited for just a few minutes, by which time local police traffic units had sealed off the surrounding area. That was followed by two full units of armed officers, approaching the target arch from the north and south. Matt and Lenny got out of the car, approached the senior officer in charge of the armed units and produced their creds. Matt spoke with her for about two minutes and apprised her of the current status. They agreed how to proceed to try and resolve the situation as quietly as possible but were sure that if needed, sufficient force, her units, were ready to extract the suspected terrorists from the arch. They decided the initial approach would be by Matt. He would do the same as before. Lenny looked at him and offered, "You know there's not even gonna be an answer this time, don't you?"

"Well, we have to try as it's the way we do things. We don't want the unnecessary loss of life, do we?"

"Yeah, well like they give a damn!"

"Well it doesn't matter what they think. This is the way we will do it."

"Okay, you're the boss."

"No, actually I am."

They all turned to find Wyndham striding towards them.

"You'll have to excuse my officers, Inspector. Obviously there's a difference of opinion, but we'll go with Mr Flynn to begin with, but my expectation is it may end up as Mr Resnick believes it will." He showed his creds to the Chief Inspector and they shook hands. He guided her off for a private word and Matt and Lenny looked a little frustrated and surprised.

"What's his problem? Does he usually feel the need to hold his field officer's hands?" Lenny said.

"No, never had this situation before."

Wyndham walked back and told them to go with the initial thought, but that would change at the first sign of trouble or if there was no answer. Lenny went to say something, but Wyndham held up his hand, with his palm facing Lenny. "Lenny, I know," he said, "But as Matt has already told you, we will follow protocol, and if the situation demands, as I expect it will, we'll go with the scenario you have suggested. So let's get this done as efficiently as possible. Matt, you're good to go."

"Okay, boss," they both said.

Everyone else kept out of immediate sight, whilst once again, Matt walked to the door of the arch. He pressed the buzzer, and, once again, there was no answer, so he tried once more. He waited, but nothing was happening. He stood as close as he could to the door and put his ear to it. There were sounds, but nothing substantial that he could make out, until he heard a familiar click. He moved sharply to his right, before six rapid-fire bullets came through the wooden door. They waited, in case there was more gunfire. In the meantime, the Chief Inspector sent two of her armed officers with a door enforcer and a black spray paint canister. They stood with Matt, and asked him if there were any other sightings of CCTV. He replied that he hadn't seen any, and that there wasn't anything obvious. One of the officers sprayed the door intercom and blacked out the camera. They listened for any further activity but, again there was nothing obvious. They went back to their respective bosses.

Wyndham and the Inspector had a conversation and agreed the next steps, hoping that would end the problem. There was a realisation that there could well be loss of life, but, as Lenny had previously commented, the terrorists wouldn't care about that, as they would die martyrs.

Matt and Lenny returned to the perimeter that had been set up by the armed unit and waited with Wyndham. The senior officer took charge and, through her comms, gained the okay from her command centre to proceed to enforcement. The armed unit had added lights to their helmets, since they were confident that the initial lighting would be nonexistent. Four of the unit stepped forward with two large metal enforcers, one for each of the large doors. Going through the small inset one was totally discounted, as being too much of a gamble because one shooter could kill each officer as they came through the door. The idea was a smaller and compact version of shock and awe.

The two with the enforcers hit the doors with great force, once, twice and, on the third hit, the doors buckled inwards. As that happened, the other two officers fired smoke grenades and stood back. When they did this, a volley of bullets flew past them. Luckily, they missed everything and hit the walls of buildings opposite. The rest of the armed unit then moved forward. Shining into the dark arch, the lights from their helmets now began to pick out the terrorists, coughing and spluttering from the smoke. The officers in unison moved in, shouting, "Armed police, put your weapons down and lay on the ground face down."

Two of the terrorists raised their weapons to fire, but their inevitable slowness only accelerated their exit from this world. Four officers, with weapons set to rapid, returned fire and didn't miss their targets. Both terrorists fell to the ground, dead in a matter of seconds. Seeing this, the other three occupants of the arch came out, guns thrown to the floor, and, with arms aloft, they sank to their knees and lay face down.

The other officers moved in to the arch and secured it, but Wyndham, Matt and Lenny held back, until they were invited in by the Inspector. Wyndham was first up to her and offered his appreciation of a job well done, with minimal loss of life and her officers all intact.

"We should, hopefully, get some good information out of the remaining three that will help us track down a couple of the Lords terrorists still at large," he said.

Within twenty minutes, the scene was flooded with Forensic Officers, plain clothes from Anti-Terrorism, as well as the Met's Commander of that unit and the Met Police Commissioner.

Wyndham spoke with all of the brass, as Matt and Lenny were guided through the arch to a back office, where they had discovered a large cache of arms: assault rifles, pistols and automatic weapons, and a number of other items. "Well, looks like we found the armourer for the attack," Lenny said to Matt, "Let's hope we can get something from the three live ones as to the whereabouts of the two females."

"Wouldn't hold your breath on that, as they've probably been warned and are now long gone."

"We'll see. I just have a feeling this isn't finished quite yet," responded Lenny.

"Well, I think you're wrong on that one. I'd have been on my toes and away somewhere far from here, by now."

They walked outside and met up again with Wyndham, who said, "I think we're done here. Forensics will be a while yet, and the three prisoners are going to a maximum-security police station where they will be held overnight and interrogated under the Act tomorrow. I understand there's a bit of an arms haul in there? We obviously found the armourer then."

"Yes, boss. Lenny and I were just saying the same thing."

"Well, that will all be bagged and taken into an evidence-holding unit, ready for any trial."

Lenny looked at Wyndham in amazement.

"Any trial? You sound like there may not be one?" he said.

"Well, Lenny. I always like to err on the side of caution. I think you can understand that?"

"Yes, I do, strangely."

"Good, so you and Matt get back to the grid and start your reports. Most can wait till tomorrow. And then get some rest. I think, and hope, we're near the end of this horror show. I'll see you both bright and early." He walked off towards the crime scene, with the Commissioner.

"See, even the boss reckons we're near the end on this one," Matt said to Lenny.

"As I said, Matt, don't hold your breath."

They walked back to the car and drove off to Millbank, where they spent an hour going through the main points of the day. By around 22.30 they decided to head home to get some rest.

It was about 23.15 when they finally pulled up at Matt's apartment block, where they parked and went up to the flat. As they went in, a car across the road that had been there for several hours started up and began to drive away.

Banu looked at the apartment block.

"So, Mr MI5, you and your Israeli friend found and destroyed my armourer and his business. Enjoy it for tonight because tomorrow, finally, I will take my revenge for all my fallen comrades, and hopefully it will be your last day in this world too!" Bilquis hit the accelerator and sped off towards Chelsea Bridge.

Matt and Lenny were up bright and early the following day, as there was much to do. The mundane came first, finishing their reports on the previous day's incident, but then they were to go back down to the site and go over anything that they had been unable to get to previously, because of the forensic team's urgent need to make sure the scene didn't get contaminated.

As soon as they'd finished breakfast, they went down to the car. It was another glorious summer's day and the temperature was already up at 22°C, although it was only 08.30. They drove off, full of thoughts of taking a well-earned break to rest and recuperate, especially Lenny, who was wondering how quickly it would be till he got on that plane where the end destination would be Ben Gurion Airport. Jody and the girls would be waiting at the arrivals, no doubt about it. He turned to Matt and asked, "So where you thinking of going on your vacation, once we're done with this?"

"Dunno. My parents have a lovely house in a place called Moffat in the Scottish borders. I think I might just go up and sleep for a long time, then do some walking and get some good old fashioned clean air in my lungs, along with some great sea food and local farmed beef and lamb to nourish me."

"Sounds great, and I can't wait to see Jody and the girls."

"Okay, enough of the day dreaming," said Matt, "We've got a busy schedule today and, first things first, we need to get our reports into Wyndham as soon as possible, so that we can get over to Bethnal Green and see if there's anything that will lead us to the two females we need to find ASAP."

"Thanks for that reality check, mate. I'd almost made it to the airport there, for a minute!"

"Sorry, Lenny, but you know, as soon as we're done, I'll take you to the plane and put you on myself, promise."

"Yeah, okay, I appreciate that."

Matt parked up and they went into the building by the front entrance on Millbank, through security, up to the grid and to their stations. The work they had begun the night before was still where they had left it. They both checked where they had got to and, once satisfying their memories, had re-engaged with the events of the previous day. They spent around an hour completing the reports that Wyndham had requested. Then they checked each other's and, satisfied that they had interpreted the conclusions correctly, placed them into separate folders and walked to Wyndham's office.

Matt knocked and waited.

"Come," said the familiar voice and they both walked in to Wyndham's office.

"Good morning, gentlemen. I hope you have rested well. We have a full day ahead at the scene in Bethnal Green, so I presume those are your reports of the events yesterday, in full and factual detail?"

Matt replied for both of them, "Yes, boss, that's about the long and short of it."

"Good, just put them on the desk, and then we can get on. Take a seat. I'll get Jennifer to come in. We need a brief discussion before you get down to the scene. We'll follow you down later. We have to see the Home Secretary and give her a brief outline of yesterday's events, along with the commander of the Armed Unit and from Anti Terrorism. But we'll be back as soon as we're done." Wyndham picked up his phone and called Hardie. About two minutes later, she knocked and walked in. After exchanging pleasantries, she sat down next to Matt. They had a brief discussion regarding the aftermath of the previous day and, again, Wyndham mentioned the visit to the Home Office. Matt was a little concerned about what would be told to the Home Secretary, as she was something of a controversial character.

"Will your report to the Home Sec be a full one, boss?" asked Matt.

"It will be as full as needs be," replied Wyndham.

"Roger that," said Matt.

"Okay, now you both need to get down to Bethnal Green. Jennifer and I have a few more things to discuss, but we'll see you there as soon as."

Lenny and Matt walked out of the building and down to their parked car.

"So you want to tell me what all that was about the Home Secretary?" asked Lenny.

"Oh, she's a bit of a strange character. She has a tendency to say controversial things and be a bit of a loose cannon."

"Shit, how on earth did that happen?"

"I can see you don't follow the political scene too closely then?"

"Are you kidding? I've never yet seen a politician that I thought had my best interests at heart, and, in any case, I didn't vote for the current lot, mainly because I'm a Jew, although I might have done if they'd had someone like the 1997 guy."

"Yeah, well, I can understand that, although things didn't go too well for him in the end."

"No, maybe not, but he definitely had a clearer view of real events worldwide."

Lenny drove once again, and they chatted generally about the case and the attack, as well as what they hoped would be the end of the situation very soon.

They arrived at the arches in Heming Street about thirty minutes later. Having made themselves known to the lead forensics officer and the Senior Police Officer, they were cleared to go back into the arch to sort through any of the evidence that had been found, before it was bagged and taken away as evidence.

Most of the documents found had already been bagged, and the hardware there consisted of several cases of arms hidden behind a false wall. That had also been labelled and made ready for removal to a secure site. When Lenny and Matt entered the back room of the arch, after they had notified the Senior Police Officer, they needed some time to evaluate the documents to see if there was more information that would take the search for the two women any further. It took them a few hours to go through it all, and they managed to extract a number of documents that gave them more detail on the one who had been the original assassin: Banu Behzadi was her complete name, and she was now not only the person of interest as the contractor who had arranged the attack, but was also now confirmed as having a grievance with Lenny from years past in Israel. The other female, who was the accomplice to Banu, was Bilquis Anzorova, originally from Chechnya.

This now also confirmed that she was the girl on the bus taking pictures of the two men that had been the target for assassination. In addition, they had sketchy details of mobile numbers and places that had been rented on short stay lets, which would now also need to be checked. That, however, would be given over to the Met Police for them to do the legwork in the morning, as soon as they'd run the findings past Wyndham.

"Not sure why this information is here," Matt said to Lenny, "But I'm glad it is, and it seems that this small ring of terrorists just got a bit bigger."

"Looks like a lot more legwork and investigation for somebody," Lenny responded.

"Yeah, us, most likely," Matt smiled back at Lenny.

Matt had a call from Wyndham to say that the Home Secretary was in need of a full briefing regarding the attack, the aftermath and the latest situation at the latest anti-terrorism action in Bethnal Green. It was of particular interest to her, as her parliamentary constituency was quite close. Therefore he would wait to see Matt and Lenny back at the grid. Matt had also told Wyndham about the latest findings, in response to which the latter had just heaved a deep sigh and ended the call.

Later, during the course of the afternoon, Matt had a call on his phone. Lenny watched Matt's face contort through a number of expressions. Finally, he finished the conversation by saying, "Okay, we'll see you later, around 22.30," and he put his phone down. Lenny looked at Matt enquiringly.

"So who we seeing later?" he asked.

"Dan, he's sounding a bit frazzled and wants to work out his exit from here and a new identity for settling elsewhere, probably away from the Middle East."

"You gonna be able to arrange that?"

"Yeah, should be able to. I'll run it by Wyndham in the morning."

They worked on for another few hours, gathered up all of the information they had gained and left the arch around 18.30.

They were back at Millbank around forty minutes later: the traffic had been bad. After parking the car, they went back up to the grid. Matt went straight in to see if Wyndham was in his office. He knocked but there was no answer. He opened the door and looked in, but the room was empty. He closed the door and went over to see if Jennifer

Hardie was there. Same routine, and the same result, no answer and the room was empty. He walked over to where the two PAs sat, and Wyndham's told Matt that the Home Secretary had wanted a full debrief on everything to do with the action yesterday and the original attack. It seemed that Wyndham had called and spoken to his PA, asking her to tell Matt not to wait for him but to go home when he was finished, and that he would catch up in the morning. Matt thanked her and went back to his place on the grid.

Around 20.00, Matt walked over to Lenny.

"Think we can call time on this one today," he said.

"Yeah, that's good for me," said Lenny, "Just got to make a phone call and I'll be right with you."

"Jody?" asked Matt.

"No, strangely enough. It's to Martin. He left a message on my mobile asking me to call him. I'll just be a few minutes."

"Okay, come and get me when you've finished."

"Okay." Matt went back to his desk, whilst Lenny found a quiet place and called Martin. They spoke for a few minutes and Lenny agreed to meet Martin at the same restaurant in King's Road at around 21.00.

Lenny went back and found Matt at his desk. He explained that he had agreed to meet Martin and told him why, but said he would take Matt home first and then go back to the King's Road to meet Martin.

Twenty minutes later, Lenny dropped Matt off and drove off towards the Albert Bridge end of Prince of Wales Drive. Once over Albert Bridge, within five or so minutes, he was parking outside the restaurant in the World's End area of the King's Road. He got out of the car, noticed that Martin's cab was there and walked into the restaurant. He saw Martin immediately and started to walk over, when he saw the same waiter as he'd seen the last time he was there.

"Buonasera, Signor, how are you?"

"Hi, I'm good, thanks, and how are you?"

"Si, Signor, I'm also good. You here to see Martin?"

"Yep."

"Can I get you anything?"

"Just an Americano, please, no milk, thank you."

"You're welcome, Signor, please take a seat. I'll bring it over."

Lenny went to where Martin was sitting and smiled. They shook hands and he sat opposite him.

"So what's up, Martin? We really did appreciate your help the other day."

The waiter brought over Lenny's coffee.

"That's okay, Lenny. Happy to help."

"So what can I do for you? It sounded urgent."

"Well, it sort of is, or least ways could be."

"Okay, I'm listening."

"Well, apart from what I told you, I've remembered something else, about the woman I picked up. There was also something that happened when I took her back to her hotel…"

"Yes, you said. So what is it?"

"Well, she was carrying the hand luggage and the box, and pulling a medium-sized suitcase too. But I notice someone hanging around at the hotel outside, possibly from the same part of the world, and they seemed to be waiting for someone. When she got out of the cab, the other person suddenly became interested, and walked towards the hotel too, also with a suitcase."

"So was it another woman, and could you describe her?"

"Never said it was a her, in fact it was a him!"

"A him? Now that is interesting. Can you describe him?"

"Yes, fairly sure I can."

Lenny took out a notebook and pen, and said, "Okay, ready when you are."

Martin spent about five minutes describing the mysterious man and Lenny wrote down all the details. When Martin had finished, Lenny sat for a while and thought about the description. There was something bothering him about it, but couldn't figure out what that was. He told Martin he was curious about the description and that he would like to get an artist's impression from the details and run it through face recognition to see if anything matched up. He thanked Martin again and said he would be in touch. Martin told him he wouldn't be around for a few days, as he was going in for some tests.

"Nothing serious," he said, and to call him next week. Lenny said he would, wished him well and left the restaurant.

As he got back into the car, he called Matt to say he had some more information on another possible suspect. Matt asked him if there was a description, and Lenny told him there was and that he would show him when he got back to the flat. Matt told him ASAP as Dan was expected very soon. Lenny sat for a few minutes and let some of the details sink in, as there was something familiar in Martin's description that bothered him. Nothing obvious came to mind, so he started the car and drove off in a hurry, as there were only a few minutes left before Dan arrived.

Pulling up to the apartment block on Prince of Wales Drive, Lenny managed to find a parking space just up from the entrance. He got out and, as he was walking up to the entrance, there came a voice from behind him.

"Hi, Lenny, you going into Matt's?" Lenny spun around to see who it was and realised it was Dan standing there.

"Dan, hi, you startled me!"

"Sorry, didn't mean to. I just walked up too. Come on, let's go in." They walked in and chatted, as they climbed the stairs.

Across the road, the driver of a parked vehicle watched the proceedings, picked up a mobile phone and text a message. It was received and the response came immediately reading, *"OKAY. THANKS."*

Lenny and Dan reached the door of Matt's flat and Lenny opened it with his key. They both entered and Lenny called out, "Hi, Matt, I'm back. I met Dan outside so we're both here." Strangely there was no answer. Lenny and Dan looked at each other and Lenny mouthed to Dan, "Something's not right, you go in and I'll follow." Dan nodded. He walked the four or so paces to the living room door and his eyes widened when he saw Matt, sat tied up in an upright chair, half conscious and blood coming from his right cheek, where he'd obviously been hit, probably with the handle of a gun. As Dan looked to his right, there was a woman with a gun, who, as he turned to her, yelped and screamed, "Y O U! Hossein, you bastard! What are you doing here? Please don't tell me you work for these infidels!"

"Banu, my dear, put the gun down and let me explain."

"Explain… what's to explain? It's obvious you have committed the most treacherous act imaginable. Now I begin to understand why they knew where everyone was on the day of the attack. You told them, you bastard. May you rot in hell for this! May your ancestors drive you there, you low life scum!"

Tears ran down her cheeks. He started to move towards her, but he wasn't quick enough. Stepping back, she shot him straight through the heart. As he fell, she went over and put another bullet in his head. Ever the assassin.

Her wits returned quickly and, hearing Matt shout for Lenny as he regained more of his senses, Banu realised there was still someone else she needed to settle with. She moved a little further back, holding her Glock 19 ready for her final kill.

Suddenly realising why Martin's description of the other person at the hotel in Paddington had sounded familiar, Lenny had to think quickly. He was now, outside the lounge door and had heard everything. He was still carrying his own weapon and decided he was going to go in low, but he would switch the lights off before he did. He knew where she was: he'd seen her through the gap at the side of the door. Banu called to him, "You've got five seconds to come in, Lenny, or your friend here dies, and you know I will, it's what I do."

Lenny thought momentarily and as she got to five, he hit the light switch. He dived in and fired six shots in the direction he knew Banu had been, but as he did so, she did the same and he fell behind a sofa.

Banu had been hit by two of the shots, one in the left arm by the bicep and the other in the fleshy part of the thigh. Just then, sirens could be heard, drawing nearer. Matt had managed to get to the panic button he carried with him in his pocket, and then passed out again.

Banu didn't know if Lenny was dead. She was very sure she'd hit him, but there was no time to find out. She made her way out of the flat and hobbled over to where Bilquis was waiting in the car. When she saw Banu, she started the engine, got out and helped Banu get into the back. She laid her down, then got back behind the wheel and sped off in the opposite direction to the sirens, back towards Kensington.

In the flat, Lenny lay there, still conscious, although he had been hit and was losing blood. His thoughts were for his wife, Jody, and his two girls, Ella and Jess. He could hear the sirens and knew they would be there any moment, but the fight weakened. In another few moments, there were shouts from outside, "Armed police! Armed police!" but his eyes closed and he lost consciousness.

The light was white, but there were shadows. He ached all over and could hear muffled sounds, like people talking. He just lay there, wondering who he was and where he was. His memory, albeit temporarily and unknown to him, was a blank but would return. His consciousness drifted back into slumber and he began to dream.

By his bedside were his wife, a friend, two doctors, consultant and registrar, as well as a nurse. It was a private wing in an NHS hospital just south of the River Thames, London.

The consultant surgeon looked at the man's wife, and said, "Your husband should make a full recovery. We have repaired the damage to the arm, as the bullet fortunately passed through and missed the bicep muscles and exited with very little damage to important tissue. It missed anything vital. The bullet in the leg, however, didn't pass through and lodged in a dense section of flesh and muscle. It missed the femoral artery by about three millimetres, so he's very lucky because had it hit, he could have bled out. So, as I have said, extremely fortunate."

There was a sharp intake of breath by Jody Resnick, now turning her gaze in the direction of Matt Flynn.

"You hear that? Lucky! LUCKY!" her voice was now raised and beginning to tremble, "Why the hell was he there in the first place, Matthew Flynn? Come on! Tell me! He should have been with his family, relaxing and without stress!" Voice still raised, "SO, COME ON, TELL ME!"

At that moment they all heard it.

"J-o-d-y, do you really have to shout so loud?"

She suddenly stopped shouting and said, "Oh my god! He's

awake!" She rushed over to Lenny, put her head to his chest, arms around his body and sobbed. Lenny lifted his good arm, which he put around the base of her neck and shoulders, and gave her the best squeeze he could. After a few minutes, Jody stopped crying.

Returning to consciousness, Lenny said, "It's okay now, honey, I'm okay. I'll be right in no time." She looked up at him, the redness of her eyes telling their own story.

"Will it, Lenny? Will you? You nearly died, for fuck's sake."

"Well, I didn't, did I?"

"And you think that's good? How come you were in that situation in the first place? Why were you there?"

"Too many questions, honey. My head hurts already."

"Look, Lenny, we've been worried sick for three days, not knowing if you'd wake up. The surgeon said you were very lucky, the bullet in the leg missed your femoral artery by a few millimetres."

"That's me, honey, lucky!"

"No laughing matter, HONEY, the girls have been beside themselves, not to mention your parents. They don't understand how you got mixed up with all this."

"Oh, shit, you didn't say anything…did you?"

"What, me? Tell your parents? What do you take me for? It'd be all over London if I had! No, of course not!"

"Oh, thank fuck for that. Don't think I could have taken that. Ooh, the questions! Can't even imagine! So, where are the girls? Are they here?"

"Yes, they're here with my sister."

"Oh, for one moment I'd thought you left them in Israel with Musha."

"No, we all came over, together. As soon as Lazar came round to tell us what had happened, we all decided to come back. He had it all arranged through work. Musha said it would be best, as she could look after the girls for a couple of weeks. She seemed to know Lazar quite well. At least that's what the girls and I think."

"Can't think why, he's nearer my age."

"No, don't think it's that sort of thing. Just that they know each other from somewhere else, I'm pretty sure of that."

"Why do you say that? Is there something else going on, that we've missed?"

"Okay, we've missed?"

"Well, yeah, she's your sister!"

"Yeah, and he's your friend, and you go way back."

"Maybe, but I don't see him or speak to him as often as you see or speak to Musha!"

"Okay, Lenny, this is going nowhere. You need to rest and, when you have recovered a bit more, you can speak to Lazar and I'll speak to my sister and then we'll compare answers."

"Looks like we'll make a spook out of you yet!"

"Hmph! I think you might wait a long time for that."

"Okay, honey, we'll both make enquiries, and then compare," Lenny started to drift back to sleep, "Really tired now, honey, just need to s l e e p for a bit."

He fell back into unconsciousness. The consultant surgeon came over and helped Jody up. She started to cry again.

"It's okay, Mrs Resnick," he said, "He's exhausted from all of the trauma of being shot and then the surgery and so on. His body needs to rest a lot more. He will recover – we are keeping a close watch on that, and will get him back to full health as soon as we can. It's just going to take a little time."

Jody nodded and walked away, back towards Matt Flynn. As she did, her sister Musha came in with Ella and Jess.

"Oh my god!" Musha exclaimed, seeing Jody wiping her eyes, "What's happened?"

"No, nothing, he's okay, just gone back to sleep," Jody quickly confirmed, "He really is okay!"

"It's okay, Mum, we're just glad we are here and can actually see him at last," said Ella. Jess just stood there, with tears beginning to well up. Jody saw this and gathered both of them into her arms and held them tightly. As they all began to cry, Jody's sister came over and put her arms around all of them.

Outside the door to the ward, Lazar Spiegal watched the proceedings. Happy that his friend was on the mend, he went out into the street and phoned his bosses back at Mossad and updated them, with some information received from Matt Flynn.

* * * * *

It was some days since she had shot and killed Hossein, after discovering his treachery, and shot her nemesis, Lenny. Although she had been injured in the process, she hoped that her injuries were significantly less than those she had meted out the Israeli cab driver, but she didn't know. However, with the help and quick wits of her most trusted friend, Bilquis, they had escaped.

Bilquis had seen Banu emerge from the apartment block, wounded and astonished that she had managed to get out, but obviously unaware that she had sustained her injuries in a very similar way to the way Lenny had been injured. After she had started the car, Bilquis left the engine running and stepped out to help her friend into the back seat, where she laid Banu down, covering her with a blanket.

Bilquis knew exactly where to go in case of any injuries: it was an event that they had calculated and made arrangements for, and she drove straight to the contact, a medical friend they knew would be able to help. Their destination was a large house on the edge of Hampstead Heath in North West London. The man, a qualified surgeon, originally from Iraq, was waiting for them in the underground garage of his house. As soon as Bilquis had text him, he started to prepare and make sure every eventuality was covered. When she arrived outside, Bilquis text again and the door had opened to the underground garage. The Iraqi surgeon was waiting for them. Once she had brought the car into the garage, Bilquis jumped out and opened the rear door. They lifted Banu out and laid her on the waiting gurney. Bilquis told the surgeon where the bullets had hit her friend and that she seemed to have stemmed the blood flow, by applying two tourniquets to arm and leg. She had also checked where both bullets had entered and exited.

The surgeon nodded and told her he would examine Banu for any other damage, but, if Bilquis was right, then the whole thing should only take a couple of hours, but he would sedate Banu and they would both need to rest, at least overnight. With that, the surgeon wheeled Banu off and into his private, underground operating room, where an experienced nurse was waiting to assist.

Bilquis took the opportunity to clean the car thoroughly, as there were some blood spatters, despite the fact that she had prepared for that eventuality by putting plastic sheeting across the back seat and on the floor.

After a couple of hours, the surgeon came back and found Bilquis. He told her that it had all gone well and that her quickness applying the tourniquets had played a major part in the fairly straightforward procedure. He said that the nurse had taken her up to a bedroom in the main house and would stay with her overnight to monitor her progress. In the meantime, he led Bilquis up to the main house, showed her to another bedroom and said for her to relax and shower if she needed. Suitable clothes were available for her to change into, and when ready she should come down and have some food. Bilquis nodded and went into the room, took her time showering and tried to unwind as best she could.

Thirty-six hours later, Bilquis and Banu were back in the car. The surgeon had given Banu enough medication to see her through her healing period. They drove off to complete the final part of their escape: to regroup, and plan for the future.

Two days later, they arrived in Beirut, having significantly changed their appearances to a more westernised look, thanks to Bilquis' skill with latex and make-up. They had journeyed on Eurotunnel, driven to Brussels and then taken a Middle East Airlines flight to Beirut.

* * * * *

Day four after the shooting, Lenny woke up with a start and looked around. The room was strange, but it was daylight outside, even though it was only 05.30. He gathered his thoughts, and tried to think back through his memory for what had led to him being in this room, with tubes, pipes and monitors around his bed.

Things began to come back. He saw in the chair by the bed, Jody, his wife, who was fast asleep. He could see her face, mainly white and drained of almost any colour, except around her eyes that were puffy and red, obviously from crying. He looked himself up and down, and thoughts and memories came flooding back. The journey back to Matt's flat from seeing Martin, meeting up with Dan, the shooting that killed Dan, and then him switching off the lights before diving into the room and firing his own weapon. Then the memory of being hit, twice, lying there, waiting and hearing the sirens as they came ever nearer.

He then had another thought.

"Shit!" he said.

That woke Jody up. Worried, she said, "Lenny, Lenny, what is it? Are you okay? Tell me!"

"No, it's okay. I'm fine. I just remembered what happened and why I'm here. Is Matt okay? The last thing I remember was seeing him bound in a chair, with blood streaming down his face."

"Oh God, is that all?"

"Well no, but is he okay?"

"Yes, unlike you, Mathew Flynn got off lightly."

"Well, I needed to know. Thank god for that."

"Lenny, just concentrate on getting yourself fit, to look after your family again."

"So how bad was I? I'm really hungry!"

"That's a little random. However, you're fine now but it was touch and go. But we've already had this conversation."

"Really? I don't remember." Jody spent a few minutes explaining how lucky he'd been, particularly the bullet to the leg and how it had been dangerously close to the femoral artery. Lenny started to well up at the thought of what he might have lost, and said how sorry he was. She got up from the chair, smiled and hugged him. She then left the room to go and find him some food and a hot drink.

About twenty-five minutes later, Jody arrived back with bags of food and coffees. As she walked in, she said, "Look who I found on the way back!" Following Jody into the room were Ella and Jess. As soon as they saw their dad, they rushed in and hugged him from both sides. They all burst into tears. After a few minutes, Lenny said, "Hey, come on, guys. I'm fine. Let's eat, I'm starving."

They took their time eating, drinking and chatting and catching up on the time they'd been apart. The privacy was broken at around 08.30 when the door opened and in walked the consultant surgeon, his registrar and a staff nurse, to check on the latest condition of the patient. They were a little surprised to see he had company, but were pretty relaxed about it.

"Good morning all," the surgeon said, "Would you mind if we had a few minutes with Mr Resnick? We need to examine him and take some of the vitals." Jody and the girls got up, said they would be back soon and left the medical team to it.

The consultant spent time talking with Lenny, whilst the registrar and nurse carried out the medical checks. The conversation with Lenny revolved around his recovery and recuperation, and what would be advisable in the short term, then the gradual build up to a fitness level that he was used to. Lenny was anxious to leave the hospital as soon as possible, but the consultant told him a few days, maybe three or four, would be necessary to be absolutely sure of him maintaining the progress to a full recovery.

None too pleased with this initial prognosis, Lenny finally relented when the registrar, who had been listening to her boss, whilst checking Lenny over, said to him, "Mr Resnick, for your own health prospect you need to listen to Mr Jacobs. He's not someone whose advice you want to take lightly. Your survival was totally down to his skill and ability." A little sheepishly, Lenny looked at the consultant and said, "Mr Jacobs? You're one of my lot?"

"Yes, Mr Resnick," he said, smiling, "Is that a problem?"

"No, no, not at all. I should have known. I bet your mother is very proud?"

There was a slight pause and then laughter broke out, just at the point when Jody and the girls walked back into the room.

"Well this is a happy little band," said Jody.

Mr Jacobs explained the reason for the laughter, and then said, "We're finished here, I think, so we'll leave you to it, Mr and Mrs Resnick. My team will be around throughout the next few days to keep a check on your progress, so we will assess and let you know when you can go home, and what help you'll need."

"Okay, doc, that sounds a plan, and thank you for all you've done," said Lenny.

"No problem, just doing what I'm trained for."

Mr Jacobs and his team left and closed the door. Jody stood there for a moment.

"So what's going on?" she asked.

"Nothing, just I'll be here for a few days more yet, until they think I'm fit enough to go home."

"Home?" said Jody, "Can we really go to our own home again, really? That would really be great!"

"Is my mobile around? I'll phone Matt and get things moving, and then arrange that vacation as soon as." Jody handed him his phone from the bedside cabinet and he dialled Matt.

Matt Flynn was back at his station on the grid at MI5, and was waiting to see the Head of Section, Mike Wyndham, for a debriefing on the events at his flat four days previously. Under normal circumstances, this would have been carried out earlier, but because of the injuries he sustained, he was given time to recover and rest, although he hadn't completely recovered by the time he returned to work. His flat had been a crime scene, so he was given the use of a safe house, until the forensic team had finished and workmen had completed the necessary repair work.

He was just gathering his papers together and printing out his report, when his phone rang. He looked at it, saw it was from Lenny and answered immediately. "Lenny, great to hear from you. How's it going?"

"Hi, Matt, yeah, it's going okay. The doc says another few days and they'll let me go!"

"That's great news, Lenny. I'm so glad you're on the mend."

"Well, that makes two of us. Listen, when I'm discharged, Jody, me and the girls want to go home. Can we do that? I mean, is there still a possible threat or are we sure enough that the danger has subsided?"

"That, my friend, is one of those imponderables that could be determined either way. The forensics team are still going over my flat and will take a while. However, they did find shell casings from where you were firing and you certainly hit her, as there was blood and flesh on two of them, so no danger at the moment? So can't really answer that, but probably not!"

"Do you want to try that again in English? All we want to do is go home and try and get our lives back."

"Lenny, I'm just about to see Wyndham for my debrief, so I'll ask him to get a risk assessment carried out in the next day or so. If you're going to be there for a few more days, I'll come visit and bring the conclusions with me."

"That's sounds great, thanks for that. See you in a day or two." They rang off.

"So what did he say?" asked Jody, "Can we go home?"

"He's gonna get a risk assessment done and let us know before I get discharged."

"So how long?"

"A couple of days, honey. They'll do it quickly. It'll depend if they think the person that shot me is dead, alive or even in the country. Apparently, they think I hit her twice. Hopefully, they'll pick up answers from the chatter they listen to as well as other intel."

"Well, let's hope the shots made it terminal! So, okay, you're here for a few more days anyway, but we're not living with Matt Flynn. I'd rather we go to my parents, in fact I'd even rather go to your parents, if it came to it!"

"Well, none of that is happening, trust me."

"Yeah, we've done that and you ended up being shot."

"Oh Jody, don't go there again. I had to help out, you know that. Getting shot wasn't part of the plan!"

"Lenny, you nearly died, for fuck's sake. Do you realise how close that was?"

"Yes, I do. Don't keep reminding me. I feel bad enough!"

Jody realised it was now upsetting him, so she kept quiet. The girls went over and sat on the bed with their father and started asking questions about what happened. Lenny was reticent at first, but realised he owed them an explanation. Not long after, he was telling other stories about the work he was doing and, at times, making them all laugh.

Matt was called in to see Mike Wyndham. With them was Jennifer Hardie. Before he started, he mentioned his conversation with Lenny, and his wish to go home, once discharged from the hospital. Wyndham nodded and then asked Hardie to action the risk assessment straight away, also to liaise with GCHQ to see if there had been any relevant chatter. He needed to check with other agencies for any evidence if the two female suspects were either still in the country, alive or had escaped. Jennifer Hardie was extremely adept at knowing where to go and who to ask. She nodded at Wyndham and left the room to get things moving ASAP.

As soon as she left, Wyndham turned to Matt.

"Thanks for coming in, Matt," he said, "You really are entitled to some leave, and as soon as we've finished and Lenny is good to move back home, you can sign off for a couple of weeks!"

"Thanks, boss. I think I'll need that by then. The last few months have been intense."

"Yes, they have, and we still haven't closed the enquiry into the original attack. Mind you, we do think the two females, with several people's blood on their hands, may be the last two of the terrorists still alive."

"So do we think they're still here or have they, more likely, escaped and fled the country?"

"Well, this is the problem: until we get conclusive evidence to the contrary, we must assume that they're still here."

"That's a problem then. Lenny and his family really want to go home as soon as possible."

"Look, we have a few days yet. Let's wait and see what happens with our enquiries and when the hospital says they can discharge him. But whatever the outcome, we'll make whatever arrangements will be right for Lenny and his family. We've imposed on them enough." Matt nodded in agreement.

They spent the next hour or so going through the whole case from the beginning, up to the attack at Matt's flat four days ago.

It was more than a recap, insofar as it incorporated a complete debrief of how the terrorist, Banu, had been able to gain access, so easily, to his apartment building, as well as how it had been possible to miss the situation with Dan. Although acting as an embedded asset, he was likely working with the terrorists, having gone native. There was also the distinct probability that he had had a hand in a number of related incidents and murders.

Wyndham had informed Matt, during the debrief, that the Home Secretary was demanding a public inquiry be set up, but she was brought back to reality by the Cabinet Secretary, who advised her to temper her comments regarding the security services as they could not be expected to reveal operational activities in public. There would, however, be a number of sessions that he, Wyndham, Jennifer Hardie and Matt would have to attend, with the Intelligence and Security Committee. Thankfully, the members of that particular body were not headstrong and could be relied upon for discretion. It was all part of the scrutiny process carried out by the government on a fairly co-operative cross party basis, but always held in camera.

Matt finally left Wyndham's office and went back to his desk on the grid, until he was cleared for active duty in the field again. Something, right now, he really didn't mind doing. It also gave him time to clear what had become a large amount of paperwork, that wasn't going away any time soon!

* * * * *

Beirut was a city once known as the Jewel of the Middle East. Although still a place with many attractions, as well as having gone through a very extensive modernisation programme, sadly the jewel effect has somewhat diminished.

It is one of the world's oldest cities, with its first historical mention around the 15th Century BC. Lying at the eastern end of the Mediterranean Sea, it is now the capital of Lebanon and also the seat of its government. It has been, over many centuries, occupied by various peoples of the region and, of course, Europe. The Phoenicians, Greeks, Romans, Byzantines all ruled the city, till it was captured by Arab armies in 635 and then, in turn, Crusaders as well as the Ottomans have ruled the city. There are also significant signs of French occupation, primarily as it came under the French mandate after the First World War.

Banu and Bilquis had been in Beirut a couple of days and had taken a luxury suite in the plush Four Seasons Hotel, but were determined that their stay would be as short as possible.

Although Banu was still in some discomfort from her injuries, realistically she was glad to be alive. No injuries were visible, since she kept her leg and arm covered by wearing trousers and a long sleeved blouse. Her mobility was only hampered by the need to use a walking stick.

She was alone in the suite at the Four Seasons. Bilquis had gone out to make arrangements for a more permanent place to stay, whilst they decided whether their stay in Beirut would be permanent, or if they would need to relocate again at some time in the future. Money was no object, thanks to Sheikh AbdulWahab. A pity he had now passed on to the afterlife, she thought, he was a very generous man, with most things.

The immediate plan was to recover, not just from her physical injuries, but also from the heartbreak of discovering that the man she had been in love with and who she had hoped to spend the rest her life with, was in fact a traitor and a treacherous liar. Hossein or Dan, whatever his real name is turned out to be, was a double agent. She now suspected that there was much more she didn't know about him. He had totally fooled her and others for many years and that made her feel stupid. Killing him had been instinctive but sickening, and something she wouldn't have been able to do if there had been time to think. What was done was done, she briefly pondered, and now was time to think of the future, and how and when to finish her business with the author of her current troubles. But rest, recuperation and relaxation away from all of the past seven months was the only thing she wanted to do. She would return to the unfinished business when her mind and body had healed.

Bilquis returned from her excursion, with an excited look and, somewhat animated, she rushed into the hotel suite, looking like she was about to burst. "What is it?" asked Banu, "What's happened?"

"No, nothing particular, but I think I have found the best place for us to live."

"Where?"

"I don't think we could stay here for too long, without going mad. We need somewhere European where we will assimilate easily, no prying eyes and somewhere safe to go to after we've finished our business in London."

"Okay, I'm getting a little frustrated by your evasion of the question, so tell me before I go completely mad and throw my walking stick at you!"

Bilquis smiled at this and said to her friend, "So you're feeling better then?...Barcelona!"

"Yes, I am...What is Barcelona?"

"It's a city in Spain."

"Yes, of course I know that, but what about it and why?"

"It's the place where we should relocate, once we've finished our work. It is a port to the Mediterranean, has an international airport, very good transport links, and there is a fast train to Marseille, if we need it. On top of that, it holds regular events when many hundreds of thousands of tourists, sporting fans and so on, come in, swelling the population enough for us to be anonymous."

"Okay, that sounds good but when?"

"That's something for you to decide when you're ready, but I would say within the next three to six months, if we can stand it here that long!"

"Okay, that sounds doable, but I'm not sure if I can manage six months here. We need to try and move there within three months."

"Yes, I agree, but we need to use the new base as somewhere to go to after our business has finished in England."

"Okay, but where till then?"

"I have found one or two places to live, just outside the city, in relative secure and secluded areas where we can arrange all that we need to with no prying eyes, and it will give us the time to rest and recover, before we can sit back in our new home and enjoy life."

Banu sat and looked at her friend, smiled and said, "Okay, let's do it, but first we need to get out of this bloody madhouse they call Beirut!"

* * * * *

Matt Flynn arrived at the hospital where Lenny had been recovering from his injuries, and was now making good progress. As Matt walked into the room, Lenny was sat in an armchair by the side of the bed, and Jody and the girls were on a sofa, with a dining chair next to an oval shaped coffee table. When the door opened, they all stopped talking and looked at Matt, as he walked in. He waited momentarily, and then said, "Morning all. Hi, Lenny, how you feeling?"

"Yes, feeling more like my old self, and hoping to go home soon."

"Hope you've got some good news, Matthew Flynn, otherwise you can turn around and walk out again!" said Jody.

"Honey, you could have waited, just a little," said Lenny. Matt intervened by holding up his hand palm out.

"It's okay, Lenny, that's exactly why I'm here. Wyndham gave me the okay this morning to come and tell you, as soon as you are discharged you can move back to your home." There were shrieks of delight from Ella and Jess, and even Jody managed a broad smile. Jody looked at Matt.

"Well thank you, Matt," she said, "That's very welcome news, and not before time, but be sure to thank Mr Wyndham for me."

"You'll be able to do that yourself in about an hour. He's coming here to tell you how he wants to maintain a security presence around your home for the short term future and also wants to know where you want to spend your vacation time."

"Thought there'd be a catch somewhere. I don't want bodies guarding us though."

"No, nothing like that. It will be a bit more discreet, but he'll elaborate when he gets here. He's just finishing a meeting with his boss and then coming over." Jody and Lenny both nodded, and Lenny motioned for Matt to come and sit on the bed.

Jody and the girls took the opportunity to go and get some coffee, and Matt spoke with Lenny, updating him on the latest situation regarding the probable whereabouts of the two females.

"The feeling is that they left the country and it is pretty firm intel as the information that has been gathered points quite significantly to them having escaped the country by car. A number of manifests have been looked through and just a couple of car registrations were of interest, from the Folkestone Eurotunnel terminal. One vehicle went north from Calais and the other went east; we are working with the French authorities and Interpol to see if they're traceable, but we've had nothing back yet."

Lenny thought for a moment and then said, "Well, it all sounds like they somehow evaded capture, so that's not great, but as long as they're a long way away, we can only hope they don't reappear!"

"True, but, as Wyndham will explain, we're taking no chances."

They carried on and chatted for a while. Then Matt asked Lenny if he had a discharge date yet, but he hadn't. Lenny was curious about Dan and asked Matt how it was he turned out to be playing both sides. Matt explained that, because he'd been embedded for so long and the fact that not enough intelligence was gathered about his past, he had found it easy to play for two masters. British security services, knowing his mother had been British and his father had worked for the embassy in Beirut, had been less than assiduous in their checks on him and too many assumptions had been made. Lenny thought for a moment or two, and said, "So really I'm lucky he went into your living room first?"

Matt just nodded. "Yes, very lucky, but for fuck's sake, don't tell Jody!" he said.

"No, that's not a good idea." They went silent.

Lenny then told Matt that he was pretty sure a few more days would be about the maximum he'd be in the hospital: he'd had some good feedback from the consultant, and, if he was okay when they checked him out tomorrow, he could leave within thirty-six hours and would get the okay to go home, which was why Jody and the girls were impatient and couldn't wait.

As they finished, Mike Wyndham opened the door and walked in.

"Morning, Lenny, Matt. How's it going?"

Lenny responded, "Morning, boss, good to see you too!"

"You had us worried there for a while, you know?"

"Not as much as we were," said Jody, as she came back into the room with Ella and Jess. Wyndham and Matt turned and saw them. Thinking quickly, Wyndham smiled and walked towards Jody with his hand held out.

"Mrs Resnick, hello," he said, "I'm Mike Wyndham, Head of the Section. Your husband has been helping out. Good to meet you at last."

"Thank you, Mr Wyndham, and good to finally meet you too! Now tell me when can I take my husband back home?"

"That's exactly why I'm here, Mrs Resnick, and please call me Mike."

"Okay, Mike, so tell me, when can we take him home, and please call me Jody!"

"Well..er...Jody, I wanted to get your permission to enhance security around the house, nothing too intrusive, but, until we are sure that there is no further threat, we don't want to leave anything to chance. Your husband has been of great help to the internal security service and it is the least we can do."

"And when do you propose these changes take place?"

"As soon as possible, and that will involve work being carried out over the next week or so."

"I thought you said the work would not be intrusive?"

"Yes, that's correct, and we will need some time to do that. And so that you are not put out by the work we need to complete, you may as well take that holiday we promised you and your family. I'm sure Lenny will appreciate a couple of weeks with you all, along with some sun and relaxation?"

Looking on in amazement, Lenny decided to intervene.

"Yes, some sun and relaxation would be just what the doctors ordered, excuse the pun!"

"Glad to hear you're recovered enough take the vacation, Lenny. I'll get everything organised, as soon as the doc says you can travel. I must go now, as I have another briefing with the Home Secretary, but Matt can fill me in with the discharge details and we'll get you booked in. Let me know what you have in mind!"

With that Wyndham turned and left.

"Well, he seems quite nice, and helpful too!" Jody said.

"Looks are sometimes deceiving, but he does have his moments," Matt offered. Lenny sat in the chair and smiled.

"Someone find the doctor! I need a holiday!" he said.

CHAPTER
45

Three weeks later Matt Flynn had got up around 06.30, dressed and had breakfast, all before 07.15. Then he made his way out of his flat and down to the parked Peugeot 5008 he had signed out from the car pool. He had a favour to fulfil. He got in the car and began his journey down to Southampton, in order to meet some passengers disembarking from a returning Princess Line cruise ship, that had began its outward journey fourteen days earlier.

He found the correct terminal and parked up in a short stay car park. Although he knew that the docking time was at 08.00, the actual time he expected the passengers to begin the disembarkation was around 09.00, as the people he was meeting were all entitled to breakfast before leaving the ship.

Matt wandered over to the terminal he needed to be at, and found a place to eat. At around 08.30, he used his phone to send a message to one of the passengers. He received an immediate response that said, *"SHOULD BE COMING THROUGH ABOUT 09.15, SEE YOU AT ARRIVAL."* He didn't reply as there was no need. He had ordered his breakfast of scrambled eggs, bacon, sausage, hash browns and mushrooms, toast, and a large cup of black coffee.

About 20 minutes later, he put his knife and fork down on an empty plate, drank the last few gulps of coffee, picked up his phone and dialled a number. It was answered on the second ring, and the person on the other end asked if Matt was there and if all was okay. He replied it was all fine, and then asked whether everything was ready as he would be back at the destination around 11.45. He was told that all was in place and he would be met there by the boss.

It was now 09.15, as he made his way to the arrivals gate and

— 272 —

waited. Unlike many drivers there with hand held signs, meeting passengers they didn't know, Matt knew his, so he stood empty-handed, waiting for his arrivals to emerge through the gate anytime soon, after coming through immigration and customs. Being a large ship, there were several thousand passengers who had finished their holidays and were now looking to disembark.

The wait lasted longer than expected and it was now 09.40. A throng of passengers had already come through, but no sign of his. The flow had slowed to a trickle, when the doors opened again and more passengers walked out, wheeling suitcases and pushing luggage trollies. Then, at last, he saw who he was waiting for: Lenny, Jody, Ella and Jess, all wearing Princess Line baseball caps, sunglasses and shorts and T shirts, and pushing two very well-laden trollies.

They saw him quite easily, as he had made his way to the front of the crowd, after the initial flow had subsided. Matt walked towards the end of the barrier, where the exit was, and waited for them. As they reached him, Lenny was smiling and the girls were still busy chattering away, but the expression on Jody's face went from happy to concerned.

"Hi, Matt," said Lenny, "Didn't expect you to be here, although it was good to get your text."

And before Matt could answer, Jody said, "Hi, Matt, what's wrong?"

"Hi, Jody, Lenny, good to see you too! Nothing is wrong. Wyndham thought it a good idea to pick you up and take you back home. The work's all done, but I'll need to show you what has been completed. Then we need you to okay it, that's all."

"But Mike Wyndham said it would be unobtrusive?" said Jody, now frowning.

"It is, but you need to know where and what it all does, and I'll show you, nothing more. I'm expecting Mike Wyndham to be there as well."

"Okay," said Lenny, "Where's the car? Hope you've got one with plenty of room. We've got a lot to carry."

"It's over in the short stay. Wait here, I'll get it. Be about five minutes." Matt walked off in the direction of the short stay car park, whilst Jody, Lenny and the girls waited. The girls hadn't taken a breath from their endless chatter, but Lenny and Jody hadn't really noticed because they were now wondering what they might find when they eventually got home.

After a short stop at a service station on the M3 motorway, they finally arrived back at their home in North London. Any fears of major disruption were soon dispelled, as, at first look, it seemed as if nothing had really changed. In most respects, it hadn't, and, until they got inside, it looked just as it was when they had left just a few weeks before.

Lenny gave Jody a set of keys to open up, but Matt said, "We had to change the locks, so they won't work, I'm afraid!"

"So much for you won't notice the change," said Jody.

"Well, nothing has changed, except for the locks and we've installed outward looking CCTV, but unless you have a very good eye, you won't see them. But I will point them out as we walk around the outside."

"And the keys you're giving us, anyone else have spares?" asked Jody.

"No, absolutely not. I supervised the work and took all the spares that came with each unit, so you have full sets and two spare sets, just in case, and you can get more cut if you need to. I'll give you the details of the locksmiths we used."

Matt and Lenny unpacked the car, after Matt had shown them into the house and how to use the new alarm system. It was a fairly easy system, mainly using a fob to set and a pin number to stop. The only major difference was that it had a panic button that went straight through to an MI5 instant response unit, instead of the police.

That wasn't something Jody wanted to hear, but Matt reassured them that it was a last resort; however, nothing at that level was expected. Everything else would be covered by the CCTV, and that would be monitored 24/7.

After they had finished getting the luggage in, Jody had made some coffee and she, Lenny and Matt sat in the kitchen and caught up with recent events. Matt asked Lenny what he was intending to do now. Lenny was pretty clear that a return to the quiet, if sometimes aggravating and mundane, task of driving a cab was the intention. He had got a cab organised and would be back on the road in a few days.

"Anything outside of that is definitely off limits now and for the foreseeable future," he said.

Just as they were finishing the chat, a car pulled up outside, and

Mike Wyndham got out. Matt went to the door, closely followed by Lenny, and opened it to let Wyndham in. Wyndham smiled.

"Thanks, Matt," he said, "Hello, Lenny, good to see you looking so well. Hope you enjoyed the holiday?"

"Yes, we all did, thank you."

"As I said, the least we could do." As he finished speaking, Jody came out. "And thank you from me, Ella and Jess too!" she said.

"No problem, Jody. We're very grateful for all of Lenny's help and glad that he's back with you. I just wanted to see you back home. I assume Matt has shown you the security measures, and I sincerely hope you don't have any need to use them."

"Yes, Matt has given us the 'tour' and, hopefully, the measures will just be a precaution," said Jody.

"We would like that too," said Wyndham, "Now I really must go as I have to, yet again, meet with the Home Secretary. Lenny, Jody, we really do appreciate all you've done." There were smiles all round, and Wyndham returned to his car and sped off.

They all went back to the kitchen table and drank more coffee and chatted. Matt looked at his watch, and then got up to leave. He said his goodbyes to Jody and the girls, and Lenny saw him out. But before he left, Jody came over once more. "Matt, I know I've been a bit of a cow," she said, "But I really do appreciate everything you've been through as well, and thank you and Mike Wyndham, of course, for looking after my family over the last few months."

He looked at her in gratitude and they hugged.

"Whenever you feel the need for some good food, call Lenny and come for dinner," Jody said.

"Thanks, Jody, really appreciate that." He turned to leave and Lenny walked him to the door. As they got outside and stood by the car, Matt turned to Lenny, but before he could say anything, Lenny said, "Just want to say thanks too, Matt, really appreciate it too."

"That's okay, but you may change your mind. We heard from Lazar a few days ago and their intelligence have found the two females. Whilst we don't think they'll be trouble, you never know. That's why we installed the panic button on the alarm. It is an added feature."

"Well, thanks for telling me. Do we know where they are?"

"Yeah, they're in Beirut. Lazar has people over there. We sent out BOLOs to friendly agencies and he called me three or four days ago.

So whilst I don't think there's any current or short-term danger, just be aware. I'll keep you posted if there are any developments."

"Okay, Matt, that sounds a plan. We'll speak soon, no doubt. By the way, do you know of any connection between Lazar and Jody's sister, Musha?"

"He's her boss!"

"What?"

"She works for him!"

"Don't joke, that's not funny!"

"Do I look like I'm joking?"

"Shit…Jody will go ballistic!"

"I don't think they want anyone to know, right now. That was also why she spent so much time with them, when they were over there. She was their protection. It was a perfect cover!"

"Okay, I'll say nothing for now, but she'll hit the roof when she finds out, and she will, you know!"

"Yeah, I'm sure she will!" With that, Matt smiled knowingly, turned and got into the car and drove off. Lenny walked back inside, where Jody was waiting.

"That was a long goodbye?" she said.

"Yeah, he was updating me on the two people they are looking for."

"And?"

"And…nothing much, really. He was just saying the intel is that they are back in the Middle East, they think Beirut, but notices have been sent out across all friendly agencies, so we'll know if they move. They'd be pretty daft to try and get here, they wouldn't get through."

"And that's it?"

"Hopefully, yes. I'm pretty sure of that!"

"Well, let's hope that's the case." Jody put her arms out and they hugged. Lenny was still dumbfounded about the news of Musha and what would happen when Jody found out.

* * * * *

Three months later: time had passed very quickly, the long hot summer had turned into early autumn and the long days were getting shorter. By the end of October, the clocks would change and the haul through to the short days and dark cold nights would begin. That cold winter feeling would soon start and last until late March.

The Resnick household had returned to normal. Lenny's new Hybrid electric cab was a really good drive, and he was now looking forward to the build-up to Christmas, work wise and with family get-togethers too. The girls were working towards their exams coming up next year and were studiously swotting in their rooms most evenings. Lenny had changed his hours, so was mainly out during the days, and Jody made sure the house ran smoothly, as well as maintaining her work as an interior designer.

The family had been together to observe the Jewish New Year, and had just been through fasting, on the Day of Atonement (Yom Kippur). It was now the weekend after and the girls were out with friends. Jody and Lenny had been over to some of their friends for the traditional Friday night meal, ushering in the Sabbath.

Whilst they were all eating breakfast the following morning, they heard the post drop onto the mat.

"That sounds like a lot of post," Lenny said, but nobody moved.

When they'd finished, Jody and the girls cleared away and Lenny went to the front door. He walked out into the porch area and picked up the letters. Taking a quick glance through, there didn't seem to be anything out of the ordinary. However, one item, a small package with a strange stamp on it, looked interesting. Hesitantly, Lenny opened one end, and, as carefully as he could, pulled out the contents. On opening the folded tissue paper, he found a short note and a black-sprayed flattened rose. The short note just said, *"Our business is not yet finished. I will return to complete the revenge for my fallen comrades so that they will be able to rest in peace."*

Lenny dropped the packaging on the floor and rushed upstairs and grabbed his phone. He found the speed dial number for Matt Flynn and pressed the button to call. There was no answer. It rang several times before going to message. Lenny had no option, but to leave a message for Matt to call him. Just in case, he sent him a text too: *"THAT PROBLEM WE THOUGHT HAD GONE AWAY, WELL IT HASN'T. IT'S JUST REARED UP AGAIN. CALL ME…LENNY."*

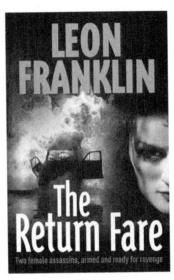

The trilling sequel to *A Fare form Hell.*

Having recovered from his near death experience, London cab driver, Lenny Resnick, cannot seem to escape his past. He is once again drawn into more danger, when his nemesis, Banu Behzadi, and her accomplice re-surface in Barcelona. At a meeting in Monte Carlo, they are given the task of avenging the death of AbdulWahab, Sheikh Hamdan al Zakani's late father.

Following many twists and turns throughout Europe, the two assassins arrive back in London. Aided by their helpers, their objective is to carry out the assassination of public figures deemed responsible for the death of Sheik AbdulWahab. Banu also enlists the assistance of a well-known IRA bomber, and the bodies begin to pile up across London.

Linked to this is Banu Behzadi's obsession for a final revenge against Lenny, for his part in the deaths of her comrades in Northern Israel years previously. The killings continue on the way to the final showdown. Will Lenny and his family survive? Will Banu and her accomplices pay the ultimate price?

Available from Amazon from April 2021

Printed in Great Britain
by Amazon